"Galenorn's imagina
—Fre

Praise for the

NIGHT VISION

"Well-plotted and cast with characters that are strong and personable, *Night Vision* is filled with taut suspense, delicious intrigue, and dangerous antagonists . . . An addictive, heady noir urban fantasy." —*Smexy Books*

"Containing gritty intensity and creative fantasy elements, this is a world to which readers will want to return again and again." —*RT Book Reviews*

"Ms. Galenorn outdid herself this time . . . An excellent book." —*Night Owl Reviews*

"Galenorn has immersed her readers in a magical world that is filled with danger and intrigue . . . A gripping tale." —*Romance Reviews Today*

NIGHT SEEKER

"Exceptional . . . A perfect blending of carnal passions, electrifying action, realistic characters, and stark betrayal. . . . If you enjoy noir urban fantasy that stretches all your boundaries, then Yasmine Galenorn is the author to buy and her Indigo Court is the series to read." —*Smexy Books*

"Filled with action and plenty of lethal roadblocks, readers will enjoy trekking the dangerous Galenorn mythological world." —*Genre Go Round Reviews*

"Richly inventive . . . full of dark characters who face difficult and sometimes virtually impossible decisions." —*Night Owl Reviews*

continued . . .

"Galenorn has created a multifaceted world full of adventure and passion!"
—*RT Book Reviews*

NIGHT VEIL

"A thoroughly engrossing series . . . Once again, Galenorn creates a magical world of both ethereal beauty and stark horror."
—*Bitten by Books*

"An engaging thriller . . . Galenorn affirms she is one of the best at Otherworld environs . . . fast-paced from the first nibble to the climactic last bite."
—*Genre Go Round Reviews*

"Will have the reader turning pages long after bedtime . . . A perfect read for any fantasy lover."
—*Fresh Fiction*

"Excitement at every turn . . . a great read for those who love paranormal romance, and a fantastic read for all the Yasmine Galenorn fans out there!"
—*Night Owl Reviews*

"Nonstop action from beginning to end."
—*Romance Reviews Today*

NIGHT MYST

"This is an amazing book. The story flows and rushes and the author makes constant incredible mind pictures . . . Lyrical, luscious, and irresistible."
—Stella Cameron, *New York Times* bestselling author of the Chimney Rock series

"An adventurous, fast read that had the right mix of tension, passion, and tenderness."
—FlamesRising.com

"Puts a unique twist on the paranormal world, leaving the reader begging for more. Yasmine Galenorn's imagination is a beautiful thing."
—*Fresh Fiction*

"A great start to a new series."
—*Smexy Books*

"This is the first in a new urban fantasy series and I am definitely looking forward to the next one . . . There is great world building here and that is one thing that I love about Ms. Galenorn's books."
—*Book Binge*

Praise for the Otherworld series

"Yasmine Galenorn creates a world I never want to leave."
—Sherrilyn Kenyon, #1 *New York Times* bestselling author of *Styxx*

"Chilling, thrilling, and deliciously dark—Galenorn's magical fantasy is spectacularly hot and supernaturally breathtaking."
—Alyssa Day, *New York Times* bestselling author of *The Cursed*

"The work is, as are all of Yasmine Galenorn's, magical and detailed and fantastic."
—*Fresh Fiction*

"A fantastic adventure that leaves the reader satisfied and yet wanting more."
—*Night Owl Reviews*

"Turns up the heat."
—Jeaniene Frost, *New York Times* bestselling author of *Up from the Grave*

"A boot to the head one moment and a full-mouthed kiss on the lips the next that leaves you begging for more."
—*Bitten by Books*

"Fast-moving, engrossing, and filled with chemistry and passion."
—*Darque Reviews*

"Galenorn hits the stars with *Night Huntress*. Urban fantasy at its best!"
—Stella Cameron, *New York Times* bestselling author of the Chimney Rock series

"Reminiscent of Laurell K. Hamilton with a lighter touch . . . Simmers with fun and magic."
—Mary Jo Putney, *New York Times* bestselling author of *Sometimes a Rogue*

continued . . .

"Pure delight!"
—MaryJanice Davidson, *New York Times* bestselling author of
Undead and Unsure

"Galenorn's kick-butt Fae ramp up the action in a wyrd world gone awry . . . I loved it!"
—Patricia Rice, *New York Times* bestselling author of
Magic Man

"A fun read, filled with surprise and enchantment."
—Linda Winstead Jones, author of *Behind the Mask*

"[A] sexy, fantastic paranormal-mystery-romantic read."
—Terese Ramin, author of *Guarding Grace*

Berkley Prime Crime titles by Yasmine Galenorn

GHOST OF A CHANCE
LEGEND OF THE JADE DRAGON
MURDER UNDER A MYSTIC MOON
A HARVEST OF BONES
ONE HEX OF A WEDDING

* * *

Yasmine Galenorn writing as India Ink

SCENT TO HER GRAVE
A BLUSH WITH DEATH
GLOSSED AND FOUND

NIGHT'S END

An Indigo Court Novel

YASMINE GALENORN

BERKLEY BOOKS, NEW YORK

THE BERKLEY PUBLISHING GROUP
Published by the Penguin Group
Penguin Group (USA) LLC
375 Hudson Street, New York, New York 10014

USA • Canada • UK • Ireland • Australia • New Zealand • India • South Africa • China

penguin.com

A Penguin Random House Company

NIGHT'S END

A Berkley Book / published by arrangement with the author

Copyright © 2014 by Yasmine Galenorn.
Excerpt from *Priestess Dreaming* by Yasmine Galenorn copyright © 2014
by Yasmine Galenorn.
Penguin supports copyright. Copyright fuels creativity, encourages diverse voices,
promotes free speech, and creates a vibrant culture. Thank you for buying an authorized
edition of this book and for complying with copyright laws by not reproducing, scanning,
or distributing any part of it in any form without permission. You are supporting writers
and allowing Penguin to continue to publish books for every reader.

Berkley Books are published by The Berkley Publishing Group.
BERKLEY® is a registered trademark of Penguin Group (USA) LLC.
The "B" design is a trademark of Penguin Group (USA) LLC.

For information, address: The Berkley Publishing Group,
a division of Penguin Group (USA) LLC,
375 Hudson Street, New York, New York 10014.

ISBN: 978-0-425-25923-8

PUBLISHING HISTORY
Berkley mass-market edition / July 2014

PRINTED IN THE UNITED STATES OF AMERICA

10 9 8 7 6 5 4 3 2 1

Cover art by Tony Mauro.
Cover design by Rita Frangie.
Interior text design by Laura K. Corless.

This is a work of fiction. Names, characters, places, and incidents either are the product
of the author's imagination or are used fictitiously, and any resemblance to actual persons,
living or dead, business establishments, events, or locales is entirely coincidental.

The publisher does not have any control over and does not assume any responsibility for
author or third-party websites or their content.

If you purchased this book without a cover, you should be aware that this book is
stolen property. It was reported as "unsold and destroyed" to the publisher, and neither
the author nor the publisher has received any payment for this "stripped book."

Dedicated to

Jo Yantz. With my love.

ACKNOWLEDGMENTS

Thanks to the usual suspects: my husband, Samwise; my agent, Meredith Bernstein; my editor, Kate Seaver; and my cover artist, Tony Mauro. To my assistants: Andria Holley, Marc Mullinex, and Jenn Price—for keeping me on track. To my Street Team for spreading the word!

A thank-you to my Galenorn Gurlz, who make writing a lot more fun with their purrs and meows. Most reverent devotion to Ukko—who rules over the wind and sky, Rauni—queen of the harvest, Tapio—the Hunter in the forest, and Mielikki—goddess of the Woodlands and Dark Fae Queen in her own right, my spiritual guardians. To the Cauldron of Changes, my coven. And to the Fae—both dark and light—who walk this world beside us, may we see you in the shadows, and in the shimmer of ice. My spiritual grounding keeps me centered and focused.

And thank you to my Moon Stalkers—my fans and my readers—for your support and enthusiasm. You can find me on the net at Galenorn En/Visions: galenorn.com. If you write to me snail mail (see website for address or write via publisher), please enclose a stamped, self-addressed envelope if you would like a reply. Lots of cool promo goodies are available—see website.

The Painted Panther
Yasmine Galenorn

In a battle all you need to make you fight
is a little hot blood and the knowledge that
it's more dangerous to lose than to win.

—GEORGE BERNARD SHAW

At the Winter Solstice, the wind is cold, trees are bare
and all lies in stillness beneath blankets of snow.

—GARY ZUKAV

The Beginning

There came a time when Myst, Queen of the Indigo Court, rode in on a glacial tide, attempting to devour all who opposed her. Battles were waged, alliances were formed, and a small faction stood the front line against her. Cicely, Queen of Snow and Ice, and her cousin Rhiannon, Queen of Rivers and Rushes, were there to meet the challenge. Behind them stood their loves, their people, and an alliance of vampires and the magic-born. Together, they faced the Vampiric Fae Queen's onslaught as Myst attempted to silence the balance of fire and ice. Some survived . . . but there were losses. . . .

From *The Last Days of the Indigo Court*

Chapter 1

I stood on a hillock near the Barrow. The land was covered with snow and ice, the horizon stretching out in a vast panorama of winter. It was the perfect picture. The snow gleamed under an overcast sky, sparkling with the cold. Here and there, patches of ice glistened, a sheen rippling across the landscape, casting pale blue shadows to blanket the world. Evergreens—firs and cedars—stood cloaked in white, the snow weighing down their limbs so they brushed the ground.

My breath emerged in puffs, visible in the early dusk, a cloud of white every time I exhaled. But the pristine chill that made the very air shimmer barely penetrated the feathered cloak I wore. And what little of the cold that *did* make it through had ceased to bother me over the weeks. For I was the Queen of Snow and Ice now, and cold was no longer my enemy.

As I surveyed the land around my Barrow, I was aware that not ten yards away, Check, my personal guard, kept watch. Beside him stood Fearless, who had thankfully recovered from his wounds. Cambyra Fae healed quickly, and Fearless had mended right up, even with the severe wounds he'd sustained from the Shadow Hunters. While he had been in great pain for several weeks, now he was back in action. I had noticed a side effect of the attack that was both welcome and curious: His attitude toward me had shifted. Where before he had simply been doing his duty, now I sensed loyalty mingled in with that duty; an impression of respect that he hadn't offered me before.

As I stood there, I plunged myself into the slipstream, searching for information. The realm of Snow and Ice might be mine to command, but we were terribly vulnerable. While Myst was still out there, we were in danger, and we couldn't let down our guard. I trusted the scouts and my advisors, but ever since my coronation, my awareness had heightened. If I listened carefully enough, I could reach out, almost touch Myst's energy. After all, we were bound together from a lifetime long before this one. She had been my mother, and I had been her daughter Cherish, the shining star and hope of the Indigo Court, until I betrayed both her and my people.

Ulean, my Wind Elemental, swept around me. She was stronger here, in our frozen realm. The winter kingdom agreed with her. While I'd always heard her clearly—from the very beginning when we were first bound together—here I had become even more aware of her.

At times, I thought I could catch a glimpse of her. Strict, my advisor, had told me it was one of the side effects of taking the crown. One more in a long line of shifts and changes that I had been going through. Some days, I looked in the mirror and wasn't entirely sure of who I was.

Cicely, there is danger close by. A looming shadow. I believe Myst is on the rise again. Ulean swept past me, swirling snow in the gust of her wake.

It was only a matter of time. We knew she was regrouping. I've been hoping she would hold off until Rhiannon and I were more settled in our positions—that it would take her more time to re-strengthen her forces, but I don't think we have that leeway. I'm afraid we'll be fighting her sooner than we'd hoped.

Shivering, but not from the cold, I pulled my cloak tightly

around my shoulders. The owl feathers used to make the cape had been gathered one by one, hand-sewn by a talented seamstress. My Uwilahsidhe brethren had gifted it to me for my wedding, an honor that meant they'd accepted me into their people. *My* people. I was half magic-born, and half Uwilahsidhe—the owl-shifters, a branch of the Cambyra Sidhe. I'd only discovered the latter half of my heritage six weeks before. Everything I thought I'd known about myself had changed in that time.

We will do as we must. If we fail, Myst will extend her reach. She will take control of this realm and drive the eternal winter into the world to blanket the land with ice and snow. She will loose the ravenous appetites of her Shadow Hunters on anyone who stands in her way. We cannot let her win, Cicely, or everyone—the magic-born and the Weres and the yummanii—will all be so much prey for the Vampiric Fae. Even the true vampires, Lannan and Regina's people, will fall to her fury if we don't stop her.

I reached out, trying to sense the danger Ulean had mentioned. It was like stretching a new muscle—not a physical one, but mental. Focusing, I sent out feelers, probing the landscape. They crept like vines through the slipstream. *There*, I could sense an arctic fox, and *over there*—the hare it was stalking. A ways beyond I felt the silent passage of a group of Ice Elementals, their focus so distant and alien that I couldn't have deciphered their intent if you paid me to. But the creatures were my subjects, they were aligned to me, and so I simply touched their energy before I passed on.

Beyond the Ice Elementals, I came to a tree line, and the dark sentinels of the woodlands whispered rumors in my ears. There were creatures in the woods—monsters who did not belong here, even though they, too, were born of winter and hearkened to the dark months of the year.

I softly began to move forward, my attention drawn by a familiar presence in a stand of snow-covered bushes nearby. As I approached the Wilding Fae—I knew who she was—Check and Fearless flanked my sides.

Ulean laughed. *Your friend wishes to speak with you. You have won the hearts of the Wilding Fae, and that is a double-edged blessing.*

The Wilding Fae were dangerous, a breed unto themselves. Ancient even by the standards of the Cambyra Fae, they were feral, belonging only to themselves, aligned with no one. But they had chosen to live in the realm of Snow and Ice when I took the throne. Bargaining with them could prove dangerous, but once they'd accepted my rule, they knew better than to try to trip me up with their deals. A good thing, too, considering my lack of bargaining skills.

I paused by the juniper bush. As I waited, a figure stepped out from behind the laden branches. She was short and dressed in a ragtag patchwork of a dress that swept the ground. Her hair was matted into clumps, draping to cover her shoulders. A withered roadwork of lines crisscrossed her face. Gaunt, her limbs were long and lean, her fingers gnarled with the knots that usually came from old age. But to be honest, I had no clue as to how old she was. The Snow Hag might be old as the world for all I knew, or as timeless as the stars.

She flashed me a cunning smile, and one of her teeth curved up from her upper jaw to rest against her bottom lip. She did not kneel, but I didn't expect her to. The Wilding Fae lived by their own rules, and while they might now make their home in my realm, they were a force to be feared and respected.

"A queen might be listening for danger, but looking in the wrong direction." She cocked her head.

I stared at her. Apparently we were dispensing with the niceties today. Usually there was a set format—a pattern with the Wilding Fae that held sway even when discussing nearby dangers.

"It would be helpful if one of the Wilding Fae could help to guide a queen as she seeks for the source of danger on the wind."

I didn't have the full cadence down, but Chatter—my cousin's husband and the new King of Summer—had been drilling us. He was adept at bargaining with the Wilding Fae. Right now, I wished he could be here to help me. But I had to learn for myself at some point, and if I made a mistake, well . . . then I made a mistake.

"There is a learning curve to this. A queen might be making good progress, however, even while she trips a step here or there. If a certain Wilding Fae were less scrupulous, there might be trouble brewing, but luck will out. One of the Wilding Fae respects the young Winter. And at times, luck has little play in matters of destiny; desire wins out instead. And there is desire to see the new rule continue."

She winked and laughed. It reminded me of the wolf out of *Little Red Riding Hood*, but then the slyness vanished, and good humor shone through. Once again, I could feel the Snow Hag's power emanate through the forest, down to my very bones. They were a crafty, cunning lot, the Wilding Fae, and were dangerous enemies to have.

I thought over what she had said and tried to pinpoint my mistake. Where had I slipped up? But right now the thought of danger lurking in my land preoccupied me, and I was having a hard time concentrating.

After a moment's silence, the Snow Hag broke a small branch off the tree. "Looking into the distance often leaves a queen ignoring what is directly below her nose. Danger can be alluring, and seemingly, the best of friends. Danger might also throw a cunning glance, begrudge good fortune, and be trapped by what was thought to be a good deed but turned into a snare. Usually, such hints will be visible if one chances to look for them."

That didn't sound good. "A spy? You're saying that I have a spy in my midst?" When she remained silent, I rephrased it as best as I could. "One might think, by your comment, that a queen might have a spy in her Court, as eyes and ears of Myst."

And with that the Snow Hag cackled. "One might think the Queen of Snow and Ice is growing into her throne. She is wise to listen to and understand the Wilding Fae. One might think the Queen of Snow and Ice is on the right trail and should look in the dark recesses of her Barrow for mice that do not belong there." And with that she vanished back into the bushes.

Hell. The last thing I needed was one of Myst's people hiding in my Court. And the Snow Hag had said the danger was right under my nose. I glanced back. Check and Fearless were standing at attention, studiously ignoring my conversation. They had learned the fine art of being present without intruding, a difficult tightrope for anyone to master. But this information meant I couldn't trust anyone, and while Check and Fearless seemed more than willing to protect me, when I thought about it, I really didn't *know* them. I'd have to corner my husband, Grieve, when I returned home, and ask him what we should do.

While I made my way back to the guards, a sudden shift in the wind alerted me as Ulean slipped past.

Cicely—move. Fly. Get yourself out of reach!

I trusted Ulean with my life, and if she said there was danger, I knew it was true.

"Danger! There's danger coming." As I warned my guards, I was already closing my arms, transforming, my arms spreading into wings. I shifted into owl form. And then I was aloft and on the wing, in my barred owl shape. Until recently, I'd had to undress in order to transform, but one of the perks of becoming a Fae Queen meant that my clothes changed with me now.

As I spiraled up into the chill evening air, I looked down to see a creature racing out of a nearby bush—and then, with a shimmer, another figure appeared. Shadow Hunters! And they had to have gained entrance to my realm via some way other than the front gate. We had guards set up, watching. *Unless those guards are corrupt and working for Myst.* The thought crept in as I circled the fray below.

I watched as Check and Fearless engaged the Vampiric Fae.

I wanted to be down there, fighting, but I was the Queen, and I wasn't allowed to fight my own battles. At least, not unless there was no other option. It felt more and more that my freedom had been pared down. Although I had more power than I ever had possessed, I also had more restrictions. I chafed at the constraints, even though I understood the reasoning for them.

The two Shadow Hunters launched themselves at my guards. They were twisting, morphing into the great cerulean-colored beasts of the Indigo Court, as they prepared to destroy. They were hungry, and unlike the true vampires, the Vampiric Fae fed on muscle and sinew as well as the life force.

Check engaged them with a jeweled sword while Fearless scrambled out of reach. One of the Shadow Hunters had snapped at him, almost catching him in its slathering jaws. Fearless had just recovered from a similar attack, and my blood rose as I watched my men struggle to keep the Shadow Hunters' great bared teeth from latching on to them.

There was no way I could survive an attack should I set down on the ground. Not even my queen's dagger could deflect the attack of one of these monsters. But then I knew exactly what to do. It was a dangerous choice, but I couldn't fly off and allow the Shadow Hunters to ravage my guards.

I spiraled up to the nearest tree and landed on the first bare branch I could find that was big enough to support me when I changed back to my normal shape. Balancing on the limb, I made certain it would be wide enough, then spread one wing so that my arm would be braced against the trunk as I shifted back. My cloak almost threw me off-balance, but I managed to catch myself and stood at the crotch of the limb where it met the trunk, bracing my weight against the tree.

Once I knew I was steady enough, I closed my eyes and summoned the winds. My hair began to lift as the currents of air rose around me, and a niggle of delight twisted in my stomach.

It was a dangerous prospect, for me to gather the winds, to stir up a tornado or a gale. Too often, they beckoned me to stay at their helm, to fully give myself over to their realm and become a mad queen on the crest of a storm. But I could save Check and Fearless—and I wasn't about to let them die.

As I glanced down at the ground, the blood channeled across the snow in a delicate wash of rose that spread over the blanket of white. Whether the blood belonged to Check, Fearless, or the Shadow Hunters, I didn't know, but if I didn't act, my guards would be dead. Or worse. Myst could offer worse fates than merely being killed by her people.

"Gale Force." I whispered the words, but the slipstream caught them up and sent them spinning into the air, and they took the form of a vortex.

A breeze wakened, starting lightly, but as I focused it through my body, the gusts increased. They were strong beyond the winds of my Winter realm. They bled directly from the heart of the plane of Air, a boreal wind sweeping down to buoy me up, to fill me full with a delicious sense of power. I rose to my tiptoes, balancing precariously on the branch.

As I raised my arms, no longer needing the support of the tree trunk, the winds lifted me into the air and spun me aloft, carrying me at the helm of a bank of mist and whirling snow. A second whisper of "Gale Force," and the winds roared into a storm, hurricane strength, only instead of driving rain along the front, in its fury it picked up the snow and used it as a weapon.

Sleet and snow pelted against the Shadow Hunters, blinding the Vampiric Fae as they struggled against the biting wind. Check and Fearless fell back, Check shouting something to me that I couldn't hear through the raging storm, but I understood his gestures. He wanted me to drop the winds, to fly back to the Barrow.

But they held me in their mania, and I couldn't break free. Each time I used this power, it was harder to rein myself in. Each time, I was one step closer to being enslaved by the chaotic forces from the plane of Air. One day, I might not be able to free myself. They summoned me, cajoled me to dive headfirst into their strength, to give myself over to them.

But a shout from below caught my attention. A handful of my guards had noticed the battle and were wading into the fray. Armed, they pushed forward to attack the Shadow Hunters, even as Check and Fearless rejoined the battle. My forces were strong, and Myst's pair couldn't stand up against them.

In that moment of clarity, I released the storm, and as the Shadow Hunters fell under the wave of my guards and the snow was stained with their blood, I transformed back into my owl form and circled to land on the field below.

I sat on the edge of my bed. Druise, my personal maid, was helping me change clothes. She bundled me up into clean, dry black jeans and laced my blue corset snugly, then brought me dry boots and a thin black cloak embroidered with silver threads. The cloak was surprisingly warm, and I wasn't sure from just what kind of material it had been woven, but it was light and pretty and would keep any chill in the Barrow at bay.

As she draped the material around my shoulders, she was careful not to touch the crown that circled my head. A diadem forged with silver leaves entwining on either side of the circlet, the vines met in the center of my forehead to embrace a glowing cabochon of black onyx. Below the onyx dangled a single diamond teardrop.

I sat on the bed, sipping tea and eating a cookie.

The huge four-poster bed was made from yew wood, the headboard intricately carved with designs and runes that I couldn't decipher. The bed was old, and I wondered just how many queens had slept in its protection and comfort. Piled high atop blankets and sheets, the indigo comforter matched the pattern of the carpet. Covering the cobblestone floor, the rug was a sweeping panorama of swirling labyrinths embroidered in silver against the indigo weave.

Over the bed, inlaid in cabochons of iolite, sapphire, amethyst, and quartz, the pattern continued. The rest of the ceiling was jet-black, and the gems shimmered against the dark background, their inner light picking up the glow from the lanterns. The shadows in the room seemed to flicker in a slow, sinuous dance of movement.

"How long before you have to be at your meeting, my Lady?" Druise refilled my teacup and I inhaled the rich aroma, grateful as the peppermint cleared my thoughts. A glance up at the clock told me it was five P.M. Of course, it was an arbitrary setting. Time always worked differently within the Faerie Barrows, but I used the clock to keep me on track with my schedule when I was here. It gave me some sense of familiarity, a touch from the outer world that made me more comfortable as I adjusted to my new way of life.

"An hour. They're conferring now, but I needed . . . I need to think over something before I meet with the others." Actually, what I had needed was a chance to decompress from the afternoon.

I inhaled slowly, my breath grounding me back into my body, lingering over the comforts of the tea and food. Finally, able to put it off no longer, I sighed and stood. Time to face the reality we had all been dreading. But we'd known she would return sooner or later. Myst was out for my blood and bone.

It had been a month since my cousin Rhiannon and I had taken the thrones of Summer and Winter. A month since I had married Grieve and she had married Chatter. Since then, Rhia and I had poured ourselves into an intensive study of the language of our people and the customs of our Courts as we desperately crammed on what it meant to be Fae Queens.

The whole concept that we were effectively immortal was still too much to deal with, although truth was we could be killed. But if we avoided accidents and murder, if no one found our heartstones, we would live into the mists of time until we were ready to let go and lay down our duties.

Gathering up the messenger bag I carried within the Barrow, I made sure my notebooks were in it, along with pens, chewing gum, my EpiPen, and everything else I would need while out of my chambers. With one last look around the bedroom, I pushed open the door. Check was waiting on the other side to escort me to the council room.

The council chamber was lit by the ever-present lanterns that lined the Eldburry Barrow. The lights within, pale blue and violet, were young Ice Elementals, indentured into service before being set loose into the world. They did not object to their service.

Within the Fae world and the world of Elementals, human rules and emotions didn't apply. In the Marburry Barrow—the Summer Court of Rivers and Rushes—the lights were fueled by young Fire Elementals.

Strict was waiting at the table, along with Grieve, my beloved Fae Prince turned King. Check and Fearless stayed after escorting me there, and several other advisors and guard leaders had straggled in. As I entered the room, everyone stood and bowed. Once again it hit me that I was the end of the line. No matter what everyone else did, it all came back to land on my shoulders.

I took my place at the table and nodded for them to sit. A servant offered me a tray filled with roast beef sandwiches, bowls of hot chicken soup, and the ever-present tea. I was weaning them onto coffee, but it was a hard sell.

The Barrow kitchen had already gone through culture shock when I banned all fish and shellfish products. If people wanted to eat them in their own homes, fine, but for me and my staff there would be no seafood at the table. I was EpiPen allergic, anaphylactic, and even though I didn't like thinking about the possibility, the fact was it would be an easy way for an assassin to get to me. That I even *had* to think about things like this still sent me reeling, but I was quickly getting used to it.

Once we were settled in with food, Grieve leaned over and placed a kiss on my lips. He was my love, the heart of my heart, and I wore a tattoo of his wolf on my stomach that responded to his feelings. Grieve had been crown prince of the Summer Court—the Court of Rivers and Rushes—until Myst had overrun the Marburry Barrow, killing hundreds of the Cambyra Fae. But he'd been caught by her, and she turned him. Even though he had control over his nature now, he was still feral and wild, a hybrid. But he was my love, and that's all that mattered.

"Myst is on the move."

The room fell silent. I had abandoned the protocol of moving through business and polite chitchat.

"Check told us about the attack." My advisor, Strict, picked up the thread, smoothing over my gaffe, but I didn't care about faux pas or social niceties. The nightmare had returned. Small talk was all well and good, but right now we didn't have the luxury to observe tradition.

"They would have bought the farm if our men hadn't noticed the commotion and shown up to help." I told them about my encounter with the Snow Hag, though didn't mention that she'd warned me about a spy in the Court. "Luckily we weren't far from the Barrow, or we would have been in a fuckton of trouble."

"Your Majesty . . ." Strict winced. My slang still bothered him. We were speaking in English because I didn't know enough Cambyra to make myself understood. I was learning, but it was a complex language and slowgoing.

"Bite me, Strict. When I speak my own language, it's going to be in my own way." I flashed him a smile.

That cracked his stern demeanor, and he laughed. "The Cambyra are definitely being dragged into a new way of life thanks to you and your cousin. As to Myst, do we know if she's within the realm of Snow and Ice?"

I shrugged. "I can't be certain, but I don't think so. When I was flying overhead, all I saw were the Shadow Hunters emerge from behind the bushes. They had to get into the realm somehow, so either we have a breach at the gates, or they've found some way to transport them over here."

"Myst could be here, however. We can't discount the possibility, Your Majesty." Check tilted his head slightly. "She might have sent them ahead as scouts. I think at this point in the game, we have to be open to just about any possibility."

Considering what the Snow Hag had revealed, he made a valid point. I leaned back, wondering how much to tell them. The Snow Hag had said the danger was under my nose rather than in the distance, and I knew she hadn't been talking about the Shadow Hunters. If we did have a spy in our midst, could it be Strict? Check? Fearless? Or one of the other members of my staff gathered around the table with me? Or even . . . my own sweet Grieve?

But as quickly as it passed through my mind, that last

thought vanished. I knew my love, inside and out. I knew that even though he would forever be a member of the Indigo Court, he had broken the connection with Myst. He would always be wild-eyed and feral, my wolf-shifter husband, but he loved me and would lay down his life for me.

After a moment, I motioned to him. "We need to talk, my husband. *Alone.*"

He followed me into a private chamber just off the council room.

Ulean, keep watch. Make certain nobody is listening at the door. Warn me if they are. And listen to what they are saying while we're sequestered. I want to know if it's anything to worry about.

I will, Cicely. But the Snow Hag is right. Danger lurks here. Not necessarily in this room, but the Barrow feels uneasy, and I think there is treachery hiding in the shadows. The edge was not here yesterday, I don't believe. Though perhaps I only notice now because I am looking for it. But I think, had it been here before, I would have sensed it. I could be wrong, however.

I shuddered and Grieve pulled me into his embrace. His long platinum hair shimmered against the dim light, and his olive skin was warm and musky. He smelled like cinnamon and autumn leaves, like the dark half of the year on a rainy, chill night. Like the blackness of stars against the snow. He held me close, kissing my hair, kissing my forehead.

"What's wrong, my Cicely? What gives you grief?"

In soft tones, so as not to be overheard by any prying ears, I laid out what the Snow Hag had told me. "Someone is playing the spy for Myst in our midst. I don't know who it is, or where to find them. Now I can't trust anybody. My father assured me that I could trust Strict. He told me that shortly before he and Lainule left for the Golden Isle. But now can I believe what he said? Do I dare trust anybody?"

"*Trust* is a relative word. You were right to keep this a secret. We can't take chances. While I doubt that Strict or Silverweb would be in Myst's pocket, we have to know for sure before continuing. If any one of the council in that room

happens to be in the service of Myst, and we talk openly
about this, she'll know we're onto her plans, and then our
advantage will be undone."

He moved back, holding me by my shoulders. "I know
you aren't going to like this, but there is a way to find out.
We have to be cautious about how we go about it so word
doesn't get around, however."

I knew exactly what he was talking about, and he was
right: I didn't like it.

The shamans of the Cambyra Fae had a procedure they
could perform. Painful and intrusive, the ritual allowed
them to delve into someone's mind, to root through their
thoughts and feelings and secrets. Essentially it came down
to a form of mental torture. But it got the job done. And
everyone in the Barrow had been through it before I took the
throne, so either someone new had joined us, or someone's
loyalty had been turned after the fact.

"I don't want to order that." Even as I said the words, I
knew that I was fighting a losing battle. There was no other
option. Simply going around asking, *"By the way, are you
working for Myst now?"* wasn't going to get me anywhere,
and I knew it. "It's mind-rape," I whispered.

"Perhaps so, but it might also save our people. Leave a
spy from Myst loose in this Barrow, and the bitch will have
a good chance of sweeping through here again. And this
time, Myst won't leave *anyone* alive. If she gains a foothold
again, rest assured the Barrow will be slick with blood and
bone and gristle."

"And she'll turn everyone who she can use. And the
rest . . . food for the Shadow Hunters." I hung my head. "I
really don't have a choice, do I?"

Grieve slowly backed away and knelt before me. "You are
the Queen of Snow and Ice. Wear your crown and wield your
power."

And so, reluctantly, I whispered, "Then how do we go
about this without word getting out?"

"We tell no one else. Not Luna, not Peyton or Kaylin."
The warning in his voice was clear—our friends couldn't

know what was going on. "We visit the shamans. They alone can be trusted. They are chosen from birth for their discipline and power." He rose, staring into my eyes. "And first, they put me to the test."

"*You?*" Startled, I began to shake my head. "Not you—"

But Grieve took my hands and gently brushed my wrist with his razor-sharp teeth. A thin red weal rose as blood welled up. Even as I responded, melting under his touch, he shook his head.

"Remember, my love. I belonged to Myst for a time. I carry her blood in my body. She turned me into one of the Vampiric Fae, and while I have gained a modicum of control, as Queen, you cannot be complacent. You cannot trust even me, not without knowing for certain."

And so, my heart heavy, we returned to the main chamber and told everyone to sit tight. And then Grieve and I made our way through the Barrow, to where the shamans lived. To where I would order them to torture the truth from my beloved husband and the rest of my people.

Chapter 2

Deep into the Barrow we made our way, past guards, past the places where the ordinary citizens were allowed. We were headed into the heart of the Court of Snow and Ice. To the very core from whence the magic of this realm emanated. My heartstone might have revived the Court, but the shamans guarded the magic, communed with the Elementals, and kept the light flickering within the ice. Without them, the Barrow would be harsh and brutal. They were the keepers of comfort, the dreamers of dreams, the visionaries who walked between the worlds. They were the eyes and ears of my land.

The tunnel was labyrinthine and long, and as Grieve and I followed the twisting passages, accompanied by Check and Fearless, I thought back to the days of my life, less than two months ago, and how different my world had been.

My name is Cicely Waters, and I'm a Wind Witch. And now I'm the Queen of Snow and Ice and the Fae Queen of Winter.

My journey down this road began at birth, though of course,

I didn't know it then. My cousin Rhiannon and I were born on the same day—the summer solstice. Rhia was born in the morning, during the waxing half of the year, and I was born during twilight, after the tide had turned and the year had begun to wane. We called ourselves twin cousins.

Aunt Heather—Rhiannon's mother—called us fire and ice, amber and jet, for Rhiannon was born tall and willowy with curling red hair, and I was born short and pale, with long, smooth, black hair. Our eyes had been different then. When she took the throne of Summer, Rhiannon's eye color changed from hazel to gold. And as I ascended to the helm of Winter, mine changed from emerald to the frozen blue of northern ice.

When we were five, my cousin and I met Grieve and Chatter out in the woods, and they taught us how to tap into our magic. The magical Fae prince and his friend became our mentors, and by the next year, when Krystal, my drunken and drug-addicted mother, dragged me off on a journey that would last the next nineteen years of my life, I was prepared for the ordeal to come. Grieve had bound Ulean to me by then, and with her help, I was able to survive the cruel underbelly of the cities through which we traveled.

We'd never stopped long in one place, hitchhiking most of our way up and down the west coast. I explored the seedy streets as my mother sold her body to vamps and to men. I'd learned quickly that she wasn't cut out for survival. Krystal was on a one-way path to self-destruction, and I didn't want to go down with her. Even at six years old, I knew that if we were to stay alive, I'd have to figure out how to keep us going.

So Ulean warned me when danger was near. She told me when to run, when to hide. I'd played hide-and-seek with rapists and thieves; I'd hustled Krystal out of the dives we lived in too many times when the landlord was on his way down the hall carrying a baseball bat, looking for his money.

When we were first on the streets, I'd met Uncle Brody, an old black man with a heart a mile wide. He'd taken one look at my situation and done his best to teach me how to survive. I learned a lot of street smarts from the man, and would be forever in his debt. Uncle Brody's Rules he called the set of guidelines he'd taught me. By the time Krystal dragged me out of that city—wherever it was, I could never keep them clear in my mind, one place was just the same as the next—I was older than I ever should have been at that age. But I was ready to play the game.

So we ran, from city to city, from man to man, as Krystal sought to escape the visions in her head. She was one of the magic-born, and she hated her ability to read thoughts. So she steeped herself in booze and drugs to escape. But there was no real way to leave it behind. If you have the power, that's it. She refused to accept my abilities, too, and so I kept quiet and used them on the sly. Meanwhile, Krystal sank so deep that no one could reach her. Not even me, her daughter.

By the time she died in an alley, drained by some vamp, I was staying with her out of a sense of responsibility. Love? What's love when you have to take over your own mothering? When you have to mother the woman who gave you birth because she fucked herself up so bad?

The day I found her, sprawled there, throat ripped out, I realized that any love I thought I had left was curiously absent. I felt sorry for her, like I would any stranger, but she was just some poor hooker who had lost the game. I fished through her pockets, took her wallet and anything that might identify her, then I walked away. When I was long gone, I called in an anonymous tip to the cops. I never looked back.

I took to the road on my own, winning a car in a game of street craps. And from there I restlessly prowled, always wanting to return home for good but never getting up the nerve to ask.

Two years later, my aunt Heather sent a message on the wind. She needed me. As a teen, I'd been allowed to take a few trips back to see my cousin and aunt. Each time I'd wanted to stay, but the knowledge that Krystal wouldn't survive without me haunted me and I always went back to her.

But now, Heather was frantic. Something was wrong at the Veil House, and would I please come home. Feeling happy for the first time in years, I rushed back to New Forest, only to find my aunt had been abducted by Myst in a war waging between ancient forces.

That was about two months ago. And now, here I was, a thousand miles away from the night I was pulled back into New Forest, Washington. I'd parked my car in the lot of a hotel, and walked into a life I'd never expected to live.

Reunited with my cousin, and now married to Grieve, I was a woman instead of a child. A woman fighting a desperate battle against the Vampiric Queen of the Indigo Court. And I wasn't all that sure we were going to win.

The tunnels through the Barrow grew narrower and darker. They were infrequently used, and few dared to come this far. The shamans of the Cambyra Courts had a frightening reputation, and they scared the hell out of people, which was just as well, because it meant they didn't get overwhelmed by curious members of the Court.

The walls glistened, and I realized that we were in a series of ice tunnels—glacial passages leading out of the actual Barrow into the depths of the ice field that spread out as far as the eye could see. We were still within the magical boundaries of my Court, that much I knew, but here the ice was illuminated from within, glowing with soft white and violet sparkles. The lights flickered, as if emanating from some cold flame deep inside the core of the ice sheet, and when I looked down at my feet, I realized the surface of the floor was the same smooth glass. But we glided over it as if it were a faint mist.

My transformation into the Queen of Winter had changed me into a creature of the snow and ice, and the elements were now my blood and soul. I belonged to Winter as sure as the flakes that blanketed the land.

Grieve moved in silence, his face set in a stony expression. Once we had married and he had taken the position of King, he had changed subtly, grown older in a way. His feral nature would never be tamed, but once he accepted the responsibility for our people, his stature had shifted. He had become regal, and to a degree, stern.

I glanced back at Check and Fearless, who walked a few steps behind us. While they were also suspect, we'd had to bring them with us. I couldn't go wandering around without protection, and to order them to stay behind would only put everyone on alert.

But Grieve and I kept our eyes open, and with Ulean following, she could warn me before they moved more than an inch to attack. Ulean had my back, and she always would.

The tunnels ran deep, a labyrinth spiraling toward the shamans' lair, and as we continued, it grew progressively colder. I watched the puffs of air hang in front of my face, freezing and then exploding into a fine powder. The decreasing temperatures told me we were reaching the outskirts of the Barrow, which meant from here on out, the wild would encroach, and even though we were still within the boundaries of the Court, we would do well to be wary.

There were no branches or forks along the way. These tunnels led in one direction only, straight to the shamans. There were no opportunities for any thing or any person to burrow in from an alternative entrance. I had no clue if there was an exit from their chambers to the outside, but if there was, it would lead into the chill desolation of the realm, where nothing could survive unless it was already acclimated to the area.

After a while, I fell into a light daze, not knowing how long we had been walking. I wasn't tired, per se; everything had just become a blur.

The Fae Courts existed in their own world. Outside their boundaries, time flowed like a river, but inside? A week spent in the realm of Faerie could easily translate into minutes in the outer world. Or decades, depending on the will of the Queen. And here, I was the one who set the pace, though I didn't know how to tinker with time yet. The thought scared the fuck out of me. What if I screwed up a friend who came to visit? What if I messed with someone's life, keeping them here too long as the outer world passed them by? But sooner or later, I'd have to learn how to adjust the flow of the realm.

"Are we nearly there?" I glanced over at Grieve, wanting to take his hand. But now that we had taken the throne, when we were in public we had to watch our decorum. A kiss? Was acceptable in certain quarters. Holding hands? Passable, depending on the situation. But snuggling and cuddling? All of those affections had to remain in our chambers now. I didn't like this part of being Queen much, but there was nothing we could do about it. At least, not yet. Perhaps in time I could change tradition, but right now we had a war to focus on. Changing the stance on how much PDA the royals were allowed, well—it wasn't exactly high on the priority list.

"We are. It takes time to reach the shamans because they wanted to avoid the chance for invaders to reach them quickly. Gives them a chance to set up defense. That's how they kept fairly immune from Myst's first attack. Same with the Court of Rivers and Rushes."

Grieve grinned. "I can feel your desire, you know." He reached out and, with light fingers, caressed my hand. I lingered over his touch, then reluctantly pulled away. My wolf let out a low rumble in response. Grieve wanted me. It was a nice reassurance.

The tattoo on my stomach was that of a wolf's head, staring out from in front of a trailing vine of silver roses and purple skulls. Running from my hip to the opposite ribs, it linked Grieve to me—he was a wolf-shifter—and I could feel his energy through it. When he was upset, it growled; when he was hungry for me, desire emanated from the core of the wolf. When he was in pain, I felt his pain.

I was marked with three other tattoos. On both upper arms I had identical bands, a silver dagger through the moon with a pair of owls flying past. On my breast, a feral Fae girl hid behind a bush. They all connected to facets of me—they all were part of my essence and core.

I nodded. "I thought as much."

A moment later, Check pointed out a shift in the color of

the ice covering the walls. It had changed from a white fading into pale blue to a white fading into purple.

"Subtle, but enough to tell us that we are within their territory. Purple is the color of the shamans' magic. I warn you, they may bow to the Queen and King, but they are beyond all laws save a very few. They live within their own world. Do not anger them. While they would not harm you, their cooperation is vital for our continued existence in this realm. While your heartstone brought the Court back to life, the shamans make that life habitable."

As he finished speaking, we came to the end of the tunnel. What waited beyond was impossible to see because a veil of energy stretched across the opening. Shimmering like the aurora, the rays streamed across the passage.

"Here we are, then." Grieve turned to me. "This will be your first time meeting them, though trust me when I tell you, they have followed you since birth. Lainule and Wrath told me that they were instrumental in setting up the circumstances of both your and Rhiannon's conceptions. While the shamans are not like the Wilding Fae, I advise you, my love, do as you do with the Snow Hag. Think before you speak."

"No jokes or snark, I take it?" I had a habit of mouthing off when I felt threatened, and it had fucked me over more than once. When I'd ascended to the throne, I had come to a swift realization that my days of free and easy speech were numbered. Everything coming out of my mouth would have to be thought out and planned in order to avoid rumor and to avoid stirring the waves. A mistake now could lead to far more than hurt feelings—one wrong word and I could start a war. End an alliance. The more power I'd gained, the more restrictions I found myself under. It was a sobering realization.

If this keeps up, in years to come, I'll be locked in an ivory tower.

Ulean whistled past. *But Cicely this is what it means to be the Queen. And yes, you will find your world narrows, even as it expands. The higher you climb, the less your life is your own. One day you'll look back, and all the days*

*before you became Queen will seem like a dream. A distant
memory.*

That thought terrified the fuck out of me, but I let it be. I
turned to Grieve. "What do we do? Do we just pass through?"

He nodded. "Yes. But Fearless, go first. Check, bring up
the rear."

And so Fearless moved to the front and passed through the
veil. I watched him go as the energy crackled and snapped
around him, sucking him in. A moment later, Grieve stepped
through, motioning for me to follow. With a deep breath, I
obeyed.

Stepping into the crackling waves was like plugging my
finger into a light socket. Even though I closed my eyes as I
entered the veil, forked lightning played across my eyelids,
spearing my vision. My skin prickled as a web of sparks
danced its way across my body; it felt like a hundred stinging
gnats. As my teeth began to chatter from the buzzing in my
head, I stumbled through to the other side and was out. Grieve
and Fearless were waiting for me. Check followed shortly
after. It took a moment for my vision and hearing to clear, and
I felt jarred, like I'd had way too much caffeine.

I looked around. "Are we in a secondary Barrow?"

Grieve nodded. "Yes, though this is still technically part
of the Eldburry Barrow system."

The chamber resembled a cave more than anything else,
with walls that glistened like frosted glass. I ran my hand
over them only to find they were ice. The illumination from
within the walls cast a dim light through the chamber, sil-
houetting our shadows against the walls as we crept along in
silence.

The room was large, with benches carved from the ice
floes and frozen tables, and everywhere there was the feeling
of stasis—as if time stood still here, even more so than out in
the regular Barrow. I looked around to see if there was anyone
in sight, but there were only shadows against the walls. And
then I realized the shades were moving on their own.

Grieve motioned for me to join him at a circular table in

the center of the chamber. Fearless and Check followed, taking their posts by our side. I kept my mouth shut. I had no clue what to do, and I'd discovered it was generally best to remain silent until I knew what I was dealing with.

As we sat there, the temperature dropped even further, and though I was wearing my cloak, a shiver of fear ran through me when the shadows stepped off the walls. They began to take form, the inky blackness falling away like grains of sand as a man—short and dark, with long hair caught back in a cascade of braids adorned with beads and feathers—stepped into sight. He was wearing leather pants with a fur cloak and bare chest. But the cold didn't seem to faze him, and he strode to the chair between Grieve and me, and sat down.

I remained silent. There was a palpable energy in the room that threatened. *Do-Not-Fuck-With-This.* By his shimmering blue eyes and the crackle of his aura, I realized that this man was one of the shamans.

Grieve inclined his head. I followed suit.

Check and Fearless bowed, looking anything but sure of themselves. I began to realize just how much power the shamans wielded in the Barrow. I may be Queen, but they were in control when it came to the inner workings of the magic that sustained this place.

"Thorn, at your command." The shaman turned to me. "I am the Speaker for our council. I am also the Elder. Instruct me."

I stared at him, unsure of what to say. First, he understood me and I understood him. I wasn't used to that with the majority of my people. Second, I realized that he hadn't spoken aloud. I'd heard him like I heard Ulean, in my core.

Stammering, I tried to figure out what to say—and how to say it. Should I speak aloud? Should I try to project my thoughts to him, or speak into the slipstream? But as I struggled, once again a whisper-light touch ran through my thoughts. It was nothing like when Kaylin had intruded into my mind, which had felt very much like an invasion. This . . . This was cautious. A gentle hello, very respectful.

A moment later, Thorn spoke aloud. "I know what you fear. I know what we must do. We will begin with the King and your guards." He stood and motioned for us to follow him.

Hesitantly, I obeyed. Grieve swung in stride next to me, with Check and Fearless behind us. I wondered if they could guess what was happening—and if they could, how they would feel. Would they hate me for what was about to happen to them? Or accept it as their duty? The shadows on the walls were standing at attention now, watching as we passed. Ulean followed at the rear.

I whispered to Grieve. "What would happen if Check or Fearless tried to run?"

Thorn turned and, without missing a beat, said, "The Watchers would come off the walls and rip them to pieces. As they would your King if he tried to avoid our summons."

Grieve leaned close. "He searched your mind and saw your need. We must all be tested in order to assure your safety. Once the Queen—you—gave the order, the shamans are bound to destroy those who try to avoid your ruling."

"They took my thoughts as an order?" I blinked.

"The Fae Queen's will is law, whether it be in word or action. Or thought. They heard your need and are responding. They live to serve you . . . and will die in your service." He reached out and gently stroked my cheek as we followed the shaman. "As do I. And as I will."

His touch was like fire, sparking off a flush of desire that raced through my body, setting off a deep, gnawing hunger. I pushed back my need. This wasn't the place, but when we were done, I needed to fuck him, to press skin against skin and feel him thrust deep, drive himself into me. While I'd always been sensual by nature, ever since I'd returned home, my sex drive had taken an exponential leap. Every step I took, every movement, every touch, seemed to trigger me off.

We veered into a side passage that forked to the right, and Thorn stopped in front of a door. He whispered something under his breath, and as the door opened, he ushered us through into a softly lit chamber. Here, a circle of chairs surrounded a raised bed. Well, it wasn't exactly a bed, but instead was a raised, padded bench covered with a fur cloak, reminding me of the place in which my heartstone had been created. Another row of chairs lined one wall.

He motioned for us to sit in the chairs against the wall as a group of men and women filed through a door on the opposite wall. They circled the bench and took their seats. Thorn motioned to Grieve.

While I had never seen this rite performed—for there was no doubt this was a full-fledged ritual—Grieve obviously had, for he silently stood and walked over to the bench, where he lay down. One of the women sitting in the circle rose to cover him with the fur blanket then took her seat again.

The shamans reached out and joined hands, creating a ring around Grieve. One of them began to hum, his voice low and resonant. The rest joined in, one by one, until they were weaving a rhythmic, sonorous tone that threatened to draw me deep, drag me under the waves. As I began to follow the thread of music, I found myself in a long tunnel. In the light that blinded me from up ahead, I could see the shamans standing, only they were once again the dark shadows they had been on the walls. They surrounded a brilliant indigo form, and I knew it was Grieve hiding beneath that glowing light.

The music began to swell into a tide, a wave that rolled far out in the ocean like the beginnings of a tsunami, biding its time before its inevitable march toward the land. It loomed over Grieve, rising up like a great shadow—roiling waves ready to crash down on him and drag him under. I could feel his fear. The wolf on my stomach whimpered, cowering down, as it watched the wraithlike ocean descend. And then, as our link tied us together, I began to feel his pain as the storm broke, ripping into his mind, tearing it to shreds with a whirlwind of questions, a flurry bombarding him as the shamans sought their answers.

He let out a long scream as they rammed into him, penetrating deeply, tossing aside every block, searching every hidden nook and cranny of his mind. They stripped away the covering to every recess protecting those private shadows we all have. I tried to break free, not wanting to intrude, not wanting to see something that I might never be able to forget.

But then, as I jockeyed for my footing, I found myself roughly shoved to one side. As our link was severed, I went reeling back into my body, slamming into myself so hard that I fell off my chair. Dazed, I allowed Check and Fearless to lift me up and help me back to my seat.

Grieve was convulsing. His eyes rolled back in his head, and he was foaming at the mouth. I struggled to go to him, but the guards held me down. He was in pain, in horrible, terrible pain, and I realized this was the most intimate of intrusions, forcing into his very essence. The shamans were raping his mind, ravaging him to shed light into every corner, uncover every secret nook.

Crying, I watched, helpless to stop them.

Check leaned over. "Your Highness, do not weep. Show no emotion. This must be done in order to ensure the safety of the Court. To ensure *your* safety. His Lordship understands this, and volunteered to do it because he cares for you. Do not fear. Do not cry. Don't make his sacrifice meaningless."

Bleakly, I looked up at him. "You and Fearless will have to undergo the same ritual. Do you understand this now? There's a spy in our midst, and we have to find out who it is." Perhaps I shouldn't have blurted it out, but I couldn't face watching anyone else get roughed up who might be innocent.

Check nodded. "And so will all who come into contact with you in any capacity. And, my Lady, while it hurts, we understand the nature and necessity for this pain. The good of the Court and the good of the realm come before our personal comfort. For your sake, and the safety of all, we willingly submit, so that we might avoid having to submit to a far more dangerous force."

Fearless nodded, and then did something that surprised the hell out of me. He reached out and patted my hand. As if realizing he'd just made a gaffe, he pulled back, but his eyes still crinkled with kindness, and the feel of his cool skin on mine managed to calm me down.

I turned back to watch Grieve. He was shaking now, though

the convulsions had calmed down. Even from the outskirts, I could still feel the racking pain that raced through his mind. Helpless, knowing this was one of those horrendous duties that I would have to face again and again, I forced myself to watch. As I did so, Ulean fluttered around me.

This is your life. This is your destiny. You must wrap up your feelings and fears and tuck them away in a box. During times like this, you must learn to observe and let be what must be. Grieve will survive. Your King will be all right. Will he remember the pain? Yes, as will everyone who undergoes this rite. But it will not harm them, unless they have dangerous secrets to hide. And then . . .

And then . . . and then if he *had* something to hide, a terrible choice loomed before me. If Grieve was my betrayer, he would die, and I would be forced to make the decree. The thought of having to condemn him to death sent me into a cold sweat. Even if he was the spy plotting against me, how could I offer him up for execution? How can you order the death of someone you love, even if they deserve it?

You will do what you must, because you are the Queen of Snow and Ice. This is what wearing the crown means, Cicely. You face terrible possibilities, and you must learn to stand in your decision without flinching. You will do what you need to, because you must. It is as simple as that.

Simple? No. But true? Yes.

I caught my breath, struggling to inhale. As the shamans continued to rip their way through Grieve's mind, I waited. Counting the seconds. Counting the hours. Time was mutable, and I lost track of how long the session went on. My emotions had become numb, and the tears stopped as time rolled past. But, just when it seemed it would never end, the energy spiraled up, away from Grieve, and vanished in a wisp of smoke.

Thorn turned to me. "He is loyal, heart and soul. He is not your spy and has not betrayed you. Nor is he likely to."

And with that the sun rose again in my life, and the terrible night came to an end. And yet, even as two of the others helped

Grieve over to the chair next to me, where he slumped, exhausted, I knew that the long night had barely begun.

Check and Fearless were next. Check volunteered to go first, and once again, I forced myself to stand witness. If they were being put through hell for my sake, the least I could do was stand in silent watch.

It was a little easier with them—I didn't have the connection I had with Grieve, but still, watching them writhe and twist, watching the shamans bear down on them, fierce lights burning in their eyes, I began to realize just how ruthless was this realm over which I now ruled. Ruthless and terrifying and harsh. My people were rugged, and they expected me to be the Queen of Ice, cold and stern and able to stomach far more than I'd ever had to face.

Slowly, as I watched, I tried to accept my place. There was no other option—if I didn't adapt, I'd fuck up and run the place into the ground.

Check was released, and Fearless took his place in their midst. As the process began again, Check and Grieve whispered together, before turning to me.

"When Fearless makes it through the ordeal, he and I will escort Strict and Silverweb here, and they shall be put to the test." Check stretched his legs, wincing. "We will simply instruct them you have ordered their attendance."

Strict was my chief advisor, Silverweb my treasurer. It stood to reason they should be next, though I dreaded seeing Silverweb undergo the ritual. Somehow, in a double-standard sort of way, it seemed wrong to order another woman into the arms of the shamans.

But you must, Cicely. There can be no weakness based on gender. The best way to exploit a vulnerability is to play up to one's fears. And whoever your spy is, they will know this.

Ulean made sense. For a brief moment, I feared that maybe Ulean had turned on me, traded sides. My feelings must have seeped through to her because she embraced me with her gentle breeze.

Cicely . . . the shamans would not allow me in here if

they thought that possible. I was bound to you when you were six years old. There is no spell, no magic strong enough to break that bond, save for death. And I do not die. The only way for you to be rid of me is to give me to another— like Lainule did when she ordered Grieve to bind me to you.

I nodded, knowing she was right. I was jumping at shadows, fearing they might be hiding Myst's hunters. I started to apologize, then stopped. Ulean knew what stress I was under. She could read my energy, hear my whispers into the slipstream.

And so we waited, silent, as Fearless underwent the long dark rites of his soul, deep into the night. And when they were done with him, the shamans bade Grieve and me to rest, while Fearless and Check went back to the Barrow.

Grieve and I retired to the chamber they provided and shut the door behind us, closing away the world. It would be some time before Check and Fearless returned with Strict and Silverweb, and we were both exhausted.

But as I turned to my love, the pain in his eyes overwhelmed me, and I fell into his arms, sobbing quietly. "I'm sorry. I'm so sorry. I'm responsible for what you went through."

He held me, his arms wrapping around my waist, and buried his nose into my hair. "Cicely, my love. It's all right. Please, believe me. This is the way of our people. I have undergone this ritual before—in Lainule's Court. And Myst put me through it, for her pleasure. But for you, I would endure so much more. I needed you to know I was true to you. I need you to *know* that in your heart."

He leaned down, pressing his lips to mine. As his hands slid over my ass and along my back, the heat within me rose, and I yanked off my crown. The only time I was allowed to take it off was when we were alone in our chamber, or when I was sleeping. It had become an anchor around my neck, and I welcomed the times when I could remove it, even though the weight of responsibility was there regardless.

Grieve pushed me back, staring into my eyes, and I lost myself in his gaze. His eyes had been cornflower blue once, blue as the morning sky, but when Myst had turned him, they had shifted to inky black, with a sparkling of stars through them. The Vampiric Fae all had eyes like the night sky.

He reached out, touched the busks on my corset, and I let him undo them. Grieve preferred to undress me, and I liked it when he did. He undid the steel fasteners one by one, easing the pressure on my midriff, and then my boobs bounced free. I had large breasts. I was five-four and a sturdy one hundred and forty pounds of muscle. As he ran one finger up my side to slide over my breasts and then pinched my nipple, hard, I inhaled sharply, gasping at the pain before the fire hit. And then, in a haze of hunger, I unzipped my jeans and kicked my way out of them.

Grieve, like all full-blooded Fae, could shed his clothes with a single thought, and did, now standing naked in front of me. He was glorious, my Faerie King, and his hair grazed his shoulder blades, pale and shimmering as the cool winter sun. Exotic and dangerous, he bared his teeth—they were razor sharp from the turning. I gasped, oh so hungry.

"Fuck me. Fuck me, please." I needed him. I wanted his hands on me, roughing me up, pushing me down, stroking against my thighs, my breasts, over the tattoo on my stomach.

He could feel my need—my wolf growled in response to his rising hunger—and he stepped toward me, gaze still fastened on me. I danced back a step, teasing him, daring him to join the chase.

"You want it that way, then?" His voice was soft, running smooth over the words, but it set me off, the sparks racing through me at a rate I could barely stand. "You want it rough? You want it dark and dangerous and deadly?"

I could only nod. "I need you to be the strong one. I need you to take control." As I said it, I knew it was true—I couldn't handle making another decision; I couldn't handle another choice in the day.

I wanted to forget, to be set free from the constant demands put on me. And the only way that I could lose myself and get out of my head was for Grieve to be strong enough to overpower my thoughts, to overpower my choices, to take me into that dark deep place where I could feel through pain that turned to pleasure. I needed to bleed onto the ground, the pain of the wounds making me know I was still alive, that I wasn't just a figurehead, a symbol, an icon.

I stretched out my arms, and Grieve slowly moved around behind me, taking my arm in his hand, stroking the skin, stroking the flesh up to my elbow. He turned my wrist upward, his lips lingering over it, and then with those razor-sharp teeth, ran them along the flesh, scoring it as he went, a thin red line welling up. The sight of the blood, the sting of his teeth sent me into a frenzy, and I cried out, my head dropping back.

Grieve moved up to stand in back of me, and he encircled my waist, stroking my stomach with his fingers as his teeth found my neck, nipping me sharply, drawing more blood. The venom in his saliva could no longer entrance me, but it sent me reeling, as strong as any aphrodisiac. I moaned as he sucked lightly, drawing drops of blood, and then he leaned around and licked my face, trailing my life force across my cheek, kissing me deeply, his tongue probing my mouth as he began to grind against me.

His cock rose up, strong and firm and thick, and I moaned again, the taste of my own blood in my mouth. But he wouldn't let go. Instead, he walked me toward the bed, his hips swiveling against mine. I ached so deep, so hard, that I could barely stand the pain. I wanted him in me, wanted him to thrust so deep and hard that I wouldn't be able to stop screaming.

And then we were at the bed, and I began to fall backward, my legs opening as he drove in toward me, finding my cunt, finding my center. I was wet, and he slid inside, fitting perfectly, filling me up. The next moment, he was moving in me, thrusting with a passion that I had never met from anyone before—not even Lannan. I wrapped my legs around his back, holding on so tight that I would have broken his back if he tried to pull away.

"Never stop, never stop. . . . Screw me till I can't remember my name."

"I'll fuck you forever. Until you lose yourself completely. You're my shooting star, Cicely, my dark queen in the middle of the night sky. And the only one I will ever share you with is that goddamn Lannan Altos . . . because he saved your life, and that is enough for me to let you take what you need from him."

Tears in my eyes, I rocked back and forth as he plunged deeper with each thrust. And with every thrust, I lost a little bit more of myself until it was all a blur of the night sky and cold fire and the silver stars in his eyes.

And then—in the darkness of his love and his fury, I came to the edge of the precipice, and as he roared to life, the wolf master of my world, I was able to let go and topple over. All thoughts of fear and guilt vanished as I gave myself up to the ecstasy that destroys us all with its passionate drive. With one sharp scream, I let go and flew, and in that flight, I knew that here was my strength—the cold fire of ice and snow, the fire of passion and pain, and sex under the dark and torturous sky.

Chapter 3

A knock on the door woke me. I had fallen asleep in Grieve's arms, but now I was on my side of the bed. I never did do well sleeping in someone's arms. A moment later, Druise entered the chamber. She looked exhausted, and I realized she'd been through the wringer. Again. But she ducked her head and smiled wanly as she tiptoed over to my side. I sat up too quickly, grimacing. I'd slept in an awkward position, and everything ached. Or maybe it was just stress. Whatever the case, I didn't feel quite up to snuff.

"Pardon me, Your Highness, but Thorn—the shaman—he asked me to come wake you and His Lordship." She held out a warm robe. I'd slept in the nude, since we weren't in our own bed, and I slid into it, wrapping it tightly around me. Though I was fairly immune to the cold, here in the shamans' lair, the chill seeped through insidiously, catching me unaware until I realized I was shivering. How they lived this way, I didn't know. It felt silent here, and tomblike, as if a stasis ran through the air, brought about by the ice itself.

"Did you . . . did the shamans . . ." I couldn't finish my question but she finished it for me.

"Yes, they tested me. I wouldn't be here if they hadn't."

She showed me to the bathroom; then when I finished washing up and returned to the bedroom, I found she had thought to bring a change of my clothes with her, including fresh underwear, for which I was grateful. I slid into the panties and jeans, then allowed her to bustle me into a warm but sheer black under blouse, over which she laced me into a silver corset. I slid on my boots as she swept my hair back with the brush. She seemed to pick up on my mood, and remained silent, humming softly as she worked.

After a few minutes, I glanced over my shoulder. "I'm sorry we had to put you through that again, Druise." She'd underwent the procedure before being hired into her position, and I knew how much that invasion had cost her.

Druise gazed at me, her eyes clear and steady. "Your Highness, may I be blunt?"

"By all means." This surprised me—Druise was usually reticent. At times, I thought her overly grateful. But then again, her job with me meant her family was in a better position than they had ever been. She wanted to keep her post and I knew she'd do just about anything in order to make me happy.

"I think . . . I don't dare to presume, but I believe your advisor, His Lordship Strict, would caution you against apologizing to the help. Or to anyone, for that matter. It is not my place to question your motives, or your orders, but to accept them as you will."

I let out a soft laugh. Lainule, the former Queen of Summer, had already had my head over that one. "I think you're right, Druise. But I'm still . . . I regret having had to order this. Allow me that much, at least."

"Honestly, yes the procedure hurts, but for you? I'd walk through fire. You treat me like a real person. You aren't cruel or demanding. I never feel afraid around you—well, not so long as I mind my manners and do my work right. Your Majesty, I would give my life for you." And with that she stopped, flushed and looking ever-so-slightly embarrassed, the brush half-raised.

The realization that I literally held her life in my hands—

every life in my Court—sank in at that moment. I was responsible for them all, and I could terminate any of them—including
Grieve—with one fit of temper or pique.

"Druise, I value the trust and faith you place in me. And
obviously you're here because you passed the challenge. The
shamans wouldn't let you near me without that. Please know
that, any time we ... I ... put you through something like
this, it's only for the good of the Barrow." And what was good
for me, was good for the Barrow. But I didn't say that.

She curtseyed, then finished brushing my hair into a ponytail, then affixed my crown, making certain it set firmly on
my head. As she finished up, Grieve woke, and even as he slid
out from the covers, his clothes appeared, forming as he
stood. Druise curtseyed to him, too, but since she was my
lady's maid, she was primarily at my beck and call.

My stomach rumbled. I turned to her. "Breakfast?"

"There will be food in the testing chamber, they said." She
reached in her pocket and pulled out a roll. "I brought you
this, though, Your Highness. I knew you'd be hungry."

Grinning, I took the bread. "You know me, Druise. You
do at that." And, biting into the soft, crumbling bread, I
allowed her to open the door. One of the shamans' guards
was standing there, and he led us back to the chamber.

Check and Fearless were there, as well as Strict, Silverweb,
and several other members of the Court. I recognized them
all by now—prime power players in my Court whom I needed
to rely on.

"Their loyalty is unswerving, Your Majesty." Thorn eased
into the chair nearest me. "Whoever the spy in your Court is,
the person is not among those here. You should also check
your magic-born friends."

I started to protest—the very thought that Peyton or Luna
or Kaylin might be working against me rankled, but then I
thought back to Leo. He'd not only convinced Geoffrey to
turn him into a vampire, but he'd then turned against my
cousin Rhiannon, to whom he was engaged. In the end, he'd

kidnapped her and put her through hell before we staked him. So Thorn was right. I couldn't very well ignore the possibility that one of my friends was no longer my friend.

"Can you . . . Will this ritual work on them, too?" I asked.

Thorn shook his head. "No, it only will work on members of the Cambyra race and on half-bloods. You must seek another method of checking the loyalty of your friends. And I advise you do so as soon as possible. Meanwhile, we will put all the guards to the test, starting with those who wield more power among your troops, as well as anyone who has any close contact with you."

"How much time are we looking at?" I couldn't stay here until they'd gone through the entire Barrow.

With a shrug, the shaman held out his hands. "I don't know, to be honest. These rituals will take time. Our task cannot be accomplished overnight—even we must rest, and this magic for this ritual requires a great deal of stamina and endurance on our part."

He motioned to the empty seats around the bench. "The others have withdrawn to rest and renew themselves while the next group of guards are being brought to the task. They are on their way now. Meanwhile, we suggest you keep your eyes open and always make certain Check and Fearless are with you, regardless of where you are."

And with that he turned and walked away. There were baskets of rolls, smoked meats—though no fish—and apples on the side tables. As I nibbled on another roll and a piece of jerky, it occurred to me that, until we'd cleared everybody, Thorn was right. I'd need to have Check or Fearless with me at all times. They were sitting nearby, patiently waiting and eating.

As I watched them, I realized that they'd be hard-pressed to catch any sleep. From now on, their sole duty would be to guard me. And that meant they would have to sleep in the sitting chamber of our bedroom in order to be at my beck and call. Another thought crept in—they'd need to watch themselves. Potential spies or assassins might target them as well.

Feeling overwhelmed, and once again slightly claustrophobic, I contemplated our next move. Myst was on the offense. She had been my mother, lifetimes ago, and we were still connected even though I didn't like admitting it. I could feel her out there. She had pulled back briefly to regroup and recruit more of her warriors from other nests where she'd left them. But the hard fact remained: She was ready to go on the attack again.

Closing my eyes, I drifted in the stillness that comes with trying to push out a world of thoughts so you can actually see things clearly. And in that second, all sound stopped, and everything around me faded.

※

I was standing at the top of a ravine as the wind whistled through my hair. The scent of snow rode in on the gusting currents, and before nightfall, the land would be white and it would be, once again, our time.

My name was Cherish, and I was the daughter of Myst, the Queen of the Indigo Court. Myst, the conqueror who had come to this land, where there was still room to grow and expand, to spread out and plunge deep roots. Like the fungi that traveled beneath the earth, that spored and spread through the ground, my mother was planting her seeds, growing a race of hunters. The regional Fae Queens ignored her—or perhaps, they took no notice or did not even know she existed. My mother was good at camouflage and recognized the value of keeping herself a secret. Crafty and cunning, she had passed those traits on to me.

We had come to this land and slowly spread from one end till now, we neared the other coast. All along the way, we laid the foundation for what would—long in the future—become a coup. We had left nests as we worked our way west, to breed and gather strength.

The yummanii who walked these forests knew very little of us, calling us the "blue demons" or the "hunger who walks upon legs." In both senses, they were right. We *were* demons, and we knew it and reveled in it. And we were constantly hungry.

The hunger churned in my stomach even now. The hunger

for flesh, for blood and bone and sinew. The hunger for life force. The hunger to chase, to corner and rip and tear into body and muscle. I licked my lips as I thought about the taste of blood on my tongue, of fresh meat.

"What do you hear? Are there voices on the slipstream?" My mother's words echoed from behind me, and I turned to see her lithe, spidery form rising up. She was lean and tall, with eyes the color of the night sky, and stars glimmering in those jet-black pools—the same as my own. Myst's hair was long, as was mine—again, the black of night—and our skin took on a cerulean cast as the shadows of afternoon lengthened toward dusk.

I did not answer, merely turned back to the ravine to listen. Her question was far from rhetorical—I had a knack for hearing voices in the wind. It helped when we were on a hunt, for I was the best at tracking quarry down, at locating our dinner.

Now I listened, closely. A whisper here, a whisper there. And then—a brief voice crystal clear and shattering to my ears.

You have a split soul, Cherish.

What? Who was talking to me? Frowning, I tried again.

Nature is full of checks and balances. When there is an imbalance in the system, she creates a counterweight to even things out again. You are that counterweight. You are the remedy to the monstrosity who should never have been born. You are the antidote to a creature who stands outside of the balance.

Startled, I reared back, opening my eyes as I searched for the source of the voice. But there was no one in sight. I shaded my eyes with my hand, trying to locate whoever it was that had been talking to me, but not a creature stirred. The birds and animals could smell my mother and me and kept still for fear we would gobble them up.

"What is it?" My mother leaned over my shoulder, resting a thin hand against my back.

Something inside warned me to keep my mouth shut. I didn't know why, but whatever it was I had heard put me in danger. I had no clue what the woman—for it was a woman's voice—was talking about, but it unsettled me. She'd been talking directly to me, and it had sounded too definite, too authoritative for comfort.

"Nothing. . . . Just chatter from the Ice Elementals. There's snow on the way, and you can gather the energy and bring up a strong storm to cloak our path." The latter was true, but in my heart, I knew that something had shifted. This was the first time I'd ever lied to my mother.

"Ah, then nothing to worry about. Come, my child. Food awaits. I saw a hunting party by the lake, and with any luck, they will still be there. Fresh sweet meat and blood." And with that Myst held out her hand.

As I took it, a niggling doubt crept through the back of my mind. She believed me. *My mother didn't know I was lying.* And that—that was almost more unsettling than having told the lie.

❧

I shook myself out of my thoughts. More and more, memories of my life as Cherish crept in. I didn't like it that they did, and the fact that they were coming in strong and clear lately scared the fuck out of me. How much of my time as the heir to the Indigo Court had stayed with me? How much of the Vampiric Fae nature did my soul still contain?

Grieve glanced over at our guards. "You know what this means for you, correct?"

Check nodded. "Yes, Your Lordship. We will be the Queen's constant companions. Even when the others are cleared, I think we should continue as her official escorts. Best to establish a core network, considering there are spies about. Too many with access to the inner Court can create an unintentional doorway for enemies to gain a foothold."

Strict let out a shaky breath as he stood, leaning on the back of the chair for support. "Your Majesty, I understand why you couldn't tell me about this before testing me, but now—we must discuss this in a private council. With Myst moving again, and with the Shadow Hunters within the boundaries of our realm, we have no time to waste. You must contact the Summer Throne and let them know. And the Crimson Court."

Silverweb leaned forward, her elbows on her knees, clasping her hands. "It's time for us to band together. We must not forget the Consortium. Your connection with Ysandra Petros may help there. Myst—"

Before she could continue, Thorn came rushing back into the room. "You must return to your throne room, Your Majesty. There is news. We can speed the way for your journey back, but you must leave now. Be cautious—evil deeds are in action, and there will be no turning back now. Here, we will rest in shifts and work our way through the rest of your guard as soon as possible. We will not fail you."

And with that another one of the shamans—we did not know his name and he did not offer it—appeared and gestured for all of us to follow him.

I looked at Grieve, an apprehensive cloud settling over me. Ulean fluttered around me with gentle whisperings.

I'll go ahead and find out what I can. I will meet you there, Cicely.

Thank you—and, Ulean? Be cautious. I know there are Elementals out there who live for chaos and mayhem, just as Myst does. And she might control some of them.

Fear not. I will watch my back. And then she was gone.

Thorn stopped us. "Van will lead you back. He will take you through the Dream Time in body so that you can be there in seconds. Be prepared for exhaustion on the other end. Eat as soon as you get there, even while you are in chambers discussing this matter. Eat protein and bread. You need the energy of both."

I nodded and turned back to Van. "We're ready. What do we do?"

He looked tired but motioned for all of us to stand. "Join hands, please."

We formed a circle. I held on to Van's hand on one side, Grieve's on the other. A moment later, I felt an icy chill begin to rise up into my feet, and from my feet into my legs. A lacework of energy, the frost networked its way through my body, paralyzing me as I stood there, unable to move.

Grieve's hand slipped away—or rather, it felt like it did,

but it was hard to say because everything began to shift and move as a mist enveloped us. Van's fingers disappeared, and there was nothing between me and the swirl of ice and chill. This was different from when I called the winds and they swept me up. This didn't suck me in. I retained control of my senses even though my body wasn't able to respond. But the cold made me lethargic, and I fell into a light somnolence as the vortex worked its magic on me.

Time vanished. I had no idea how long I'd been dozing, but a quick jolt startled me, and I realized we were standing in the council chamber back in the Eldburry Barrow. As I tried to shake the fog out of my head, my knees gave way, and I tumbled to the ground before Grieve or Van could catch me.

I landed on the floor and the hard stone woke me up—or rather, made me all too aware of where I was. Groaning, I rolled to a seated position, and Grieve reached out a hand. He pulled me to my feet.

"So much for graceful." Yawning, I managed to make it over to a chair. I turned to Van. "You said we'd be exhausted, but I had no idea to expect this."

"That's why you must eat. Food won't wake you up, but it will give you stamina and replenish the energy from transferring through the Dream Time." He stepped back. "I must return. Thorn will be in touch. We will begin testing the warriors en masse and work around the clock until we are done." And with that he vanished.

The others weren't hit as hard as I was. Full Cambyra Fae were still more resilient than I, even though I was the Queen. But everybody looked like they'd been dragged home by the cat after a long night on the town. Druise headed for the door, but I stopped her.

"Druise, you're going to get food?"

She curtseyed. "Yes, Your Highness. With your permission."

"That's fine—we all need it. But remember: No one must know what's going on or that the shamans are testing people. News will filter out soon enough; there's no help for that, but we want to keep it secret as long as possible." The longer we were able to keep the matter quiet, the less chance there was the spy would be able to report back to Myst that we knew she was out and about.

Druise nodded. "Yes, my Lady." And then she slipped out the door.

I leaned on the table, resting my chin on my elbows. The others looked as wiped out as I felt. "So . . . what do we do next? I'd send out a scouting party, but if the spy is among the guards . . ."

"You make a good point. And you cannot afford to risk Check or Fearless on the pursuit." Strict frowned, tapping his fingers on the table. "We may have to wait on that. Unless . . ." He paused. "There is one possibility—the Wilding Fae? The Snow Hag seems to be firmly in your Court. Myst can trap them but not turn them, as far as I know."

"Courting favors with them is a tricky business. What about my father's people? The Uwilahsidhe? Is there any there we might trust? They could fly in owl form, scout out from above." I would have done it myself if I thought they'd let me get away with it, but I knew better than to even make the suggestion.

Strict frowned. "You might be onto something. There is"— he paused, as if searching for the right words—"I must walk softly on this one. There is someone we can trust, but . . ."

My advisor wasn't usually so reticent. In fact, he was downright bossy and domineering at times—but always in a respectful way. I wasn't sure what to make of his pussyfooting around. Rather than push, I decided to wait.

After a moment he shook his head. "I have an idea, and as soon as I determine whether it's viable or not, I will inform you. After I've eaten, I will feel it out." And with that he pressed his lips together, and I realized we weren't going to get anything more out of him at this point.

Grieve cleared his throat. "We should talk to your cousin—the Court of Rivers and Rushes must know that Myst is back in the area. If she's infiltrating the realm of Winter, you know she'll be after Summer's heart, too."

"We'll go after we've eaten. And, as much as it pains me to agree with Thorn, we do have to figure out how to make certain Peyton, Luna, and Kaylin are on our side. I believe I know a way. While the shaman's ritual won't work on the magic-born . . . Kaylin's night-veil demon can invade minds. He did that to me once." It had been horrible, but he'd done it to help me.

"Yes, but who will vouch for Kaylin?" Grieve smiled softly. "There's the question."

At that moment, Druise returned with food, and I insisted she sit down and join us. She was as tired as we were. As we broke bread and passed around the venison cooked with juniper berries, I couldn't help but feel the weight of the overwhelming odds we were facing. But this time, there would be no reprieve. We were headed to the final battle. I could feel it in my bones.

✣

As we stood at the edge of the Twin Holly trees that sheltered the portal into the Golden Wood, I steeled myself. The bracing energies raging between the trees were buzzing like a hive of bees, a network of sparks that raced through the body. The energy jarred me, but I was getting used to it.

We'd sent word ahead to Rhiannon that we needed to meet at the Veil House. It seemed easiest to go there rather than face the risk that spies might also be in the Summer Court.

As Check and Fearless moved to flank my sides, Grieve took the front. We had to make it to the Veil House on our own. We didn't dare put our trust in the other guards until we knew they were safe. Though, it occurred to me that if they were out to assassinate me, they'd had plenty of time.

Maybe they aren't aiming for a simple assassination, Cicely. Remember, Myst has a long memory. She prefers to toy with her quarry before she swoops in for the kill. She might be saving you for herself because she considers you a traitor, even though it was several lifetimes ago that you turned your back on her. Ulean was with us—she was sticking to my side like glue, for which I was extremely grateful.

The thought that Myst might be out for more than just my blood was almost more terrifying than the thought of actually fighting her. What she could—and probably would—do to me was more horrific than I wanted to think about.

"Come on, then. We'd best get a move on." The Golden Wood was still covered in snow even though it was early February. Normally, New Forest, Washington, claimed some snow during the winter, especially out in the woodland areas, but nothing like this. This season had been like no other. Myst had rolled out her long night and blanketed the town with perpetual snow. But after spending a month in the realm of Winter, the weather felt almost balmy to me. While it was colder than normal in the forest, it was far colder in my new home.

We glided across the snows, running atop the four-foot-deep banks that filled the forest. The woods here were like most of those around western Washington. A playground for cedars and towering firs, the undergrowth grew so thick you needed a machete to get through the bracken and brambles, huckleberries, and waist-high ferns.

The ground beneath the snow was spongy during the spring and autumn, soft and filled with detritus from the long seasons gone past. Moss blanketed the sides of the trees and spread across the fallen logs and over the boulders that had tumbled through the valleys during the slow retreat of the glaciers during the last ice age.

But a new ice age was what Myst sought to bring about. Not content with the balance, she was looking to rule over the world, creating a snowy hunting ground for the Indigo Court. And the Golden Wood was her chosen place to make her stand. Home to both the Summer and Winter Courts of this region, the Twin Hollies led into my realm—the Court of Snow and Ice. Twin Oaks led into my cousin Rhiannon's realm—the Court of Rivers and Rushes.

We shared the wood, and the balance entailed handing over rule on the summer and winter solstices, with each of us guarding our half of the year. Mine was the waning half, hers was the waxing. But Myst had destroyed the balance before we came to power. She had managed to wrest it away from Lainule, the former Queen of Rivers and Rushes, and Tabera, the late Queen of Snow and Ice. She had destroyed Tabera's heartstone, killing the Winter Queen, and had managed to drive Lainule back to the Golden Isle.

Skimming the top of the snow was still a novelty for me. I hadn't gotten used to being able to traverse the wintery fields as if I were gliding on air. Suddenly, for pure joy, I twirled, skating on the crust, delicate in my movements for the first time in my life.

Behind me, Check laughed gently. "Be careful, Your Highness. You can still slip and hurt yourself."

"I've fallen so many times in my life it's second nature." And it was true. I'd spent my youth honing my skills in running away, dodging danger, and sneaking into apartments in order to ransack them for money. I'd learned how to climb through windows, drop down fire escapes, and edge out onto ledges in order to avoid people coming home before I was done pilfering their apartments. But, given all that, while I'd developed muscle and speed, I'd never considered myself graceful.

"Be that as it may, perhaps the skating should wait until we're safely at home in our own realm." Grieve glanced over his shoulder, a smile spreading across his face. He stopped suddenly, staring at me. "Cicely, you are so beautiful—look at you, in a mantle of white."

I glanced down. I was wearing the owl-feather cloak, but the softly falling snow had blanketed me in a layer of flakes, freezing against my skin, against my hair. I was outlined in frost, in winter's lacework shawl. I held out my hand and watched as the snow landed on my palm, not melting—but sitting there, crystalline and pristine.

The realization slowly filtered through that I was now colder than the snow. Colder than the dead. I had truly become the Queen of Snow and Ice, and though my heart pumped and blood raced through my veins, heat no longer translated through my body. I was winter incarnate, as frozen as the icicles hanging from the eaves.

Grieve moved to my side, reaching out his hand. In the

same silence, we turned and began to run again, heading toward the Twin Oaks.

We were nearing the turnoff leading to the Marburry Barrow when a flutter of wings caught my attention. I glanced up. A great horned owl—looking much like my father, though I knew it couldn't be—swept past. I shaded my eyes to gaze up at the circling form. As the owl swooped lower and lower, a noise of rustling bushes sounded behind us, and Check whirled, pulling out his sword. But it was Strict sweeping out of the trees, taking long strides.

He was almost to us when the owl suddenly spiraled down to land on a nearby log. Strict passed me with a perfunctory nod, then knelt by the owl and waited. My heart fluttered. I knew it wasn't my father, but for Strict to kneel to anybody meant this was someone terribly important.

The owl was larger than my father was in owl form, with a wingspan that must have stretched over five feet in width. He was white, mottled with brown markings, and I had the feeling this bird had seen the decades come and go. I knew he was Uwilahsidhe—I could feel the connection between us even though I was only half-blood.

Strict motioned for me to come forward, and so I did, slowly approaching, all the while wondering whom I would be facing. Grieve followed behind me, as did Check and Fearless. We formed a semicircle around the log, with Check and Fearless holding our backs, keeping an eye out lest anything should come out of the undergrowth to attack us.

I closed my eyes, inhaling deeply. The scent of winter was all around—the smell of ozone from the storm tinged the air with its acrid scent. The tickle on the back of my neck told me we were expecting snow-thunder. The world felt on edge, poised and waiting. Ulean swept around me, and I could sense she was both excited and nervous.

Who is this? What's going on?

I cannot tell you.

You know, though?

I do, but I was bound to silence by Wrath. Now, though,

*you shall know. I did not believe this day would happen—
and I am both overjoyed that it is happening and filled with
trepidation. I don't know how you'll feel. Or what you will
think about this.*

Yet another thing she hadn't been allowed to tell me. Over
the weeks, I'd discovered that Ulean knew far more about my
life than Lainule had allowed her to reveal, and it appeared that
was still the case. Ulean was bound to me, yes, but she was still
enjoined by promises to the former Fae Queen.

I was about to push her for further information when the
owl began to shift form. As we watched, he morphed, shimmering as wings shifted to arms, beak to nose, tufts to ears.
A moment later, there, sitting on the log in front of us, was
one of the Uwilahsidhe. His jet-black hair was streaked with
gray, which told me he was incredibly old—the Fae didn't
gray the way magic-born and yummanii did, not until they
had reached a great age. The man in front of us had probably
lived for centuries, if not longer.

As Strict slowly stood, hands patiently folded behind
him, Check let out a gasp and stepped forward, kneeling in
the snow. Fearless looked as clueless as I felt, but Grieve—
my beloved Grieve hung his head and slowly knelt before the
aging man.

"Am I the only one left out of the loop?" I didn't like
being the odd one out when it came to things like this. I
never liked surprises—be they a birthday party or an unwel-
come trap. I'd dealt with too many unexpected snafus and
bugaboos over the years.

The man stood, his clothes shifting to take on the appear-
ance of a feathered cloak like mine, beneath which he wore
brown trousers and a tunic. There was something oddly
familiar about him. He looked . . .

"Oh my gods . . . Wrath . . ." This couldn't be my father,
and yet the resemblance was uncanny.

"No, I am not your father, Cicely. My name is Hunter, and
I'm Wrath's father. I'm your grandfather."

And with that the world fell away.

Chapter 4

"Grandfather? You're my grandfather?" I didn't know how to react. I'd barely gotten a chance to know my father, let alone learn anything about his heritage. The only thing I knew is that he had been born into the Court of Snow and Ice. Check had been his oath brother, pledged to marry Lainule, but the moment she laid eyes on my father, the rest was history. Wrath had fallen in love with her and changed his loyalty to the Court of Rivers and Rushes. That my guard leader bore them no ill will both humbled and amazed me, but Check had become their most loyal supporter.

Hunter slowly circled me, eyeing me up and down, his expression carefully set to neutral. I restrained any impulse to throw my arms around his neck and give him a hug. One thing I'd learned the hard way, starting with my mother, is that blood didn't always mean fealty.

"My son did you a disservice by not telling you about your heritage early on." Hunter did not look pleased. "You have much to learn. You know nothing about your people—my people. I know"—he held up his hand when I started to protest—"I realize this is not your fault, but you must spend time with us, to understand what your heritage and lineage means."

My heart leaped. This is what I wanted, though I wondered

if the Uwilahsidhe would resent me, considering my background. Hell, when it came down to it, I knew very little about
the history of the magic-born, either. Krystal had kept me in the
dark. Whatever she'd been taught, she'd repressed with the
booze and drugs, and a deep disdain for her own abilities.

"You wouldn't mind teaching me?" As I spoke, my voice
cracked, and I realized this meant more to me than I could
ever have imagined.

The only family member who'd ever truly loved me was
my aunt Heather, and she was long gone now. I'd had to play a
part in her death, which still hurt. Rhiannon and I were
rebuilding our relationship—so far, so good. But when it
came down to it, Ulean was the closest thing to family that I
had left. She alone I trusted not to let me down. While Grieve
was my husband and I loved him with all my heart, I also
knew how fragile love could be. It was hard to let myself
believe that we might have our happy-ever-after ending.

I guess Hunter sensed my need because he paused, staring down into my eyes, and his face filled with a compassion
that I seldom saw in any of the Cambyra. He placed his hand
on my shoulder.

"My granddaughter. I know your story, and I know what
you've been through so far in your short life. It's never easy
to be destiny's pawn, nor to believe that your existence was
engineered merely to fill a need. You are Wrath's daughter.
You are *my* blood. Beyond the crown you wear on your head,
beyond the title you assumed . . . you are my family, and I
will do what I can to help you connect with your roots." He
backed away then, turning to Strict. "I have scouts I trust.
They are wild and feral, belonging more to the wing than to
any Court or allegiance. I will send them on reconnaissance
to see if we can search for the upstart and her armies."

And with that he turned to go, but stopped. He glanced over
his shoulder and, looking at me, said, "I will be in touch, girl.
Now is not the time to begin your studies, though I know you
are champing at the bit. But after this war is over, we will take
wing and fly together. You will learn what it truly means to be
one of the Uwilahsidhe. Half-blood . . . is as good as full."

And then he shimmered and in a blur, transformed back into his owl form, and winging his way through the falling snow, he vanished into the depths of the Golden Wood.

I wanted to cry. I wanted to laugh. I had a grandfather. I had family and roots. Krystal and Heather had spoken very little of their parents. My mother and her sister had been closed mouth. After Heather died, Rhiannon had confided that she'd found nothing about our relatives in the trunks that had remained undamaged during the fire at the Veil House. Our mothers had been chosen by the Fae. Rhiannon's father was also Cambyra Fae, but a snake-shifter.

Neither of us had known the truth about our fathers until the past few weeks. We were still navigating our way through the labyrinth of what felt like a conspiracy surrounding our birth. And truth was we *had* been bred for the thrones of Winter and Summer. Hunter was correct in his statement that our very existence had been engineered. We were created to fill a need rather than conceived out of love. So many unanswered questions remained, that I doubted we'd ever know the full story.

I turned back to Grieve, who smiled at me. He held out his arms, and I slipped into his embrace, pressing my head against his chest.

"I have a grandfather," I whispered.

"I know." He kissed the top of my head. "Hunter is very old and very wise, and from what little I know about him, he seldom takes form in human shape anymore. He's one of the elders of your father's people, you know."

"I didn't know, but it doesn't surprise me." The wind was picking up, and the snow was starting to fall harder. As much as I wanted to shift into owl form and follow my grandfather, he was right—now was not the time.

When—*if*—we all came out of this war intact, then I would try to forge a relationship with him. A spark in my heart told me that I'd be very disappointed if it didn't work out. Family had always been important to me, but I'd had to push the desire into the background in order to put my focus where it had mattered: surviving day to day, and sometimes hour to hour.

"We'd best get a move on. Rhiannon will be waiting for

us—I sent word for them to meet us at the Veil House, and though I said it was important, I gave no clue as to what, in case the messenger . . . well . . . in case whoever carried the message happens to be the spy we're searching for."

"What will you do about the others? About Luna and Peyton and Kaylin?" Grieve let out a heavy sigh. "We have to figure out a way to test them."

"I know what to do about everyone except Kaylin, but in a sense he's the most important. He can examine their minds, but who can look into his heart and find out if he's safe?"

A little voice inside me whispered, *How can you ever trust anybody? Sometimes you just have to step away from the fear and take a leap of faith.*

With that thought ringing in my mind, I nodded, and we headed out again as Strict made his good-byes and returned to the Eldburry Barrow.

✴

The Veil House had belonged to my aunt Heather, and before her my grandmother and great-aunt. From what little I knew, the house at the end of Vyne Street had belonged to the women of the family for generations. It was also centered over a major ley line—an energy vortex. Aunt Heather had figured that out from notes in a journal we'd found. What she'd planned to do with that knowledge neither Rhiannon nor myself had figured out, and we might never know, but even if we couldn't reason out why Heather had researched it, we might be able to make use of the knowledge in the future.

With Rhiannon and myself living in our respective realms, Luna, Peyton, and Kaylin had taken over the house and were keeping it safe for us. Luna had assumed the business I'd planned to open—Wind Chimes, a magical emporium. Peyton was working hard to open her magical PI firm—Mystical Eye Investigations. They would host them from the house to avoid having to rent out space in town.

A part of me mourned the loss of my plans and the loss of the life I'd started to lay out for myself. Whoever said you can never go home again was right. No matter how good—

or bad—your home was like, when you try to revisit the past, you find that everything has shifted.

And for me, that shift had been drastic. On one hand, I had a purpose; I had a new life and an amazing one at that. On the other, I'd been dragged in from a ragtag existence, but one where I understood the game. I knew how to hedge my odds on the streets, but coming back to New Forest, I'd plunged into a surreal nightmare. As rough as things had been walking the underbelly of the cities, I'd never had to kill before. I'd never had to fight a war.

The edge of the Golden Wood opened into the backyard of the Veil House, which was at the end of a cul-de-sac on Vyne Street. Seeing the house standing there, rebuilt from the fire that had destroyed part of it, made me long for my old life even more. I'd never aspired to be a queen. I'd never once played the princess when I was a child. Now the neighborhood and the house looked so cozy and inviting that I let out a soft sigh. Grieve put his hand on my arm, and my wolf shifted on my belly, letting out an anxious huff.

"I'm all right," I told him. "Just . . . nostalgic. But I'm nostalgic for what might have well been a dream. I only miss the life I had before I was six, before Krystal dragged me away. I remember it through a child's eyes. For all I know, it might have been hell on earth for Heather and Krystal. Maybe Krystal left for a good reason. I'll never know, not now. Everybody who could tell me the truth is dead."

"You miss what might have been." Grieve gazed at me, his eyes black as night with glittering stars. "But love, that's not a bad thing. I, too, think of what might have been. . . ."

I nodded. He had his own demons. He'd been born to the Court of Rivers and Rushes, and Myst had taken him forever into the ice and chill. My Summer Prince was now as bound to the Winter as I was. Together we would rule a land neither one of us would have picked, if given a choice.

Check stood guard by my side while Fearless reconnoitered the area. Ulean swept past, also checking for hidden threats and dangers. A moment later she was back.

The area is clear, but they have been past. The Shadow

Hunters. I can feel their energy on the slipstream. Their
hunger is strong. And Cicely? In town . . . there is trouble.
Horrible trouble.

Vampire trouble?

No, Lannan's people still sleep—it is not yet dusk, even
though the storm holds the light at bay. Myst's hunters . . .
They are feeding.

Her thoughts were tinged with pain, and I cringed. New
Forest, Washington, had already seen a decrease in popula-
tion recently, as people fled from the attacks that had run
rampant through the city. A few people had started to trickle
back, but fresh murders might destroy the city for good.

New Forest was a small town near Snoqualmie,
Washington—nestled between the larger urban areas that com-
prised the GSMA—the Greater Seattle Metropolitan Area—
and the Cascade Mountains. But sometimes it seemed as
though New Forest was off the grid. The town felt so discon-
nected from the other cities and communities. I couldn't
remember if it had been that way when I was a child, but ever
since I'd returned, the city felt severed from most of the world.

I steeled myself as Fearless returned. While he didn't
have the same information regarding the town that Ulean had,
he verified that he'd seen no sign of the Vampiric Fae around
the perimeters of the land. Nodding, I motioned toward the
house, and we strode out of the woods into the clearing and
raced across the wide lawn separating the Golden Wood from
the town.

The door opened as we neared it. Luna stood there. Short,
plump, and curvy, the yummanii bard motioned us to hurry
in. She stood back as we burst through the door. The television was on, and she held her finger to her lips as she bustled
back into the living room.

We followed.

There, Luna, Peyton, and Kaylin were watching the news.
Peyton was part Native American. She was half werepuma
and half magic-born. Rex, her father, had recently reentered
her life, only to be struck down by one of our enemies—a
vampire named Geoffrey, who was now dust. And her mother

had betrayed us and almost managed to kill me. She, too, had died at the hands of the vampires. Peyton had taken both losses hard, but she was stoic, as usual, and doing her best to weather the situation.

She waved at us, but her gaze was still glued to the television. Another moment, and I understood why, as the newscaster returned.

"We repeat—stay inside your homes. Lock the doors. The attacks continue and a representative from Lord Lannan's estate has informed us that the danger we face still stems from the Vampiric Fae—from the Shadow Hunters."

Lannan must have had a speech prepared for this eventuality. As much as I loathed the vampire, I had to admit he was smart, especially for someone who hadn't wanted the responsibility of being Regent. But the Crimson Queen had decreed him in charge, and he would obey because, as loathsome as he could be, Lannan was loyal to the throne, and to his sister Regina—the Emissary for the Queen. He was also Regina's lover, but that was beside the point.

"I repeat, the Regent requires that you stay indoors. Defend yourselves should you need to, but be aware: These creatures cannot be reasoned with; they are cunning, intelligent, and out for blood. Do not approach them. Do not attempt to bargain with them—they are ruthless killing machines. Hide yourselves, and tonight, the patrols will be out in full force to counter their attacks. During the meantime, the city council is appealing to the Courts of Winter and Summer to send aid, and to the Consortium."

Rhiannon was standing to one side, and when the newscast ended, she crossed the room, arms out. Without thought for decorum, I gave her a tight hug, and the warmth of her skin almost burned me. I stood back, gazing at her.

"You feel like you've got a fever." Cocking my head, I searched her eyes. She looked worried, but beneath the worry, I could sense happiness, and also exhaustion.

She returned my gaze. "And you feel like you're chilled to the bone. You look as tired as I feel."

"We've both got a lot to learn and not much leeway as far

as time." I paused, feeling oddly unsure what to say next. We hadn't seen each other for a couple of weeks, and a subtle distance had grown between us.

"We should respond to their request." Rhiannon looked as uncomfortable as I did. Her hair was flame red, and she practically crackled as she moved. While I could control the winds, she had power over flame, and the sparks arced off her body, a flickering of pale orange that haloed around her.

I glanced at Luna and the others. "Can you give us a few minutes? I need to talk to Rhiannon and Chatter about something."

There was a flash in Luna's eyes that told me I'd hurt her feelings, but she motioned to the others and led them out of the parlor, followed by Rhiannon's guards. Check and Fearless stayed behind with us. I closed the door and locked it.

"What's going on?" Rhia sounded more like herself, and as I turned, her gaze flickered toward the door. "Something's up, Cicely. I didn't want to give away anything in front of the others, but I can feel it. My advisor, Edge, told me that Strict contacted our shamans. They put her and my private guards to the test this morning. They also searched Chatter's mind. Just *what* were they looking for?" A hint of anger colored her voice. I didn't blame her.

"Thank gods. We are at least a leg up, then. The guards you brought with you? They all passed the loyal test?"

"Yes, and I don't mind telling you, it wasn't any fun watching the process. Now tell us, what's going on?" Sitting on the sofa, she patted the cushion beside her, and Chatter joined her.

Grieve and I sat opposite, on the loveseat. I glanced at the closed door, then lowered my voice. "There is a spy in my Court working for Myst. We don't know who it is, yet. But we also encountered Shadow Hunters in my realm, and we know Myst is on the move again. For all we know, there may be spies within your Court as well."

Rhiannon was silent for a moment. Then, "Dear gods . . . she's back, already?"

"We knew she wouldn't take long. She just managed to regroup faster than we feared." I gave a little shrug. "So we have to find this spy, and any more that might be hiding in the shadows. I think we should go on the offensive." Pausing, I looked into my cousin's eyes. She was nodding. "Also, on the way here? I met my grandfather."

"What?" She leaned forward. "Would that be . . . my grandfather, too?"

I realized she thought I was talking about our maternal grandfather, whom neither one of us had ever known. "Oh, no, sweet. I'm sorry. I didn't mean to get your hopes up. I met Wrath's father. His name is Hunter, and he's one of the elders in the Uwilahsidhe. He's going to scout for the Shadow Hunters' hideout while we try to clear the rest of our guards through the loyalty ritual." Once more, I glanced back at the door.

Ulean, can you check the other side and make certain nobody is listening at the door?

A moment later, she swept around me, a faint gust lightly ruffling my hair. *No one there, Cicely. They wait in the kitchen, and they worry.*

Thank you. I hate that I have to keep them out of the loop, but it's imperative until we know what we're dealing with.

"That's not all. My shamans told me that we must verify that Luna, Peyton, Ysandra, and Kaylin are loyal." Before she could say anything I held up my hand. "No, I know—how can we question them? But remember what happened with Anadey. And . . . Leo."

Rhiannon hung her head. "Yeah. I'd rather forget Leo, but I get your point. You're right, of course. But how do we do that?"

"I think Kaylin can do it—especially since his demon is so much stronger now. He can enter their minds and sort through their thoughts." Even as the words came out of my mouth, I cringed. I knew how it sounded. Hell, I knew how the others would take it.

But to my surprise, Rhiannon nodded. "I agree. But how do we verify Kaylin's loyalty? We can't just take his word for it."

"Therein lies our dilemma. The shamans can't test him—he isn't Fae. He isn't even half-Fae." And then I stopped. Maybe . . . there might be one person we could turn to. A seer. An oracle, actually. But he wasn't human, and hadn't been for thousands of years. And whether he'd help us . . . that was a sticking point.

"You are thinking something. I know it. What are you thinking?" Rhia leaned forward and took my hands. "Tell us."

I looked from her to Grieve to Chatter, wincing. "I don't want to suggest this. *Please* know that this is the *last* thing I'd suggest if I could think of any other way."

"The Consortium?" Rhiannon frowned. "I'm not so sure about them."

"No. We can't trust them any farther than we can throw them."

"Then who?" Grieve sounded suspicious, and I realized that my wolf was transmitting my nervousness to him. No matter what, I couldn't lie to him—I couldn't hide things from him. We were linked in too many ways.

"I'm thinking . . . we take him to Crawl."

A beat passed, then another—and then they all burst out in loud shouts, just as I thought would happen. I said nothing. Let them tear the suggestion to shreds, and then I'd explain myself.

"Cicely, are you crazy?"

"You can't be serious!"

"After what Crawl did to you, you seriously are suggesting turning Kaylin over to him?"

After a moment, they fell silent, staring at me. I stared back, unwavering.

"Got that out of your system? Okay, seriously, do we have a fucking choice? The facts are simple: We're facing the end of our world if Myst wins. Suppose she manages to find our heartstones? Then, not only do you and I die, Rhia, but so do our people. We have thousands of lives resting in our hands now. Do you want to risk it all?"

"I guess . . . you're right about that."

"You bet I'm right. We aren't playing penny ante poker anymore. We're in the big leagues, playing for high stakes. We can't afford to be squeamish. We can't afford mercy." I winced. "The truth is, we can't afford to spare our friends a little pain."

I fell silent, leaning forward as I pressed my hands against my knees. My jeans felt rough under my palms.

"But he tried to kill you." Grieve's voice went cold, and his lips were curled back, baring his teeth. He looked ready to shift into his wolf form at any minute.

"Of course he tried to kill me. Crawl's a fucking freakshow. But he's *also* an oracle, and he also hates the Indigo Court. Crawl can't lie. Or at least, I don't think he can. We don't even know if he'll do it. But if we take Kaylin to him, chances are good he'll be able to tell us if we can trust him. Crawl can see into the future, to some degree. And into people. He looked into me when the vampires first took me before him."

"I still don't like it, but you may be right." Chatter surprised me, being the first to take my side.

"After we verify Kaylin is still on our side, then he can probe Luna's, Peyton's, and Ysandra's minds." I began to feel the breeze pick up around me as the winds responded to my mood.

"Why not take all of them to him, then? Why just Kaylin?" Rhiannon sounded genuinely confused.

I sighed. "Kaylin's the strongest. He can withstand having that freakazoid in his mind. I don't think the others could. Crawl . . . You don't know what he's like. I do. He's like an insect that won't stop. Ruthless and alien. But Kaylin . . . Well, ever since his demon woke up, he's changed. He can meet Crawl's inspection and pass through."

So much had gone on. We were all changing; we were all shifting. The world would never be the same again, and we'd all have to man up.

Rhia let out a soft sigh. "I can't argue with your logic."

"Do you really think I'd hand Kaylin over to the Blood Oracle if I didn't think he could make it through?" I stared at my hands. But then I shook my head. "You don't have to answer me. I am honest enough to admit that I might do it, if I thought it were the only way to save the day."

"Oh, Cicely—we know you wouldn't do that." Chatter tried to cheer me up, but I shook away his support.

"Yes, I would. And don't tell me you wouldn't—any one

of you. Too much rests on our shoulders. We don't have the leeway to be merciful anymore, not if it means we endanger everyone around us."

"You're right." Rhiannon stood. "I stand by you. Chatter, you are my consort. You will abide by our wishes?"

Chatter merely nodded.

Grieve looked torn, but then he shrugged, giving in. "Okay, then. How do we work this? If there's a chance that Kaylin is a spy, we can't forewarn him. Or the others."

I frowned, thinking. Grieve was right. We couldn't take any chances, especially after the speech I'd just given. I crossed to the window and stared out into the snowy afternoon. It was nearing dusk.

"We talk to them as if everything's normal. When they ask what's up, we tell them . . . We'll tell them that we needed a break. That the adjustments to life in the Barrows is daunting, and we are taking a few days out, to regroup. I'll call Regina and have her summon us to talk to them. At dusk, we'll all go over to Lannan's estate. I'll talk to him and Regina in private, and if they agree, we can take Kaylin to the Blood Oracle right then, before he'd have a chance to get away. And then, while still there, he can check the others. We'll need to get Ysandra over here on some pretext though."

"That shouldn't be hard; she wanted to talk to Luna about some sort of magic they're cooking up." Rhiannon grimaced. "I dread the aftermath of this, though. I know it's necessary, but the fallout is going to be problematic, at best."

"I know, Rhia. I know. I've prepared myself to lose friends. I hate the thought, but there's nothing else we can do."

"Your Majesty, if you don't mind me interjecting a thought: Kaylin is still weak from the attack a month ago, but he should be able to handle himself." Check had been listening in, but now he moved forward.

"Do you think he's well enough to handle the Blood Oracle?"

"Is anybody ever well enough to handle him, Your Highness?"

As Check posed the question to me, I closed my eyes and

once again found myself in the grips of the Blood Oracle as he sought to drain me dry, to feast on my blood.

He was like an insect—long and lean and gangly, with limbs like hollow husks, except they were strong. Oh, so strong, and oh, so dangerous.

Crawl scuttled, shifted without seeming to move. He was a vampire—a dangerously old and mad vampire. He had been sired by the Crimson Queen herself, and he lived in a prison because he had long ago forgotten how to listen to orders, how to keep from being a one-man scourge on those who still walked with blood pumping through their hearts.

Crawl, the Blood Oracle, the seer of the vampires, the father of vision who foretold the future and who remembered the past. He was mad as a hatter, mad as a hare. Lost in a world of his own, he spoke in riddles, doling out dribs and drabs of information in return for the sacrifice of life, the sweet force of the veins.

Locked in his prison, a world between the worlds, he waited for an opportunity to free himself. He'd been loosed on the town not that long ago by the renegade vampires Geoffrey and Leo, and he'd fed and fed, drinking deep and casting aside the bodies. But Crawl hungered for more; there was always the thirst, the burning need to feed, and so he had driven his way through the people of New Forest, as ruthless as a spider spinning her web for flies.

People were chattel—food and nourishment. Our lives, our hopes and dreams, our desires were moot in the face of the Blood Oracle. He fed off pain, licked it up like a delicious syrup on top of ice cream or cake. He reveled in it, without care, without worry, without any shred of guilt.

It had been so long since Crawl had been human—yummanii—that he'd lost any semblance to the people on whom he now fed. He was beyond the scope of most of the vampires, and even the Emissary and her brother feared him. Crawl could just as easily stake their hearts, cast them aside, and move on, as he could feast off their slaves.

And the Blood Oracle had, three times, had me in his

grasp. He'd fed off of me—the last time nearly killing me. Lannan had stepped in, brought me back at a cost that I could never forget. As much as he disgusted me, the hedonistic golden boy had been responsible for saving me, and I owed him a great debt.

And now I was planning on turning my friend over to the monster. That's what Crawl was: a monster, a creature, no longer anywhere near human. I knew he would ravage Kaylin's mind.

But . . . but . . . a small voice whispered. *Kaylin is demonic. He can handle this journey, and he will understand why you did it.*

Kaylin's soul was wedded to a creature as alien to the yummanii as was Crawl. When we had woken the night-veil up to consciousness, we had not only saved Kaylin's life but opened the door for him to change. He would never be the same—could never be the same.

And Crawl? Crawl would strip him down and sift through his psyche, but Kaylin was resilient. And he would come through intact.

And if he's the spy?

The question raced through my mind. I didn't want to think about it, but I already knew the answer. I knew what would happen. If Crawl told us that Kaylin was our downfall, I would leave him there. Let the Blood Oracle bleed him out, tear him to pieces, rend his soul even as he ripped at his body. Because if any friend of mine had turned sides, had voluntarily aligned themselves with the Indigo Court, they had automatically forfeited all protection, and my love for them would shatter like crystal.

I looked up. The others were waiting.

"Let them in. They'll know something is up, but we *have* to lie. I'll step out and call Regina's day-runner in a moment, then we'll leave for Lannan's estate shortly after. Dusk will fall by the time we get there. I think I can convince Regina and Lannan to play along with us."

At that, Grieve gave me a dark look, but I merely stared back at him. I would do whatever I needed to, and he knew it. And I knew he supported me. Even if it meant handing myself over to Lannan again. Even if it meant sacrificing myself at the altar of the hedonistic vampire.

"Open the door," I said. And Check did.

❧

As we neared the estate where Lannan and Regina lived, I shifted uncomfortably. We'd stopped on the way to pick up Ysandra, the last member of our inner Circle. She gazed at me, silently, and I had the feeling she knew something was up, but she said nothing.

The others had been less than thrilled about the idea of visiting the vampire compound, but there wasn't much they could do. They deferred to us now that we'd taken the thrones.

I'd called Regina to tell her that we were on our way and to ask her and Lannan to wait for us—that we had something important to ask them. By the time we arrived she'd be awake and get our message.

A few minutes later, we pulled into the compound. It was hard on Grieve and the other Fae, for they couldn't ride in cars so had to run along beside the vehicles. My father had done his best to ride in my Pontiac one time, but it had jarred him greatly, and he'd hated every minute of it.

I was driving Rhiannon and myself. The others followed in Kaylin's car—if one of them was betraying me, not such a good idea to be alone in a car with them without my guards. I'd had to play some fancy footwork to explain why we were riding separately, but again, it seemed that making up stories on the spot was becoming a strong point of mine, even though it made me feel like a louse.

As the estate—a magnificent mansion that rose three stories aboveground, and who knew how many below—came into view, I let out a soft sigh. The grounds were exquisitely kept, though they lay below a cloak of snow, and the borders of the estate were patrolled by armed guards—vampires during the night, and their day-runner guards during the day.

We pulled in, and I turned off the engine. I glanced at Rhiannon. Even though we were half-Fae and had been transformed by our coronations, we weren't affected by iron like our people. The magic-born blood in our veins helped prevent us from succumbing to the pain of the metal.

"You know I wouldn't do this if I could think of anything else." I wanted my cousin, above everyone else, to understand how much this went against my nature.

But she reached out, put her hand over mine. "I know. Cicely . . . when I burned that little girl to death . . . even though I didn't *intend* for it to happen, the fact is that on that day, I realized I could never go back. I could never again be the person I'd been before then. No matter what I did, I'd always be affected by my actions that day. My anger had been my undoing."

"I'm not angry at him, though." I bit my lip, hurt that she might think so.

But she merely smiled. "No. You aren't angry at him, not at all. And yet you are ordering that he undergo a painful and dangerous test. The reason you are doing this? Because on the day we accepted the crowns, on the day we created our heartstones and took the thrones, we changed who we were. We'll never again be just Cicely and Rhiannon. We'll always—forever—be affected by the choice we made that day. And every action we take will be affected by those choices. It is what it is."

It was then that I began to understand something about my cousin. I'd been worried she might not be strong enough to withstand the changes we underwent. But now I saw that Rhiannon had developed an inner strength. Yes, it was a quiet strength, but it was resilient. Rhia had landed smack in front of her demons long ago, and even though she'd run from them for a while, she finally had turned to face them, and to own them.

I lifted her hand to my lips and kissed it gently. "Twin cousins, forever."

"Fire and ice."

"Amber and jet. Summer and Winter." With a soft smile, I unbuckled my seat belt and slid out of the car, meeting Check and Fearless as they raced over to my side. Rhia's guards joined her.

As Kaylin and the others fell in behind us, we turned to the mansion and—with a cloud looming over my shoulders—I led the way into the ambush we'd set for our friend.

Chapter 5

The maid who opened the door recognized me. She'd been there the night Lannan brought me back to heal me from Crawl's last attack. When the Blood Fever had taken me in thrall, I'd needed sex—rough and wild and as feral as I could get, and only Lannan could offer me the intensity that would shake the fever loose from my system.

She ushered us into the mansion. The great hall had taken on some renovations, though it still sported the sweeping staircase to the upper floors, nestled between two halls that ran the depth of the mansion. Large, luxurious rooms veered off from the hallways. We'd been in two of them. I'd been in one other room in the house—Lannan's suite, though I doubted it was where he slept during the day.

To either side of the staircase spiraled massive, heavily pruned junipers, sculpted into coiling snakes that gazed over the hallways in their glistening green finery. Marble benches and tables made of heavy dark wood lined the walls at intervals, and the floor was polished tile, gleaming so brightly that I could see my reflection in it. I'd hate to be on the cleaning crew for the Regent's mansion—it was expected to remain spotless and meticulously groomed. As were most of the vampires making their home here.

I motioned to the maid as another servant took Luna, Ysandra, Peyton, and Kaylin's coats. Pressing a note into her hand that I'd prepared while still in the car, I whispered, "Please, give this to the Emissary now—before we're shown into her office."

The maid glanced at me, quizzically, but simply curtseyed. "I'll be back for you in a moment," she said to everyone. "Please be seated while I make certain the Emissary is prepared to receive you." She tapped away down the hall, her kitten heels tattooing a quick beat against the floor.

We waited a moment—then two, before she returned. "Please follow me." And she led us down the left hall to the office of the governing Regent.

Behind the heavy double doors, Lannan and Regina were waiting for us. Regina was sitting behind the desk; Lannan was sprawled in a chair next to it.

Twins with hair as golden as sunlight, spun straight and silky, the pair were as depraved as they were gorgeous. Regina was statuesque, curving in all the right places, and she wore a red pantsuit with a black corset beneath the blazer. Her hair was swept up into its usual chignon, and sparkling rubies studded her ears. Lannan, on the other hand, had hair that swept past his shoulders, and he wore black leather pants, tight and formfitting—showing off every attribute he had. He had on a brilliant blue button-down shirt, open to the naval, and an ornate black leather vest.

They were true vampires—not Vampiric Fae, but truly the living dead. Their eyes were black as pitch, but no stars swirled within, and they ruled the town, even though there was an ostensible city council.

As a pair, they were stunning.

Lannan stared at me, his eyes taking me in with one sweep. I blushed—I couldn't help it. He was obsessed with me, and I'd been bound to him by a contract until I was chosen to transform into the Queen of Snow and Ice. I'd knelt at his feet, forced to grovel and beg him to humiliate me. Vampires had glamour, and most of them didn't care what their chosen subjects felt. They were top-of-the-food-chain preda-tors, and they knew it and used it, although there existed a delicate balance between the governments of the Vampire Nation and those of the yummanii and the magic-born.

"Your Majesty, please be seated." Lannan stood and gave me an exaggerated flourish of a bow. While technically showing respect, I knew he was goading me. Ever since he'd fucked the Blood Fever out of my system, his obsession with me had grown.

"Brother . . ." The cautionary note in Regina's voice echoed through the room. While Lannan might be Regent, his sister was the Emissary, and her word held sway over everyone in the Vampire Nation, save for the Crimson Queen herself.

"I'll behave myself. Don't get your bun in a twist." Lan-nan motioned for us to sit down. "Please, be seated."

I paused, wondering how this would unfold. My note to Regina had asked her to please find something to occupy the others while Rhiannon, Grieve, Chatter, and I talked to her in private.

But Regina was smooth. She stood. "I have official busi-ness to discuss with the Courts of Fae before we all make ourselves comfortable. My servants will escort the rest of you to the drawing room, where you will find tea and refresh-ments. While you are there, perhaps Luna can look over the arrangement on the piano. I've attempted my hand at a com-position. While I'm pleased with it, I would welcome your input on ways in which to strengthen the intermezzo. Your musical eye would be highly appreciated here."

Luna blinked, clearly surprised. "Of course, Emissary."

"Thank you. I respect your skill." Regina smiled at her, a cunning beautiful grin that was hard to resist.

I blinked. "You play piano?" I don't know why this sur-prised me. But after I thought about it, it seemed like a skill I'd expect Regina to have.

"I have played for well over two hundred years and am fairly accomplished, but I've never before attempted my own compo-sition." She smiled at me, her fangs showing ever so slightly.

Luna looked a little puzzled, but she motioned to the oth-ers. Warily, they edged out of the room, following the maid.

Once they were gone and the door closed behind them, Regina turned to me. "You needed a private audience?"

"I did, but we needed to bring the others, to have them here on the estate, in case you agree to what I'm about to ask." Here I paused. What I was about to ask was turning me into a traitor to Kaylin, but once again, my heart told me there was no other way.

Lannan searched my face. "What weighs so heavily on the Ice Queen's heart?" Again, his words were punctuated with just a hint of snideness—a soupçon of snark.

With a glance at Rhiannon, who nodded, I launched into what we had learned, and what we needed to ask. By the time I finished, Regina was staring at me, jaw slightly open. Lannan was shaking his head.

"That crown truly has changed you. How does it feel, now, to be on my side of the tracks? To play the sadist—for you know that's what this will end up being, should we agree?" He let out a faint snort. "Sweet Cicely, you truly do have a heart of ice now, don't you?"

I wanted to slap him but held myself in check. A quick glance at Grieve told me he was close to doing the same. My wolf shifted and growled, and I knew Grieve was pissed out of his mind.

Regina, however, simply sat there, as pale as porcelain. She folded her hands together on the desk. "You're truly serious about this? You would have us take the night-veil to Crawl? To let the seer peer into his heart and future to see if he's loyal?"

I bit my lip, wanting to hang my head. But Lainule had taught me well, and I forced myself to meet her gaze. "Yes. We have to know. Then he can test our other friends. There is far too much at stake to risk putting our trust in anyone unless we know for sure that trust is warranted. We know you will not side with Myst—it's inborn in your nature to go against the Vampiric Fae."

And truth was I was right.

✳

Eons ago, Geoffrey, before he had taken the name Geoffrey, had attempted to turn the Fae of the Unseelie Court. He had taken Myst down, drank her to death's door then fed her his blood, hoping she would turn when she died and come back to life. But Myst had not died.

Instead, she regenerated at a vastly increased rate of healing, and along with her own dark powers, she now possessed the powers of the vampire, along with others that had developed out of the unholy union. The whole idea had been a conspiracy between the pair, but once Myst found herself growing more powerful than Geoffrey, she had cast him aside as she turned others of her kind.

The Vampiric Fae fed on life force and body, as well as blood, and they evolved into the Shadow Hunters: ruthless killing machines. Worst of all—the Vampiric Fae could breed. With no more need for Geoffrey's help, Myst turned against the vampires, creating her own empire. And eventually I had been born, her daughter Cherish, and we came to the New World in search of land in which to breed, and conquer.

Now, the Vampiric Fae had grown strong, and they were rising, not only to fulfill a long-prophesized war against the vampires, but to spread their disease throughout the land. Turning the magic-born and Fae as they went, they set out to enslave the yummanii and the magic-born as their cattle, and to destroy the balance between Summer and Winter.

Regina glanced at Lannan, who gave her a subtle nod. "We can do this thing," she said, "but it will require a price. You know the Blood Oracle requires a sacrifice of—"

"Of blood. I remember. I will pay it." I hated the thought of seeing him again. He'd almost killed me. He'd had more of my blood than I ever wanted to give him, and the thought of coming into close contact with him again gave me the creeps. What if he managed to catch hold of me again? What if he tried to finish the job he'd started?

Grieve must have caught my fear because he stood. "I will go with her. I will not allow her to go there alone."

I turned to him. "You can't. We can't afford to chance both of our lives. The Barrow must have guidance."

"You are the heart of the Barrow, so if anyone remains behind, it must be you." Grieve's eyes gleamed in the dim light of the shadowed room. Outside, the snow fell silently, blanketing the already whitened lawn.

I turned to Regina. "He'll demand my blood, won't he?"

She nodded, a solemn look spreading across her face. "None other will do. I know the Blood Oracle too well. He is . . . unswerving. You escaped him. Now he thirsts for you—to drink you up and leave you a shallow husk. Like all spiders, his thirst never abates. But once we caught him after Geoffrey and Leo set him free, we keep him on a short leash. There is no way to fully guarantee your safety, but we will do as much as we can to keep you from harm."

Lannan, for a change, turned serious, and the smarmy look vanished. "Definitely. Regina will guide you there. If I go with her, it may set him off. He remembers that I freed you from his grasp, and he's not taken it well. The Blood Oracle would as soon drink me down as he would you. I am now his enemy."

I hadn't expected that, but it made sense. Crawl might put the true vampires above everything, but if someone crossed him, I had no doubt that he would waste no time in eradicating them if at all possible.

"So, by saving me, you put yourself at odds with the Blood Oracle. I'm truly sorry about that." And for once, I meant it.

The politics of the Crimson Court were complex, a minefield of hazards. This could make it dicey for Lannan if Crawl had supporters who might not appreciate Lannan rescuing someone who wasn't a vampire. However, the fact that I was the Fae Queen, and that he had managed to avoid a dispute between the Fae Courts and the Vampire Nation probably swayed opinion to his side more than anything else.

Lannan caught my gaze, holding it. "Do you think I care what anyone thinks about me?"

"That's precisely why the Crimson Queen questions your ability as Regent," Regina said, walking behind him. She stopped to cuff him lightly on the head. He snarled at her, showing his fangs, and she laughed. I had the feeling this was foreplay between them.

"Then she should choose someone better for the job. I never once expressed an interest in wearing this hat. I much prefer my job as professor at the New Forest Conservatory." He arched one eyebrow at me. "All those lovely young coeds, both magic-born and vampire. But none, none can hold a candle to the Queen of Ice."

Grieve stiffened. I could feel his reaction through my wolf, but he said nothing. Truth was Lannan was to thank for me still being alive, and we both knew and accepted the ugly truth. We owed the vampire a favor, and Lannan knew it as well.

"Back to the subject at hand. When can we go? And Kaylin doesn't have a clue about this. We didn't dare take a chance, just in case—"

"Just in case the night-veil demon is your spy. Of course." Regina motioned to Lannan. "You will summon the man. Leave the others where they are and make certain they are protected."

"As you wish." Lannan slipped out of the room, softly shutting the door behind him.

Regina followed him out the door with her gaze, then brought her attention back to us. "Rhiannon, you and both consorts will remain here. Cicely and I will take Kaylin to the Blood Oracle. Check, you may come as your Queen's guard, but you will obey *me*. Do you understand? If I say jump, you jump. If I say drop down on the floor—"

"I will drop. Yes, Emissary." Check snapped to attention, clicking his heels together smartly as he straightened his shoulders.

The fact that Regina addressed neither of us by our title didn't bother me, and I knew it didn't irk Rhiannon, either. Regina had known us both before our coronations, and somehow, rebuking the Emissary to the Crimson Court for overlooking a few words would just be borrowing trouble. There was no disrespect in her voice, and I doubted any was meant.

As she finished speaking, Lannan reentered the room, Kaylin in tow. I caught my breath, wondering how the fuck we were going to explain what was about to happen. We couldn't just drag him along with us and then throw him to the wolves, so to speak.

Regina took care of that problem. She motioned for Kaylin to take his place in front of her. "Kaylin, I'm afraid we have a problem."

He looked at her, a quizzical expression on his face. "Have I done something to offend you?" While a faint smile played on his face, a feral light flickered in his eyes. With his demon fully emerged, Kaylin had turned into a highly dangerous adversary, though there was no way to know just how powerful he would become as he evolved.

The Emissary shook her head. "No, you haven't. I think, perhaps, the best tactic to take is the truth. Cicely, you do owe him an explanation, considering what we are about to undertake."

I dreaded the thought, but she was right. How could I ask him to undergo Crawl's scrutiny without knowing why? And if he was the spy, and tried to bolt now, then we'd be able to stop him. But . . .

"What if there's a mind link?" I asked Regina. "What if . . . what I fear turns out to be true and there's a link there?"

"Good point. That, however, we can solve simply enough." She took hold of Kaylin's arm. "Check, Cicely, follow us."

Kaylin, looking confused now, allowed Regina to lead him over to the bookshelf. Check followed close behind, ready to stop him should he try to turn on us. If Kaylin *was* the spy, he either didn't suspect anything or was furiously plotting what might happen next.

Lannan pressed a book on the bookshelf behind the desk. A secret door slid open to reveal a passageway lit by a dim light. We passed into a room where a table sat in the center, and a single bulb hanging from the ceiling illuminated the space. On the table—which was shaped like an octagon—a crystal hovered above a two-inch-thick crimson block of glass.

As soon as the door slid closed behind us, Regina let go of Kaylin and motioned for us to gather around the table. Still looking bewildered, Kaylin did as asked. Check stood next to him on one side, Regina on the other. I stood opposite him.

"Here, you may tell him. We are between worlds now,

and I doubt if any message could reach through the veils."
She nodded at me.

"Tell me what?" Kaylin was beginning to look worried.

"Kaylin, I'm so sorry. But we have . . . I have . . ." I
paused, uncertain how to verbalize my thoughts, but then
they spilled out of their own accord. "I have to do something
that's going to be horrible. I have no choice." In a flood of
words, I told him what we were doing and why.

The expression on his face passed from angry to incredu-
lous, and then—resigned. "I understand."

I didn't want to look into his eyes, to see the betrayal that
had to be lurking there, but I forced myself to meet his gaze.
I owed him that much.

To my surprise, Kaylin seemed calm and collected. "I
understand," he repeated. "You have a spy in your Court;
you must find out who it is. Your shamans can't perform
their rituals on us, so—"

"This is the only way," I finished.

"We are so far past being able to trust anyone's word. Look
at what Anadey did. To you. To Peyton, her own daughter."

And then I realized that he really *did* understand, and that
almost made me feel worse. I would have felt better if he'd
yelled or screamed or cussed me out. But instead, he stood
there stoically, and it made me almost want to say, "Forget it,
I trust you." But I couldn't take the chance.

"Yes . . . so, when Crawl verifies you are what I believe
you to be—a trustworthy friend—then we will have you
examine Peyton, Luna, and Ysandra. I know how you feel
about Luna, but . . ."

Kaylin had fallen hard for the bard, and I knew it wasn't
going to be an easy thing for him to delve into her mind. And
I knew what he saw there might not sit well. Luna cared for
him, but she was wary—not willing to dive off the cliff,
romantic though she might seem to be.

Kaylin made no move to try to escape. Instead, he turned to
Regina. "Tell me what to do. I will listen. I've no desire to have
Crawl any closer to me than need be, so let's get this over with."

And with that Regina traced some sort of symbol over the

crystal then said, "Hold hands." She took Kaylin's hand in her right, mine in her left. Kaylin reached for Check, and I completed the circle by holding my guard's hand. As the world began to spin, twirling like a Tilt-a-Whirl, everything fell away, and a rush of wind swept us into the churning slipstream of time.

✤

Time went whistling past, the centuries turning back—or perhaps we were moving sideways, hopping realities as the creak of trees echoed in the howl around us, and the scent of smoke from burning wood swirled to surround us. A shadow of spiders crept past, on tiptoe, and I wanted to whimper. Then a flurry as a murder of crows rose up and vanished through the turbulent currents.

We traveled between worlds, through portals in a way unlike the Twin Oaks and the Twin Hollies. Those portals shifted us, body and soul, through a crackle of electricity. This vortex swept us up and cast us to the raging winds, letting them buffet us against the jutting rocks of the static-filled ocean, bruising our psyches until—with one final howl—the winds dropped and we were standing in a gigantic chamber, dimly lit and echoing with every sound, every breath.

We were around a table identical to the one in the secret room back at the mansion. I slowly turned, all too aware of where I was.

Regina waved us toward her. "Follow me and do not step off the path or you will not live long enough to regret it. When we come to Crawl, do not speak directly to him. Do not answer him. Answer me if he asks you a question, and let me take the lead. Do you understand?"

Kaylin and Check both nodded. I already knew the drill. We set off, behind Regina, following single file. Kaylin walked behind her, then me, then Check.

Thirty feet high, the ceilings loomed overhead, painted to mimic stained glass, with portraits of battle and sex, a glorious beatitude in vivid color to the art and consequence of war. Below the ceiling, a rich, crimson wallpaper covered the chamber, and the light source remained hidden, but dim light flickered through the room. Marble benches lined the walls, their feet lost in a heavy mist that wisped along the floor in scattered strands.

The floor was, as I remembered it, a grid of magical symbols. A narrow pathway led through the etched tiles. Tuscan gold in the center with thick black border lines, each of the blank panels was a safe place to step. I remembered enough to know the magical runes engraved on the rest were to destroy the unwary. Setting foot off the path was painting a bull's-eye on your forehead.

As we neared the front of the chamber, my heart leaped into my throat. There, a dais ran the width of the room, about five feet high. Regina lithely jumped up onto the platform and took a look around. Then she turned back and motioned for Kaylin to join her. He scrambled up as Regina offered me a hand. Check simultaneously hopped up to join us.

I quickly glanced around, on high alert. And there, about ten feet away, crouched Crawl, the vampire of my nightmares.

Twisted and bent in a low squat, Crawl was near a cushioned seat, but he ignored it as he sniffed the air. He was an insect, a walking stick, with skin that had been blackened and crisped. His face was wet with rivulets of blood. Viscous and sticky, they trickled down his jowls. A swollen tongue snaked out from his mouth, hideously long, to flick at the droplets as they neared his chin. His eyes were black as night—vampire's eyes, yes, but the lids had long ago been burned away, and his gaze was hollow.

Yet I had the feeling he could see through me to my insides, see my bones and blood and muscle and sinew. When I'd first encountered him, he'd had clumps of matted hair, but now his head was smooth, and that made him look even more alien.

I glanced to the left, and yes, there was the fountain I remembered. It bubbled brightly with blood, echoing with the merry sound of splashing. A circle of flames surrounded the font, and it was from here that Crawl drank, forever burning himself to reach the sweet blood he craved. It seemed terribly sadistic of the vampires—to punish their oracle by making his food so painful to reach—but the ways of the Crimson Court eluded me, even though I was beginning to understand the need for authority to bear a certain ruthlessness . . . even cruelty at times.

Crawl let out a slow hiss and leaped toward me, but then, as I stumbled back, he stopped short. It was then that I saw the iron chain around his neck. It blended in with his skin, and it gave him a certain amount of leeway while keeping him at bay. He could reach his fountain, and his cushioned seat, which was large enough to sleep on, but he could not reach me.

He let out a garbled shout as rage and disappointment filled his face, but it passed as quickly as it had come. "Regina, Regina. My wayward child and lovely daughter of the vein. Your brother is forbidden in my presence, you know."

"This is known and accepted. Lannan is not with me. I come seeking information. I bring you sweet offering in return for your sight. This matter concerns the Vampire Nation . . . the Crimson Court, in a peripheral manner." She slid a narrow dagger out from a sheath hidden at her ankle.

"The only offering the Blood Oracle accepts from you is the sweet blood of Cicely. Such a sweet, warm taste. I would have it from her neck." He licked his lips, looking at me. I turned, trying to avoid his gaze.

Regina cleared her throat. "The Blood Oracle remembers what the Crimson Queen has decreed, does he not? For escaping from your prison, you may not press lips against flesh. I will give you her blood, but in the offering font, and only with your promise to read the omens and seek the answers."

I stole a glance at Kaylin. He had never encountered Crawl—not up close. Kaylin had been wounded during the last battle and had not been there to see the Blood Oracle attack me. But he'd witnessed the aftermath in my scars.

He was staring at Crawl with a revulsion that I seldom witnessed on his face. After all, he was connected to the Bat People through his demon, and they were an odd race in themselves, alien and terrifying. But Kaylin grimaced as Crawl leered at me, licking his lips again.

"The Queen in her madness gives me no quarter, does she now, my dear daughter? You pain your father thus. . . . But you must do what you must. I will accept the pittance and be satisfied with that." The sad, puppy-dog voice sounded contrived, a spider spinning a web. Crawl's only pain was that he wasn't allowed to rip me to pieces in a feeding frenzy.

Regina stared at him for a moment, then in a rare show of temper, blurted out, "Old Father, do not push me. I may carry your blood within my veins, you may be my sire, but I will not stand for this. We are facing dangers that could lead to the downfall of all, including the Crimson Court. Your personal whims and desires? They are nothing in the face of she who seeks our demise."

Crawl blazed up, a rearing back, hissing at her, his fangs down and ready, but then he paused, and—simmering at a low boil that I could feel from where I stood—backed down.

"Very well, *daughter*. Make your offering, and I will do my duty and give you my sight."

I followed her to the font as she watched to make certain Crawl stayed the distance. He moved too fast and could be on us in a heartbeat, but her warning seemed to have staved him for the moment. I hurriedly held out my hand, and she sliced deep, across my palm. I turned my hand palm down over the fountain, my arm wavering between two of the flames, and my blood spurted into the font. A moment later, Regina bade me remove my hand and then lifted it to her lips, licking it slowly, every touch of her tongue sending shudders through me. And they weren't unpleasant.

Crawl watched with greedy eyes, and Regina quickly moved me out of his reach again. "Old Father, drink and be satisfied. Then tell us what you see."

In a blur, the Blood Oracle was at the font, his tongue dipping into the blood as the flames licked his face. He showed no sign that the pain was hitting him, though I knew it must be. But maybe time had seared his nerve endings; maybe he simply no longer cared.

"What say you?" Regina motioned for Kaylin to come close

while I moved back to stand by Check. "Old Father, look into this one—is he loyal to Cicely? To the Court of Snow and Ice? Has he pledged his help to the Indigo Court?"

Crawl cocked his head, leaning close to sniff at Kaylin. "You smell like demons, like bat guano. You smell like a cold autumn night, and like ghosts of the past. I hear spirits around you—they follow you and watch, waiting to see what you do. But . . ." A pause, while the vampire seemed to take stock.

With a shake of the head, Crawl moved back to hop up on the cushioned seat. He hunkered down, his feet on the cushion in front of him, bony knees thrusting up near his chin. "Come here, young man."

As Kaylin approached, Crawl grabbed him by the head and pulled him close, licking him across the eyes and face. Kaylin let out a cry but went limp as the Blood Oracle's hands held him tightly. And then, as a low beat began to resound through the chamber, Kaylin began to scream, writhing in Crawl's embrace. But the vampire held him firmly, not biting him, but breathing on him, his gaze fastened on Kaylin's unblinking eyes.

He twisted as Kaylin struggled, but never let go. Crawl's voice was raspy as he sank into a trance, and the words echoed off the walls of the chamber.

"This one is no danger to our sweet Cicely. He craves nothing . . . save for one young woman. But his threads of destiny lead in a different line than hers, so hearts afire will fizzle and love will wither. However . . . there are alliances being formed, but not the ones you fear—and not ones *to* fear. This one . . . He is destined for great things but not in this realm. Your destiny lies in a dim and distant land, boy—so prepare to leave your home. Your destiny will plunge you into the heart of the darkness from which your demon was spawned."

And with that Crawl curled up on the cushioned seat and turned away, falling into a silence that echoed louder than his words.

Chapter 6

Kaylin slipped into a fugue as Crawl let go of him. Regina dragged him back for Check to carry—though she easily could have done so—and motioned for us to follow her quickly. We headed back through the maze of plain floor tiles as Crawl let out a shout that reverberated through the chamber. It was a howl, a guttural cry of frustration, and it scared the hell out of me.

We made it to the table, where Regina passed her hand over the crystals, and once more we took hands, with Kaylin draped over Check's shoulder. The room vanished as we fell back into the swirl of time, rushing every which way to return to the mansion.

I shuddered as the room began to materialize again—we were back in the small chamber, safely away from Crawl.

Turning to Regina, I gazed at her softly. "What happens if he ever gets free again? Can he get loose from his prison now?"

She regarded me quietly. "We have built in safeguards against that happening again. To be honest, we thought he was safely locked away the first time. It never occurred to us that anyone would be foolhardy enough to ever set him free.

Geoffrey showed us that we cannot afford to trust even those closest to the Crown." Regina passed a hand across her eyes, and I thought, for a moment, she looked almost human. Her lip twitched, and a vague wash of pain swept across her face.

I took a stab in the dark. "Geoffrey was a surprise to you, wasn't he?"

The Emissary stared at me, her hand back by her side. For a moment, I thought she wasn't going to answer, but then she gave me a faint nod. "We did not expect his disloyalty. We all go through loyalty tests—those of us within close proximity to the Crown. He passed his last. . . . There is unrest in the Vampire Nation because we now realize that at least some of the Vein Lords can—"

"Fake out the test."

"Yes, that is one way of putting it. We never realized that was possible. So one of our tasks now is to develop a new form of testing that eliminates the chance for deception." She paused, then glanced at Check who was studiously ignoring us. "You yourself now understand the nature of what it means to be a royal—and what it means to not know whom you can trust. Cicely, when you take a position of power, it means leaving activities, and people, behind. You can never be as free as you were. Even when you were under contract to my brother, you were freer than you are now."

I nodded, absorbing her words. She was trying to help me. For whatever reason, she was doing her best to give me advice, and I'd be a fool not to pay attention. Regina might be harsh, and frightening, but unlike Lannan, she was all business, and she thought in terms of power and how to play it. She respected me more now because I had taken the throne.

Even though the thought rankled a little, I wasn't letting myself take offense. There was a mindset that went with power. And there was a mindset that went with being a vampire. Something about the turning brought it out, that much I understood. Though we might not like it, it was simply a fact. With the ability to destroy others, to turn them into the living dead, with the ability to control through glamour, came a certain arrogance. It was what it was.

I thought carefully before I spoke, because what I was about to say would affect the Court of Summer, too. But it seemed a good time to broach the subject.

"Will the vampires stand with us against Myst? And if we do defeat her, will we be able to forge an alliance afterward? As bad as the Indigo Court is, given what we saw down in the sewer system—with the creatures from the depths—we must think of the possibility that there are more dangerous beings in the world. In New Forest. I would prefer we work together to keep the town safe."

Regina regarded me quietly, then said, "I cannot give you an answer—the final word must come from the Crimson Queen, of course. But I will do my best to convince her that such an alliance would be the best way for us to move into the future. The Fae Courts are changing. The Consortium must follow suit. And the Vampire Nation? It would do well to heed the signs of evolution."

With that she moved to open the door, and we were once again back in the Regent's office.

�֊

Kaylin was beginning to come around as we schlepped him onto the sofa. Rhiannon, Grieve, and Chatter turned to me. I was about to speak when Chatter interrupted.

"I take it he's loyal to the Courts, or you would have let Crawl slurp him up?" The callous note in his voice startled me, but he just shook his head when we all turned to look at him. "You know I'm right. As much as I know this pains you, Cicely and Rhiannon, I also know we cannot allow our Courts to be endangered."

"Chatter is right." Grieve stood back, folding his arms across his chest. "So Kaylin passed the test?"

I nodded, thinking back to what Crawl had said. "Kaylin has a destiny that is going to take him away from us. And, I think, away from Luna."

"I think I may know what it is." Kaylin sat up at that moment, wincing. "I never want to see that freak again, but I'm glad I went. There was something playing in my mind—something

I've been dwelling on ever since I was hurt. I haven't said a word about it, because I didn't know if it was just my imagination or not. But Crawl . . . he confirmed what I thought."

"Are you all right?" I rushed over, kneeling down by his side.

"Well, it wasn't a walk in the park, and I feel like I've been hit by a sledgehammer—my head feels bruised inside and out—but I'll be okay." He accepted the glass of water that Regina offered him, drinking it greedily. "I feel dehydrated."

Regina motioned for Lannan to get the pitcher and refill the glass. "You probably are. The Blood Oracle . . . well . . . Let's just say he has more than one method of attack. And his touch is as unpleasant as his presence."

"What did he confirm, Kaylin? We heard what he had to say, but what was he talking about?" I had a nasty suspicion but was hoping I was wrong.

Kaylin was unusual. We'd been in the Court of Dreams, talked to the King of Dreams who was the lord of the Bat People. The night-veil demons had chosen the Bat People as their children, but with Kaylin, it was a little different. His mother, one of the magic-born, had been possessed by one of the demons during her pregnancy. It had died, but its soul bonded with the child in her womb. The King of Dreams had told us there were a few others like him—a new generation.

"I must return to the Bat People and learn from them. There are things I need to know for my future. While I don't know what that future is, I knew in my heart long ago that it would lead me far from New Forest into a different realm."

"I had a feeling that might be it. You have to return to the Court of Dreams, don't you?"

He nodded. "There are things only the Bat People can teach me. I think . . . it's the only way. They said I'm part of a new generation. I think I'm going to be at the forefront of . . . whatever my people will be called." He hung his head. "I should never have led Luna on. I don't want to hurt her."

Biting my lip, I decided to just be upfront about what I knew. "Kaylin, Luna cares about you, but she's still uncertain. She's held back. I asked her, while you were hurt. She told me because the future is so tenuous, she wasn't letting herself fall for you." Even though I knew the news might hurt him, I hoped it would alleviate any guilt he was feeling.

Kaylin's gaze flickered to meet mine. "I hope you're right."

With a heavy heart, I asked, "Are you feeling up to helping us? I know it's going to be hard for you to check Luna. Probing anybody's mind can't be pleasant." And having Kaylin's demon in my mind hadn't been pleasant, either.

He pushed himself fully to a seated position. "Yeah, I'm ready. But . . . are you going to tell them first? And for me, it helps if they're asleep—or drifting off. I work better during that time, being a dreamwalker."

Kaylin could travel the astral, in body and in spirit. That was how he could get into people's minds. The night-veil demon just made the process easier for him. I still wasn't entirely clear on what a dreamwalker was or how they became one, but I had the feeling he'd been born that way. Most of the magic-born had one innate ability over the others. I was a wind witch; Rhiannon worked with fire. Leo had been gifted with herb crafting. Anadey, Peyton's mother, had been an anomaly—she'd been adept with all four elements. Peyton's magic came out in divination.

I turned to Regina. "I hate to ask this, but is there a way to put them to sleep? Ysandra will be difficult, given she's so strong in her magic."

Regina glanced at Lannan, who said, "Visotine."

"What's that?" Kaylin stood and stretched.

"A safe knockout drug. It shouldn't hurt them. The stuff can flatten a horse." Lannan shrugged. "We have occasion to use it on members of our stables. It will quiet even the most magical person."

"You're sure it's safe?"

Regina nodded. "As safe as any drug can be. I have never seen anybody have more than a slight hangover from it. Should we administer it to them? It's simple, tasteless, and the dosage is easy to control."

With a heavy heart, I okayed it. As Lannan left the room, I crossed to the window. It was snowing up a gale outside.

When we had pushed Myst back, the winter had died down a little—felt more normal. But today, I closed my eyes and I could feel Myst on the winds. She was out there, no longer waiting but beginning her advance. The snow was a directed force, swirling in a frenzied dance, eager to gobble up the land.

For the first time, I began to think by the time this battle was over, I wouldn't have any friends left. Those still alive would probably hate my guts. As I stood there, contemplating what felt like a bleak future, Rhiannon joined me.

She put her hand on my shoulder, leaning against me. "We will win this. Don't fear. We'll win, and free New Forest of Myst."

"But what then? The town is dying. People are being murdered on the streets. You saw the news reports. Will there be anybody left?" I turned to Regina. "We heard the news. What's going on in the town?"

She let out a soft whisper, as if to someone by her side. Then she flipped on her computer and quickly tapped something onto the screen. Another moment and she met my gaze.

"There were fourteen deaths today—the Shadow Hunters are in the town. Lannan and I already dispatched a group of men tonight to hunt them down and eradicate them. They seem tougher than before. I think Myst has been recruiting for strength rather than numbers." She pulled out a file and tossed it across the desk. "I think you should see this."

I picked up the folder. "What is it?"

"What we have managed to gather on Myst and her cronies the past few weeks. We noticed that attacks on animals near the town were growing—yes, we keep track of things like that." Regina drummed her fingers on the desk. "The remains were . . . few, and viciously ripped to shreds. We're not stupid—we know Shadow Hunter attacks when we see them. So Lannan sent out scouts and began to find traces of them. They're cagey though, and good at hiding in the woodlands surrounding the town. Then, yesterday, the attacks on people began."

"Yesterday? How many, total?" Rhiannon turned from the window, where she'd still been standing.

"Twenty-two deaths. Sixteen wounded, six severely." Regina leaned back in her chair. "We can send scouts out into the woods, but the Shadow Hunters can hide by night and come out in the day. They know we can't chase them down during daylight hours."

"I may be able to help there. I met my grandfather today. He said he'd send out reconnaissance to look for Myst's warriors. If the Indigo Court is holing up in the Golden Wood, we'll find them." Though I said it with more confidence than I felt, I still felt that at least we had some hope.

At that moment, Lannan returned. He motioned for Kaylin to follow him. "They're all asleep and will stay that way for the next few hours. How long do you think it will take you to examine their thoughts?" Though he spoke to Kaylin, he looked at me, and in his face was hunger mingled with a strange sense of loss.

For once, I met the vampire's gaze, and—even though I didn't want to admit it—the thought of his touch appealed to me. The more stressed I was, the more I welcomed his slam-bam attitude. My darker nature hid in the shadow of worry and regret, and when the gloom grew thick, it came out to play.

Kaylin glanced from Lannan to me but only said, "Not long, though it will be harsh and penetrating. They will wake with the full knowledge of what I've done. I'm prepared for their anger, as should you be. This is a deliberate mind-fuck, Cicely. I agreed because it truly is the best option in the situation, but even my demon is squeamish at the intrusion. And it's hard to make a night-veil demon squeamish."

I patted him on the shoulder. "Yeah, I know. Just . . . go. Do what needs to be done. We'll deal with the aftermath when we get there."

Kaylin followed Lannan out the door. As it closed behind him, I turned back to Regina. "I don't know what my grandfather will be able to do, but I'll let you know as soon as he contacts me."

I didn't want to sit around waiting, but there wasn't much

else we could do. We couldn't just head out in the streets looking for a fight. And once I knew for sure that the others were
on our side, we could start to plot our course of action. I wandered over to the window again. Rhia had taken her seat next
to Chatter, and they were holding hands, softly whispering.
Watching them, I wondered how she'd ever let herself get
involved with Leo. He'd been so wrong for her.

Chatter leaned over, softly nuzzling her ear, and their
connection was so tangible it was hard to ignore. Did Grieve
and I look like that? Did my pull toward Lannan interfere
with us, or did it simply exist in a different light? I didn't love
Lannan, and I never would. Grieve was my heart. He was my
center. Lannan fed the darker side of me, the side that I
didn't want Grieve to go near. If Grieve stepped into those
shadows, then my rock would vanish, and I would be fully
swallowed up by the abyss. Lannan allowed me to be vulnerable with Grieve.

The snow continued to fall in the growing dusk, and it
called to me. I wanted to be out in the chill and gloom. I
turned back to Regina. "I need to go outside for a breath of
fresh air. Will it be safe?"

She considered, then nodded. "The French doors will
lead you to the patio. Feel free to walk out on the veranda for
a bit. No one will harm you here. Not unless they launch a
full-scale attack, and then war would be upon us all, and no
one would be safe."

I motioned for Grieve to stay where he was. I wanted to
be alone with my thoughts. As I stepped out into the chill
night air, the winter braced me up and quickened my blood.
I straightened my shoulders and shook back my hair. How
fast this transformation had changed me. And how much I'd
taken to it.

I walked atop the drifts, gliding over the crust that had
formed on the surface. The air caught me short. Not nearly
as cold as it was back in the realm of Snow and Ice, it was
still harsh and austere. A snowflake fell into my mouth and
landed on my tongue, but it did not melt.

The patio—or veranda—extended some fifteen feet out

from the mansion and was surrounded by a low stone wall, high enough to sit on but not so high that it impeded vision or could easily conceal someone crouching behind it. I wandered over to the edge, staring out into the wintry darkness.

Guards were patrolling the compound, and more would be making the rounds, watching over the perimeters of the land. They were vampires, all of them. During the day the Vampire Nation had to rely on their day-runners—not nearly as powerful but almost always loyal without question. Though, after the incident with Crawl and Geoffrey, I had a feeling that all the day-runners would be under scrutiny as well.

I passed the wall and walked out onto the lawn, the full brunt of the snowstorm landing on my cloak. The owl feathers softly wafted in the breeze, and as I stared up into the sky, the barren trees loomed overhead, black silhouettes against the silvery night. In one of the trees perched an owl, and I recognized it immediately. Hunter. My grandfather.

He flew down, circling to land on a nearby bush. The bough bent under his weight, and within seconds, he stood there, a pale glow against the night. He was wearing soft white leather buckskins and a matching tunic, and a pendant around his neck emanated a silver light. It looked to be moonstone, though it was surrounded by a black onyx ring of stone. Hunter's hair was caught back in a ponytail. Something inside quivered.

Blood recognizes blood.

At first I thought Ulean had spoken, but then remembered she was not allowed within the compound. Vampires didn't like the magical creatures—Wind Elementals could read a vamp's thoughts, where most of the magic-born couldn't. And vampires couldn't sense them very easily. So they banned them from the premises, and we respected their wishes.

"No, I spoke to you." Hunter took a step toward me. "You are my blood, even with being half-breed. My blood sings when you are near, as it did with your father. As it does with all of my children, and their children."

There were so many things I wanted to ask, so much to learn. But I'd come to learn one lesson as Queen—patience.

Even though I hated waiting, I'd learned that there was an order to all things, and trying to hurry them up didn't work.

I smiled and held out my hand. I wanted to reassure myself he was real. Hunter seemed to understand—he took my fingers in his and drew me out fully under the blowing gusts. We stood there a moment, listening to the soft hiss as snow met snow. There was music in the fall of the flakes, hard to hear unless I listened for it, but it was there, and the song was melancholy and haunting.

After a moment, Hunter turned his face from the sky to me. "I have sent my men out into the woods and the fields. We are searching for the lair of the Indigo Court. We will find it, know this."

His words inspired confidence, and I nodded, as certain as he was. "Do you miss Wrath?" I asked, wondering why that was my first question to him, and yet it seemed fitting. He had lost his son, first to the Court of Rivers and Rushes, and now back to the Golden Isle.

Hunter pressed his lips together, and for a moment, I thought he wasn't going to answer. Then he placed a light hand on my shoulder. A flicker of remembrance and recognition ran through me. I gathered it close, cherishing the feeling. It felt like . . . *family*.

"Your father left home so long ago. I have seen him, of course, and we talked and we flew together. But he followed his heart into Summer, and I could not go there—Summer is not my realm, and I had no desire to cross over. His mother died long ago. Some might say her heart was broken when her son turned his back on the Winter, but I know better."

Wrapped in his words as though they were a cloak, I could only ask, "How did she die?"

"Your grandmother died of disappointment. She died because I could not love her like she needed. I'm a hunter, Cicely. I carry my emotions in check. I'm a hunter, and I cannot allow myself to feel too deeply about anything or I will disrupt the objectivity I need in order to carry forth my duties. I could not love her enough, and it destroyed her, in the end. She stayed in owl form one day, and by sundown, she swept too close to a wolf, and he caught her. She engineered her death, but she did so on her own terms."

He sounded sad, as if recounting a ballad from a lifetime back. But when I glanced at his face, there were no tears, no wincing grimace. Just a calm, serene nature that might be mistaken for coldness.

"What was her name?" I needed to know. I needed to understand her better. She'd loved him too much, and she'd paid the price.

"Her name? When she was born, the seers took one look at her and whispered her name to her parents. They didn't need time to confer. They didn't need a consultation. Instantly, they knew that her name was Loss." Hunter let out a slow sigh. "I will try to have more information for you about the Shadow Hunters by tomorrow. I cannot promise, but we are doing what we can." And then, before I could say another word, he turned back into an owl and flew away, and I was standing alone.

Or at least, I thought I was alone. As I hugged myself, watching my grandfather vanish into the air, a low, sensuous voice slithered over me.

"Oh, sweet Cicely. You have too much pain in your life."

I whirled around to find myself staring at Lannan. He was watching me, his hair a nimbus that fell softly around his shoulders. I caught my breath, not wanting to look at him. Not wanting to react the way my body reacted. But my blood quickened despite myself, and my hunger for his touch grew.

"I have no more pain than many others . . . and less than some." I stayed where I was, not trusting myself to be within arm's reach. Lannan wouldn't drink me down, and now that I was Queen, he wouldn't humiliate me either—not without my permission. But he could make me want him. He could brush my cheek with his fingers, and I'd be a quivering mess.

"Kaylin is with the others, finishing up. What do you think their reactions will be, Cicely? What do you think they'll do now that they know you've ordered their minds raped so violently? And how will they react to the night-veil? You gave them no choice." He lingered over the words, and

I could hear the pleasure he felt in saying them. "You are beginning to understand the nature of power, and you revel in it."

And then he was next to me, leaning down, staring at me with those deep, obsidian eyes that glistened like dark diamonds in the night. There was no life in him, no pulse racing through his body. His heart did not beat, nor did he take breath. And yet . . . and yet . . . Lannan was perhaps more alive than anyone I knew. He glorified his hedonistic lust; he exulted in it, bathed in the pleasure and pain that he caused others. There was no quarter with Lannan. I knew exactly where I stood with him, and that knowledge both thrilled and terrified me.

"I am not your toy." I wanted to step away, but that would be giving him power, and I wasn't willing to acknowledge that he could make me flinch. I'd done too much flinching at his feet.

He grabbed my wrist. "Queen you may be. But I know you, Cicely. You belong in my world—vampire or not. You're one of a kind with Regina and me. You just haven't acknowledged the depths to which you're willing to dive. You teeter on the edge, playing with fire, coaxing the flames and then running from them. But you forget, I've seen you wanton. I've seen you abandon yourself in my arms, in my bed. I've seen your dark side, and I answered the call. You can never shut the door on me again."

I stared at his hand. I'd thought myself free from him. I'd thought that once I'd let him fuck me, I could walk away unmoved. And I had, for a few weeks. But now, tonight, under the snow, with him so near, I felt the pull of his intoxication. I felt the drive to abandon everything and throw myself into his arms. To drag him down on the ground until the world with all its cares vanished in a puff of mist and smoke.

"You can't resist me, and you know it. Run with me, let me bring you into my world. It doesn't have to be like Geoffrey and Myst. I'm not asking you to rule the world by my side—I have no interest in so much responsibility. We can blaze through the nights. Regina would welcome you into our relationship. She likes you." Lannan's words coiled around me, all too tempting. Even the thought of Regina—she was luscious, with her perfect ruby lips and long, curvy legs. She had kissed me before, unnerving me with desire.

But . . . but . . .

"I can't do this, Lannan. I can't let you keep creeping in. I am married to Grieve, and while he understands our connection, he hates it. We both owe you a favor, given you saved my life. But I'm not leaving my post. I'm not turning my back on my people. They need me. And Myst—she's out there, waiting. She's coming for me. I can't just run away and leave New Forest to her. I can't run away and leave my world behind."

My heart ached. I loved Grieve; he was my passion and joy, but Lannan called to my shadow self, and right now, here in the snow, I wanted him. So help me, I wanted him even without the Blood Fever driving me, and that scared me more than anything.

"You think this now. But when you are facing the mad Queen, then tell me that you're still willing to sacrifice yourself for your people. Wait till she has her hands around your throat, and her horrible jaw unhinges as she begins to eat you, gristle and bone, while you still live. You were her daughter, *Cherish*. You were her betrayer. She will never let you die easily. Enjoy what life you can now, for the end will be painful and racking."

I struggled to get out of his grasp, starting to panic. Lannan was good at painting a terrifying view of the future, and the feeling that Myst was watching us and laughing raced through my thoughts. Was Lannan her spy? Was she using him to get to me? He seemed to tower over, looming like a dark shadow against the snow.

"Let me go! Let me go, please!" I managed to break free and, panting, stared at him as I backed away into the snow. "Are you her spy? Are you her eyes and ears? Somebody is, and until I find out who, I can't trust anyone. I won't let her win. Do you hear me? If you are her mouthpiece, you turn around and tell her just that. I'll fight till the end. I'll destroy her."

And then I fell to my knees in the snow and began to cry, overwhelmed with everything.

Lannan pulled back. He stared at me, an odd mixture of emotions crossing his face. Another moment, and he knelt beside me, pulling me into his arms.

"Hush, hush, Cicely. I am not in Myst's pocket. No one owns me, no one controls me. I answer to the Crimson Queen, but only as much as I must. I am neither Myst's shadow nor her puppet. Come to me, feed me your pain. Feed me your anger and your fear."

As he spoke, he pressed his lips against mine, and then, his tongue playing over mine, his death chill met my own cold, and I kissed him, deep and dark, falling into the icy fire that sparked between us, letting him drag me under as I gave up my fear to him.

Chapter 7

The kiss went on and on, drawing me in. Lannan's hands slid around my waist. I should have pulled away right there, but I couldn't. He was comforting in his strength. I didn't have to worry about hurting him—about loving him. He pulled me closer, his hair draping down to tickle my cheek. A slow heat began to rise, from my belly, snaking up through my breasts so that I could barely catch my breath. I throbbed, wanting him. Slick now, wet and moist, I shifted, spreading my legs slightly. My jeans chafed against me, suddenly feeling too tight.

"We could sneak away to my room." His words were gravelly, low in my ear.

"I can't. I can't do this, Lannan." I tried to pull myself out of the mesmerizing hold he had on me, but his grip grew more insistent and he slid one leg between my thighs, prying them open. As I rode his knee, rubbing my crotch against his pants, hearing the faint squeak of denim on leather, I prayed Grieve wouldn't come out here. He had to feel what was going on—we were too bound for him not to. How could he not know I was ready to spread my legs, to fuck Lannan again?

Lannan tried to slide his hands under my corset but it was

laced too tight. He tugged at the strings. "Take this off. I want to feel your breasts. I want to—"

"Kaylin is done." Regina's voice cut through the haze that had risen between us.

Glassy-eyed, feeling wanton and slutty, I gazed over Lannan's shoulder, into her eyes. She moved forward, circling around behind me, and slid her hands around my back to reach around and cup my breasts. Beneath the leather of my corset, my nipples stiffened and I let out a gasp.

"If you still feel up to playing later, I would happily join you." Regina's voice tickled my ear, and I let out a soft moan as she snaked one hand down to grab my crotch, holding it tight, her fingers pressing through the denim against my clit.

Lannan laughed, then. "We could have ourselves quite the party, couldn't we?"

"Is it a private party, or can anyone join?" Grieve strode up, pulling Lannan off me. He glared at the vampire, then stared at me. The stars glistening in the depths of his eyes glittered harsh and cold.

Stammering, I disentangled myself from both vampires. "Grieve—I . . . I . . ." What could I say? *This isn't what it looks like* wasn't going to cut it.

"Never mind. Kaylin is done. The others are returning." Grieve turned to go. I shrugged away from Regina and Lannan, hurrying to catch up with him. Behind us, the vampires laughed, and once again, I felt dirty and tainted. I tugged on Grieve's arm, and he gave me a cursory glance. "You weren't in the throes of Blood Fever this time, and you're no longer under contract to the bloodsucker."

"No . . . no . . ." I didn't know what else to say. There was no real way to defend myself. The Fae weren't normally monogamous, but Grieve had a special hatred for Lannan.

"We'll discuss it later. You are the Queen. You are free to do as you choose, even though I am your consort." And with that Grieve slammed through the French doors.

I wanted to grab him, make him stop and talk to me, but I could see Kaylin and the others through the window. It would be bad enough facing them, let alone Grieve.

"Cicely—he will come around." Regina had caught up to me, and now she leisurely draped an arm around my shoulders. "And if not, you always have a place here. Right between Lannan and me." And with that she entered the office, and I followed.

✤

As I tentatively entered the room, I didn't know what to expect. I knew they wouldn't be happy with me, but had I just lost every friend I had?

There was an uncomfortable silence, and then Luna stood. Flushed, her lip trembled as she held on to the back of the chair for support. I waited, not wanting to defend myself. What I'd had Kaylin do was both necessary and yet—indefensible. I wouldn't apologize, but I wouldn't try to force them to understand why I'd done what I'd done. I'd explain what was going on, but if they couldn't see where I was coming from, that was the best I could do.

"Myst has planted a spy in my Court—somewhere among those closest to me. We have no idea who it is . . . yet." I glanced at Kaylin, who shook his head, giving me the all-clear sign.

Peyton let out a long sigh and crossed her right leg over her left. "In other words, you need to know if anybody close is betraying you."

"Essentially." I tried to stand tall—which wasn't easy at five four. After a moment, I gave up, dropping into a nearby chair. "Don't you see how dangerous it could be if—"

"If one of us had turned on you." Luna's words were soft.

Ysandra dusted her hands, sitting as prim as a librarian on Saturday afternoon around a bunch of screaming kids. Looks were deceiving, though. She was actually a powerful witch, one of the magic-born, and a prime member of the Consortium. "You did what was necessary, but you have so much to learn about how to approach matters like this. Cicely, you might have lost us all."

"She might still have. At least me." Luna glared. It was hard to meet her accusatory stare. I was as guilty as she thought I was. "I can't believe you . . ." And then her voice dropped away. "If you would have told us, and one of us was the spy, we would have alerted Myst."

Nodding, I gave a helpless shrug. "I was between a rock and a hard place. I had to do what I felt best. For the Barrow. For me. For this war. My people are being tested as well. My guards, the Court advisors, everybody. Rhiannon's, too. Myst is dangerous, and she's on the way back in with fresh Shadow Hunters."

I didn't want to ask their forgiveness, but I did need to know one thing. "Are you still with me? I'm not going to ask you to like me or like what I did. But are you still with us?"

Peyton scuffed her boot on the floor. "Yeah, I'm in. But I'm pissed, Cicely, and it will take me some time to get over it."

Ysandra shrugged. "As what you need—I'm here. And I'll do what I can to make certain the Consortium stands with us."

I turned to Luna. She blushed again, glancing at Kaylin, who studiously ignored her. Something had gone down between them, but I knew better than to ask in public.

After a moment, she gave me a "whatever" shrug. "Yeah, I'm in. But don't think we're friends. Allies, yes. But friends? If you can do that to me, then we never were."

I wanted to yell at her, to tell her to stop being so stubborn, but the truth was, she had every right to feel the way she did, and I wouldn't take that away from her. I did what I had to, but I couldn't allow myself to invalidate her feelings about it.

"I just hope you can someday understand my position. I'll settle for allies, right now. But I still consider you a friend, and I've hurt you." That was as far as I could go, at least in public.

At that moment, a servant entered and handed a message to Regina. She read it, her lips pursed, then she motioned for the maid to leave. As the door closed behind the girl, she turned to me. "The Shadow Hunters have swarmed the police station. Two or three officers escaped, but except for those who were out patrolling the streets, Myst's people have turned the law enforcement of New Forest into supper. We have to get in there, and rout them."

⚜

I slammed my hand on the table. If we alerted the guards at home, then the spy would know we were onto them. But then the absurdity of that statement hit me. "It doesn't matter now if the spy is among my guards. We're going out after them. Check, how do we get word back to the Barrows without going there ourselves? We need everyone who's been tested on board, and we don't have the time it would take to get back there."

He looked at me. "Your Wind Elemental can take word to the shamans who can contact Strict. They can also contact the shamans at the Marburry Barrow. But Your Majesty, we can't make it common knowledge. Dispatching the unit? Will have to be done privately."

Ulean could go. That meant I had to leave the confines of the estate to contact her. I whirled to face Regina. "You hate Elementals, but surely you can make an exception and lower your defenses this time?"

She shook her head. "No, I can't. The barrier is built into the estate. She couldn't make it through even if we gave her leave. I will drive you to the gates, and from there you can contact her."

"Let's go." I motioned for the others to stay and begin discussing strategies, while following Regina on a dead run to the front door. Check came running behind me. "We're going in the car—you can't ride in it or you'll feel sick. Wrath did once, and he swore he never again would voluntarily enter one."

"I will deal with the consequences, Your Highness. I would not allow you to go alone—even with a vampire." He cast a dark eye at Regina, who ignored the slight.

"I'll go with her." Kaylin motioned him aside. "I'll protect her, and you know I'm safe."

Check glanced at me, and I nodded, so he gave way. Kaylin followed Regina and me, and we climbed in her limousine. Moments later, we were at the front gate, and the car eased out, guarded by the patrols watching over the estate. I didn't have to get out. Once we were beyond the barrier, I was able to focus on Ulean and call to her.

Ulean, I need you now. Are you here?

Yes, I'm here. What do you need, Cicely? The slipstream is rocky with energy and emotion. There is danger on the wind, and violence and bloodshed from so many quarters. She came rushing in, swirling the snowflakes in her wake.

I need you to go back to the Eldburry Barrow and talk to the shamans. They can hear you. Tell them we have to marshal our efforts and send troops into town—the Shadow Hunters are feeding. They've taken over the police station, and any officer not out on patrol has either been turned or killed by now. My guess is killed. Yummanii aren't as much use to the Vampiric Fae as are magic-born.

I can do that, Cicely. Anything else? It will take me only minutes to reach the Barrow.

Yes, you must instruct the shamans to contact their counterparts in the Court of Rivers and Rushes and tell them the same. This must be done secretly—with only the guards who are tested through for loyalty being dispatched, and they must tell no one where they are going. We need all the help we can get. Tell them where we are at, but that we don't have an estimate for when we're coming back, nor are we sure of our plans at this point. And even if we were, we still can't take chances that spies wouldn't report back to Myst. It's one thing for the Shadow Hunters to know that we are striking back. Quite another for them to know where the Fae Queens are. I paused, then hung my head.

Do you want them to report to you at Lannan's estate?

I suppose they'd better, though check with me first. We may be back at the Veil House by then. Send one of the shamans with the guards so that you can talk to him—at least if they're on their way before things are settled. And tell them to hurry. I paused for a moment, the sobering reality of the situation hitting home. *Ulean, it's begun, hasn't it? Myst has come, and only one of us will walk out alive.*

I think so, Cicely. And that someone must be you, or the world is doomed. And with that, Ulean sped off, only a faint hint of mist trailing around my feet to indicate she'd ever been here.

I turned back to Regina. "I've put out the call. Now what?"

"We go back to the mansion and plan our attack. It will be all hands on deck. I'm afraid that New Forest will be slick with blood before morning. And thick with the dust of vampires as well. My people will fight alongside yours, and we will shake the town to the core with our resistance."

And with that the driver turned the limousine around, and we returned to the mansion.

⚜

By the time we got back, Lannan and Grieve had put aside their differences and were deep in discussing the layout of New Forest. Chatter was adding his opinion. Rhiannon was in the corner, looking pensive. Ysandra was on the phone, and Luna and Peyton were arguing over something.

As we entered, Ysandra finished with her conversation and slid her phone back into her purse. "I have convinced the Consortium to send a group of our elite fighters—they did not want to, not after losing so many last time, but I told them if they didn't, they might lose the entire Seattle branch, should Myst win out. They'll be here in a few hours, providing they can get through the town."

"Most likely, they'll face Myst's Shadow Hunters coming into town." I tapped my chin. "Once our guards get here, we'll do our best to post lookouts in order to keep watch for them and help them get here. Or to wherever we happen to be at that point."

Luna looked up. "I can help. I can summon the dead. They speak through me now, and I can be a conduit for some of the more powerful spirits."

That sounded dangerous. I started to shake my head, then stopped. "What can these spirits do?" At Peyton's protest, I held up my hand. "We need all the help we can get. New Forest appears to be under a full-scale attack, and with the police out of action, we have to do something before morning. The vampires can't fight during the day, and bluntly put, we need whatever help we can get."

"You'd pay the devil to kill the demon." Peyton stared at me.

"I'd *be* the devil to kill the demon we're facing. And I may well have to be at some point." I stared back at her, and she grumbled but nodded.

Luna twisted the hem of her blouse, and it was obvious she was nervous, but there wasn't much we could do to stem that. We were *all* afraid. "Some of the dead know powerful rituals. Some of them can summon spirits to do their bidding—on the physical plane as well as the astral. If I can contact a woman named Dorthea, who is one of my ancestors, she may be able to bring us a host of spirits to fight on our side." She shivered. "I will do whatever you need me to, Cicely. I realize how bad things are."

"What do you need in order to summon her?" Ysandra took Luna's hands in hers, calming the bard. "I can help."

"I can't do it here—the vampires have a very effective dampening field in place. We'll have to move off the estate. I suppose we could do so at the Veil House—it's not that far from the center of town." She shifted, uncomfortable. "I'd feel safer here, but I suppose there really isn't any place that is truly safe. Not anymore, is there?"

Shaking my head slowly, I said, "No, there isn't. We'll go back to the Veil House, then. Lannan, Regina, will you come with us?"

Regina held my gaze. "As Emissary, I cannot. And neither should you and Rhiannon. But we will send a contingent of our men with Luna and Ysandra. They carry weapons that can destroy even Myst's creatures, but . . . it will still be dangerous."

"Life's dangerous." Ysandra stood. "I will go with you, Luna, and we will do what we can from there. We must stay in contact, though. Make certain your cell phones are charged."

I jumped up. "On it. Ysandra, can you speak with Ulean?"

She cocked her head. "I might be able to, if she's willing to try. When she returns, we can give it a go."

"I will go with Luna and Ysandra, too," Peyton said. "I can be of use there—even if it's just to fetch and carry."

I turned to Grieve, who gave me an impassive look at first, but then he ducked his head and I slipped over for a quick kiss. "My love, what are the plans so far?"

"We take soldiers and head to the town. We kill every Shadow Hunter we find. There's no way to attack Myst directly yet—not until we find out where she's hiding. Basically we're on a seek-and-destroy mission tonight, to save as many of the townsfolk as possible."

"My grandfather is looking into where she's hiding. If he's able to find out, he'll contact me. I can always call the winds and rage through the town. It will destroy homes, but I can also destroy a number of the Shadow Hunters with a tornado." I frowned as Rhiannon broke in.

"You can't use that power much longer without being swept up by the winds themselves. Not until you're taught properly how to control it." She had the same tone her mother used to have—unbreakable, undeniable. I stared at her, and for the first time, I saw how closely she resembled Aunt Heather. It made me smile, and yet feel sad at the same time.

"I can't *not* use every power at our disposal. But I'll save it for when we truly need it. If it looks like we're outnumbered, I'm pulling out all the stops."

"We *are* outnumbered, my love." Grieve pushed away the blueprints. "I think Myst probably raided every camp the Indigo Court had set up for hundreds of miles around, if not farther. I would not expect this to be an easy fight—we are facing a monster and her minions here."

"Perhaps we are, but all monsters have weak points. We just have to find out what Myst's are." I glanced out the window. "It's snowing heavily. That will help against any fires that my winds stir up should I need to ride the gale through town."

"I can help with that, too." Rhiannon smiled at my questioning look. "Among other things, I've been learning not only how to control my flame, but how to control other flames as well. I can bend most of them to my will, if I try hard enough, now. I can use flame as a weapon, and I can quench it when it's used against me."

"Then we are even better equipped." We were going to need everything we could possibly put to our advantage.

Kaylin slowly crossed over to where we were standing. "I, too, have something to offer. I might still be weak from my wounds, but I'm strong enough to let my demon loose."

I stopped. Truth was I had no clue what Kaylin's demon could do when he let it loose—I didn't even know that it was being tamed, per se. "You mean that . . . you can let it take control? I thought that we put a stop to that when we fully woke it up so you could come out of your coma?"

The demon, when it first merged with his body in utero, had died—but it had left behind a hatchling. Once the hatchling began to wake up, we'd had to fully help it emerge from its slumber, or Kaylin would have been lost forever, caught in the world of dreams into which he'd slipped.

"I can release it if I need to. We did merge, so there will always be part of me in it, and part of it in me, but I can give it more control. And Cicely, my demon can be horrific when roused. But if I do give over control, there's always a chance that it won't retreat so easily, and then . . ." He paused, his gaze meeting mine, and I knew what he wasn't saying aloud. If he couldn't rein it in, then he would be more demon than Kaylin, and our friend would retreat from us.

I held my breath, wanting to beg him not to go there, not to chance it. The risk was so great, and the potential loss, hard to think about. But even as I started to say something— to dissuade him—my voice faltered, and the words died on my lips. There were people dying all over town. There would be far too many following if we didn't stop this.

The best I could manage was, "Keep it in reserve, Kaylin. Like my power over the winds, we unleash these as a last resort. We may have no choice, but don't play the hand too quickly. Both of us have too much to lose if things go wrong."

He leaned toward me, ignoring Check's glower, and pressed his head against mine. "When we first met, I thought I might . . . we might . . . Cicely, I'm glad we met. I'm glad I have the chance to fight alongside you. I've been alive a lot longer than you, but in the distant scheme of things, with you being half Cambyra, and more importantly, one of the Fae Queens, a hundred years isn't going to make a dent in our friendship. I hope always to know you, Your Majesty. And I will always owe you my life."

Feeling like he was somehow saying good-bye, I turned away. "What do we do now?"

At that moment, a knock on the door brought another servant, with the word that our guards were waiting outside. Which meant Ulean had gotten through to them.

"You should wait here with Regina," Grieve started to say, but I held up my hand.

"Rhiannon and I are going along. This is our battle as well, and we will have plenty of protection with you and Chatter and the guards. We won't take the helm without it being absolutely necessary." I was getting used to stepping back, though I still didn't like it.

"You might as well let them come." Check laughed, but there was no joy in his voice. "We can protect them better while there—otherwise, Fearless and I, and the Lady Rhiannon's guards, would have to stay here to watch over them. And your lordship and Lord Chatter would be too worried and unable to focus."

Grieve let out a grunt, but shrugged. "Fine, but they need protection. What do we have for them?"

"We bring the Queens' leathers, Your Lordship." The guard stepping through the door held up a suit that I had only seen but never worn. Or rather, I'd been fitted for it, but never had the chance to put it on other than when it was being made. Another guard held a similar suit, only it was forged from green leather with gold accents where mine was black with white.

We'd been fitted for them shortly after our coronation, and given the circumstances, the seamstresses had pushed them through, and the shamans had enchanted them quickly.

They weren't foolproof, but they would give us more protection by far than what we were wearing.

I pulled off my cloak and stretched out my arms. Fearless and Check began fitting the gear on me. They had adapted their usual style to my tastes—well, to both Rhiannon's and my specifications—and now to go with the leather tunic, we had leather pants as well. The pants weren't quite as protective as the top, but then again, we had to be able to move and run in them. As it was, the outfit was heavy, and chafed annoyingly beneath my arms. The sleeves were a softer suede, again, to allow for movement, but overall, we were a lot more protected in the clothing than out of it. Though one good bite from one of the Shadow Hunters might pierce the hide, it would be hard-pressed to pierce us as well.

When we were decked out, we looked ready for just about anything. Rhiannon shook her head. "I can't believe we're here. We're here, in the Regent's office, Fae Queens, wearing leather armor, ready to go fight monsters taking over the town. Two months ago, I would have laughed in your face if you told me this was all going to go down."

"Come on, Monster Fighter! Let's go out and whip us some Shadow Hunter ass." Sounding braver than I felt, I sheathed my Queen's dagger that Regina had ordered brought in—she'd had the guards bring in all our weaponry that we normally left at the gate—and turned to face Check and Grieve. Fearless and one of Rhiannon's guards had gone to marshal the troops.

"I guess . . . we're ready?" Not wanting to go but knowing that if we didn't, the town would be a bloody mess by morning, I motioned to my cousin. "Let's take the lead, at least until we hit the gates. We need to offer moral support to our soldiers. Remember, some of them fought Myst when she first ripped through the Eldburry Barrow, then worked her way over to the realm of Summer. I doubt if they will be eager to face her and her monsters again."

"Good point." Rhia sheathed her dagger, too, and then—with one last look at the others, who were getting ready for their own part in our private little war—we headed out the door, ready to face the monsters hiding under the bed.

✦

Once we were out of the gates, Rhia and I moved back into a protective circle of guards. They had all been vetted through by the shamans, so we were relatively safe where we were at—at least from our own people. Grieve and Chatter took the lead, and we raced through the night toward the town, with Lannan's people guarding our flanks. Lannan himself was up front between Grieve and Chatter, and whatever differences the men had, they pushed them aside for now. We couldn't afford to fight among ourselves.

As we sped through the night, through the streets heading toward the center of New Forest, we began to see the signs that the Shadow Hunters had been there before us. There were blood splatters staining the ground, and here and there, cars had skidded off the road, their doors hanging open. From where we were in the middle of the street, we couldn't see inside of them. For that I was grateful, but the scent of blood was thick in the air along the route.

Scattered houses were lit from within, so we knew that the electricity still held. Some looked barricaded, with smoke still drifting out of their chimneys, and to our thoughts, the people within them were probably still safe. At least, for now. But here and there, a house stood, lights on, but door busted open, or windows broken, and there were no sounds coming from within. And those homes—well, we knew what had happened. It was obvious.

As we were passing one house, we heard a high-pitched scream coming from inside. A girl was begging for help. Immediately, Grieve, Chatter, and Lannan veered, leading our men toward the house. Rhiannon and I were swept along, near the front but not close enough to immediately see what was going on. But we rushed inside, along with the men, and there, the carnage became evident.

The bone and gristle on the floor spoke to wholesale slaughter, and there were at least five Shadow Hunters in various stages of transformation. And then, I saw her—a little girl of about ten, crouching atop an entertainment hutch, bleeding from one arm and a gash on her forehead. How she'd gotten up there, I couldn't tell, but one of the Shadow Hunters was trying to swing up after her.

The girl had hold of a gun and was unsteadily pointing it at the creature. A glance to the floor showed that she'd already managed to hit one of them—he was back in his Vampiric Fae form, shot through the stomach, lying on the floor growling and bleeding. But he wasn't dead. It took one hell of a lot to kill the Shadow Hunters.

Our men swarmed the group while Check, Fearless, and Rhia's two guards pushed us toward the back, keeping us from joining the fray. The Shadow Hunters were whirling dervishes, violent as devils. They never gave ground, never ran, but in their savage fury, rent and tore at the guards. One guard went down with a scream, and his arm disappeared into the mouth of one of the creatures.

Their terrible jaws unhinged, the Shadow Hunters were like blue lions, only they knew no fear, focused only on the fight and the potential for food. They lived to destroy, lived to feed and drink the blood of their enemies, driven on by their need and hunger, and driven on by their love for Myst, who enslaved them all. Mother of the unnatural race, she was also their tormenter.

The little girl atop the hutch caught my eye, and in her expression I saw both horror and hatred. She would carry this for the rest of her life, if she made it through. She had seen them destroy her family, and right there, I knew she'd grow up with vengeance in her heart—it would be her way of surviving. The hope that she might one day return the favor, should any of the Indigo Court survive,

Cicely—there is another. Ulean's soft whisper hit me full-on. The slipstream let me hear things that were too quiet to overshadow the noise going on around me.

Another what?

Another child. He is upstairs, in a crib—and he will die

shortly if someone doesn't get up there and save him. There's a Shadow Hunter nearing his room, and the boy is crying loud enough to be heard.

I tried to make myself heard over the din, but Check shook his head, indicating he couldn't understand me. Frustrated, I shoved him aside and bolted for the stairs. Check and Fearless were on my heels then, and within seconds Check had scrambled by me to take the lead. I shoved at him, indicating that we needed to continue upstairs, and that, he understood.

We came to the hallway, and there, near a door at the end of the passage, stood one of the Shadow Hunters in his creature form. The sound of the baby was clear enough here, and we could hear his piercing cries over the shrieks of the fighting downstairs.

I pushed forward, but Fearless caught me back. Check engaged the Shadow Hunter as it lunged down the hall, and they fell to the fight. But one against one—not so good of odds, not with Myst's warriors. And so I shoved Fearless in front of me.

"Help Check! I'm getting the baby." I shook off his hand and raced into the room as both of my guards began to struggle with the Shadow Hunter. A toddler—possibly a year old, maybe a bit more—was standing up, clinging to the side of the crib. His screams pierced the air. I raced over and swung him into my arms.

As I turned around, I saw the Shadow Hunter dart into the room. Fearless and Check were on his ass, but he covered the space between us in one great leap, and I found myself, baby in hand, facing the ruthless monster.

Chapter 8

Oh fuck. What the hell was I going to do?

The Shadow Hunter growled, his eyes luminous black with swirling stars—the stars of the Indigo Court. I froze, mesmerized for a second, but then instinct took over, and in one swift motion, I turned to drop the child back in the crib with one hand, while with the other, I yanked out my dagger. Smoothly, I stabbed at the Shadow Hunter's face, even as Check plunged a sword into his back, then quickly out again.

The creature yelped, snarling as it turned, and I took that moment to whip my dagger back and plunge again, this time catching him between his shoulder blades where Check had stabbed him.

Check had managed to keep hold of his sword, and now, he ducked to the side, bringing the blade up into the belly of the Shadow Hunter. The creature let out one last howl and toppled to the side, still. It was dead.

I picked up the child and looked back to Check. "We can't take him through the fighting down there. Check the rest of the upstairs, and if it's clear, I'll lock myself in this room with him until you let me know everything downstairs is safe again." I didn't want to leave him alone—it was far too dangerous.

Check didn't look all that happy, but he nodded. "As you wish, Your Majesty. But if something should happen—"

"That's why you check and double-check the upstairs here. To make sure it won't." I nodded toward the door. "Out, and I'll lock the door behind you."

He glanced over at the window. "First . . ." He hustled over and shoved the armoire in front of it. The only other exit was the door, so he'd effectively sealed me in, and any rogue Shadow Hunters, out. "There. I'll feel better now."

And with that he left the room. I locked the door, pressing my ear to it until—a few minutes later—I heard him knock from outside. He announced himself, and I cracked the door.

"I checked the other rooms and blocked the windows as best as I could. I can't lock the doors—they lock from the inside, so the minute I'm out that door, please latch it. I've done everything I can think to do. I'll be back for you as soon as we clear the downstairs." And then he pulled the door shut, and I locked it as he headed for the stairs.

Turning back to the child, I stared at the boy. He was still crying, though more softly, and he reached for me. "Mama . . . Want my mama."

"So you can talk?" I had little doubt his vocabulary was still quite limited—he seemed very young—but at least he could say a few words. I picked him up and looked around. A rocking chair nearby offered a good seat, and he leaned his head against my shoulder as I rocked him. The thought of children scared me, though I knew Grieve and I would someday have them. They were so vulnerable, and they needed so much.

"What's your name, little one? What's your name?" I wasn't sure if he'd understand me, but he blinked his huge blue eyes and sniffled.

"Andy. Where's mama?" The sobs coming from him were quiet, almost eerily so, and I realized the boy was exhausted. Probably over-exhausted, if my guess was correct.

He doesn't know. He's too young to understand what's

going on. Ulean swept past, blowing a gentle breeze across his wet, red face.

I know. And there's no way I can explain that his mother's probably dead, caught in the carnage below. Chances are his father is there, too. I wonder about the girl.

I fear she was wounded, Cicely. Who knows how badly? Do you think she'll live?

I cannot say, but the Shadow Hunters make no differentiation between adults and children when they attack. At least the boy is unharmed.

Yes, terribly frightened but alive and well.

At that moment, he whimpered and stuck his thumb in his mouth. I gazed into his face—he looked so scared, and so alone. So I did what anybody trying to comfort a scared baby would do.

"Andy, your mother is asleep. She was tired. You should sleep, too, honey. Go to sleep." And I began to hum, gently rocking him back and forth, until he dropped off in my arms as the fighting raged below.

※

Shortly after I'd slipped him back into his crib and covered him up, making sure his teddy bear was next to him, a knock sounded at the door. Pulling my dagger, I crept over to it, edging to one side as I waited.

"Your Majesty, we've routed them all. It's safe to come out."

Ulean? She had stayed with me, watching over me. Now she blustered away, but was back in seconds.

It's Check. The fighting is over. The Shadow Hunters are dead.

I unlocked the door and stepped back, pressing my fingers to my lips. "We need to get this little guy out of here. There's only one place I can think of where he'll be safe, and that's back at the Barrow."

Lannan and Rhia joined us, along with Chatter. One look at the boy, and she raised her hand to her lips. "There's something about him . . . I don't know what, but he looks so familiar to me."

As I watched her lean over him, an odd feeling swept over me. "Rhiannon, you be his foster mother. I don't know how— I don't know why, but I think . . . Andy's meant to be with you."

I wasn't used to premonitions that didn't deal with death or destruction, but this one felt life affirming, and when I closed my eyes and tried to project ahead, I could see a tall youth in a field of flowers. He had long, flowing golden hair and a smile like the sun, and he was standing under the glow of midday.

"It's important you take him. More than ever, I see him as having a place in our future." The feeling was overwhelming, and I prayed she'd listen to me.

Rhiannon lightly ran her fingers over the side of his cheek. "My son? Well then, we'd best make sure he gets home safely and is watched after. I wonder what he'll grow up to be." She looked at me. "We need to get him back to the Barrows. Help me?"

I motioned for Check. "Summon Fearless. Have him choose two men he trusts and ask them to take Andy back to the Barrow. Have Druise look after him, and make certain nobody else has access to him. Tell her . . . Tell her I said he's to be treated as if he were my son."

Check bowed, then raced out of the room. I turned to Grieve. "He's our nephew, my love. We will keep him safe— and for some reason, it's important he stay in Winter's domain until this is all taken care of."

"Our people are more ruthless than our Summerkin." Grieve smiled, but there was an edge to his voice. "Rhiannon, your realm is far lighter than ours—no less dangerous, but more inviting to those who would plunder it. Until we destroy Myst and set our homes in order, best rely on Winter for the protection of innocents like the boy."

Rhia shrugged. "I'm not going to argue. I know you're right."

Fearless returned with two guards whom I recognized. "Your Majesty, we have been through the shaman's testing. We are safe."

Fearless nodded. "They tell the truth. All who joined us have been tested."

"Then take the boy and run back to the Barrow. Stop for no one, stop for nothing. Avoid all confrontations until he's safely in Druise's arms. Tell her I said he is to be treated as my nephew—to be watched over at all times. No one is allowed to come near him save for her, and the shamans, and anyone they trust. Keep him safe for our return. His name is Andy."

Rhiannon gently lifted him out of the crib, and he was so tired he merely blinked for a moment, then fell back asleep. She bundled him into their care, and within a blur—a motion of speed and silence—they vanished with him.

Ulean, follow them to make certain they reach home safely. Help them in any manner you can. If they need help, summon the shamans. Return to me when the boy is safely back at the Barrow.

I will. Cicely—you are right. He is part of the future of both Summer and Winter's realms. And with that she was gone, following the guards.

I turned to the others. "What's the damage down below? What about the little girl?"

Fearless shook his head, his lips set grimly. "I'm sorry, Your Majesty. By the time we reached her, she had lost too much blood. All inhabitants of this house except the boy are dead. Torn to bits and a good share of them eaten. From what we can tell, there were five adults and two older children. The Shadow Hunters destroyed them all. And we killed fourteen of the creatures."

Fourteen. In a sea of how many? "How many of our men did we lose?"

"One, only. Another wounded, but he's still able to fight. We're ready to move out." Check straightened his shoulders. "At your command."

I glanced at Rhia. She gave me a nod.

"Then let's get a move on. We've got to get into town and rout them from the police station so the officers who are still alive can return to their headquarters and regroup. How many patrols are still out there?" I turned to Lannan. "Do your men know?"

"I will find out." He took off. One thing I could say about the vampire. When we were pressed to the wall, he focused on business and getting things done. He kept his sleazy nature for when we weren't in immediate danger.

As we headed downstairs, the smell of blood was overwhelming and my stomach lurched. But what made me queasier was the fact that I was getting used to it. The sight of shattered corpses and the slick feel of blood under my feet were beginning to feel like a normal way of life.

The room was thick with bits of offal scattered here and there, along with splintered bones, arms and feet and hands that had been severed and tossed aside. Rhiannon stood as steady as I, and I reached out and took her hand. Together, we entered the room and surveyed the damage.

Nothing had been left standing—the furniture was gone, all of it. But over near the fireplace, I caught sight of a small trinket box. I picked it up. The glass was intact, and inside was the diorama of a small child skating on a pond near a winter landscape. As I lifted the lid, the Skater's Waltz tinkled out, the tinny sound catching at my heart. This was important to someone who had died here—it had been a birthday gift or a Christmas gift, or some such token. I slowly shut the lid and handed it to Rhiannon.

"Save it for Andy—give it to him, to remember his life by."

"He's magic-born, you know." She cocked her head, running her fingers over the box. "I don't know what gifts he'll have, but I could feel the magic around him." As she slid the box into the bag she'd slung over her shoulder, she gave me a sad smile. "I wish we knew his parents' names . . . to tell him when he gets older and wants to know."

"We don't have much time, but let's . . . Here . . . look." I picked up an envelope that had fluttered off one of the tables or desks. It was a doctor's bill, from a pediatrician. A bill for treating Andy for a cold. "His mother and father were Roy and Rebecca Chase. That much you can give him. Later on, we can check the city records and find out if he had any brothers or sisters, and hopefully figure out who the others here were."

Lannan sauntered back over. "We put out a call. There are fourteen units, each with two men, still prowling the town. So we have at least twenty-eight officers alive. We should go. We are nearing the police station, and the sooner we evict the Shadow Hunters, the sooner they can return and secure it. I'll have some of my men stay through most of the night to help them reinforce it."

We headed out, our makeshift army of vampires and Fae marching through the street. True to his statement, we were only about six blocks from the precinct headquarters. As we jogged through the snowy streets, no cars glided down the roads, and the signs of struggle were everywhere. Houses with their lights on stood silent, some obviously barricaded, some plundered. I thought I saw once a face staring at me from an upstairs window—watching us as we hurried through the night, an army to fight back the darkness.

About a block away from police headquarters, one brave—or perhaps foolhardy—man raced out of his house. He was older, and he was carrying a shotgun. "You're going to fight them, aren't you? I want to help."

I looked at him. He was old enough to be a grizzled grandpa, but his gaze told me he'd seen his fair share of trouble. "It's dangerous out here. You should go back inside and bar the door."

"If we don't stop them, there won't be any door they can't break down, or any barricade strong enough to withstand them. I want to help. I'll take orders." His jaw set, he gave me a steely-eyed stare.

I glanced at Check, who nodded.

"Fine, but you do as you're told. Is anybody inside your house?" I nodded at the open door.

"No. Bastards took my wife this morning. I managed to get inside before they caught up to me. There wasn't anything I could do to help her." His voice quavered. "Forty years. Maddy and I withstood fights, we broke up three times and got back together. Our son died overseas, and our daughter was in and out of jail all through her teen years, but now we have three grandchildren from her. I bounced back from a heart attack, and Maddy made it through breast cancer. But here, in what's supposed to be a safe and cozy town . . . in our front yard . . ." His voice trailed off, and he dashed his hand across his eyes.

"What's your name?"

"Trevor. Trevor Grant. My wife was named Maddy."

"Welcome to the front lines, Trevor." I would have smiled, but there wasn't much of anything to smile about at this point. He gave me a short bow, and I realized he knew who I was.

"Thank you, Your Majesty."

"Get in line, soldier." Grieve clapped him on the shoulder. "You're with us now."

The older man seemed to appreciate the order, and he proudly marched back to Fearless, who showed him where to go. Chances were he wouldn't make it through this alive, but if he did, he'd have a place in my Court if he wanted one. Yummanii though Trevor might be, he had what it took to be a member of the Winter Court.

As he worked his way to the center of the line where Fearless had assigned him, another call startled me. I turned, as did the guards, in time to see several men and women straggling out from behind a thick patch of brambles. They were scratched and bruised, with some bleeding, but they were alive.

"We want to join you, too." The man in front stepped forward. "We're magic-born and have a smattering of spells that might help. We'll do whatever you need."

Grieve tapped me on the shoulder. "They could be spies."

I gave them the once-over. Could be, might be . . . But if they were, what better place than to have them where we could see them?

"Report to Fearless. You do what he says—that's the one order. You break it, I won't vouch for the consequences." I held the man's gaze, challenging him slightly, but he merely nodded and led the brigade of ten back along the line, where Fearless interspersed them, making certain our guards were surrounding each one of them. He also perfunctorily patted them all down to make certain nobody was carrying anything like explosives. Once they were in place, we quickly covered the remaining distance to the edge of police headquarters.

The building was functional, yes, but the architect had also had vision. New Forest's police headquarters was crafted out of concrete, but with pillars and an embellished façade that gave it a feeling of importance. No run-of-the-mill building, this. A statue of a woman holding the scales of justice stood out front, ten feet tall and towering over the courtyard. Because the police were headquartered in city hall, there were concrete benches and picnic tables surrounding the courtyard, and what looked like sculptures—all buried under the heaping mounds of snow.

The lights were blazing from inside, through the open double doors. One of the heavy metal doors had been ripped off its hinges, and an uneasy feeling hit the pit of my stomach. There were bound to be Shadow Hunters still in there, though I doubted they would deliberately set out to occupy the building. They weren't like a regular militia, and Myst wasn't attempting a political coup. At least, not in the usual sense of the word. No, she was out to destroy the existing structure, not just take over. Myst wanted a new world order, where her people were free to hunt as they desired.

As we strode through the courtyard—they had to know we were coming—signs of butchery were everywhere. Blood galore, and bits and pieces of what were once people littered the snow, turning the pristine white fields into gruesome burial mounds.

I shivered. Myst was taking no prisoners this time. She might keep someone she thought would be useful to her—turn them if they worked magic or had special abilities—but the rest of the populace? Cattle food.

We strode through the snow toward the open doors. Rhiannon and I fell back a bit, allowing some of the elite guards to go in front with Grieve and Chatter. I looked at my cousin.

"Are you ready?"

She shrugged, a mirthless smile on her face. "Are you?"

"Always and never. Is this our life then? After Myst, will there be another upstart? Or will things quiet down?" Feeling particularly grim, I stared at the future as an unending string of battles and blood. Maybe we'd luck out, but right now, I had the uneasy feeling that leading a kingdom meant that we would always be at war with somebody, somewhere. Maybe I was just tired, or scared—or both, but for a brief moment, I just wanted to change into my owl form and go flying away, into the night.

But then we were through the door and into the mess that had been city hall. The Shadow Hunters hadn't just destroyed police headquarters and the officers within: it looked like they had ravaged most of the building. Which meant that, considering they had come in during the day, most of the city workers had probably lost their lives. At least the ones who hadn't managed to get away. The blood smeared on the walls and floors attested to that. The smell was stuck in my nose by now, and I wondered if I'd ever get rid of it.

Here and there, the Shadow Hunters were still feeding— one munching on a hand, another on what looked like someone's cheek. Our men fell to them while Rhia and I were cloistered against a wall, guarded by our personal guards. As we watched, there was a noise to our left, and suddenly, a group of three Shadow Hunters broke through the barricade of guards, surprising them from above as they dropped through the ceiling tiles.

Rhiannon shouted, and the next thing I knew, she held out her hands and let loose with a volley of fire, aiming it squarely at the center of the trio. The flames were white-hot, and they scorched skin as they hit the Vampiric Fae. They did not extinguish, however, but clung like gel, the heat blistering as the Shadow Hunters screamed and began to stagger.

Rhia's face was contorted, her eyes ablaze, and I could feel her anger rising. "You will not win—do you hear me? You will never win!" And with that she sent another bolt of fire at them, and this time, our guards fell back as it landed in front of the creatures and exploded, showering them with the smoldering gel. The minute the goo touched their skin, it exploded, and they became fiery pillars, dancing back as they tried to free themselves of it.

I felt my own fury rise to match hers. I caught sight of more Shadow Hunters above in the crawl space and called up the winds. As they buoyed me up, I began to spin, the vortex created by my wake sweeping into a twister. I was becoming a tornado—no longer simply riding at the helm but creating my own tidy funnel cloud. I spun up and into the crawl space, turning, sweeping through, shrieking as I went. The Shadow Hunters there tried to scurry out of the way, but there was nowhere for them to go, and I barreled through them, sending them through the ceiling to the floor below with my force. As they hit the floor broken and battered, I began to lose steam. The next moment, I doubled back and dove through the opening to land near Rhia as I once again took control of the currents and shook away the rage.

Our men finished off the injured Shadow Hunters, taking them down before they were able to come to their feet.

I turned, shaken. "I've never done that before."

"You became the tornado. I saw it—you weren't just controlling it." A look of fear crossed her face, but it was immediately replaced with a fierce pride. "We're evolving."

"That we are." I wasn't sure how I felt about it, but there was no way to stop this train ride we were on. Whatever we were becoming, it was our destiny, and we had accepted it. "Come—we're done here. Let's go."

Grieve caught my gaze, as did Lannan. Both men stared at me, silent, unspeaking. I said nothing but motioned for us to move forward.

"Fan out and search for both survivors and more of the enemy. Destroy any Shadow Hunters you find!" Grieve ordered our warriors and the vampires to spread out and begin searching for any of the Vampiric Fae still hiding in the shadows or corners of the rooms as we passed.

Shrieks and screams punctuated our passage as our warriors routed the remaining Shadow Hunters. We killed every one we found, giving them no opportunity to escape. There would be no mercy here, or compassion. Full-scale war demanded ruthless precision.

An hour later, we held the building and radioed for the cops to return. As we waited, our men began fortifying the entrances and boarding up windows and unnecessary doors. The fewer chances for the enemy to penetrate our defenses, the better. By the time all fourteen units returned and had checked in, we were ready to turn it over to Lannan's men and some of our warriors, who would sleep till morning and take over when the vampires had to return to their lairs at daybreak.

Lannan walked us to the door. "I can take this from here for now. I suggest that you call me when you get back to the Veil House. We need to know what Luna and the Petros woman are doing. It's imperative we keep in contact at this point, and I'll have Regina pick one of our strongest and most trusted day-runners to take any messages during the day so that we get them upon first moment's waking."

"Makes sense to me. How many do you think we killed today?" I stared at the bloodstained floors around me.

"Not as many as they took out. Probably fifty . . . maybe sixty. But I estimate they killed at least two or three hundred townsfolk. Make no mistake, Cicely—this is war. Outright war. There's no room for mistakes." And with that he shook his head and turned away.

We trailed out the door, leaving twenty of our best there. Whether it would be enough, who knew? But we'd have to chance it. As we stepped out into the darkening night, a howl echoed through the air, from far away. A woman's shriek, but it wasn't pain. No, it was anger and fury and madness. And right then, I realized Myst knew we were on the offensive, and she was letting me know that she was aware of our actions.

❧

We left those who had joined our army behind with Lannan and his men, and now, as one mass, we began to run.

When the Fae run, it's like the Hunt. A blur of motion, a blur of speed. Fleeing treachery and danger on the wind, we flew. Racing through the snow, we sped through the town. The Summer Fae ran right alongside us, though they traveled through the warmer months of the year faster than us, and we traversed the Winter realm in the blink of an eye. But we ran as a group, faster than any magic-born or yummanii could hope to see or even keep up with. The guards caught Kaylin and our other yummanii troops up and carried them with us.

We raced the length of town back to the Veil House. When we came to the end of Vyne Street, where my aunt's house stood at the end of the cul-de-sac, we dropped out of the slipstream and stood, filling the yard, listening for any sign of Shadow Hunters. But none were about the property. Ulean checked and verified that fact for us.

While the warriors waited outside, Check, Fearless, Rhiannon's personal guards, Grieve, Chatter, Kaylin, and I went inside. As we entered the house, a cloud seemed to descend—a darkness I'd never before felt in the Veil House. It wasn't gloomy, but dense, and alive, and prickling at the back of my neck.

One of Lannan's men nodded for us to go on through to the living room, and we did, cautiously approaching the Circle in which Luna sat. Ysandra stood outside the chalked outline, on the left, and Peyton on the right. Both were dressed in black dresses, and Luna was in a silver gown. Ysandra glanced over at me and the look on her face was enough to freeze water. There was no warmth, no compassion in her expression. Peyton's expression matched Ysandra's.

Luna turned then, her arms outstretched. The gown shimmered across her full breasts, caught at the waist by a simple black belt. Her hair was down, cascading around her shoulders, and the look on her face was feral and fierce. Her eyes gleamed with an unnatural light, and I had the feeling we weren't facing Luna at all, but someone who had taken possession of her.

"Who are you?" I stepped forward.

"I am not harming your friend, so do not interfere." The voice echoing out of her plump, crimson lips was not her own—was not even human, but lush and opulent.

"What are you doing here?" I cocked my head, knowing better than to intervene before I knew exactly what was going on. There were rites and rituals that you just didn't go stomping into—no matter how afraid they might make you feel. One wrong move and whatever—whoever—this was, might turn back on Luna and hurt her.

"I was summoned. I am Dorthea. Luna's great-great-grandmother. And I will be taking possession of this body as needed, until my task is done. My help has been requested, the price has been paid, and so I fulfill my end of the bargain."

My breath catching in my throat, I stepped to the very edge of the Circle and stared into the silver-tinged eyes of the woman whom I considered my friend. "*What* are you?"

With a dark laugh, Luna let out a long volley of song, a trembling array of notes so beautiful that they hurt my heart. They spiraled up and around, echoing off the walls, ricocheting from door to ceiling to floor to center of the room. It was an orgasm of sound, magic weaving through voice, through sounds so primal they could form no words. But the music spiraled up, like the minarets on a mosque, into the night.

The next moment, I was on my knees, weeping at the song's beauty. She was singing of death, and darkness, and falling into decay—I could see it all, see the dark forms spiraling around her, shadows of the past clinging to her aura. They infused her with their essence, shoring her up. They empowered her as she slowly danced—weaving her song, weaving her magic.

Ysandra slowly crossed to my side, helped me to my feet. She looked almost as entranced as I was, but tears clung to her face, and I knew there was something dark and terrible here—some secret we hadn't been told yet.

Luna came to rest again, so light on her feet it looked like she might be floating an inch above the floor. "I will help you fight this queen of darkness, and my army of shades will move with me. We will move as a blight. You tell us what we are to destroy, and we will seek them out and hunt them down and drain their life from their bodies and souls."

I staggered back a step. "Such power . . . Luna . . . I didn't know she possessed this ability."

"She does not—not without our help. But she paid the price when she first opened herself to speak to the ancestors. And she guaranteed a new price tonight, in exchange for the ability to call the spirits. She belongs to us now, and we will give her everything she needs." Dorthea laughed then, and Luna's expression followed form, turning vicious and malevolent. "We will destroy those who seek to destroy our daughter."

Ysandra pulled me away past the others, who were staring at the whole scene with horror. As we stumbled into the kitchen, I whirled on her.

"What is going on? What the hell is happening in there?"

"It is as she says. Luna summoned her great-great-grandmother. And Dorthea was apparently a witch of tremendous power. She's working through Luna now and won't desert us until we either win or go down in flames."

But there was something else. Ysandra's face was normally pale, but I'd never her seen her look like this. Not horror, but a healthy amount of fear and—something more.

"What's going on? Tell me. You know something—that much is obvious. What aren't you telling me?" I grabbed her by the shoulders, not caring whether she could deafen me with one shout.

The witch stared at me, then slowly shook her head. "The price she paid . . . the price she promised . . ."

"What? What is it?"

Ysandra's brow furrowed as she rubbed her head. "Before I could stop her, Luna promised them her life. If we lose, they will let her be. If we win . . . she dies when they choose." And with that a high-pitched bout of laughter echoed from the living room, going on and on and on.

Chapter 9

"What the fuck did you say?" Before I could help myself, I hauled off and slapped Ysandra across the face. "How could you let this happen?"

"I had no say over the matter. *She* was holding the Circle. *She* called them in. *She's* the one who made the deal. If I'd tried to break in, the spirits would have been free to come and go as they please, and you do not want the spirits riding free, Cicely. They are dark and dangerous and vicious. They will do as they promise because they made a deal, but do not expect them to befriend us, or to be anything but treacherous outside of the bargain they have made."

I stared at her, horrified. "Why? Why did she do this?"

This time it was Ysandra who grabbed me by the shoulders. "Because we are facing a monster. Because we are at war. Luna was doing what she could to help. And . . ." She stopped and shook her head.

"No, tell me. What is it?" Whatever it was, I wanted to hear.

"You couldn't trust us. I understand why you did what you did. You had to. But Luna . . . having Kaylin—of all people—force himself into her mind and sift through her innermost thoughts? It changed her, Cicely. Consider her a casualty of the war. Because even if she comes through this . . . Even if she makes it out alive somehow, she'll never be the same. And I doubt if she'll ever be your friend again."

I crouched on the floor, hands over my face. "I broke her. I broke her."

Ysandra yanked me back up. "Never kneel. You are a queen. You did not break her, but your actions changed her. She was determined to prove herself true to her word. But in doing so . . . she signed her own death warrant."

My heart plunging, I stumbled back. "How can I fix this? How can I make this better?"

"You can't. Face it—this is what war is like, Cicely. This is what it means to lead a nation and that's what you're doing. You are going to lose people along the way. You just hold on as best you can, and do what you need to do. There is no win-win scenario in a situation like this. Luna, even in her mis-guided anger, actually did us a favor."

"A favor? How the hell do you see that?"

Ysandra lowered her voice. "With the dead on our side, we stand a better chance. They can drain the Shadow Hunt-ers' life force. They can't be killed; they're already dead. We have a small army of very deadly soldiers on our side now, thanks to Luna's sacrifice. Don't let it be in vain. Accept what she did and quit whining about it. You can grieve later. There's no time for tears now."

Grabbing me by the elbow, not giving me any chance to say another word, Ysandra dragged me back into the living room where Luna—or rather, Dorthea—was waiting. She cocked her head, a wicked smile on her face.

"And so, she is back. The Winter Maiden. What say you now: Will you accept our help, or do we ride free of our prom-ise, using my great-great-granddaughter as our mare?"

She'd do it, too. I could tell. She'd take over Luna and rage through the world doing whatever it was that she'd left unfinished. I had no doubt that Dorthea was an intensely powerful witch, and I had no idea what kind of magic she could work. Especially with a host of the dead on her side.

"We accept your help. But I beg you to reconsider—don't take Luna's life in payment. Surely we can think of something else you might want even more."

"Enough. The body must rest. I will vacate till the need is here, and then I will come and bring my legions with me, and we will decimate your enemy." And with that Dorthea vanished, and Luna crumbled to the ground as the Circle broke. We could tangibly feel it snap, and the chalk outline on the floor swept open.

"Luna! Luna? Are you all right?" I was by her side, on my knees, before anyone else could move. She stirred, sitting up slowly, holding her head. "Luna, can you hear me?"

"Yes." Luna pinched her nose between her eyes, grimacing. "I feel sick, and I have a horrible headache." Then she focused on my face, and her look turned to icy. "Cicely. How did it go in town? I hope everyone's all right."

I slowly backed off. I knew she meant what she said, but the tone of voice left no question as to her mood. I bit my lip, wanting to beg her to forgive me, but one glance at Ysandra, and I knew I couldn't do that.

"We came through with minimal losses. We took back city hall, and some of Lannan's men are there with the police and some of the Fae." I reached out to help her up, but she ignored my hand, instead struggling to stand on her own. Grieve gently took my arm, drawing me back as Peyton entered the Circle to help her. Luna let Peyton guide her over to the sofa, which had been pushed out of the way.

"I'm glad everyone's all right." She was staring at Kaylin as she spoke, but again, her look was cold as ice—cold as my realm—and I realized Luna had erected a wall between us. She was on our side, but she'd never be my friend again. Or Kaylin's. Not unless something happened to shift the balance. "I'm afraid I feel queasy. Ysandra can give you all the details. Peyton, would you take me to my room? I need to rest."

Peyton gave me a sad, understanding smile, then helped Luna out of the room. As soon as she left, I whirled on Ysandra.

"Tell me, what now? What do I do?"

"I told you. I doubt she'll ever trust you again. Not unless mountains fall and the earth quakes and fire rains from the sky. Or some such miracle. Luna will hold your back, though. Don't ever doubt her loyalty again. She will fall in service to you, even if she curses you doing so." With a long sigh, Ysandra motioned for us to sit down. "Let me make some tea. It's been a long and grueling evening for everyone."

"We cannot keep our men so long from the Barrow." I looked up at Grieve. "What do you think?"

"I will talk to Olrick. He leads the brigade. Stay here."

As he and Chatter went outside, Rhia and Kaylin joined me on the sofa, and I leaned back, suddenly realizing that I smelled. Looking down at my clothes, I saw the spatters of blood covering me, and I shook my head.

"I honestly don't know what to do next. We can't keep waiting for Myst to make the next move. We can't keep running from fire to fire, cleaning up after her raids. We have to find out where she is and then go on the offense. It's really our only hope." I wearily accepted a plate of cookies from Peyton as she returned to the room. She sat down opposite me, leaning forward to prop her elbows on knees, hands crossed between her legs.

"That means planning out how to kill her. Finding her won't be the hardest part." Peyton's gaze flickered over to Kaylin. "Let's get this out of the way, shall we? What you did? I hate you for it, but I understand why you did it, and unlike Luna, I can let it go. So you know my secrets now. But I trust you to keep them to yourself unless you feel they breach some security around Cicely and Rhiannon."

Kaylin sauntered over. "I would never have done what I did had there been another way. But we have so little time, and so many enemies facing us. Cicely needed me to help, and so we chose the only path we had at the moment. If we'd told you about it beforehand and you *had* been a spy, you could have warned Myst we were onto her. As it is, by now she probably knows, but we needed every second we could buy."

Peyton shrugged. "I realize that. I may be angry now, but I'm not shortsighted. I know what needs to be done. Luna though . . . you . . ."

"I realize that—the minute I broke through her shields and saw what was there, I knew how this was going to end. It did one thing for me, though." He shook his head, sounding resigned. "I've accepted there will never be an 'us'—not with her and me. As much as I hoped there would be, it can't happen. And that frees me to do what I must, once this is over."

Terribly curious, but realizing that asking would probably make me not only a bitch but a nosy one at that, I waited for a beat. "But Luna poses no danger to the Courts, right?"

"Right." Pausing for a moment, Kaylin considered a thought, then he motioned to Peyton. "Can you leave us alone for a moment? I know Check and Fearless won't go anywhere, but the rest of you please step outside the room."

They did, after some grumbling. When they were gone, Kaylin turned to me. "I would normally never tell you what I'm about to, but I think you need to understand something I discovered, in order to fully determine what to do about Luna. I've lived a lot longer than you, so far, and don't throw anything in my face about how you're the Fae Queen now, yada, yada, yada. The fact is, I've seen a lot of life, and too much of people, generally."

I waited, not sure if I really wanted to hear what he had to say. But he leaned forward and took my hands, and I realized that he really wouldn't tell me anything if he didn't think it was absolutely necessary. Kaylin didn't gossip. He didn't run around spilling secrets.

"When I went through her mind, I came across a memory that Luna had secreted away. Oh, she remembers it, all right, but she keeps it under lock and key, repressed to the point that she rarely ever thinks about it. In fact, she's built up so many layers trying to hide from the memory that she truly, actually believed she'd managed to rid herself of it. Until I dredged through . . . until I raked her mind over the coals and uncovered it."

Fuck. "Do I really need to know this? Isn't it just going to make it worse for her?"

"No, because you will never tell her what you know. You will go on acting just the way you did tonight, but perhaps it will stay your tongue if you feel the need to bitch at her or question her stance." He let out another sigh. "When Luna was a teenager, her uncle came to visit. He was a telepath . . . a slimy bastard. He's dead now, or I'd hunt him down and kill him myself once this war with Myst is over. But, long story short, he sneaked into her room one night, and he raped her."

When I started to gasp, Kaylin held up his hand. "That's not the worst of it—if you can believe it. He not only had his way with her, but he got inside of her mind. He not only convinced Luna she asked for it, but he filled her mind with self-loathing. He taunted her weight, her looks, her voice—and he convinced her that she'd given him the go-ahead to do what he did."

"Oh fucking hell. And we drugged her, and then you . . . at my command . . ."

"Oh, it's worse than that. It took Luna five years for the spell to break and her to realize that she hadn't agreed to it. That he'd actually raped her and then made her believe it was her own fault. But while he was in there, he tore through every thought, and he taunted her for years after about her secrets. About her private desires and thoughts."

Tears welled up as I realized what I'd done. "You pawed through her mind—looking for her secrets. We were looking to see if she was loyal to me, if she was a spy, but that doesn't matter. You . . ."

"I told you it would be a mind-fuck. And it was. And she's been the victim before. This . . . How can either one of us expect her to ever forgive us for this?" Kaylin's voice trembled, but he stayed steady. He shook his head. "I could have loved her and been there for her. . . . But it won't ever happen now. And while I was in there, I understood why it can never happen. And it's not because of what I did. It's because of who I *am*."

I frowned. "What do you mean?"

"I'm afraid that Luna looks at me like I'm a freak, Cicely. A nice one, a talented one, but she sees me as a freak. My demon scares the hell out of her. She could never love me, not the way I want her to, because she could never love my demon. I don't think she even realizes that this is what's been holding her back. It's buried in her subconscious."

Realizing just how far down the rabbit hole we'd fallen, I sat there as Kaylin called the others in. No matter what Luna said to me, no matter what her reaction, I wouldn't raise a voice or take offense or even protest. How could I? Knowing what I now knew, if she said the sun was blue and the stars were gold, I'd agree.

Ysandra brought in the tea and looked quizzically from Kaylin to me, then back to him, but we both just shook our heads. As Peyton fixed another plate of cookies, the back door opened, and a moment later, Grieve entered the room.

We were eating silently when he came over to my side. "Love, Cicely? The Snow Hag is outside. She wants to talk to you."

Exhausted, but relieved for the chance to get outside and stretch my legs, I followed my husband to the yard, weighed down by the knowledge of just how much damage I'd done to so many lives.

⚜

The snow had let up, and overhead the stars were peeking out, crystal clear and twinkling. I slowly descended the back steps and crossed into the yard where the Snow Hag waited for me. She was standing frozen, a sparkle in her eye.

"The snowy night seems to agree with you." I was too tired to play all the games required, but I'd do what I could and hope for the best.

"A queen might be weary and tired, and forget herself with lessons in communication so recently learned, and one of the Wilding Fae might recognize this to be exhaustion and not disrespect." And with that the Hag gave me an out.

She stared up at the sky, a bemused look on her face. "One might think we chance never to see the stars again, and one might be right at there being a chance, if the long winter is to come. But there are ways to prevent the winter from lingering. There are ways to find weaknesses in an enemy, if you are a queen who was once a princess."

I froze. The Snow Hag knew something, and I needed to know what it was. My tired brain scrambled to put together my question into the right format. "If one were a queen who was once a princess, one might wonder what a Wilding Fae knows. One might be wondering what the price for such information would be." Crossing to one of the low bushes, now a mound of white, I felt wrapped in a cocoon, muffled from the world. Everywhere, the snow reigned, and it was now my life, my world, and even after we had destroyed Myst, my realm would remain a frozen chrysalis—perpetual winter encased in ice and frost.

The Snow Hag followed me, somehow managing to keep atop the crust. She was short enough and squat enough that I'd expect her to sink deep in the drifts, to be encumbered by them. My thoughts must have been at the top of my mind because she let out a tinkle of laughter—it sounded young to her age, and fell pleasantly on my ears.

"The Wilding Fae belong to seasons. A Snow Hag might belong to the winter, wouldn't one surmise? She might embody the chill nights and frosty skies. Her form might be an illusion, wouldn't one think?"

I glanced at her sideways, a tired smile creeping across my face. I nodded. "One might think so, indeed."

After a moment, she raised a handful of snow to the sky. "Snow falls from the clouds. It freezes to the ground, then melts in the natural cycle of things. Come the spring, it flows into waterways where it evaporates with the heat of the summer, and returns to the sky. When winter rolls around again, it falls once more. The natural order of life. A cycle—a circle."

I said nothing, just listening. She was teaching me things, even if I didn't recognize what they were just yet.

"A queen may ask a question and ask the price of the answer. She understands there are always costs for information. Answers require the questioner to pay a price. Whether to life, or to one with knowledge, this is always true, even if the price is not agreed upon in advance."

"Never anything for free," I murmured.

"One might be a queen and be correct. Nothing is free.

However, there are costs . . . and then there are costs. And sometimes, the sum cannot be determined because the one holding the answer is not she who determines it. At times, the price is roundabout. One asks, one gives, the price is taken by some other force, the payment is given through yet another. Roundabout we go—twists and turns in the path."

Mulling over her words, I thought I understood what she was saying. "Then, perhaps a queen may ask a question, and an answer is given, but the payment takes place behind the scenes. And neither the queen nor the Wilding Fae know what it is to be, or when it will be given."

The Snow Hag turned to me. "One understands, one does. One wonders, then . . . does a queen still wish an answer to her question, not knowing what the price will be, or to whom it will be paid?"

I stared at her silent form. The snow on her hand wasn't melting. She was as cold as I. Suddenly grateful she'd aligned herself to me, I nodded.

"Yes, a queen might still want an answer, given those circumstances."

Abruptly dropping the snow, she turned to face me. Her eyes, so beady during the day, had grown luminous and bright, and I could see the outer edges of the brilliant creature hiding within the old crone's body.

"A queen must look to the past—must actually travel into days gone by. She must look to the time when she was a princess, and seek out the vulnerabilities of her enemy. She must journey back to when she lived with starry eyes and cerulean skin, to when she knew the secrets of the one who now holds her fate. She must look for chinks in the armor—only through that means will she know how to proceed in playing the final move. Check might be found without this journey . . . but checkmate? Only can be accomplished by taking a step backward before moving forward."

The swirl of singsong words danced in my brain . . . and then I understood what she meant. I'd had several flashbacks to my time spent as Myst's daughter. I was Princess Cherish then—my time when I was a princess, not a queen. If I was able to travel back, I might discover what Myst's vulnerabilities were. *Find the chink in her armor,* so to speak.

"But how do I do that?" The words slipped out without me thinking.

The Snow Hag merely tapped her finger to her nose and vanished out of my sight into the darkness. Ask a straight question, and the Wilding Fae would turn a deaf ear or vanish. They lived in a world of riddles and rules and bargains.

I watched her fade, as if into the landscape itself, as Grieve came up behind me. He wrapped his arms around my waist, and I leaned back against him.

"I know what I have to do, but I don't know how to do it."

"And what is that?"

"I have to return to the past—I've done it via flashbacks, unwittingly, but I have to go back to when I was Cherish and look for anything that makes Myst vulnerable. The Snow Hag is convinced I know something—or *knew* something— that can give us an advantage against the Vampiric Queen. But I can't remember it as I am now." I rested the back of my head against his shoulder.

He kissed my hair, his arms gentle around my waist. "Hypnotic regression? Would that work?"

"I don't know, but it might be worth a try. I wonder if Ysandra can help me. It's worth asking. Or . . . Kaylin. I wonder if his demon might know of a way."

Grieve didn't like that idea. "Kaylin's demon is chaotic and dangerous. Trusting him might be stretching our luck, Cicely."

"We live in dangerous times." I closed my eyes and reached out into the slipstream. There, on the currents, was a cacophony of whispers. The rush of recent dead slipped past—they were loud tonight, and I could hear the murmurs of confusion coming from them. And the voices of people hurrying home, trying to get off the streets, terrified that they might be targeted for attack like so many others had been. A rush swept by—a Wind Elemental I didn't recognize, but it paid no attention to me, just soared past in a frenzy of movement.

As I lowered myself deeper into the ever-changing river of

energy, I could hear the sounds of forest animals scurrying through the snow and the footsteps of the guards patrolling the land and the Golden Wood. From the house, I could hear the pacing of Ysandra's thoughts—she was worried about Luna, about me, about the world. And in another room, I could hear Luna crying. Fear seeped into her voice as she settled into the realization of what she had promised Dorthea.

And then, from farther out, I began to sense a disturbance. It wasn't an energy I recognized, at least not well—I thought I might have felt it before but couldn't be fully certain. But it was covert and covetous, and . . . jealous. Envy? Or jealousy? The two emotions were very much akin to one another, but there were subtle differences. . . . Jealousy was more dangerous.

A moment later, the focus zeroed in on me. Someone was horribly jealous of me and . . . just as I was about to home in on the source, she pulled back, like a snake coiling, rearing to strike. But instead of lashing out, she turned tail and slithered off, faster than I could follow. Whoever it was had picked up on my energy. She knew I was out riding the currents.

I shook myself out of the slipstream. *Ulean! Ulean, are you here? I need to follow an energy signature. Someone I think might be the spy in my Court.*

I'm here, and I heard it. I'll see what I can find.

I turned to Grieve. "Someone is out there who hates me. She's jealous. I think I felt the energy of whoever is our spy. Ulean is following her signature to see if she can track her down."

"Then we let her do her job. Come inside. We will discuss how best to send you back to discover Myst's secrets." He led me toward the door. As we neared the homey Veil House, I realized that I was lonely. Lonely for our realm, for the stark lands and the austere luster of the Barrow. For the heat of the fireplaces that kept the chill at bay. And yet, even with the roaring fires, there was always a chill there. It had seeped into my bones, into my soul. It was who I was.

"I want to go home," I whispered.

"So do I, but we have things to do. We'll go soon enough. We aren't far from there. Just a skip through the woods, my love."

And yet, it seemed like we were half a world away from our home. With a start, I realized that the town—New Forest, and the beloved Veil House—were beginning to feel alien to me. They no longer belonged to my life, and while I was still adapting to life in the Court of Snow and Ice, a part of me had already adopted it for my own.

As we entered the house, I realized I was a guest here now. I wondered if Rhiannon was feeling the same way, and that made me sad. It was her childhood home, after all. She'd spent all her life here. Her memories of her mother were locked within these walls. That it might no longer be a welcome haven for her hit me in the gut.

I found her in the kitchen. She was staring out the window.

"I was watching you out there. You look so at home under the night." She turned. "What are you thinking?"

"About my home. I finally have a home, and it's not the one I expected it to be. I always thought I'd return here, to this house, and that we'd be a family again." I shook my head. "We're so far from where we started; there's no way to calculate the distance, is there?"

She bit her lip, but it wasn't indecision. A drop of blood welled up, and she licked it off, deliberately, holding my gaze. "The initiation changed me. It changed you. How can we ever think to be the same? Even when Leo was holding me in that cage, I was not the woman I was when he walked out on me. Cicely, you worry too much about me."

Rhia looked around, motioning to the kitchen. "I lived my life here, but when it burned, it burned away my connection to it. When you and I killed my mother, we severed my connection to the past. I've had to let it go to stay sane, to forget what we had to do to Heather. To let her go, I've had to let the Veil House go. You never had a foundation like I did. I think sometimes you place too much value on it. I think, like I've had to let go of my past, you need to let go your idolization of actually having one."

I leaned against the counter. What she said made a lot of sense, but it was hard to see through the layers of hope I'd built up around coming home. "Maybe I'm so caught up in losing what I never had, that I'm struggling with what I have now. I feel guilty for loving my new home. I feel guilty for moving into that dark, icy realm, and leaving everything behind."

"But you're not leaving *anything* behind. I'm still here— and we're closer than we've been since we were little. You have Grieve. All you left behind was a life on the streets. You didn't have Heather, Cicely. You didn't have the Veil House. You didn't even have Krystal. She wasn't your mother; you couldn't rely on her. If anything, she treated you like the adult. All you had was your car and your memories of being dragged from city to city. The only thing you're leaving behind is your old life." She laughed gently and reached out to stroke my cheek. "You've got more now than you ever had in your life."

I knew she was right, but there was something I couldn't seem to verbalize. And then I knew. "Kaylin, Luna, Peyton. They were . . . I thought they'd be my family."

"And you feel you've lost Luna. And you aren't sure about the others." Rhia pulled me close, resting her forehead against mine. "Kaylin will follow whatever path he needs to. Peyton will return to her father's pride to learn what she needs to know about that side of her heritage. Luna . . . Luna might hate you forever. They each have their own journeys. It's hard to accept, but people leave us along the way. People don't always stay with us until the end of the story."

I let out a long sigh. "I know. I just thought maybe I was done with losing people. I lost you for so long, Rhia."

"And you found me again. But Cicely . . ." She stood back and a pained, sad smile crossed her face. "We will outlive them all. Unless we're murdered, we're going to outlive all of them. Did you think about that?"

And there it was. The crux of our transformation. Except for our new families—Grieve and Chatter—we would out-live everyone we ever knew. We were headed down a one-way path to virtual immortality, and other than the vampires, anybody we'd ever known would be dust before we could even blink an eye.

"Immortality. What a bitch, right?" I glanced at the staircase. "And Luna . . . She may go sooner than we thought. I wish she hadn't made that pact." But there was nothing else to say. Nothing to make it better. Sometimes, we did what we had to, even when the end result was devastating. Sometimes, we played the devil, because playing god was out of reach.

Rhia handed me a sandwich. "Eat. You need food. What were you doing out there?"

I bit into the roast beef with Swiss, and smiled. Simple comforts meant a lot when times were dark. Even with all the riches of my Court, sometimes the best cure to sorrow was standing by a kitchen counter, a roast beef sandwich in hand, talking to my cousin.

Licking the mayo off my fingers, I shrugged. "Talking to the Snow Hag. She gave me advice on how to find Myst's Achilles' heel, but I'm not sure how to proceed." I ran down what I needed to do. "So, I have to travel through time, in a sense. Not like a time machine, but go back in my memories—and that's one hell of a tumble into the abyss."

"Yes, it is, but I can help you." Ysandra was standing at the kitchen door. She swept into the room. "It won't be easy, and the ritual has its own dangers, but I can help you regress to that time period. The question is are you ready?"

I glanced at Rhiannon and swallowed the bite of sandwich in my mouth. "The question isn't am I ready. The question is how soon can we get this show on the road?"

And with that Ysandra led me into the living room so I could travel into the past to face down our enemy.

Chapter 10

Of course, as soon as I agreed, fear crept up and hit me over the head like a sledgehammer. "Myst won't really be there, will she? I mean, whatever I see will be a memory, won't it?"

Ysandra let out a long sigh. "While I want to say yes, and I believe that's the way this works, there's always the chance that—in this life—she'll sense something going on. Magic is nebulous. You know how unpredictable it can be, and there's always the chance something will go wrong. But if you have to do this, and it sounds like it might be one of our best chances to find a way to defeat her, then I'm going to say that I think we should go for it."

Grieve entered the room. He stopped at the sight of us. "What's going on?"

"Ysandra can help me go into the past, to look for ways to battle Myst." I brushed my hand across my face, weary beyond belief. "Does it matter that I'm so tired that it feels like I'm about to drop?"

Truth was all I wanted to do was crash. I didn't even care if I managed to get my clothes off, though sleeping in blood-stained leathers wasn't all that appealing. In fact, now that I thought about it . . . I began to unbuckle the sides of the tunic, and as I did, the smell of dried blood wafted up, and I had to get it off.

"Help me, I need this off now!"

Ysandra jumped to help me, and I noticed that Rhia had already removed hers. Within a couple of minutes, I was standing there, devoid of the armor, but my corset and jeans felt sticky and ripe. The blood hadn't soaked through to them, and I hadn't really sweated—I really didn't perspire much anymore, ever since the initiation—but the feeling of death clung to them.

"Is there anything in the house I can—" I stopped as Ysandra put a hand on my shoulder. She turned me toward her.

"Cicely, breathe. You are panicking. I think . . . So many changes in such a short time . . ."

I wanted to protest, to be the strong Cicely they deserved. But the truth was she was right. Too much death, too much betrayal and betraying. The dominos were falling, and now there was no stopping the chain reaction. I'd been the fuse on the bomb . . . and now the shockwaves were reverberating faster than we could cope with them.

But something about Ysandra's touch was calming. I closed my eyes and found myself breathing in sync with her. A few moments later, the panic slid from my body, and I opened my eyes. Rhia and Grieve were watching, as Peyton entered the room.

I turned to her, mutely holding out my hands, willing her to understand and forgive me. I couldn't say the words, but I prayed she could hear them.

She paused, then slowly walked over to face me. "I understand. I can't forgive you, not quite yet, but I do understand."

With light fingers, she lifted my hands to her lips and kissed them lightly. "My mother almost killed you. You thought you could trust her, and she turned out to be a traitor. The stakes are so much higher now. We thought we could trust Leo, and he almost killed Rhiannon. This town runs on treachery. You did what you had to. Luna will come to understand. Someday, she'll understand."

"Not if she dies first." I winced, but held my head up, remembering what Lainule and Ysandra had both taught me.

"Maybe . . . Maybe it will take death to help her see. We can't make choices for other people, Cicely. They have to walk their own paths, even when those paths are dark and fearsome. And Dorthea's help? We need every hand on board. Even when those hands are shadows from the other side." She glanced over to Ysandra. "What do you need me to do? I heard everything from the kitchen."

Ysandra motioned to the sofa. "Cicely, you can lie down for this. Indeed, the fact that you're already tired will only help us take you into the trance that you need to be in. Peyton, will you get my bag?"

Chatter suddenly popped into the room. "Just got word that the crew from the Consortium are on the edge of town. I've sent a contingent of men to guide them back here. Apparently they ran into an altercation a ways out and were held up. They have wounded, but no dead."

"How long till they get here?" I glanced at the clock, dazed. It felt like we'd been on our feet for days, but it wasn't even midnight. So much had happened in such a little time.

"Half an hour maybe. I'll have some of my men get the parlor ready for them—they'll need a place to stay." He vanished back into the kitchen.

"Lie down, Cicely. Rhiannon, can you get me a throw to cover her with? Something warm. Even though she belongs to Winter, she needs to keep her body temperature within reason."

As Rhia left the room, Peyton entered it, handing Ysandra a black bag, like an old-fashioned doctor's bag. Ysandra opened it, fishing around until she came up with a small bottle that had an eye dropper in it.

"This tincture will help you sleep, and it will make you vulnerable to my suggestions. Therefore, Grieve—you and Rhiannon must be in the room at all time. I don't want there to be any questions as to what I've done, or am doing. Do you understand?"

Rhiannon, who had just returned with an afghan, nodded. "Of course." She pulled a chair up to sit near my side.

Grieve moved to a stool beside Ysandra. "Make no mistake. If you even make a move that seems like it might hurt her, I will kill you right then and there. No questions, no regrets. Do you understand me?"

Ysandra flashed him a mirthless smile. "Of course I understand. I also know that what I'm about to do won't be very pleasant for her, but I will explain to you and Rhiannon every step of the way. However, when it comes time to draw her back, I may have to slap her—or otherwise startle her. Cicely, if you get caught in the trance, if you go too deep, I have to be ready to yank you out. There are no guarantees that this will work, but I'll do everything I can to facilitate it."

I looked at the bottle. "Will that hurt me, with the fact that I've made the transformation to Fae Queen?"

She shook her head. "No—I know for a fact that Lainule used these herbs herself. And there are no fish products in it. There should be no reason why it would harm you, unless you drank the whole bottle. Then it might send your mind into a tailspin, but I doubt it would poison you."

I accepted the dropper. "How many drops?"

"Let's start with ten, and see where we go from there. Peyton, kill the lamps, please. And light a couple of candles." Ysandra held my hand, gazing into my eyes. "Take the tincture, Cicely, then lie back and close your eyes."

I grimaced as the drops hit my tongue. "Tastes like I'm drinking toad water. Or dirt."

"It's the valerian and kava kava. There are other, stronger herbs, but the valerian is pungent and ripe from the earth." She paused. "Luna?"

I opened my eyes and sat up. Luna was standing there, staring at the proceedings. Her gaze fell on mine.

"What are you doing?" She turned to Ysandra. "Do you need my help?"

"Can you keep your personal feelings out of the way? I could use someone to sing the song of spinning time."

I wanted to protest—Luna hated me. It had to affect the spell. But Ysandra patted my hand when I reached for her. "Give her leeway, Cicely. Luna is not your enemy, even if—"

"Even if I hate what you did." Luna finished the sentence. "I can sing the song for you. I won't do anything else."

Grieve let out a little growl, but she turned to him. "Your wife is our only hope against Myst. Do you really think I'd do anything to fuck that up? Give me a little credit. I may have little to lose now, with the bargain I've pledged, but do you really think that I'd make such a bargain if I didn't think we needed the help? If I didn't believe this war was worth dying for? Sit down, *Lord Grieve*, and let us do our work. Cicely is willing to go through this ritual. She knows what we have to gain from it."

I wanted to ask how she knew about it, but the tincture was making me dizzy. I lay back again, moaning slightly. But then Ulean was there, by my side.

Luna, is she safe? Will she sabotage this rite?

No, she is not your enemy, Cicely. I found out who it is— but . . . Cicely? Cicely? Can you hear me?

And then, there was a rushing of wind as the world around me began to fade. I couldn't hear Ulean anymore, but only Ysandra's voice, droning on and on from a distance. In the background, Luna began to sing, in a language I didn't understand, but she kept a steady cadence, and I thought I could hear a drum accompanying her. Her voice grew almost shrill, more insistent, as the drums rose in volume, and then I was hearing voices echoing in the drumbeat.

"Listen to me, Cicely, and follow my voice. Follow my thoughts—follow the thread. Can you see the thread of my voice on the slipstream? Can you catch hold of it, focus on it? Let it lead you along."

I searched the currents, and there—there it was, a silver cord rippling with every word she spoke. It wrapped around me, like a snake, like a lasso, and another tendril rose up to beckon me on. I began to follow, seeing myself in a deep woodland covered with snow. It was not the Golden Wood, though, but darker and deeper—an ancient winding path.

"Follow me down the path. Follow my voice, let it lead you into the past. Let it lead you through the years. See them fly by, the past speeding forward, becoming your future. See time

streaming quickly, a blur of motion, as you journey through
your past. Back to when you were a child, then to when you
were a babe in arms, and then . . . before you returned to this
world."

I wanted to dance, the song was leading me on as much
as Ysandra's words. The music became a focal point, and it
seemed to open up the path, making it easier to skate past
the years, to travel into history.

And then I saw through my eyes as a child. The world
was so new, and yet I had been here before—I could feel the
connection to the spirit world out of which I had just
emerged. And then—

"Go back, go back, and let the path lead you into the time
before time. To the time when this life was only a flicker of
possibilities."

And I was no longer Cicely, but a soul wandering the currents, wading through the slipstream. The wind blew past as
I walked through the mists, searching for . . . searching
for . . . who was I looking for? I lost track of my name, lost
track of my goal. I was floating, wandering, beyond the scope
of anyone I'd ever been, too far from the person I would
become.

"Hear me—don't lose track of my voice. Pay attention to
my words. Let them lead you back through the gray time,
through the time of mist and shadow and uncertainty. Keep
moving. You are crossing the path of transition. You must go
beyond. There is another door coming up. Go through that
door."

The voice was familiar, but I was no longer clear about
who was talking, or the singing that echoed from beyond the
veil. But up ahead, a door beckoned, and I slowly, cautiously,
opened it. There, on the other side, I saw a young child. She
was playing with flowers in a meadow, sitting next to a pond.
I stepped into the world, but something felt off. Leaning
down, I reached out to touch her chubby fist, which was
holding a bouquet of freshly picked daisies.

"Who are you?" I whispered.

She gazed up at me and, with eyes no longer those of a

child's, she shook her head. "We came back too soon. He's not here. We have to go now, to look for him." Before I could stop her, she picked up a fat mushroom—red with white spots. I wanted to tell her, *Don't eat that, it will poison you*, but the words died in my throat.

She held my gaze, deliberately, slowly putting the fungus in her mouth and chewing. "Don't worry," she said. "We'll find him again. I promise."

And then she clutched her stomach, and I felt myself being drawn back toward the door. She stood up, leaving her body behind, and ran toward me, running through me—into me— and I felt her essence merge with mine, and we turned to exit the door.

Together, the girl and I moved back into the slipstream— only she was part of me now, and I realized I'd left her behind because she'd seemed so minute, so splintered off. But truly, when I examined her thoughts, young as she was, she was bright and joyful and fiercely brave for her age. She knew what we had to do, and she took my hand, deep in my heart, and promised me that it would be all right.

"What was your . . . my name?" I couldn't just call her "little girl," especially when she'd been a part of me.

"Violet."

We continued through the slipstream, through the winds that were now howling, stirring up the wild mist rolling past like a thick blanket. It smelled of mildew and mold, of grave-yards and dusty bones and hopes left in dark closets to wither and die. By now I could no longer hear the voice guiding me, but the song continued, the song of time, the song of spells, the song that spun the thread of my days.

"There." The little girl's voice echoed. "A door."

I turned to see a dark door, cloaked in shadow and dusk. This was our destination. This was our goal. What I was seeking lay beyond. I held tight to her hand. "This is going to be scary. I don't think you're going to like it."

"I don't think *you're* going to like it. You've run from it every time you've found it before. The story behind it scares you." Violet didn't seem afraid, though, and that confused me.

"Why aren't you frightened? There's something dark and dangerous behind there." I hesitantly put my hand on the knob.

"It's only dangerous if you let it overpower you. You have to be the one in control. I'm not afraid, because I'm already dead. There's nothing behind there that can hurt me." Violet's logic made terrible sense, but it didn't do much for me.

"But I'm not dead yet—what's there *can* hurt me."

She laughed then, both at me and with me. "Silly goose! You're not even *born* yet. Come to think about it, *I'm* not even born yet. How can something from the past hurt us when we aren't even alive?"

Her logic made an odd sense. I tried to work my head around it. When I touched lightly on the thought, I knew she was right. We were traveling into the past. How could the past hurt us when we were mere flickers of what might be? But when I tried to reason it out, to wrap my mind around the concept, I lost all sense of reality, and everything became a blur. I decided to take Violet's advice.

"Okay, then. I guess we just go in. Do you know what I'm looking for? I seem to have lost my memory."

Violet shook her head. "No, but you'll know when you find it. That's how these things work, right? Otherwise, why would you be here?"

Pausing, I mulled over her words. "Seems good to me. Let's go then." And with that I put my hand on the shadow-cloistered door and opened it. And as Violet and I went tumbling into a world of snow and ice and silvery spiderlike beings, she blended into me and became a part of my heart and soul.

❧

Inhaling deeply, I opened my eyes and realized I was seeing through someone else's body. And yet, the body felt incredibly familiar. I wasn't sure who I was, or why I was here—wherever here was—but there was something I was searching for, and I could only discover it in this place, in this time. The memory of a song lingered, and the memory of a voice guiding me down a long hallway encased in mist, and there was the whisper of a little girl echoing in my head, but other than that, I had no clue as to what I was about or where I was.

I looked around. I was standing outside a hillock—a Barrow of sorts, and it was covered in deep snows. The trees surrounding it were weighed down with heavy blankets of white, their branches frozen to the ground. The air was clear, so clear it hurt my lungs, and the sky was that pale eggshell blue of dawn, but a storm was coming in—I could feel it in my bones. The energy of the storm was bringing heavy snow and snow-lightning, and it promised a renewal, recharging with its fury.

As I spread my arms wide, welcoming the coming fury, my stomach rumbled, and I realized that I was aching, so thirsty and hungry I was. A cunning swelled up, a desire to seek, to chase, to hunt, and I cast my eye around for possible prey. As I scouted out, following a faint scent that I caught on the wind, I saw him. He was tall and lean, and his clothing was barely enough to keep him from turning blue.

I squirmed as I stood there, and when I looked down, I realized I was naked—or nearly. A gossamer gown, silver threads loosely woven in a lacework pattern, hung lightly from my shoulders, but I could see through it the weave was so loose. My breasts, my stomach, my legs—my entire body was faintly cerulean, and with wonder, I ran my tongue over my teeth, feeling their razor-sharp edges pierce the flesh. Drops of blood welled up on my tongue, and their salty, metallic tang increased my hunger.

I lowered myself behind a nearby bush, as the man began to come my way. He hadn't seen me yet, and I had the feeling that if he knew I was here, he'd be running. All the more reason to be patient—to lie in wait like the snow weavers my mother kept as pets.

My mother? The image of a tall queen rose up, stretching over the sky, blotting out the morning light. Thinly jointed, with angular eyes and a pale, dangerous beauty, her visage was imprinted on my heart, and I realized I loved her with a passion. She was my everything. She was my all, my role model, my goddess. And I was her beloved daughter.

Cherish. That was my name. I was Cherish—and I was my mother's daughter in every way.

Well, almost every way. The voice inside annoyed me, and I tried to push it away, but it wasn't so easily silenced. *You know I'm right. You know that you have something your mother doesn't, and that something might someday be her downfall when you rise up to take your rightful place as her heir to the throne.*

A flash of anger raced through me.

"I'm no traitor. I will never betray my mother. If the throne comes to me, it will be through her choice—not mine." My whisper barely touched the wind, but the slipstream caught it, carrying it deep onto the currents racing around the world.

You have no choice. Destiny will out. The strong always overcome the weak. It's evolution. It's what created your mother in the first place.

"Hush." I shoved the thoughts aside as my prey neared the bush. He paused, and I realized he had sensed something was wrong. Maybe he heard my whisper, maybe he caught my scent. Whatever the case, there was no time to waste. I leaped out, landing in front of him, in a crouch.

He took one look at me and screamed, turning to flee. As I began to change, morphing into my beast, I reveled in the power of my jaws, of the bones shifting and lengthening. My head grew, my jaws transformed into a death vise, and I let out a laugh while I still could, from deep in my belly. A laugh of joy, pure and wallowing in the pain that I knew would follow.

My stomach rumbled, the hunger pushing me on, the lust for his blood and bone and life force so strong that there was nothing more in the world. The only thing that existed was my desire—and nothing, no plea for mercy, no stray thought, could assuage the hunger. Nothing except the feel of his gristle in my mouth, of the hot blood sliding down my throat. I lunged, jaws agape, and his screams punctuated the birdsong echoing through the early morning.

Later, satiated with a full belly, I used the snow to clean myself off. The hunger was at bay for now, and it was time to go home. My mother was waiting for me. There was something she had wanted to discuss with me earlier, but I'd blown her off in exchange for a little time outside by myself. Sometimes the din in the Barrow seemed overwhelming, and I had to get away from the noise.

I headed into the Barrow, ignoring the milling throng of our people. They were all descended from my mother, in a way. Myst had given birth to our race; the first ones were turned by her after the mad vampire had come up with his scheme. But he'd been weak, and my mother had grown stronger than he.

Once she told me that, after the turning, she'd realized he could never be her match, and so he became her enemy. And now, all vampires—the true vampires—were our foes. We were the rightful heirs to their lineage, we'd evolved far beyond their archaic powers, but they wouldn't accept that we were the next step in their evolution, and so we were always at war with them.

They didn't know we'd journeyed to this new land, though. Myst had kept it a secret, leaving some of our people behind to build a community in the old world, even as we'd discovered the vast, unspoiled wilderness here. There was room here, room in which to spread and breed.

Our kind reproduced slowly—and painfully. Mothers sometimes died in childbirth, their children ripping their way out of the womb. But I hadn't done so to my mother. I'd come into the world easy enough, though who my father was remained a mystery and always would. It didn't matter, though. I was Myst's daughter, heir to the Indigo Court, and I would help her reach out and take control of this land. Together, we would build an empire of blood and bone.

As I made my way into our private chambers, I looked around for Myst, but she was nowhere in sight. There was a serving girl nearby and I grabbed her by her hair and yanked her over to my side.

"Where's Queen Myst? Do you know?"

She sputtered, letting out a little growl, but I fisted her hair tighter and let go. She dropped to the ground at my feet. "Last I saw of her, she was in her bedchamber, Princess."

"Go, then. Get about your work." I kicked her out of the way, lightly though. It furthered nothing to damage the help. Put them in the infirmary and somebody else had to do their job.

I headed to my mother's chamber and was about to knock on the door when I heard something from inside. It was a groan—the sound of pain. Worried, I cracked the door and peeked inside.

There, lying on her bed, was my mother. Two Ice Elementals stood over her, and to the side, one of our healers. The Elementals were standing to either side of her, their arms outstretched over her body, and she was writhing, a look of pain sweeping across her face. Sparkles flickered in the air above her chest—a spray of magic filtering through the room, silver and white, and the color of the deep indigo that hits right before dusk. They swirled, like the stars in our eyes.

Slowly, I closed the door behind me and edged my way behind the floor-length curtain that draped over the wall. No one had noticed me; they were so focused on Myst and what was happening. The healer looked nervous, and he was muttering something beneath his breath.

I focused on the slipstream, trying to catch his words.

I don't know if this will work. . . . Please don't let her die. . . . Please let this work. . . . He was frightened. That much came through.

Wanting to burst out into the open, to ask what the hell they were doing to her, I caught myself and kept quiet. If I interrupted, whatever they were involved in might go awry, and my mother would be furious with me. So I stood back, watching and waiting.

The thrumming in the room grew stronger, so loud it was like a flurry of bees in my head. Wincing, I covered my ears as my mother's cries grew stronger. But I couldn't look away.

And then I saw it—the swirls began to coalesce and take shape, forming into a pool of liquid energy over the center of her heart. A stream of light poured from her body into the pool as it whirled, turning like some mad dervish in the thrall of his dance. I'd seen them, somewhere, when I was very young, though I couldn't remember much about it. In some street somewhere, before we raced in and ravaged the townsfolk. He'd been spinning like a top, spinning like he was centered on a string that dizzily wavered round and round.

The energy over my mother shimmered, a diamond forming in blue and silver, but there was something about the whole thing that felt off—something was out of kilter.

I struggled to remember what she'd taught me about her early days, before the Turning. Before she'd founded the Indigo Court. She'd been a member of the Unseelie—the Dark Fae, and she'd watched as her sister ascended to the throne to become the Queen of Winter. My mother had thought the honor would go to her, but she'd been overlooked. Story after story flooded back, her resentment and anger echoing through my memories.

And then I realized what she was doing. My mother was creating her own heartstone. She was mocking the Courts of Fae by using their sacred ritual on herself. Somehow, she must have stumbled across the information on how this was done, because it wasn't common knowledge—that much was for sure. And now she was removing part of her essence to a sacred gem, to hide it and keep it safe. She was assuring her immortality.

As I watched, she let out a piercing scream as a white-hot pinprick of light shot up from her chest to the center of the sapphire. The stone began to take physical form, an emerald cut that was so dark blue it was almost black. But inside, sparkles of silver and white gave it life—my mother's life force, encased within the heart of the jewel. As long as it survived, so would she.

Another moment, and the Ice Elementals placed the jewel in a silver box and stepped away from the bed. Myst slowly sat up, groaning, as the healer hurried to her side. He checked her pulse, her eyes; he pressed his ear to her chest to listen to her heart.

"Well, is it done?" Myst smiled down at him, a gentle tone in her voice. He was her favorite. He'd been with her for many years and had brought me into the world. I liked him, as much as I could like anybody.

"It is done, Your Highness. Your heartstone has been created, and now one thing remains. You must hide it." He gave her a faint smile. "You know what will happen should the Court of Rivers and Rushes or the Court of Snow and Ice find out what you've done. They will hunt it down and destroy it. You cannot let the information out that this ritual has taken place."

She gave him a solemn nod. "I do know that. We've broken every rule the Greater Courts set forth. Over the years, we've torn the rules to shreds and then destroyed the remnants. But you are wrong about one matter, dear friend. Old friend. More than one thing remains to be done before I am safe."

He cocked his head, staring at her. A look of pale recognition crossed his face, and I knew what was going to happen. My mother hadn't noticed me yet, nor had the Elementals or the healer. Myst was so preoccupied that she wouldn't feel me near.

"Old friend, the Ice Elementals are loyal to me, and unswerving, and they will never speak. But the problem with secrets? When two people know about something, that thing is no longer sacrosanct. No longer a secret. You know this, don't you?" She slipped off her bed, already healed from her ordeal. Our kind healed incredibly fast.

He stuttered, stepping back. "I give you my word, Your Highness."

"Unfortunately, words are only as good as their speakers. And while I love you, I can never trust you." And with that I watched as my mother fell upon the healer, ripping him to shreds with her great jaws. She was a most magnificent creature, huge beyond the rest of us, and by the time she finished, there was neither bone nor drop of blood left. She licked the floor clean before returning to her form.

The Ice Elementals stood unwavering, waiting for her. With one last look at the bedchamber, she depressed a place on the wall and a secret door opened—one I'd never seen before. I stayed where I was. I loved my mother, but I knew, instinctively, that if she even so much as *thought* I might know about this, she would kill me. I'd be as dead as the healer, her daughter or not.

Followed by the Ice Elementals carrying the silver box, Myst stepped into the passageway. As the door closed behind her, I realized that I now knew what my mother's vulnerability was. She was as vulnerable as every other Fae Queen now. Find her heartstone, and she was a dead woman.

And with that as I turned to exit the chamber, I heard a voice calling my name. Only it wasn't my name—close, but not the same. But I couldn't resist. The pull was too strong.

"Cicely? Cicely! Can you hear me?"

The voice began to blur the world around me. Who was Cicely? And yet, a part of me answered, *"I'm Cicely."* But then, the image of a little girl flashed in front of my eyes and I thought, *"No, I'm Violet."*

Stumbling, I turned to the door, but it wasn't there. Instead, I was standing in a current of mist, and I blindly fell into the slipstream, following the siren song luring me on.

Chapter 11

"Cicely? Cicely! Can you hear me?"

The voice echoed through the mist again. I stumbled forward, knowing that I had to follow the voice. And then, behind the voice, I heard a song. It sounded familiar. The melody was haunting and made me want to follow it, no matter where it led me. I looked around, wondering where I was.

And then another memory hit me and I *knew*. I was in the slipstream. I wasn't sure why, but that was the name for this place. I was in the slipstream, journeying through a darkened passageway filled with mist and fog. I thought I saw the silhouettes of trees as I began to speed up, and then boulders hidden by the fog. A pale light streamed down from overhead, but whether it was the moon or sun wasn't clear in this monochromatic land.

And then I was running, following the voice, suddenly eager to get out of this place and back to . . . *Where was I heading back to?* I didn't know, but wherever it was, it felt like home. I was going home, and once I arrived there, I'd know who I was and why I'd made this journey.

The mist began to thicken, until it surrounded me, and I

felt like I was choking. Another minute, and I was breathing fog soup. I stumbled out, into what seemed a very bright light, and lastly, I opened my eyes. I was in the living room, and I remembered my name—I was Cicely. And I had been Violet. And I had been Cherish.

And . . .

. . . now I knew what Myst's vulnerability was. And I knew how to destroy her. The only question left was: Where would I find her heartstone?

❧

I struggled to sit up, dazed and wondering what time it was. Squinting in the candlelight that had just a few minutes ago seemed bright as the sun, I realized that the candles were half-melted, and there was a faint light outside.

"What time is it?" My voice sounded like it was stretched, my throat was parched, and I felt like I'd been screaming for hours.

Ysandra brushed the hair off my forehead, and then she pressed a cool cloth to my cheeks. The chill felt comforting against my skin, which was hot and inflamed. As I struggled to sit up, Grieve sat on the sofa next to me and braced my back. I leaned against him, the cool of his skin a welcome respite.

"What time is it?" I couldn't quite focus on the clock—my vision was blurry, and I wasn't seeing all that well, but I knew it would wear off as I pulled further out of the trance.

"Four thirty in the morning. You were out for several hours, and I was worried that I wouldn't be able to bring you back. How are you feeling? Are you nauseated? Ears ringing? Headache?" As she listed off the symptoms, I could tell Ysandra was searching for something. Probably a clue as to whether I'd permanently damaged anything.

I sucked in a long breath, examining my body. How *did* I feel? Pinpricks where it felt like I had lain in one position too long. Tingles ran through my arm as I moved off of it. But that was nothing to worry over. Headache? Slight one, yes. But no ringing of the ears. And my stomach, while a little upset, wasn't in danger of losing my dinner.

"I feel like I have a mild hangover, but that's about it. Mild queasiness, a slight headache. Nothing major that I can tell. But I do know one thing." I gazed up at the ring of faces gathered round.

They waited, expectantly.

"I know how to destroy Myst. I'm just not all that certain on where to find what we need in order to do so."

Of course, my statement incited an outpouring of conversation. Luna, even in her anger, which I could still see seething beneath the surface, hurried over to the sofa to listen.

Peyton appeared, a cool glass of water in her hand. I downed it and asked for another, and after that—a third. When my throat was no longer parched, I told them what I'd seen, and what I'd discovered. And as I spoke, I felt something inside had changed. There was a part of me that felt like it had always needed to be there, but had been missing.

Violet. For some reason, I'd needed to be reunited with Violet.

Who she'd been, when she'd lived, remained unclear. But the fact was I'd returned to life too soon—before Grieve— and I'd known about our pact. I'd taken my own life again to go in search of him. Violet had known very well that the fly agaric would poison her. But in whatever wisdom her— my—soul had possessed, she'd swallowed them down and sped out into the slipstream again.

You need to know me because I can give you something you never had—a happy childhood. I was happy, until I realized I'd come back at the wrong time.

Her voice echoed in my head . . . or perhaps it was my gut. The words were muffled, but the feeling came through loud and clear. And the tattoo of the little Fae girl on my chest suddenly laughed, and tickled me. She'd woken a few times, but only briefly. My owl tattoos had woken when I'd discovered the owl-shifter within. My wolf had always been connected to Grieve. But my belladonna faerie? She belonged to me, to a part of me that had been cut out too quickly, if out of necessity.

I laughed at her tickling; it was playful and joyful and with a

slightly wicked sense of humor. Everybody stared at me, and I
realized they had no clue what I was laughing about.

"I'm just glad to be alive. Even with everything we're facing, I'm grateful I'm here and that I have all of you. And that
I've found . . . a part of myself that I never knew about." As
I said the words, I knew they were true. I'd never felt particularly joyful about my life, but now, here in this room at four
thirty in the morning, facing one of the most dangerous
adversaries we could be facing, I didn't care. All I wanted to
do was hug everyone dear to me and tell them I loved them.
So I did just that. And when they stared at me like I was off
my rocker, I laughed again.

And then I slept like the dead.

※

By the time I woke, it was nearing noon. I was in my old bed,
and Peyton was sitting near me. She was knitting something—
I couldn't tell what it was, but I hadn't even known Peyton
could work a needle.

I struggled to sit up, and squinted. The snow was holding
off but, as usual, the skies were overcast. Stretching, I sniffed
my armpit and grimaced. I needed a shower. Bad. Though my
clothes had been removed and I was in a long nightgown, the
fact was I smelled like I'd been in a bar fight. The combination
of the fighting, the blood, and the herbs in the tincture did not
for a pleasant combination make.

"Shower?" Peyton smiled, holding out a towel and some
bath gel. "The bathroom's empty. Go to it."

I slid out from beneath the covers, the cold floor no longer
bothering my feet. I smiled softly. For so many years I'd hated
waking up because of cold tile or cold hardwood. Now, I'd
never mind it again. One of many blessings in disguise.

"Peyton . . . how are you doing? Your mother . . . Rex . . ."
Both of her parents had been killed by the rogue vampire
Geoffrey. In the intervening weeks, I hadn't had a chance to
ask her how she was coping.

Her doe-eyed gaze was solemn, but she seemed to be holding the tears at bay. "I'm managing. Some days are harder than

others. I've contacted my father's Pride, and when this is over . . . when Myst is found and defeated, I'll visit them to take my vision quest. Then I'll return here and run my investigations agency. I'm going to be okay, Cicely. I'll be all right."

I wanted to say something to help, but at this point, only time would heal. She knew how I felt. I'd been with her both when Rex, and then Anadey, died. "What about the diner?"

"Up for sale. Asking a song and a prayer. Half of what it's valued at, but it's worth it to me. I hated working there, and Mother . . . I've still got so many conflicting emotions surrounding her death. She tried to kill you, Cicely. She tried to have my father killed. Even though she protected me at the end, it's rather difficult to have much sympathy at this point. I'd rather just let her go quietly. Forget my life with her and make a new one."

I nodded. I knew exactly what she meant. When I'd found Krystal dead in an alley, I'd pilfered her pockets, closed her eyes, and turned my back on the past as I walked away from her body. After calling the cops—anonymously—I'd taken off and had never seen her again. I didn't even know what they'd done with her remains. Now, a pang raced through me. Did the mortuary still have her ashes? If so, I could claim them. Lay her to rest in the woods where we staked Heather, so the two sisters could be together again.

You know they aren't around, Cicely. Their spirits have moved on.

I know, Ulean, but the poetry of it . . . Sometimes the gesture is more important than the meaning behind it. I don't know if I'm explaining that right, but sometimes . . .

I know what you mean. Let it rest, girl. Take your shower. There is much to do today, and just because you now know how to destroy Myst, doesn't mean that it's going to be a walk in the park.

I nodded; then, feeling I needed to say something to Peyton, I opened my mouth. But by then she was back to her knitting and looking quietly content, so I picked up my towel and cinnamon-scented bath gel, and headed in to take a long shower.

As I lathered up, I ran over what I remembered about the night before. The images from my journey were clearer now. A good night's sleep had provided enough distance to give me insight to everything I'd seen.

The Barrow in which I'd seen Myst hide her heartstone? I knew the lay of the land around it. I vaguely remembered seeing an area deep in the Golden Wood that resembled it. Had Myst created the Barrow centuries ago? Thousands of years ago? Even if she'd deserted it, chances were I could find it again. And if I did . . . could I possibly find the entrance to where she had taken her heartstone?

I scrubbed my body thoroughly as I thought over everything that had happened. Violet—she'd been important to meet, and while I still wasn't sure why, I felt whole now. Meeting that part of myself seemed to have given me back some joy robbed from me during my childhood in this life. Violet hadn't been unhappy. She merely realized she was in the wrong time period, and so she had found a way to leave it.

By the time I finished lathering and rinsing my hair, I was deep in thought, trying to sort out where and when I had seen the area surrounding Myst's Barrow. It was definitely deep in the Golden Wood, long before there had been a New Forest to border it. Long before there had been a Seattle . . . or a United States of America to mark borders and territories.

I knew it was farther back into the wood than the Twin Hollies. So deep that we never routinely passed by it. And then . . . then, a memory tugged at me. I knew where it was. One day, a long time ago when Rhia and I were five and just starting to know Grieve and Chatter, we'd gone for a walk and gotten lost in the woods. We kept going, certain we'd be able to find our way out again.

The drowsy bees had bumbled by, a deer had brought her fawn out for us to see, and she had stopped, allowing us to pet the young doe. We were totally unaware of how rare a gift she'd given us. At one point, we lay down and took a nap around noon, in the shade of a giant cedar. An hour or so later, we were worried—home seemed so far away, and we'd gotten turned around, no longer sure of where we were. So we kept walking.

By early evening, we came to a stream and followed it, and then . . . A flash of memory showed me a mound in the earth nearby. We were headed toward it, pulled toward it, but the next thing I could remember, we were back at the edge of the Golden Wood. Dazed, but none the worse for wear, we raced out across the yard, safe into the house.

"I had totally forgotten that memory," I whispered to myself. "The Barrow—that had to be Myst's Barrow. We were far too deep in the woods for it to be the Marburry Barrow, or even the Eldburry. And we didn't make it through any portal. There was no shift there that I can remember."

Focused, I hopped out of the shower and quickly slipped into clean underwear, jeans, and a pre-laced corset that Druise had sent from home. This one had a zipper and I quickly zipped it up and then slid on a pair of ankle boots. Sturdy, they had a platform heel that I could run in. I pulled the brush through my hair, sleeking it back, not worrying about drying it, and plopped my crown on my head, then—sans makeup—ran downstairs.

"I remember! I know where her Barrow was!" I skidded to a halt in the kitchen, staring at the group of solemn faces sitting around the table. "What's going on? What's happening?"

Ysandra put a plate of eggs and bacon in front of me and poured me some coffee. "The Shadow Hunters hit again, though this time they left the police station alone. But they've attacked over in Snoqualmie. They are branching out, and there seem to be far more of them now. Myst has called in all her reserves."

"What about defense? The police? The National Guard?" Even as I spoke, I knew that the National Guard would be of no earthly use against them. The Shadow Hunters could be killed by bullets, yes, but they were deadly foes, and crafty, and they were adept at culling their victims without being seen.

She shook her head. "You know as well as I do that the police don't know what to do, and I gather they were talking about calling in the military, but you see . . . a blizzard has sprung up near there. And I do mean a blizzard. The storm is moving in quickly, spreading over the entire northwest. No helicopters can fly in it, or planes. Driving is hazardous at best. We'll soon be in whiteout conditions as it spreads. Myst has started her march, and if she can hold the weather steady, she has a good chance of gaining a stronghold before anybody can do anything."

Nature could still put a stop to even the most devilish of mankind's machinations. Blizzards, hurricanes, tornadoes—not much of our weaponry could do anything against the natural forces of the world, and it seemed that the more we tried to control it, the more the world fought back. This time, there just happened to be a mad queen at the helm.

"Have you contacted the Consortium? Have they gotten off their asses about this matter?" I was growing very weary of the noninterference policy the magical group was taking.

"We do have the warriors they sent—the Elite Unit. I was in charge of one just like this, you remember, not long ago. But they are few, and the enemy is strong. I called the council again this morning, but the phone lines are down. The storm is close enough to be driving static between us and the outer world. I expect the winds and snow to pick up within the next couple of hours." Ysandra stirred a spoonful of sugar into her coffee, frowning.

I dug into my breakfast, needing the fuel. Between the fighting and the journey I'd taken last night, I was famished. "Regina and Lannan are asleep, of course. Did they contact you last night after I passed out? Do we have any news from them that I should know about?"

Rhiannon cupped her hot tea, and the longer she held the sides of her mug, the more it steamed. I laughed when I noticed it. "You can warm up your food no problem now."

She snorted. "Yeah, but you should see me with ice cream—not quite the effect I want." With a laugh, she raised her mug in salute.

I grinned at her. "Well, you ever need me to freeze it again, just call." Sometimes it took a joke, however feeble it might be, to lighten the mood.

After that, she leaned back, her eyes crinkling. "Lannan sent word this morning, before dawn. They've got one of their strongest day-runners on the switchboard. If anything comes down, anything, call her—her name is Dakota—and she'll get the information to them as soon as possible. She also has the authority to dispatch day-runners to us, should we need them for anything."

"We'd better send her the info on what's going on near Snoqualmie, if you haven't already done so." I paused, then looked up. "I suppose you're waiting for me to ask *'What's our next move?'* but the truth is I know what we have to do. We're taking the offense. We have to find that Barrow, see if we can unearth Myst's heartstone, and then destroy it. Even though I think I know where it is, this is going to be a rocky journey. We can traverse the wood, no problem, but if she has any clue we're on her trail, then you can bet we'll be facing a gamut of her monsters. And this time, it might not be just her Shadow Hunters."

And then something from the mayhem and chaos of the night before broke into my thoughts. *Ulean, you were following the energy signature of the person I thought might be my spy! Did you find anything?*

Ulean swept around me. *I think I know who it is, but I can't prove it. And I hesitate to accuse without proof.*

Who, then? Who do you suspect? I promise I won't haul ass over there and slit her throat without any proof. I knew what it was like to be falsely suspected of something—I couldn't just kill and ask questions later. Not in this case.

Well, then. Zoey. Luna's sister. Luna has no comprehension this might be the case. I followed the signature back and found evidence that it might be her.

Zoey! It couldn't be! *But Zoey is one of the Akazzani, and she returned home after helping us.*

Did she, Cicely? We all thought so, but now I believe her to be still lurking in the area. Ask Luna if she's heard from her sister since Zoey left. Don't tell her why, but ask.

My blood ran cold. Zoey was from a group of those who watched over history—a secret society. She had magical powers—in a sense, she was a witch, but not like Rhiannon or me. Zoey had helped free Grieve from Myst's control using a magical ritual. While she could not break the spell binding his blood to the Indigo Court, she'd reached out, touched Myst's energy, and unwound it from Grieve's. Oh hell . . . she'd touched Myst's energy. Had something happened during the ritual that we didn't know about? Something that connected Zoey to Myst? We'd invited her to stay on, but she went back to the small island on which the great halls of the Akazzani stood. *Or so we'd thought.*

I looked up from my eggs and bacon. "Luna, I know you'd rather not talk to me, but I have a question for you and I really need a clear answer."

Luna bit her lip. "No, I'd rather not talk to you. But until this is over, until we win, I'm willing to stop qualifying every sentence or question."

Nodding, I dreaded asking what I was about to ask. "I was just wondering, have you heard from Zoey lately?"

Her head jerked up, and she frowned. "Odd you should ask. The answer is no. In fact, I got a strange call from my family this morning. The Akazzani contacted Mother a few days ago to ask where Zoey was. It seems . . ." She let out a long sigh. "It seems she hasn't been heard from for a few weeks. In fact, the word is that she never returned after leaving here. I didn't tell Mother about her visit here, of course, or what we were doing. But the timing matches up."

And then I knew it was true. Zoey had somehow latched on to Myst during the ceremony, and Myst had won her over. That was the only answer. But if there was a spy in my Court that must mean . . . that Zoey was hiding in the Court of Snow and Ice.

I grabbed Grieve's hand. "I have to talk to you. *Now.*" Nodding to Check and Fearless, I added, "You too, both of you. Come outside with me."

Once we were out in the backyard, I quickly briefed them on what Ulean had told me. "Don't you see? With what Luna said, it *has* to be Zoey. She must be hiding in the Court of Snow and Ice. I'm sure she could figure out how to blend in."

"But why? What happened? She was so adamant about returning to the Akazzani." Grieve frowned.

"Something had to have happened during the ritual—something she didn't let on about. While Kaylin and Luna held Grieve's feet and head, somehow Zoey got swept into the energy of the Indigo Court. At least, that's my best guess."

Who knew what really had happened? And unless we found Zoey—and even then, only if she told us—we'd probably go to our graves without knowing.

"So she's jealous of you?" Grieve cocked his head. "Why?"

"I have no idea. Maybe it has to do with you, or my place as Fae Queen, or what. But there is danger there. She works for Myst now. Ulean couldn't be sure, but this rings a bell deep within me, and I'm going to trust my intuition. If we find her, we'll have to question her as quickly as possible. I won't have her harmed on sight—because we don't know for sure, but it's looking more and more like we've found our spy."

Check glanced over to Fearless. "We must dispatch someone to the Eldburry Barrow. Have them begin searching for her. If she's hidden out, chances are she's keeping below deck. Probably with the scullery staff or other menial workers. That would be the last place to look, given the high profile of the nobility."

Fearless nodded. "Your Majesty, you cannot return to the Barrow till we find her. There's too much danger."

I wanted to go home, but with all that was happening, chances were I wouldn't see my own bed again till we were done with Myst. As we stood there, the snow began to flake down and the sky clouded over. I glanced at the horizon. Silver-gray clouds banked up, so thick it was hard to see anything else. No scrap of sky peeked through, and the snow that was just beginning felt a precursor to a much larger storm.

"We're headed into the thick of things. The blizzard is approaching. Any travel is bound to be dangerous, and the Shadow Hunters will be out thick as thieves. We need to contact Dakota and ask her to issue radio and television pleas for people to lock themselves in their houses and not come out." I turned to go inside. "Oh, and until we know what's going on with Zoey? Not a word to Luna. I've already turned her world upside down once. I don't need to do it again, until we're certain of the facts."

They nodded, and we turned to head back inside, but a flutter of wings stopped me. I whirled around to see my grandfather land on a nearby bush. The heavy layer of snow cascaded to the ground as the bush shook from his impact. The great horned owl was beautiful in the lazy fall of the snow, but the flurry was strengthening, and it was becoming harder to see more than a few yards in front of us. A haze of white was beginning to blow up as the winds gusted by. I thought about using my powers to try to calm them, but I did better raising the winds, and the last thing we needed right now was a gale.

The owl shimmered, changing form into Hunter, my grandfather, who then rose to his feet to stand atop the four-foot drift that blanketed the outer yard.

"Cicely, I promised you that I'd bring word when I knew where Myst is headquartered. I'm not sure, my girl. I wish we could have more answers for you." He strode over to me.

"What about deep in the Golden Wood? In a long-unused Barrow?"

"I know what you're talking about. No, she is not there now, but she may be close—her energy is around the area, and we examined that neck of the woods in-depth." He gazed into my eyes. "How do you know of it?"

I let out a long sigh. The story was too convoluted for a quick explanation, so I simply said, "I revisited the time in which I was her daughter. I saw the Barrow, and I saw her hide a heartstone deep within its heart. We must journey there. I have to destroy her heartstone before she realizes that we know about it."

"The blizzard is hitting, Cicely. It's going to be dangerous."

"Maybe so, but if we go now, she won't be expecting it. She's narcissistic, she's going to be focused on the havoc she's causing over in Snoqualmie. We have the time right now to get there. Yes, even for us it will be dangerous, but I think we should take advantage of this window." I looked over to the Golden Wood. It was hard to even see the border of it now through the whirl of snow, but the dark silhouettes of the trees were a blur against the white.

Hunter surprised the hell out of me. He stepped forward. "I will go with you, then. If my granddaughter does not fear the blizzard, then I will follow. You are the Queen of Snow and Ice. I am part of your realm, as was my son, before he fell in love with the Summer."

"The Queen will not travel without her guards. When do you want to head out?" Check stretched, shading his eyes from the storm.

"I think as soon as we gear up and eat a little more. We shouldn't waste any more time than necessary. I have a feeling that we are in the grace of a window right now. We can make haste. Once Zoey is found, if there's a way she can communicate with Myst, you know she will." The more I thought about it, the more urgent I felt that we make our move. I was antsy, and nervous, and as I looked up at the sky, I could almost imagine Myst staring down at me.

"Listen to the Queen," Grieve said, and as he spoke, my wolf shifted. "I can feel her uneasiness. Let us go. Now."

And so we entered the house again. I chose not to wear the leathers—they were heavy and would bog me down in the snow. We needed to move fast, and light. I motioned for the others to gather around the kitchen table.

"Where did Ysandra go?" She wasn't around anywhere in the house.

"I'm not sure, but she mentioned something about attending to an urgent situation and took off with her crew from the Consortium. I thought they were just headed outside." Chatter frowned, looking around. "Has anybody else heard from her?"

Rhiannon shook her head. "No—she can't have been gone long."

"Well, we'll have to start the meeting without her." I was irritated. People needed to check with me before running off to take care of errands. "Okay, here's what we're going to do. We have to split up. I don't like it any more than you do, so keep your complaints. But this is how it's going to be. I will lead a group into the Golden Wood. We go in search of Myst's heartstone."

"We're going with you." Peyton set her jaw. I recognized the stubborn streak in her rising.

"You can't." I didn't want Luna and Peyton prowling the woods. I didn't want them out there, endangering themselves. "We need to fly through the forest, my friend. And very few can match our speeds. Besides, somebody needs to be here to guard the Veil House and wait for the vampires to wake."

"What about Rhiannon and me?" Chatter cupped his mug of tea. "What would you like us to do?"

"We will leave most of our Fae warriors here to guard the house and, if needed, scour the town. They will report directly to you and Rhiannon. Rhia, you're in charge. If you have to, you and Chatter can lead another routing on the town. But be cautious—this storm is going to become far worse before long. A whiteout is nothing to get caught in. And very hard to navigate."

"I need to go with you, Cicely." Kaylin cocked his head. "I have to go with you."

I stared at him and something deep inside whispered, *Let him.* "All right—but my men will have to help you. No bitching about it."

"Understood."

As we armed up, my cell phone rang. It was Ysandra. I quickly punched the Answer button. "Yes?"

"Cicely? I need your help."

"Where are you? What's going on?"

She sounded frightened, and when Ysandra was afraid, that meant there was trouble, big-time. "I'm over at the school a few blocks away. Dakota—Lannan's day-runner—texted to let me know there were children trapped in the school. Parents have been calling the emergency vehicles but nobody can get through. They thought we might be able to do something since we're near. Everybody was busy, and the school is so near the house that I decided to bring my group of Consortium guards over to gather the kids up—it's only a few blocks away, and I thought it would be easy enough. But it's all gone horribly wrong."

Oh fuck, no. "What's going on? Shadow Hunters?"

"I wish it was just them. No, Myst sent in more than the Vampiric Fae on the snows. We have snow weavers building webs outside the school, and they are trying to get in. I heard rumors that some houses in Snoqualmie are covered with webbing. They've come in force, Cicely. This is Myst's full push. It's now or never. Either we defeat her this time, or she will lay waste to this region and pick up steam."

I stared at my phone. "I'm putting you on speaker, give me a second to fill in the others on what you've said so far."

As I ran down what she told me, then tapped the button to put Ysandra on speaker phone, the enormity of our situation was beginning to hit me and my stomach clenched, thinking of the kids trapped in the school.

"Go ahead. You're on speaker."

"Thanks. As I said, Myst is making her push. It might seem a far cry for her to blanket an entire city, but reports coming in from Seattle say it's snowing heavily there, too, and they're expecting extreme ice and snow within a couple of hours. The long winter has begun. Ragnarök is rolling in, not on the shoulders of the frost giants, but on the wings of a crazed queen. Can you come get us?"

I bit my lip—we needed to get out to the woods, but the children were in danger, and so was Ysandra. "We'll be there. How many kids?"

"Fourteen. The others made it out, but how many made it home safe, I cannot tell. I do know that we can't hold out much longer. We've locked them out for now, but there are so many ways into the school. I have the children huddled in a class-room, and my guards are blocking the doors and trying to keep the snow weavers from breaking through the windows. Hurry, Cicely. Or we aren't going to be here when you arrive."

And with that her phone went dead. The bars on my phone vanished. I picked up the house phone but it, too, was dead.

"I suppose the television is out?"

Luna nodded, pale. "We're cut off, then."

"Yes. It won't take much to bring down the coast. The grid isn't all that stable and the infrastructure of this country is already strained and weak. Come on—we have to go rescue Ysandra and the kids. All hands on board, and we're fighting Myst's spiders, so be prepared."

With that, leaving a small contingent of men at home, the rest of us armed up and headed out into the storm.

Chapter 12

We moved into the storm, leaving behind enough of our men to guard the house should anybody decide to try to invade. My bets were that Myst was still focused over in Snoqualmie and turning her sights on Seattle, but she'd given her minions a free hand in branching out. I also had the feeling she'd ordered them to leave me alone. In other words, *leave me for her*. She wanted her revenge as much as I wanted mine.

The streets were so clogged with snow there would be no other way of getting there except on foot. As we turned the corner, about twenty yards down Second Street we saw flames. The school was still several blocks off, so we knew it wasn't that, but a house had caught fire, probably from some-one trying to stave off the cold, and it was blazing brightly. The fire department was nowhere in sight. Maybe they were trying to plow through the streets to get here. The snow was piling up so fast and thick, that even the fire engines would have trouble navigating New Forest. We were here, though, and so I sent over one of my men to see if there was anybody still trapped inside.

He returned. "No, they are all safe, at least from the fire.

But Your Majesty, if we continue on and leave them here, while waiting for the emergency response . . ."

I saw where he was going. "The Shadow Hunters may attack them. Or the snow weavers. Or worse. I see your point. How many are there?"

"Five—a father, the mother, and three children. Two cats and a dog."

I thought quickly. We didn't dare take them along with us. "Take three men and get them back to the house. Then catch up with us as best as you can. But be wary. We have no clue what other monsters Myst has managed to dredge up while she's been recharging. For all we know, she might have discovered an abominable snowman or two."

He gave me a curious look, clearly not understanding what I was talking about.

"Yeti? Bigfoot's cousin? A form of *Sasquatch*?"

"Oh! The Old Man. Yes, we know what they are, and they are highly dangerous and unpredictable. We will be cautious, Your Majesty." He gave me a quick but decisive bow and then chose three other men and headed over to the family. Satisfied they'd have at least a decent chance at safety, I motioned to the others, and we moved on again.

As we moved farther into the town, the extent of Myst's snow weavers was obvious—houses were covered in thin sheets of icy webbing, and I could only pray that those within were able to withstand the siren song of the snow spiders. Here and there I caught a glimpse of one, sparkling in the night. They were fierce and terrible, milky white with golden sparkling stripes that ran their length. Orb weavers, but with a deadly venom and an even deadlier ability to lure their prey into their webs.

As I eyed the houses covered in webbing, my first thought was to rush in, to rescue whoever might be trapped within. But then reason dawned. We couldn't stop the snow weavers, not until we stopped Myst. We had to focus on our task at hand and not get sidetracked.

The going was rough—the snow was deep and even for those of us used to the snow and ice, the storm raged like a crazed animal. Hunter was skimming the surface—my grand-father seemed able to skate across the snow like a water skip-per on a pond. But Luna, Peyton, and Kaylin were not faring as well, and my men were helping them along. Rhiannon, Chatter, and the Summer Guards fared somewhat better but they, too, were bogged down by the heavy snows. Finally, in frustration, Rhia moved to the front of the pack with Chatter, and the pair joined hands, motioning for the rest of us to stand down.

We sidled back as the sparks sizzled and popped around them, and then—in one long streak—they sent out a burst of flame through the snow in front of us. It traveled a good twenty yards before sputtering out, melting away some of the ice and snow.

Rhia shook her head. "Takes more energy than it does good. Might as well just slog through."

And that's just what we did. We drove our path through the clogged roads, pushing against the winds, which were gusting heavily now and whirling the snow into a blinding fury around us. By now, we could see no more than an arm's length away from our bodies and were doing our best to continue in a straight line so we wouldn't get off track.

"How are we going to know when we get there? We can barely see the side of the road, let alone anything beyond it." I had to shout to be heard over the wind.

Check, who was leading us, moved closer and leaned in. "Can Ulean go ahead and lead us, Your Majesty?"

Ulean, did you hear him? Can you lead us to the school?

That I can—it is easier for me to navigate than you. Hold for a moment and let me scout out where you're at.

We paused, huddling as the storm raged. I thought I could hear howling in the slipstream, and for once prayed I was wrong. Because if I was hearing a howl, it was one of the Shadow Hunters—and that meant they were on the rampage. Shivering, I leaned toward Grieve and he wrapped his arm around my shoulders. We waited, counting the seconds, counting the min-utes. I was beginning to worry, but then Ulean was there, sweep-ing around me in a succession of quick gusts.

We are near the school. You will want to verge to your right—about twenty-five degrees—and you will be on-target for the front doors. They are about one thousand feet ahead—you will be going through the front lawn. There are Shadow Hunters in there, and they have spiders with them, and goblin dogs.

Oh fuck. Fuck, fuck, fuck. What about the children and Ysandra? Are they okay?

They are barricaded in a room—the first hall to the left, first door to the right. There are large windows, and right now, Ysandra and her Consortium allies are managing to hold a force field against those attempting to break through, but they won't be able to for much longer. They are strong, but the Shadow Hunters are stronger.

Fuck. We need to get there now. How many do you estimate?

Shadow Hunters? I cannot tell you. But they have at least a dozen, if not more, of the snow weavers with them. Remember: They can mesmerize you, Cicely. They can lure you in, even now.

I remembered all too well. We'd encountered them several times out in the woods, weaving their massive webs, hiding, waiting for victims. They were beautiful and terrifying, and they could hypnotize their prey, as well as poison them. Deadly and quick, the snow weavers were creatures of nightmares.

If we head straight, we'll run right into the school?

Yes, you're directly on track now.

Then, damn the torpedoes and full speed ahead.

"Let's move. Check, head directly to that direction." I pointed. "We'll be facing a bundle of Shadow Hunters and snow weavers, and I think some goblin dogs—so be alert. They'll be as blind as we are, though, at least before we get into the school. Ysandra and her crew can't hold out for much longer." I pulled out my dagger. Even though I wouldn't be on the front lines, I wasn't about to go in unprepared.

Luna tapped me on the arm. "Before we go . . ."

"Yes?"

"Let me . . ." She stepped back and closed her eyes. Within seconds, a shadow began to descend on our group, and a mist settled into her body. She looked up, slowly, a cunning in her eyes that was abnormal for her. As her eyes met mine, she let loose with a hearty laugh, and the next thing I knew, we were surrounded by shadows.

"We have backup," she said.

I stared at the army of the dead that filtered in and around us. Shades in muted tones of shadow and light darted between the snowflakes, barely there, and yet their silent hush carried the weight of a hundred soldiers at our command. They were a darksome force, fierce and feral, and the look on Luna's face scared the hell out of me. The gentle Luna had faded, and the wild-eyed Dorthea had taken her place. Full and robust, the spirit had taken over and now I could feel her unspoken orders filtering through the ghosts who joined our company. They would move at her slightest word. I could feel their loyalty, and it scared the hell out of me. What if Dorthea took it into her mind to sic them on us, instead?

But as I stared at Luna, at the spirit inhabiting her body, Dorthea cocked her head. "Why would I want your position, girl? I have all the power I want right where I am. What's more—Luna has given her oath to you. And I must abide by that."

Then I realized—regardless of the fact that two spirits now inhabited one body—our friendship, which I'd probably forever destroyed, would carry Luna through on my side, and anybody hitching a piggyback ride on her.

Olrick and a band of the strongest took the forefront. Check, Fearless, Hunter, Grieve, and I came after. Behind us, Kaylin, Luna, Chatter, Rhiannon, Peyton, and Rhiannon's guards hedged us in. The force of the dead swelled behind them. And at our backs, holding the rearguard, marched the rest of our warriors.

The wild tangle of energies charged the air. Summer and Winter, the spirits of the dead, the forces of our friends—all combined to create a whirlwind of static as we forged onward toward the school.

We counted down, with Ulean guiding us through me. And then she told us we were on the grounds, and there was an insurgence of movement as snow weavers appeared on the front lines, backed up by the ghostly figures of Shadow Hunters caught in glimpses through the strengthening blizzard.

The snow and mist were so thick that we could only fight whoever was directly in front of us, and our warriors spread out, a core group surrounding Rhiannon and myself. Once again, I found myself chafing against the restrictions, but I also knew that for us to take down Myst, I had to stay alive. So I let myself be protected; I reined in my frustration and thought of the bigger picture. The fighting was a blur of snow and blood around me, and I longed to be doing something productive—something helpful.

Rhia tapped my shoulder, and I leaned close. "I know—I know what you're feeling, but this is our life now. You have to bite the bullet on this one, Cicely. You know how much we need you later on."

Grimacing, I wondered if I should have even come. We were tying up resources protecting us that could have been focused on fighting instead. Though our personal guards would have stayed home, it would have made things easier if we weren't here. Unlike the Fae Queens of history, Rhia and I weren't strong warrior women . . . yet. We were more liability than help.

"You should wipe that look off your face, Your Majesty." Check leaned close, pressing his lips near my ear. "You look defeated. The men take their cues from you. You show depression, they will follow suit. We need you to stand tall, to claim your place and prove to us why we want you with us in the field."

I cocked my head. "How'd you get inside my mind, Check?"

He grinned. "It's my business to watch you, to anticipate your needs and moods. I'd be remiss in my duties if I didn't pay attention to things like this. Now straighten your shoulders and rally the men. Encourage them. They will need all the encouragement you can give before this war is over." He glanced over at Rhiannon. "And Mistress of Summer? Might you do the same."

With a glance at Rhiannon, I shook away the lacework of frost and cobwebs that had been weaving their way in my mind and stood tall. Rhia followed suit. I wasn't sure what a rallying cry might be, but then I decided we'd just have to do it my way. I wasn't a warrior queen of old, I was Cicely, and I had to be myself—and that had to be enough.

"Beat the freaks back! Make spider stew out of them! You are my troops and you can do this. The snow weavers belong to Myst, and Myst's ass belongs to *me*!"

Ulean caught my voice in her currents, sweeping it through the troops, sweeping it into the slipstream so it echoed through the schoolyard. It hung in the air for a moment, then shattered like crystal and my warriors surged forward again. The dead swarmed through the blinding snow, adding to the fray, and though I couldn't see what was going on, the clashing of swords mingled with screams, and I knew our men were taking down the Shadow Hunters.

A few moments later, and I found myself moving on, Check and Fearless guiding us forward. We worked our way relentlessly toward the school. Ulean told me we were nearly there, and then—suddenly—we were at the doors, and they opened. My men surged forward, and the next moment, we were inside. The power still held, so entering the building, coming out of the storm, was like emerging into daylight from darkness. There was blood on the floor, but the halls were relatively empty. I remembered Ulean's instructions.

"First hall to the left, first door on the right!" My voice echoed off the high ceiling and the empty corridors, and we moved in a wave. The dead went ahead of us. By the time we reached the hallway there were bodies littered everywhere: Shadow Hunters, their life force sucked out of them. Some still remained on foot, it seemed the dead could only feed so much, but my men made quick work of them, and when the last one fell, Olrick pounded on the door.

"Open in the name of Queen Cicely!"

A moment later, and Ysandra's shaking voice called out, "Are you there, Cicely? Is it really you?"

I pushed to the front, Check and Fearless by my side. "Yes, it is me. We're here."

The door slammed open, and we took in the scene. Ysandra and her Elite Consortium Guard were standing watch over fourteen children. The windows were straining with the blows on the other side—Shadow Hunters and snow weavers, no doubt. Two of the Consortium witches were holding a force field—strained to the limit—that prevented them from breaking through, but they couldn't hold it for much longer. The stress on their faces was horrible, lining their brows deep with the exertion.

Several of my men rushed forward and began escorting the children out. The rest formed a line at the wall of windows, readying their swords. The moment the force field broke, the Shadow Hunters would burst through into the building. As soon as everybody was out except for the guards, the Consortium witches dropped their spells and raced out of the way.

I watched from outside the door as the glass shattered and Shadow Hunters and snow weavers scurried through. At that moment, the dead swarmed in to help, and Check pulled the door shut, hurrying us away from the room. Ysandra looked exhausted, but she and two of her other elite joined hands. A moment later, a circle of protection rose around us, the energy undulating in concentric waves to encircle us, like ripples on a pond. A group of my guards surrounded them, protecting all of us from disturbance.

As seconds stretched into moments, we waited, poised to fall back. The sounds of fighting echoed from within the room, steel clanging, snarls and shrieks and growls. Finally, I couldn't wait any longer.

Ulean, please tell me what you can?

She swept past, vanishing into the room. A moment later she was back. *Your men are winning. Hold fast—it should not be long now. But there are casualties on our side. The dead are working swiftly, but they can only feed so much before being satiated and unable to siphon off any more energy.*

I wondered how that worked. I'd never had much interaction with spirits, or with ghosts—if there was even a difference between the two. Hell, I hadn't even realized they could feed off the living. Unless these were very different from the typical Halloween ghost.

Another moment, and the door opened. Olrick stumbled out, bloody but alive, followed by the rest of our men and a swarm of the dead. The stench of blood ran thick from within the room and from what little I could see, the carnage was spread everywhere. It looked like a slaughterhouse.

"Did we lose anyone?" I gritted my teeth, praying the answer wouldn't be too bad.

"Four men dead, and one seriously wounded. Considering the odds, not a heavy loss. We cleaved down thirty-five Shadow Hunters and a dozen or more snow weavers." Olrick did his best to salute without splattering me with blood—he was slick with it, but still managed to present himself properly.

I nodded. Four dead still hurt, but I had to get used to thinking in terms of relative victories. "Very good." I glanced around. "I suppose we should get the hell out of here. We need to get the children safely away."

"You are correct. With all respect, Your Majesty, we can't waste more time here. Myst, no doubt, has still larger forces in the town, and while we have been victorious so far, the storm is worsening. We should fall back and regroup, and yes— guide these children to safety." Olrick punctuated his words with a formal bow.

"You're correct. Let's get back to the Veil House while we are all still in one piece—well, mostly all." I closed my eyes. *Ulean, are you here?*

Yes, Cicely. What do you need?

Please, lead us back to the Veil House via the most direct, easiest route you can find. The storm has picked up even more since we got here, and I don't want anybody lost or left behind.

Come, then, follow me, and I will get you home safely.

Ysandra and her crew dropped their spell and we swept out the door, into the night. The trip home was rough, but if there were other Shadow Hunters who saw us on the way back, they left us alone. Chilled and soaked through from the storm, we made it back to the Veil House.

✤

We needed a rest before setting out after Myst's heartstone. While my endurance and stamina had shifted dramatically when I took on the mantle of Winter, I desperately wanted a plate of hot food and some dry clothes before we took off again.

Luna immediately went about heating up some soup and biscuits.

I lingered in the kitchen beside her. "I know I'm probably the last person you want to talk to right now, but I have a few questions."

She glanced at me, her expression bleak. "I wish I felt differently. I wish I wasn't so angry with you. I understand, I really do, why you did what you did, but that doesn't change the fact that . . ."

"That I forced you into something against your will and it brought up some really bad memories." I bit my lip at the swift jerk of her head. "Yes, Kaylin told me—but only me."

"I wish he hadn't done that. There are some events that you don't want people to know about because they always look at you differently after they find out." She stared into the pot, stirring the soup more than it really needed.

"Luna, you know I'll never say anything to anyone. But it made me realize how rough this was for you. I hope you know that I'd do anything to be able to change what happened, to be able to undo it—but . . ."

"But you were looking for a spy and you had to know. I understand." She paused, then said, "Did you find out who it is?"

Oh man, here it came. The conversation I really didn't want to have. I bit my lip and stared out the window. The outside world was a blue of darkness and white—the sky and snow glimmering silver in the night as the flurries whirled out of control.

She must have sensed something was up, because she rested a hand on my arm. "Tell me. Please. What did you find out? Is it very bad?"

She'd have to know sometime, though I really hadn't planned on having it out at this point. But since she brought it up, I couldn't very well lie and later on dash her spirits again. Given everything that had gone down, it was probably better I tell her now.

"Yes, we know who it is. We still haven't found her, but she's hiding in the realm of Winter, and my men are searching for her now."

"Who is it?"

Exhaling softly, I pressed my lips together and shook my head.

Luna frowned. "Cicely, I know I'm mad at you, but you know you can trust me. Why won't you tell me? Do the others know yet?"

"Only Grieve and a few of my trusted warriors." I stared at her, trying to gauge what her reaction would be. Her loyalty to her sister ran deep, but I also knew they were at odds over a number of things. "The question is: Do you trust *me*? Do you really trust me to tell you the truth, Luna? After everything that has happened, I need to know. Never fear, I know you won't betray us. I also realize that you summoned Dorthea and the dead to prove your loyalty, but . . . what will you do, I wonder, if I tell you who the spy is?"

Paling, she backed away. "Please, tell me it's not Peyton or Ysandra?"

Shaking my head, I attempted a feeble smile. "No, neither one of them. But you know who it is—I mean, you know the person. And the news will not go down easily."

Luna hesitated, then went back to stirring the soup. The irritation seemed to fade away as her shoulders slumped. "Zoey. It's Zoey, isn't it?"

Both startled and yet—oddly unsurprised, I rested a hand on her shoulder. With that lead-in, it made sense she would guess correctly. "Yes, we are almost positive. My men are searching for her now. So, what do you say to this? What are you feeling . . . thinking?"

"I would like to say I can't imagine her doing anything like this, but the truth is, I don't know Zoey anymore. I was honestly surprised she helped us with Grieve." Without turning around, she mumbled, "What do you think happened?"

"We think she connected with Myst's energy during the ceremony where she helped free Grieve, and that somehow Myst managed to snare her in. Ulean traced the spy's energy signature back to her. We . . . I'd like to say I'm not sure, but the truth is, we are." I dreaded the next question, which I knew had to come. And I was right.

"What will you do with her, when you find her?" Now, Luna did turn to face me. "I know the punishment for spies."

I had no clue what to say. Truth was I hadn't thought that far ahead. "I don't know. I really don't know what to do. She's your sister, Luna, but she's working for an enemy who could destroy all of us. What would you do?"

Luna hesitated, then shrugged. "I'd have her killed. If Myst can see through her eyes, unless you keep her under lock and key in some bare cell that is magic-proof, then she's a danger."

That was an idea. "Maybe we can rig up something like that."

"But what then, after the war? If we win? She will have endangered us all. What the hell are we supposed to do with her then? Just let her go? She might be my sister, but a traitor is a traitor and I'll never be able to forgive her." She slumped, suddenly, and her shoulders began to shake. I could hear the sobs well up in her throat and, whether she wanted it or not, I slipped my arms around her back and hugged her gently.

"I'm so sorry. I've ripped your world apart, it feels like."

She shivered, and I turned her around, taking the soup spoon out of her hand and setting it on the spoon rest. I turned the burner to low, then moved Luna over to the kitchen table and pulled out a chair. "Sit."

She did, leaning her forehead against her hand, staring at the table surface. "No. You didn't rip my world apart. Myst did.

Everything was fine until she came along. She's to blame, Cicely—not you. You saved my life, and I'll never forget that." She looked up, her tearstained face pale. "You saved me that first night I came to you for a reading. You kept me here, and we both know what would have happened if I'd left. I'd be caught in her webs by now, most likely dead."

I reached out, took her hand in mine. "Luna, can you get out of the deal with Dorthea?"

She gave me a bleak look. "No, and it doesn't matter. My fate was sealed when I cast the spell to find Rhiannon. Once you make a pact with the ancestors, they own you. I think something like this would have happened sooner or later, anyway. I was always destined to work with them—I just didn't know it. In a terrible, frightening way, all of this feels right. Even the deal with Dorthea feels like a destiny I'm meant to fulfill."

There wasn't much I could say to that. I had just handed her the information that her sister's life was up for forfeit. That Zoey was a traitor. And Luna was accepting it with a resignation that was almost as frightening as her acceptance of Dorthea's terms.

I rubbed my hand against her back and let out a soft sigh. "Myst has sure screwed the pooch, hasn't she?"

Luna snorted. "Understatement of the year, Cicely. Now grab some bowls and let's eat. You have a long and dangerous journey ahead of you." She crossed back to the stove and took a taste of the soup, adding salt and a little pepper. The scent of chicken and rosemary rose from the pan, making me hungry. "I wish I had time to make a real soup. The canned stuff works, but it's nothing like mine."

"I believe you on that. I know what a good cook you are."

She smiled at me, and then, just like that, we were back to being friends, even if things were a bit strained. As I began to set out the bowls, Rhia and Peyton joined us, and soon we were all gathered around the oak table, holding hands. It felt like an ending. If we could find Myst's heartstone and destroy it, the town would be freed, but things would continue to change, and Luna would still be forfeiting her life. If we couldn't, then we faced a long, arduous battle, and chances were we wouldn't win the war. And we might all forfeit our lives.

Wrapped in the melancholy cloud of thought, I forced my attention back to the table. *Focus on now*, I thought. *Focus on this moment, right here. Focus on the soup and the biscuits, focus on your friends and the warmth of the house as the storm rages outside. Focus on these things—this is what you are fighting for. Get lost in what might be, and you'll lose your will. You have to remember that friends and loved ones, and this way of life, this . . . this is worth fighting for. This is worth the struggle. Myst can try to defeat us, but don't give her any quarters—don't give her more power than she already has.*

A gentle gust of warmth surrounded me. Ulean was by my side. She embraced me in her ethereal arms, soothing me as I bit into the bread. I forced myself to breathe, to ground and come back to the present.

My grandfather was with us at the table, and I realized how much I'd lose if I didn't talk to him while I had the chance. Tomorrow was iffy—yesterday, gone. There was only today.

"Hunter, have you always lived in the Golden Wood?"

He looked up at me from his plate. "No, young one. I came east, from the Olympic Peninsula. I lived in the heart of the ancient groves there. The trees are so large, their roots sink down to the center of the world, and it rains so much you think you might drown. The trees are so old they've forgotten their names, and there are days where you think the sun is a faerie tale."

Peyton put down her spoon. "You must be very old, sir."

Hunter grunted. "As old as the upstart queen. I've watched the yummanii come and go, and watched the forests dwindle. I've watched the turn of the tide as the landscape has shifted. I've watched the cities born, and men die in the woods, and I've seen the rivers change course over time. One day I will return to the Golden Isle, but my time is not yet. I have things here to do, and one of them is to watch over my granddaughter, since her father had to leave."

He smiled then, and laughed. "You are so solemn, all of you. And well you should be; Myst is a blight. But Myst is not all-powerful, and together, you possess far stronger abilities than she. You need to acknowledge your fear, then dismiss it. Fear will kill you faster than the Shadow Hunters, any day."

"Have you ever fought them before?" Kaylin asked.

"No, demon. I have not. But I've watched them, seen them feed, watched as they bred slowly but surely. She tried to gather the Wilding Fae to her, many centuries ago, but they would give her no quarter, and the only control she's ever had over them is through entrapment."

"Like the Snow Hag. We freed her from a snare that Myst had set."

"Yes, entrapment and slavery. A true leader breeds love, as well as respect, and Myst doesn't have what it takes to inspire love. She's a demagogue. A wayward, temperamental child. Cunning, yes, but still . . . a child who cannot accept her place in the scheme of things. This is why she will fail. She oversteps her reach, and she forgets. Cicely, you must find her heartstone before she realizes that you know she has one. Before it occurs to her that you know where she buried it."

"After dinner, we'll leave. You said you'll come with us?"

"Yes, but we cannot take a great force—too much chance for notice. Bring your guards, Grieve, the demon, and a couple of your vampire friends." He gave me a look that said, "Don't argue."

"Vampires?"

"They are your allies, whether you wish this or not. They can be very useful. I have a feeling . . ."

I didn't want to agree, but he was my grandfather, and without Wrath and Lainule here, I needed an advisor who was blood related.

"Then," I said, holding out my bowl for a refill on the soup, "I guess I'd better give Lannan a call in a few minutes and have him meet us here." Ignoring Grieve's disgruntled expression, I once again tried to focus on my friends. This might be our last gathering together, and I wanted to make the most of it that I possibly could.

Chapter 13

With Lannan and a few of his men on the way, we moved into the living room to discuss what the others would do while we were gone. While taking such a small contingent was dangerous, it would attract far more attention to go as a larger group.

"We can set up a protection grid for you." Ysandra motioned to the members of the Consortium who had joined her. "We'll keep you under our cloak as long as we can. Once you enter the Barrow, the energies there will negate the spell, but we should be able to help you make it through the woods without attracting too much attention."

Luna leaned forward, resting her elbows on her knees. "I'll let Dorthea send the dead into the town to hunt down the Shadow Hunters and snow weavers. They can feed often, so they should be able to take more of them on."

Olrick smartly clicked his heels and bowed. "With your leave, I will take a unit of men into the woods and begin hunting down Myst's people."

Rhiannon motioned to him. "We will go with you. We'll take some of Summer's warriors, too. We may not move as quickly in the snow as you, but we can still make haste."

"As you will, Your Highness." Olrick bowed to her. I often wondered just how tired our men got of bowing to us, but it was a tradition we weren't going to be able to break them of, and frankly, given that we truly did need their respect, I had thought the better of trying to put a stop to it.

Peyton shrugged. "I guess I'll stay here and help Ysandra and Luna. I can't make it through the storm very well, I know that much. And I don't want to be a hindrance. So I'll do what I can here." She was still very quiet, even compared to her usual stoic nature.

"I guess we're settled, then." Antsy, wishing Lannan would get here so we could start, I walked into the parlor to stretch my legs. Grieve followed behind me, closing the door to give us some privacy.

"Cicely?" His voice echoed with uncertainty. As I held out my arms, he pulled me into his embrace, covering my face with kisses.

"I'm so sorry. I'm so, so sorry." He sounded rattled, and I looked up at him, startled by the pain in his expression.

Worried now, I reached up to stroke his face. "What for? What did you do? What's wrong?"

"What's wrong? Everything. Myst . . . the fact that you were supposed to be the Queen of Summer and live in a land of warmth and beauty. . . . I feel like my love drew you back here, and look what happened."

He held me so tight I almost couldn't breathe. "I blame myself for getting you and your cousin involved in this mess. Chatter and I were assigned to guard you while you were young. I knew you were my Cherish, from before, so I never thought about what loving you now might mean. I almost think it would have been better if I hadn't reminded you of who you were. If I hadn't fallen in love with you all over again."

I struggled back a step, pushing him by the shoulders so he could get a good look at my face. "Listen to me, and I do mean *listen*. None of this is your fault. We bound ourselves together eons ago. Our love has existed down through time. I've seen the past, and I know that at least once, I killed myself when I was a little girl because I realized I'd been born in the wrong time and you wouldn't be there with me."

"But everything is a mess."

"Of course it is. Myst is still alive, and she's the one to ultimately blame. *She* turned you, *she* took over the Summer and Winter Courts, *she* made the halls bleed with the life of your people. And of my people. Rhiannon and I were born for this—you know that. We were destined to take our places as the Queens of Winter and Summer. You certainly aren't to blame for our births."

"I know, but I can't help but feel . . ." He stopped, and I realized what was going on. But I'd lay odds that Grieve didn't even know.

"You know what's eating you? You feel guilty over the fact that she turned you. Somewhere in there," I touched my hand to his heart. "Somewhere inside your heart, you really do believe that you could have somehow prevented her from turning you. You think that maybe you could have stopped her from destroying your people if you'd only—"

"If I'd only been smarter . . . stronger . . . had seen her coming." He finished the sentence for me, as I knew he would.

"The fact is, love, you couldn't have done a damned thing. She took everybody by surprise. If she was able to pull a fast one on Lainule and Wrath, how can you believe—for even one minute—that you could have made a difference? She's strong. Not invincible, but Hunter is right—she's cunning. And old. Add in that insatiable drive for power she has, as well as the jealousy she feels, and it makes her the most dangerous foe we're ever likely to face. And that doesn't even begin to factor in her thirst for revenge against me." I smiled then, and though it felt pale, at least it was a smile.

"Grieve, my sweet, Myst was set up for this. She was bred for it. When Geoffrey turned her, he miscalculated. He turned an unstable member of the Dark Fae who had a thirst for power. How could Myst *not* be the adversary she is, given her breeding?"

Grieve looked at me for a moment; then his shoulders relaxed and he pulled me down onto the sofa with him, wrapping his arm around my shoulder. "This is the strangest life. . . ."

"And I'm the strangest wife you could probably ever have." I snuggled into his arm, resting my head on his shoulder. "So, when this is all over and done with, what do we do? Settle into a long, happy, boring life?"

Laughing, Grieve planted a kiss on my forehead. "Life with you could never be boring. No, I foresee children . . . ruling your kingdom—"

"Our kingdom."

"Our kingdom. You will learn our customs and we will try to learn yours. And if Lannan tries to touch you again, I will stake him through the heart. Or better yet, I'll cut off his balls and feed them to the one pet Shadow Hunter I'll have kept on the end of a leash. Or . . . if you need him, we will figure out a way to make it work." Grieve chuckled. "You, my sweet, are the most beautiful Ice Queen there could ever be."

"The Snow Queen . . ." I mused. "With a heart of ice and a silver dagger in hand."

Grieve placed his hand over my heart. "You may run cold now, the transformation changed your body—this is true— but your heart is as hot and passionate as the sun." He pulled me close and his mouth met mine, lingering as he gently bit my bottom lip and worried it with his sharp, razor teeth.

I murmured his name, my breath meeting his, and he laid me back onto the sofa, shifting so he was on top of me. The weight of his body was warm and inviting, sending spirals of hunger through my legs, torso, deep into my cunt. I wanted him, now. We were facing a harsh journey, and if we didn't return, I wanted the memory of one last passionate night with my love.

"Do we have time?" Grieve's whisper was so soft I could barely hear it.

"I don't care. They can wait. I want you now." I struggled to pull down my jeans. The corset be damned—it could stay on, but as Grieve lifted up, I unzipped my pants and pushed them down past my knees, then slid one leg out to drape over the edge of the sofa. My ass rubbed gently against the afghan covering the leather and itched ever so slightly against my skin, both irritating me and yet, arousing me further. My nipples pressed against the lace of my strapless bra, chafing, and I wanted to tear both bra and corset off, to free my breasts for Grieve to bite, to suck, to grab hold and revel in.

He slid his hand down between my legs, fingering me, sliding one finger along my clit as it engorged, pressuring me to catch my breath. He began to rub, slowly at first, then fast, twirling his fingers lightly so that I didn't have time to breathe between the spasms that began to drive me harder and higher. As I wrapped my arms around his back, his jacket and tunic vanished and my hands were sliding along his smooth skin, feeling the muscles ripple beneath the taut flesh. I trailed my touch down to his butt—his pants vanished—and grabbed hold of his ass, cupping his cheeks firmly in my hands as he pressed against me.

The smell of his body—of spruce and cold northern woods, of cinnamon and bonfires from the darkest night—sent me reeling. He intoxicated me, made me want to lose myself in his embrace, to let him do whatever he wanted with me. I was his to play, to stroke, to manipulate, and the knowledge that he wanted me made me hotter than hell. Desire was an aphrodisiac, and being the object of desire, a heady drug.

"Hold still," he ordered, and I froze, obeying. Three fingers slid inside me, driving with a deep pulse, widening me up, making me hungry. I wanted his cock, plunging into me to fill me thick and full with his hot, salty cum. As he thrust his fingers in and out of my pussy, I could feel the liquid sliding around his hand, along my labia, down the sides of my cunt.

I gasped as he suddenly pulled away, but before I could look up, his head was between my thighs, his tongue playing across me, licking, sucking, biting ever so slightly. The sting from his teeth sent me higher and I bucked, my legs pushing upward, but Grieve grabbed the sides of my hips and held me firm as he kept going.

The pressure grew. I tried to moderate my breathing but

then he rose over me, and the look on his face was dark and fierce, his eyes a swirl of stars against their inky background. His cock stood firm, thick and rigid, a few drops of pre-cum glistening on the tip of it. I struggled to sit up, and he lifted me, his hands sliding under my arms.

I quickly slid around, on my hands and knees, so I was facing his shaft, and as he braced against the back of the sofa, I took his rod in one hand and guided the pulsing flesh into my mouth, pressing my lips together so that he had to push hard to force himself through them. I tightened, creating a delicious suction around the head of his penis, and began to trace my tongue around the salty flesh, reveling in the feel as he expanded my mouth.

Grieve moaned, his head dropping back, his platinum hair draping down his back. I closed my eyes and began to take him deeper as he thrust gently with his hips. I relaxed my throat as I swallowed him down, my head bobbing as I sucked, drawing back and then forward again as I slid along the length of his cock, stopping to tickle the ridge with my tongue before wrapping it around him.

His breathing increased as I sped up, and he fisted my hair, letting out a strangled cry as I matched the pulse of his heartbeat, milking him with my lips, not letting him rest.

His cock began to twitch, and I could feel he was on the edge, so I sucked harder, and then, with one deep thrust, he came, filling my mouth with his salty seed. I swallowed, caught in the passion, drawing every drop out onto my tongue and licking him clean. A moment later, he lifted me up and tipped me back, still ready to go. I opened my thighs. Nothing else existed—nothing but Grieve and me, and this moment.

His eyes were glimmering now, a triumphant expression on his face, and he drove down, his cock sliding deep inside me, penetrating to the hilt. As my cunt expanded to welcome him in, he brushed against my clit, and I came, sharp and hard, not expecting it yet. I let out a sharp cry, and then he was fucking me quickly, driving deep with each thrust.

"Fuck me. Fuck me hard. Do anything you want to me." I shifted as the feel of his body against mine once more began

to send me spiraling. He was my prince, my lover, my deadly
protector, and he had died for me—with me. I began to come
again, the waves of orgasm spread through me in long concentric ripples, and once again I lost myself in the love of my
wounded king.

❋

Lannan was waiting in the living room as Grieve and I came
out of the parlor, a smug look on his face. I stared at him, and
it hit me like a ton of bricks. I had a love-hate affair going on
with the vampire, and he was in my life for good or ill,
regardless of how I felt about it.

He stepped forward, stopped inches from me, then gave
me a faux bow, his lip curling up at one edge. He was so close
that I could have felt his breath on me, if he were to breathe.
But he was cold, still, no pulse, no beat of the heart. I raised
my eyes, stared into his face. He caught my gaze, leaned
down so a mere fraction of space separated our lips.

"Cicely . . . pardon me . . . *Your Majesty*. So we are going
hunting together, are we?" The jibe hit, but even though it
pissed me off, we had more important things to focus on.
"Your friends have filled me in on your plans, while you
were *occupied*." Lannan could imply a world of innuendo
with a single word, and the whisper of disrespect behind the
word promised everything and yet nothing.

His voice brushed over me like a rough shirt, one that irritated just enough to arouse, but not enough to hurt.

Beside me, Grieve bristled, but I quietly touched his arm and
he stood down. "Now that you're here, we should start out."

Lannan sobered. "First, word from the outside." His
abrupt change of mood made me nervous.

I motioned for everyone to sit down. "What's going on?"

"The electricity? Several major transformers have gone
down—nobody knows why—and Seattle is black. And from
what I've been able to ascertain, the Shadow Hunters are
moving into the city."

Fuck. A major city, dead in the water. Seattle never fared
well in snow anyway—a few inches of snow was enough to

grind the wheels to a halt. A blizzard was bad enough, but now without power, and with an influx of predators? Things were going to get very bloody, very fast.

"The Consortium is over there. Can they do anything?" I glanced at Ysandra. "What will they do?"

She paled. "Whatever they can. They may be able to take the city into a magical lockdown, but it will take everything they have, and they have to know what's going on in the first place in order to plan out anything." Turning to Lannan, she asked, "Is there any way you can send someone in to contact them?"

He considered her question for a moment, then a slow smile crept across his face. "I already did, Ysandra. When we realized what was happening, I contacted some of our people over there and asked them to get the fuck *into* Dodge and take care of alerting everybody who had any possibility of helping. It's up to them now—the cell towers over there went down shortly after. We have no idea what the fuck's going down now."

"If Seattle falls . . . If she turns all the magic-born there to help her . . ." Just like Myst had turned Heather. The Vampiric Fae could turn the magic-born and control them, and they would retain their powers while under Myst's control. A city that had several thousand of the magic-born in it? Taken by the Mistress of Mayhem? Her armies would be unstoppable. And what if she managed to overpower the Consortium? With the best of the best under her control? The world really *could* fall to her rule.

"Exactly. But that's not all of the news." Lannan was looking bleaker by the moment.

"There's more? Worse?"

He nodded. "You know the Indigo Court has pockets of Shadow Hunters tucked all over the place, right? They've had thousands of years to breed."

I didn't want to hear this. I knew that I didn't want to hear this.

Ysandra pushed to her feet. "They're launching unified

attacks, aren't they? If so here—on several cities at once—
why not in several areas of the country at once?"

Lannan gave her a nod as the silence in the room thick-
ened. "Not just several areas of the country, but several
countries. Several of the other regional Fae Courts are under
siege. They are fighting to their best—"

"And so the long winter extends her grasp." Grieve stood.
"We'd best be off, then. The sooner we discover her heartstone, the sooner we can end this."

Lannan inclined his head to me. For once, there was no
sense of animosity between the two men. "We await your
lead, Winter."

I inhaled a deep breath and let it out slowly. Turning to the
others, I scanned their faces, one by one. "So, we are here at
last. Ysandra, you and your crew will surround us with protection for as long as you can. Luna, you and Dorthea send the
dead through the town to take down Myst's forces. Rhia—you
and Chatter will oversee our forces heading out through New
Forest. Peyton, work with the guards here to watch the house."

And then it hit me. This might be it—anything could happen
through the night, for good or ill. We might not all come
through tonight, and tomorrow either Myst would stand triumphant, or we would have destroyed her heartstone. Because if
she won this battle, chances were she'd win the war.

By the looks on the others' faces, they knew this, too. We
stood, staring at one another in silence for the better part of
a minute.

And then, slowly, Rhiannon reached out and took Chatter's
hand. He took Peyton's, then Ysandra, Luna, Lannan, Kaylin,
Grieve, and I joined in. As I took Rhia's hand, completing the
circle, we stood in silence. I wasn't sure who started it, but a
line of energy began to snake through our fingers, linking us
strong, linking our hopes, our goals, our fears, and our prayers.

As the energy increased, swishing through us like a
whirling snake, Ulean joined in, and for a brief moment, we
were one—linked by a common goal, linked by our pasts,
linked by our hopes for the future. With a swift *whoosh*, the

energy spiraled up into a cone, and I realized I was holding the tether. I focused it on Myst—on driving the force toward her heart. As it peaked, with a sharp break, I cut it loose and let it fly.

Dizzy, I stumbled back, as did the others, but then Lannan stepped away while the rest of us cheered and cried and held one another.

I held Rhia by the shoulders. "You know I love you."

She smiled, the summer sun beaming through her eyes. "I know. We'll win this, Cicely. We'll win this because we have to win this. And then . . . the future will take care of itself. You and I will guide the Barrows into a new day." She leaned in, gave me a kiss on the cheek. "We are fire and ice."

"Amber and jet."

"Summer and Winter."

As I slowly pulled away, I turned to Chatter. "Take care of my cousin . . . just in case I don't make it back."

He gave me a soft smile, so strong in himself compared to the Chatter I'd first met a few weeks ago. "No need, Lady Cicely. You will be here to do that yourself."

"I hope so." Sucking in a deep breath, I called for my owl cloak. "We'd best go now."

Ulean swept in close to me, and Grieve took my left side. Hunter and Lannan guarded the right. The guards—nine total, including three vampires, and six of my men led by Check and Fearless—surrounded us. They were helping Kaylin, who couldn't walk atop the snow. The vampires were light on their feet when they wanted to be—and so we headed out the door, into the blinding storm, silently moving into the swirl of white that had become the night.

The shadow of the Golden Wood helped protect us from the storm to some extent, though the drifting dunes left our world a barren landscape of white mounds against the black shadows of the trees. The silence was punctuated only by the hiss of the falling snow, and the scent of ozone crackled in the air. I caught my breath—the temperature was icy, but it didn't bother me, not now.

Whatever animals made the woodland their home were gone—in hiding from the storm or hunted down by the Shadow Hunters, and the forest felt empty, like an abandoned house; but the abandoned house was a trap and we knew it. The woods weren't really empty. Myst's forces were out here: Shadow Hunters and snow weavers and, no doubt, goblin dogs. She still managed to control some of the Ice Elementals, too, the ones who hadn't fallen out from her spell and under my rule. So the forest wasn't empty by any means, but full with our enemies.

Ulean swept ahead of us to help keep us on track, since the path was buried far beneath the snow and landmarks were almost impossible to read. As we silently passed through the trees, I fell into a light trance, moving forward on autopilot, as my thoughts drifted into the slipstream. And then . . . I was standing on a hill, in another snowstorm, and once again, I was running from Myst.

❧

The hilltop was exposed under the night sky, but the storm was raging around me, and I anxiously looked for Shy. He was here somewhere, waiting for me. We'd made the agreement some time ago. There was no choice—no other option, and we had to go through with it now that we'd both run from our people.

And then, stepping out from a huckleberry bush that was covered by the snow, he came. Shy, my love. My one connection with Summer. This was the man who kept me from spiraling into the depths out from which I'd dug myself. My heart leaped, and I rushed forward, into his arms, as he wrapped me in his embrace and kissed me.

"Cherish, my love, you were afraid I'd change my mind?"

I didn't want to admit it, but the fear had been there. We were from such disparate backgrounds, and our natures were an antithesis of the other. He was the morning light, and green grass, white wine on a summer night, wanting to play and lounge in the fields. And I was the night sky during winter, blood on snow, ready for battle, willing to destroy and maim. My hunger was fierce, and the drive to carve through flesh ran deep in my veins, but somehow, this son of the Summer had caught me in his web, and I had lost my heart to him.

I kissed him, edging his lips with my teeth—the needle-sharp edges severing skin till drops of blood appeared on them. Licking them off, I let him slide his tongue in my mouth, probing deep, unafraid of me. And that was one thing I loved most—he didn't fear me. He accepted me, all of me, my bloodlust included. And that lack of fear had become an aphrodisiac. He danced with death and loved it, and in turn, he had sparked in me emotions I never knew I possessed, and I'd offered him my heart on a silver platter.

"Oh, my Cherish. Are you ready? We can't linger long here. They'll be after us soon." Shy's eyes were haunted. It had taken everything he had to turn his back on his people. I was far more fickle; it was easier for me because cunning and deceit were born and bred into my blood, but I understood what this meant for him and that made me love him all the more.

"I'm ready. Whatever happens, Shy, we'll face it together. Whatever the future brings, we'll walk into it side by side."

And with that we were off and running.

It took two days of us racing through the forests for the slip-stream to fill with whispers that we were being followed.

I'd hoped for a longer head start. Sometimes I was gone for a week at a time from the Barrow, and Myst, my mother, knew that I would return. But she had been watching me closely as of late. A few weeks back, she stumbled on my secret and ordered me to end the relationship. To be exact, her orders were harsher than that. She'd demanded I bring Shy's heart to her; that I destroy what I loved the most to prove my allegiance to the Indigo Court, and to her.

And Shy had been ordered to put an arrow through my heart.

The Court of Rivers and Rushes had known about my

people for some time now. They had been watching us as we swept through and hunted the yummanii who inhabited the area. We were cautious in our culling. You just don't decimate a herd, or you destroy your easiest food supply. So we took animals and Cambyra Fae to supplement our diet. But after years of hiding out, we came to the notice of the Summer Queen, and she'd been quick to alert the Winter Court.

Which meant the Indigo Court was preparing to go into hiding. Before, when it became necessary to escape before we attracted too much notice, my mother had left a few of our people to populate a small nest in the area as we vacated. And so we managed to create a network through this new land that had become our home not so very long ago. We had pockets of allies strung across the continent, left behind as we worked our way northwest across this massive spread of land we'd discovered when the Great Fae Courts had forced us to take to the ocean and leave our old world behind.

And now we'd reached the edge of the ocean. But we still weren't strong enough to take the locals, so my mother had planned our next move—to retreat into the shadows and build our strength. But she wasn't about to let me keep any ties to the Summer Court. My love for Shy was a weakness.

"You are a disgrace—worse than a disgrace! You are a blemish to the name of the Indigo Court. You will end this dalliance immediately, and to prove that you honor your Queen—your mother—you will bring me the boy's heart. Rip it out of his body. You are Vampiric Fae. You cannot love! I didn't raise you to be a traitor."

I'd always admired my mother, emulated her—until I met Shy. In that one meeting, my world changed, and everything I ever thought I knew dropped away, like a cloak of snow that melted in a sudden sunbeam. The ice around my heart had melted, too, and I'd been forced to make a choice. And my choice had surprised even me.

Now, having defied our respective peoples, we had taken our love and were on the run.

Two days in, and the hounds were after us on both sides. And we had some decisions to make. In my heart, I knew they'd catch us. But not before we blazed a trail through their forces. We'd burned our bridges, and the only way forward was to destroy anything and anybody that stood between us and our love.

"What happens if they catch us?" I turned to Shy as we stopped to rest. We'd run a hundred miles or a thousand, maybe. I had no clue where we were, but we were headed north—that much I knew.

"I guess . . . we fight till the end." Shy's beautiful blue eyes were cold as steel. He might embody the sun, but the sun could burn and crisp as well as warm and illuminate. "I've been thinking . . ."

I turned to him. "We aren't going to make it, are we? Be honest with me. Neither my mother nor your queen will let us go. We've stepped too far beyond the boundaries, and they intend to make an example out of us."

He paused, then his lip trembled. "I think you're right. I don't know if there's anywhere we can get to where they won't hunt us down and send their assassins after us. We broke the rules damned good, woman." And he pulled me to his chest, engulfing me in his arms that felt like they could keep out the world. "I am thinking of something. There is a way . . ."

I looked up at his face, and I saw the certainty in his expression—the finality. "If we have to die, I don't want them to separate us."

"There's a way we can keep that from happening. I have a potion . . . I bought it from a sorceress I know. She is the most powerful of the magic-born. The potion will bind our souls so that we can return in the future. Return to each other at a time when our love won't be forbidden."

My heart thudded. I wasn't afraid of death—hell, I was death incarnate by nature. But I was afraid of losing Shy. He was my all, and now the only fear I had was of seeing him hurt or taken from me.

"I like that. We'll fight to the end. Maybe there's some way we can survive and escape. Maybe some miracle will allow us to win through, but if we can't . . . If we can't, we'll drink the draught and flee into the future."

And just like that, we agreed that, to ensure our life together, we'd do whatever it took. Even if it meant dying to do so.

❧

Snapping out of the flashback, I looked around. We were deep into the heart of the Golden Wood, past the turnoff for both the Marburry and Eldburry Barrows, headed toward the higher elevations. The going was getting tough, even for us, and I glanced back to see how Kaylin was faring, but the guards were making sure he stayed atop the snow, helping him along. They were able to go at our normal speed by carrying him under the arms. I had the feeling he wasn't too happy about this, but there was nothing for it. While the vampires could keep up with us if pressed, Kaylin couldn't, and he'd been warned to expect this.

As we curved around a thick patch of trees, a figure glistened through the veil of falling snow. And a second—and a third. Ice Elementals. They turned toward us and began moving. Were they aligned with Myst? Or were they my own?

I stepped toward the front, pushing through the guards. There was only one way to find out. Holding up my hand, I struggled for that odd mind link that I'd had to learn when dealing with the sentinels of the ice. It was like the slipstream, only a few steps removed. Once I found the current, I could speak into it, project my intentions and communicate with them that way. But it had been a tough path to master because the frozen giants were so alien in their nature that I had to think in a pattern to match their frequencies.

I gathered my thoughts, then projected out a question, probing their intentions cautiously. If they were bound to Myst, she might immediately know that we were here, and she would guess what we were searching for.

Waiting for the answer, I held my breath. Would they be friendly? Would they obey me? Or would they attack? At that moment, one of them caught the current and turned, followed by the others, and began to walk toward us. Now, we would see.

Chapter 14

As the Ice Elementals moved closer, the guards raised their swords, waiting. But then, with a rush of cool wind, Ulean flowed around me.

They are unaligned. You can take control of them. They are not bound to Myst, so better you make them yours than let them run free for her taking.

I knew the spell to bind them to me—Strict had taught it to me first thing, but it took concentration. It also took a confidence I still didn't have down pat.

But you'd better get with it girl, or you'll never manage Myst. The thought echoed in the back of my head, and I realized that there was no more time to learn, no more time to question myself. I motioned for the others to stand back as I moved toward the approaching creatures.

Ice Elementals lived in a world of their own. I had several bound to me at such a level they would die—cease to exist—before betraying me. During the formation of my heartstone, they had become my own guardians. They stayed back in the realm of Snow and Ice, though, waiting by the outer door of the Barrow should I need them.

Elementals were so far from human that they might as well be aliens. They lived in a world bounded by their own element, and while they often showed up on the physical planes, they still ran true to their natures. Fire Elementals would never be found in the snow, and Ice Elementals would dissipate and return to their own plane of existence if they were suddenly transported to the desert.

Elementals were inherently neutral; they were neither good nor evil—they couldn't even think in those terms. If someone bound them, they would obey, but there was no malice or goodwill in what they did. They had no emotions, not of the human kind. Oh, they hungered, and they had their own agendas, that much I had learned, but jealousy? Anger? Love? These were generally foreign concepts to their worlds, as were their motives to us. Elementals simply were.

Avatars of the forces making up the whole of life, Elementals encapsulated energy—and that energy could be harnessed and directed. And while all things seemed to have some desire for freedom, the Elementals didn't resent their use any more than a frying pan resented being used to cook food.

I was still tapped into the current of communication that had been established between us, and now I began to sing the charm of binding that Strict had taught me. It would bring them under my control, and since I was the Queen of Snow and Ice, they wouldn't resist like they might normally do. But it took focus, and confidence. I had to prove to them I had the right and power to take control, and once that was done, they would be mine for life.

The energy wove between us like a frozen tendril branching out, a vine of ice that came from deep within me to swirl around the group of Elementals—and the notes of my song froze in the air, a bluish vapor that narrowed into a beam of light to entwine around the shimmering creatures who now watched me with what seemed to be utter fascination.

They stood still, having stopped their movement, as the icy fire began to burrow into their chests, the tendrils burying themselves into their very core. I pushed harder and the ice tendrils glistened as they blended into the energy making up their bodies. Another push—there was minor resistance but it was nothing to worry about. They were simply curious and hesitant, having never been bound before.

So deep in the spell casting was I that I didn't notice the movements off to the side. It was only when Ulean gave me a shout that I wrenched my attention away from the Elementals. The charm had taken, though, and they were mine. I could feel the bond there, the obsessive focus they were giving me. They would await my every command.

Cicely! Tell your men to watch out!

At Ulean's cry, I whirled around. Out from behind a stand of trees to the left emerged a sparkling cloud. It was hard to discern it from the falling snow, except for the fact that it glistened and shimmered—illuminating itself like a neon haze, the color of LED blue lights. What the hell?

What is that? Ulean, what the hell is going on?

It belongs to Myst's realm, whatever it is. I sense a sentience, and a malevolence, but I have no idea what the thing might be.

We backed away—by now my men had seen it—watching as it drifted closer and closer. The Ice Elementals shifted, and I sensed their discomfort. I couldn't easily ask them what it was, but they were loyal to me now, and they moved in front of me, forming a barrier between whatever the cloud was and us. I turned to Hunter.

"Do you know what this might be? Have you ever seen anything quite like it before?"

He frowned, cocking his head. "Once, but it was a long time ago. And I'm not certain it's the same thing."

"What was it you saw, then?" A half guess was better than nothing, and right now, the vapor made me nervous. "Ulean says this thing has a nasty feel to it, and the more I look at it, the more uncomfortable it makes me."

"It was like some spirit in the woods—not a ghost, but a being that belonged in the forest. It had been awakened when something went out of balance and allowed it to enter the woodland. I don't know where it came from—some chaotic portal a step away from our own realm, perhaps? But whatever it was, we knew that it was an astral entity." Hunter stared at the cloud. "We didn't know it was hiding among our people until too late. We lost ten men and fifteen of the women and children that day before it had sated its hunger and vanished. We never did find out what happened, or how it killed them, or why it showed up."

The cloud had stopped, it was paused just yards away from us, but it seemed to be pondering. I frowned, lowering myself into the slipstream as I tried to figure out what it was and what to do about it.

As I searched for its energy—if Ulean had been able to tap into it, I should be able to as well—the austerity of the forest hit me.

I could sense the crystalline presence of the Ice Elementals, though their thoughts ran on their own current, and the hush of the trees—deeper still. And I could even feel the spirit of the storm, driven by Myst. Brooding and powerfully hungry, it was eager to gobble up the forest for its own. And then, a layer below that . . . Yes, there it was—the cloud that faced us.

The energy was alien, just as alien as the Elementals, but in a far different way. While both were sentient and aware, the cloud had an agenda, though the hungers and desires present on the slipstream were jumbled and hard to read. But it wanted at us—it wanted in. It wanted *me*. Which brought me to the question: *What was stopping it from attacking?*

The more I examined the currents running between the cloud and us, the more I was able to pick out something. I began to see a barrier—a shimmering field of energy that surrounded us. Then I knew. I knew what was keeping this being in check.

"Ysandra and her crew have managed to erect a protection field around us. The cloud can't get through. I don't know what that is, but if the protection spell is broken, it's going to attack us the first chance it gets. And while I'm not certain what damage it can do, I am not eager to find out." I turned to the others.

Hunter shook his head. "I think it's the same type of

creature we faced so long ago. As to the damage: It can kill. Easily, swiftly, and without warning."

"Since Ysandra is protecting us, if we leave the area— walk on by—will it follow us or just wait for the next unsuspecting person to come along?" Not that there would be anybody meandering through the woods today. Hell, the way this storm was going, anybody not from the realm of Snow and Ice would die out here without help. Kaylin was surviving because of us.

"I believe that it will follow us. But there's not much we can do about it. I don't know how to fight it. Neither do you." Hunter shook his head. He looked worried. I could vaguely see his expression—our eyes were better suited for the night than most other races. Even Kaylin was able to see in the night more easily than most magic-born or yummanii. His demon had given him some pretty hefty adaptations when it had wedded itself to his soul.

I debated trying to attack it here and now, but that might break the spell. And if we didn't even know what it was, but we *did* know that it was deadly, blindly rushing in was something better left to fools. I might be stupid sometimes, but I didn't have a death wish.

"I guess we just have to accept that it's going to be on our tail, then. Check, have one of your men keep an eye on it as we travel. Let's get a move on. We have miles to go, and the storm shows no sign of letting up."

Lannan, who had barely spoken since we started out, surprised me by saying, "The storm won't let up till that bitch is dead." He wore no coat, only a leather jacket. Vampires had no fear of the cold. But beneath the jacket, he was wearing a heavy sweater and jeans that would offer him some protection in case of a fight.

There didn't seem to be a need to answer him—we all knew he was right. So we headed out, toward the Barrow that I remembered from so long ago. It was hidden deep in the forest, but as we plowed through the maze of trees and mounds of snow, I began to feel a sense of familiarity. I'd never been back here, not since I was a little girl and only that one time, but there was something about the feel of the area that rang a bell somewhere in my core.

Once again, I felt the past intruding into the present, only this time, it was like I was walking in two worlds at once. Here, with Grieve and my men, and yet . . . and yet . . . I was walking in another age, as well.

⚜

In a dream state I walked atop the deep snow. The land here was fresh and new. Mother had settled on it because we were close to the Fae Barrows. They'd had no clue we were near, not for a long time. And then, even after, they'd ignored us until I'd changed everything by falling in love with Shy. Now they hated us—their dark cousins who walked in blood and shadow.

And yet . . . and yet . . . I was not here—not really. I glanced around and realized that everything I looked at seemed to be filtered through a vapor that rose up to cloak me in mist. Then the sound of snuffling startled me, and I whirled around to see an ancient elk break free from the trees. But instead of sensing me—instead of turning to run—he ambled past, not even glancing in my direction.

I looked down at my hands—they were as translucent as the ice of the Elementals. They shimmered, as did my gown and the air around me. Confused, but knowing this was my home, I continued on, following my instinct until I saw the Barrow Mound ahead.

Out of that mound stepped a woman. The Barrow looked covered with broken branches and in a state of disrepair. And the woman? She was tall as the sky with hair the color of raven wings, and her eyes were jet with swirling stars in their core. She was like a spider, thin and jointed but beautiful in a terrible way. Her dress was the color of twilight, covered with silver embroidery. Something about her struck a chord in me, and then . . . with one look at her tearstained face, at the look of fury filling her eyes, I remembered.

Myst. She was my mother. And yet, she didn't seem to recognize me. In fact, she stared past me as if I weren't there. As if . . .

A guard scuttled up to her, kowtowing at her feet. I couldn't hear what he said to her, but she kicked him in the face, knocking him back, and then he hunched his way to the side, darting terrified glances over his shoulder.

Another moment and Myst straightened her shoulders as four more guards emerged from the woods, carrying a stretcher over for her to inspect. My stomach dropped, and I had the feeling that I knew who was on that stretcher. As they passed by me, I saw I was right. There, stretched out in a silver gown, dead to the world, was my body. *Cherish. Daughter of Myst.* Killed by my own hand—by a drink that was both poison and a promise for the future.

Myst stared in silence at the body for a moment, then spoke the last words I would ever hear from her in that lifetime.

"This is the body of a traitor—give it to the hounds to feast upon, and if they die from the poison in their veins, throw them in the lake. I have no daughter. Not anymore. And if her spirit should ever return . . . I will banish her to the depths of the abyss."

As she turned, her dress swishing against the snow, I wanted to lunge forward, to fall at her feet and tell her I was sorry, that even though my heart had won out, I still loved her. But then she was gone, into the Barrow.

※

With a sudden rush, I fell through the snow, swirling, finding myself back on the hilltop with Shy. We were bloody—I had mowed down guards on both sides with a vengeance, long enough to give us this respite. We had managed to hold them off for three days after they tracked us down, but we knew this was the end of the road. We wouldn't survive the night. This was our last stand—our ending. Only it wasn't happily ever after.

Shy held out a flask. "They're coming. It's time—or we will have no more choice. Put your hands on the flask with mine."

As I did, the energy within the fluid shifted and it loomed dark and ominous—deathly seductive.

Flash . . . a swirl of energy, beckoning me forward, beckoning me in. *Flash* . . . a pool waited, so dark and deep that I could never see the bottom, and I knew that once I fell in, a journey would begin that would take me through time, a journey that would never end. *Flash* . . . sparkling stars filled the void, and Shy and I were rocks, waiting to drop in the vast ocean, where we would send ripples out to change the course of the future. *Flash* . . . the smell of belladonna and wolfsbane rose up, the scents of hemlock and yew and all things earthy and whispering of the sweetness of death. *And one last flash* . . . and my energy blended with Shy's, and together we changed the structure of the potion within the bottle.

And then . . . they crested the hill, a row of shadows against the barren snows under the full moon that lit up the night. Lining the ridge, their leader stepped forward. Shy's brother led the pack. A fierce warrior, he hated me with a passion and had vowed he'd do whatever needed to keep us apart. I wanted to rip him to shreds, to take him down, but now there would be no opportunity. He would think himself victorious.

But we will be the winners. We'll be free of the hatred between our people.

I turned to Shy, suddenly afraid. "I'm not afraid to die—not with you—but I don't want them to hurt us. I don't want our last moments on this world to be in pain. I want to go out thinking of you. Loving you."

He pressed the flask into my hand, his gaze never wandering from my own. "I love you. Cherish, I will love you till the end. I will love you beyond the veils of time. We were meant to be together, and all the hatred and borders and queens of this world will not keep us apart. One day, we'll find each other again. I promise you this, on the honor of my soul, on all the stars in the sky."

"Then let's leave this world, leave it to the hounds and the snows and the flames. They haven't won, my love. They haven't won—we aren't giving them the chance. We have our love. We set the game. We make the rules."

As the hounds bayed and surged down the ridge toward us, I

grabbed the flask and drank half the potion, feeling the liquid burn my throat as it filled my body with its dark and passionate promise. Shy drank the rest and then grabbed me, laying me down in his arms, and our lips met. He tasted of death, of bonfires and the darkness of the grave. He tasted like sweet poison, and I rested my head in his arms, still kissing him.

They were almost upon us, but the sky began to glaze over, and as I stared up, the stars whirled, mirroring the stars in my own eyes. I saw myself reflected in Shy's gaze, and I pulled back, smiling. This was it. Our love would last forever, and they could never separate us, no matter how hard they tried. Our souls would be bound throughout time, and twin sparks, we would fly free from our bodies.

"Cherish . . . I will meet you in time." Shy's eyes began to flutter shut, and he struggled to keep them open. "I would not change this for the world—the day we met, my fate was sealed."

"I meant to kill you that day . . . but you ripped out my heart and kept it for your own. You are my hope and my passion and my everything. I never understood what it meant to love—not until you came along. I would kill a thousand soldiers to stay with you."

"I can't hold on much longer. They're almost here. Let go, my love. It's time to let go." Shy pressed his lips against mine one last time.

"If you get there first, wait for me. I will know you . . . I will know who you are." And then the stars began to spin faster. As the sound of our tormenters grew closer, I took one last breath . . . and let go, closing my eyes as I slipped into the void, racing toward the future where I knew my love would wait for me.

✦

"Cicely, are you all right?" Grieve caught my elbow as I stumbled over a hidden root buried in the snow.

Startled, I looked around to find that I'd totally zoned out. How long we'd been walking since I'd taken my little trip back in time I didn't know, but it must have been long enough for me to lose track of what I was doing.

"Fine. . . . I'm fine. Sorry—I just . . . I had another flashback."

"They've been happening too frequently for comfort." Grieve frowned, and as I stared at him, I could see his features superimposed over an image of Shy. A sudden well of emotion swelled up, and I stopped in my tracks. "Are you all right? You look like you just saw a ghost."

I caught my breath. "I might as well have." I reached out and took his hands, the emotion from the past bleeding through. "I . . . Grieve . . . no matter what happens, this is all worth it. We started something in the past, and somehow, I think that our connection goes far back in time, long before we were Shy and Cherish. But know that, whatever comes . . . I love you, and you are my passion. Here, then . . . all times."

A worried look filtered across his face. "Lower your voice, my love. I know what you are feeling, but we don't want to dishearten the men."

At that moment, my wolf shifted, both in satisfaction and in concern. Grieve could feel my need, my love for him, but my ability to shift back and forth into Cherish's mind scared him.

I understood what he meant. If I spoke too loudly, my words might sound defeatist and discourage our men. I nodded, then softly leaned forward to lightly brush his lips. We had no time for a lip-lock, but a single kiss—embodying my passion and love—there was always time for that.

Standing back, I looked around. "How close are we?" Even as I asked, I knew—we were around the bend from the Barrow. I took advantage of the pause to seek out Ulean.

Can you go ahead, see if there are any Shadow Hunters there?

I'll be back in a moment. Meanwhile, you know that cloud creature? Still it follows you. It's hanging back right now, and I don't know if your men can sense it from where it's at. But it is there, and possesses a great cunning. It plans for some course of action. Of this I'm sure.

Thank you. I'll warn the others. Meanwhile, go check out the rest of the way to the Barrow, if you would.

As Ulean swept off, a cold blast of wind in her wake that stirred the snow into even more of a frenzy, I turned around.

"That creature we encountered? Still out there, following us. Ulean just told me about it. I'm not entirely sure what it's doing but she thinks it's up to something, so we'd better keep an eye open. I sent her up ahead to scope out the rest of the path. We're near Myst's old Barrow. I dread to see what she's got in store for us there."

I swallowed a lump that rose in my throat as I realized that getting to the Barrow? Was the easy part. The hard part was coming right on down the road at us. Myst would have trapped the way to her heartstone. All Queens did. I had. Rhiannon had. So, barring anybody standing between us and there, we'd be facing the gauntlet shortly enough.

Hunter grunted. "There are ways around traps, though it will never be easy. But you have me with you, and I know more tricks than you could imagine, girl. I was scouting through the woods before there were people here. I watched the settlers come in from the very beginning. There was a time, when I walked with the yummanii shamans who first walked these paths. I was the one who showed them how to access the path into the Dream Time. I've seen the years roll by, the decades come and go like whispers on the wind."

Before I could say anything, Ulean was back, settling around me like a cloak of winds. She embraced me gently.

The Barrow stands unguarded, and I sense no Shadow Hunters in the area. I cannot vouch for what lies within—I was hesitant to enter. But Cicely, when you walk through that entrance, you will break the protection spell that Ysandra is keeping around you. And once it's broken, whatever that cloud is out there, it will have free access to you. I can't tell you if it will be able to get into the Barrow, but I can't see why it shouldn't.

I let out a long breath. There was no help for it. *We'll have to take that chance. There's nothing else we can do.*

I know, Cicely. Just be cautious.

I warned the others about what Ulean had told me, and we girded ourselves for the possibility. As we headed out again, I glanced over at Hunter.

"You said you can't remember how the cloud killed them?"

He brushed his hands across his eyes. "Not precisely. I don't think we ever figured out just how they died. One moment they were alive, and the next, the cloud enveloped them and . . . they were dead. Blood running out their noses and the corners of their mouths. Not savaged—not like the Shadow Hunters kill—but . . . just dead."

Hmm . . . maybe this thing fed on life force—sucking the energy out of a person. Or maybe it disrupted the body's systems, shut it down? Whatever the case, it was a hunter and therefore must have some motive for killing.

When we turned the corner, the abandoned Barrow mound came into view. Deep in the forest, surrounded by fallen logs piled thick with snow, in the heart of the Golden Wood, Myst's renegade mound still existed. Here it was I had lived and died, a thousand years before.

As I stared at the Barrow, buried by drifts until it had become one large hillock of snow, a wave of panic rolled over me. Fear and betrayal, lust for blood, lust for Shy . . . It all bombarded me in one instant memory. I struggled against the sensation that I was drowning as my worlds of the past and the present collided. My wolf howled, shuddering against me, and Grieve let out a harsh cry and fell to his knees.

The next moment, he was standing again, but when our eyes met, I knew we were seeing both lifetimes superimpose, one over the other. We were back to where it had begun. Or, at least, as far back as we could remember. We were back to where I'd reveled in the bloodlust, and where Grieve had been Summer's child.

Letting out a whimper, I reached for him, and he dragged me into his arms. "I've been waiting for this," he whispered. "I knew it was true, but now . . . now it's really, fiercely, true. We've made it back, my love. We're back."

I began to sob in his embrace. "We made it. We really did. And now, we're fighting against my mother again."

"This time, we have armies on our side. This time, our love isn't forbidden. And Myst is no longer your mother." Grieve pushed me back, holding my shoulders. "It's time to put an end to this. Are you ready?"

I wiped away my tears, nodding. "Let's do this thing." Turning to the others, I said, "We're going in. Keep watch, and especially keep watch for that fucking cloud monster."

I silently thanked Ysandra for helping us get this far, then ducked my head and slipped into the Barrow. I took the lead—there was no question, no argument.

As I stepped through the entrance, it was as though a protective cloak was suddenly stripped away and Ysandra's spell vanished.

It was darker than pitch, darker than night inside, as if something had sucked every drop of light from every corner, leaving a void behind. Taking a deep breath, I flipped on a small flashlight that I had hooked to my belt, and looked around. And right then, memories came tumbling back, memories from another life, and I knew exactly where I was.

I was standing in a large chamber that used to be Myst's throne room. The Barrow wasn't large, as Barrows go, because Myst had built it on the sly, and it didn't have the backing from the Fae Court to truly make it grand.

The throne—built of wood as black as night—had long overgrown with tree roots and now sat, a living creature of root and limb over deadwood, in what seemed a grotesque parody of my own throne room at home.

Everywhere I looked, time had ravaged the Barrow, but memories crept through: the bloody lust and thirst that Myst had birthed in me. A glance at one corner, and I remembered devouring a young fawn there, holding its heart in my hands as I marveled at the life running down my throat. Another corner, and a glimpse of me beating a servant who moved too slowly. Everywhere, the memories of vicious joy overwhelmed me.

Something began to wake inside, a fierce drive that made my stomach quiver. With the hunger came the fear. I was thirsty, I wanted blood, I wanted battle. The same feelings that the obsidian blades of the Shadow Hunters had awakened in me slammed back full force. Just being in the Barrow was waking a part of my soul I'd hoped would stay sleeping forever.

"Grieve—I'm afraid. I'm . . ."

My wolf shifted, and Grieve caught me by the wrist. "Focus. I can feel the hunger. I know that hunger because I fight it every day. Listen to my voice. *You are in control*. The Indigo Court still lives within your soul, but you control it now. You are no longer bound by Myst, you are no longer bound to her or the Vampiric Fae by blood. Soul memory is strong, but you are stronger."

His voice wove a sonorous thread through the waves of panic that swirled around me, and I caught hold of his words, using them like a string through the labyrinth into which my mind had spun.

"Lead me out. Lead me out. Bring me back to myself." Moaning, my knees buckled, but then another hand caught me up, and Hunter, my grandfather, was holding me fast on the other side.

"I am your lineage this life, girl. You belong to my people now. *We* lay claim on you. While the Indigo Court may leave its mark, it will not claim you. You are the Queen of Snow and Ice, and regardless of who you were, this is who you are now. Do you hear me?" His voice was commanding, and I struggled to stand, to throw off the cloak of the past that threatened to swallow me up.

Cicely—come back to yourself. We need you. Myst cannot win, and if you give in to the woman you were—to the woman who was Myst's daughter—then you are handing her a victory over you and over all that you love and protect and stand for.

Between the three of them, between the voices of reason who battered me with a continual barrage of support, I wrestled with the Shadow Hunter inside of me. With the Vampiric Fae I once had been. I'd never be fully free of her. My memories were too grounded in the past, and the ritual that Grieve and I had performed had left us inexorably bound to the

Indigo Court, but this was a new life, a new day, and I would not let Myst win after all this time.

As I fought my way through the clouds, my vision began to return. I opened my eyes, breathing heavily. But as I was about to reassure them that I was regaining control, a sound from the front of the Barrow startled us.

The cloud creature that had been following us had entered the chamber, and was making directly for me. Without thinking, I threw myself back into the mists, back into the energy of Cherish, and raced behind Kaylin. I knew how to kill it, but I didn't have the power. As the shadows of the past held sway, I gave in to the tempestuous blood lust that raced just beneath the surface of my heart.

Chapter 15

This creature and I had met before, long ago, in a land far less populated. In fact, I knew this *thing* from an intimate perspective, given that my mother had created it. Myst had dredged it up from the depths one day, a shadow of one of the Wilding Fae. She had turned it, taken it down to its essence, and out of that void, a life-stealing vampire had been created. Only this vampire fed on energy alone—for the Wilding Fae had been so old, so stretched, that his body simply vanished as my mother fed on him.

I couldn't remember what his name was, but he'd disappeared from Court one day, shortly after a rash of murders among our people. Myst had promised everyone that she'd killed the creature. He was too wayward and unable to be controlled. But in reality, she'd simply chased him into the forests.

Over the years, he became a legend in the forest, feared by the yummanii who came to live in the area. They'd turned him into a creature sent by the gods, but I knew the truth. He fed upon every sentient life force he could find, but he preferred the Shadow Hunters and the Fae, for our magic was strong and he thrived on magic.

I circled to the left as the memories of my mother's dark ritual to create him filtered back. She had snared the Wilding Fae in, and against all odds had managed to convince him to let her turn him. She would have stood no chance without his permission. He was dark and toadlike, squat and yet stretched out from the years that had passed through his life. And he'd been thirsty to collect more power, hungry to dance through the forest, eating his fill. He was darker than dark, a match for my mother, and she'd never suspected his plan to double-cross her.

The cloud shifted to the right, but a wave of malign delight rolled off of him. Thirsty he was, and more—he remembered me. And then—another memory crept in. I'd been out dancing through the snow, looking for quarry to hunt, and I'd met a strange little man. I recognized him as one of the Wilding Fae. He'd been watching me, and the leer on his face turned my stomach. I had no use for lovers or mating rituals. Life was all about the hunt for me.

He made it clear what he wanted, and I rebuffed him as he came toward me, cock out, his member huge and glistening with cum under the night sky. I kicked him square in the balls, and he cursed at me. Laughing, I leaned down to spit in his face.

"Little man, you will never have me. Be content with keeping your life. Be content you aren't the chosen prey of Myst's daughter, for I would tear you to pieces and suck your bones. I would bleed you out and wear your corpse like a cloak and braid your hair into a rope for my servants."

"One would think a daughter of a queen would know how to speak to one of the Wilding Fae. One would take offense, if such a girl was smart enough to know when she put herself in danger. But dance away, mayhem's daughter. There will be meetings to come, and one day a Wilding Fae may have his revenge." And with that he vanished into the woods.

I laughed, then, thinking nothing of his warning. I had no clue how strong the Wilding Fae were. And later, when he came to the Court and my mother turned him, I thought it was simply an experiment gone wrong. When the sparkling cloud vanished into the forest, I thought no more about it. Only as the legends built up around him did I wonder if I'd ever run into him again. But surely, as a cloud of energy, devoid of form, he'd have forgotten who I was. And that I'd laughed at him after bruising his balls.

✤

Now, facing him down, I realized that he recognized the part of me who had once been Cherish. Fuck. That made everything ever so much better. But with the memories of how he'd come to be, I also had remembered one very important thing. I backed up now, glancing at the others.

"We have to fight him on the astral—on the Dream Time. We can't win against him in a physical fight. I wish we had some of Luna's death ghosts with us right now."

Kaylin pushed his way to the front. "Then I have to go in. I'm the only one who can dreamwalk. My demon can fight him."

I let out a cry. "No. He's too dangerous and wily—" but Kaylin shook his head.

"*This* is why you brought me along. I know it. Cicely." He took me by the shoulders, ignoring the glares from Check and Fearless. "You have to let me do this. If you don't, the creature will attack you. There's only one reason it's holding back right now."

I glanced over at the cloud. True enough, it hadn't attacked, and I wasn't sure why it was hanging back. "Why do you think that is?"

"Because he can sense what I am—and he knows that I can face him down. He's waiting to see what our next move is. I'm going in, and you cannot stop me, girl."

"Then I'm going with you."

"No." The word was an order, and he turned to Check. "I won't allow it. She may be your queen, but she's not mine. If something were to happen to me, there would be no one to bring her back."

Check nodded. "Understood."

And with that he lay down, and a couple of the vampires

gathered around him, including Lannan, who was staring at the cloud monster with fascination. As I let out a short cry, Kaylin closed his eyes, and a faint mist began to gather over his body. He was going dreamwalking, taking his body out on the astral. I'd gone with him a couple of times, and each time it had been like journeying through a foreign land.

As we watched, he began to shimmer, and I remembered how it had felt, like becoming a river of silver, molten and fluid, then vanishing into the shadows as one of their own. And then—in a flurry of smoke and mist—Kaylin vanished. I whirled around to see what the cloud was doing, and sure enough, it had moved. It was backing up, and I caught a blur of movement going toward it.

Ulean, can you see them? What's happening?

Yes, I can feel them on the slipstream. Kaylin—his demon is coming out—

Before she could finish the thought, a dark shadow with large wings dove through the cloud—we could see it clear as day—and there was a loud wail. It was almost more of a sonic screech, barely within hearing range but enough to send all of us to our knees. I pressed my hands to my ears, trying to stifle the noise, but it rang like a sonorous bell, on and on, reverberating in my head.

I heard the sound of scuffling, but when I tried to look up, to see what was happening, all that was visible was a blur of mist, a haze of sparkling energy swirling around the shadow. But they were fighting, that much was apparent. The shadow and the cloud struggled, creating a vortex between them, a tornado of cross-energies. I had a horrible feeling this was all going wrong. Kaylin was in danger and there was nothing any of us could do unless . . .

Ulean, is there any way you can help him?

I'm sorry, Cicely. I can see them clearer than you, but not to help. Not to intervene. But I can tell you, that sound is dangerous to you and the others. It can harm you.

At that moment, I realized my nose was bleeding. *This was what had killed the people Hunter had seen*! I knew it in my core.

"We have to get out of range—the sound, it will kill us!"

Check immediately yanked me to my feet and began barreling out of the chamber toward the outside. The others followed us, as best as they could, and we stumbled into the open, where the sound faded. My head was pounding, and I fell into the snow, gasping with the residual pain. Grieve joined me, holding his own head, and the others did as well.

Hunter knelt beside me. "That's what killed them. You were right. No wonder we found no signs of violence. They didn't think to get out of the way in time. Or . . . they couldn't. My guess is back then, the creature wasn't distracted by someone attacking it."

Kaylin! What was happening with Kaylin? I struggled to stand, but my stomach lurched, and I turned to the side, coughing until I spit up a mouthful of diluted blood. My throat felt raw, but my stomach quieted and my thoughts began to clear.

"Its sound . . . It causes internal bleeding. Your friends, your people, they all bled out when it attacked." I leaned against my grandfather, and he wrapped an arm around me.

Grieve struggled, moving over to sit by us. "Are you all right?"

I nodded, faintly, and looked around. Lannan and his men weren't anywhere in sight. "Lannan! Is he still inside?"

At that moment, the vampire appeared at the mouth of the Barrow. The look on his face was chilling. I'd never seen Lannan look so shaken.

"It's over. Cicely, you'd better come see."

Slowly, not wanting to see whatever it was that had put that expression on his face, I started forward. Check frowned, but Lannan shook his head.

"The creature . . . the cloud . . . It's gone. I believe Kaylin vanquished it." And then the Golden Boy turned and walked back into the Barrow, still looking oddly strained and bewildered.

With a nervous glance at Grieve and Hunter, I set out, escorted by Check. The others fell in behind us. As we entered the Barrow, once again the desolation and age hit me, but this time I didn't feel the inner push from Cherish to reclaim my place here. This time, all my worries and thoughts were with Kaylin. Lannan was standing against a half wall, and he nodded for us to join him.

I glanced around. "Where's Kaylin? Where did he . . ." But my voice trailed off as someone stepped from behind the wall. Kaylin? Or was it . . . Holy crap. I couldn't take my eyes off the creature that stood in front of us.

When we'd gone to the home of the Bat People in search of the charm to waken Kaylin's demon so he wouldn't slide into a permanent coma, we'd met them. The Bat People were the children of the night-veil demons, a hybrid created by the creatures. The Bat People were shadowy, tall, and gaunt, with skin stretched thin as if over a skeleton and wings resembling those of a bat. They had faceted, bulbous eyes. Though they were called the Bat People, they weren't shifters. Not like the Cambyra Fae. They lived in the shadows, in the Court of Dreams, where everything flickered in a perpetual state of half light.

Now, the creature that emerged from behind the wall looked like a morphed picture of Kaylin . . . and one of the Bat People. Not as tall as they were, for Kaylin was fairly short, the figure stood there. Wings had emerged from his back, and though the face he wore was Kaylin's, and his hair was still long and ponytail bound, he had taken on an otherworldly look.

"Kaylin? Is that . . ." I didn't know how to ask my question. Hell, I didn't even know what to ask.

But he knew. He laughed, and I realized I'd heard that laughter once before: when I woke up his demon and brought him back to himself. I'd heard the laughter before Kaylin had regained control over himself, before he'd harnessed the night-veil.

"You know who I am, Cicely. You know me."

"You're Kaylin's demon." No question, just an acknowledgment of facts. I knew I was right, and my heart began to shatter, just a little.

"Yes, I am Kaylin, and I am his demon, but Kaylin is now the one in the background. I don't know if he exists separate from me now. How can he? I've fully emerged." And then, Kaylin—or his demon—softened, and a faint smile flickered on his lips. "Kaylin would have died unless I took over. Together, we vanquished the cloud creature."

"Can you . . . Will you let him return now? Kaylin, that is?" Again, I knew the answer and didn't want to hear it, but I had to know for certain.

"How can I? When I emerged, when we threw ourselves into the fight together, his only chance was to give way to me fully. He now lives in my body, rather than the other way around." He stepped back. "Kaylin knew that you couldn't fight the creature. He knew that he was the only one who stood a chance of defeating it."

Horrified, realizing that we'd just lost Kaylin—that he was gone from us, and probably forever—I sought for something to say. But there were no words there. *Thank you* wouldn't suffice. And *I'm sorry* would only make the night-veil laugh. He wasn't sorry to be in control of Kaylin's body.

Hunter stepped forward, his hand on my shoulder. "Demon, tell the girl the truth. She needs to know, for her conscience."

"What?" I darted a glance at my grandfather. What was he talking about?

But Kaylin-the-demon knew, because he let out another laugh. "All right, Father Owl, I'll let her off the hook."

Turning to me, his wings fluttered softly in the dim light as he crossed his arms. "Cicely, this would have happened anyway, eventually. Night-veil demons, when implanted in the soul of one of the magic-born, evolve. After we waken, we metamorphose into our final forms. Kaylin's transformation just came far sooner than it would have if he hadn't given over control to me. On a conscious level he didn't know this would happen, but deep inside? He knew."

As I continued to stare at him, Kaylin ducked his head. Once again the sly, sweet smile I so keenly recognized broke through, and I caught a glimpse of him peering through the night-veil's eyes. "I guess it's a good thing Luna wouldn't have me after all. I would have broken her heart." And then he turned toward the entrance of the Barrow.

"Kaylin, where are you going?" My paralysis broken, I took off after him. "Don't leave. Night-veil or not, you're our friend."

Tears gathered at the corners of my eyes. I wanted desperately to do something—to change what was happening. I'd always been a control freak, and not being able to make a difference in a situation like this was terribly painful for me.

Kaylin turned, his wings almost whipping across my face. He stepped closer, and I realized that he'd retreated again, and now it was the night-veil facing me. He reached out and pulled me close.

"You, too, went through a transmutation, Cicely. You are not the same person you were a month ago. Everything changes. Everyone evolves."

"I know but . . ." There was nothing I could say to that. He was right, of course. I just didn't want to say good-bye.

"I would thank you for freeing me, but that would only make you feel worse. So I will say this once. Remember it well: There was nothing you could do. You could not fight your opponent, and Kaylin and I . . . *we* could. Kaylin made the choice. He knew what had to be done. Don't tarnish his memory with your tears. He chose to help you in this war you fight. Let him claim his victory."

And then he let go of my shoulders.

"Where will you go?"

"First, I must return to the Court of Dreams. Then . . . I don't know. I doubt our paths will cross again, but there is never anything certain in this world, so for now, I simply say farewell, Queen Cicely Waters. May you destroy Myst and all her kin, and live happily ever after in your icy realm." With that he turned and ducked out of the Barrow, and Kaylin Chen was gone from my life.

I turned back to the others, feeling bleak and worn. I wanted to cry but felt numb all the way through. And we still had a quest ahead of us. There wasn't time to mourn someone who hadn't died. Kaylin was gone, yes, but he still lived, and he had become who he was destined to be.

"Let's go. We have to find Myst's heartstone."

Nobody said a word, but we fell back into our marching order, and I led the way through the Barrow, following the hollow and empty passages by what seemed to be rote memory. I didn't know where we were going, not really. If you pressed me to tell you how to get there, I wouldn't be able to give directions. But I knew the way, as sure as I knew my own heartbeat.

"Cicely, Kaylin saved our lives. His demon is right, let him have the victory, and let him claim his sacrifice." Grieve reached out to take my hand and we walked in silence through the tunnels. Lannan and Hunter were a step behind, and for once, Lannan kept his mouth shut, a taciturn look on his face.

The labyrinth of passages led us deep into the heart of the Barrow. As we neared what felt like should be the center, I realized we were almost to Myst's old bedroom, the place where I'd seen her heartstone being created. I swallowed my fear and pointed to a set of double doors.

"Through there. Myst's bedroom, and the place where she vanished with her heartstone. I don't exactly remember what to look for in order to trigger the secret chamber, but whatever it was, it should still be there."

And then we were at the door. Check and Fearless went first, opening it. As soon as they gave the all clear, I followed them in, and everything came flooding back.

The room was still beautiful, done in silver and black with brilliant blue accents. The bedcovers had long vanished, as had the upholstery. But the ebony frame of the bed was there, as were the swirling designs on the walls and the other assorted pieces of furniture that had withstood the ravages of time. In the Barrows, though, the years flowed differently, and so it was like stepping into a time capsule where anything might still exist.

I closed my eyes, searching for ghosts, searching for shades from the past, but nothing had happened here to the people of the Indigo Court. The only blood to stain our walls and floors had been that of our meals. We were the ones who had perpetuated the slaughter, not the victims.

The quiet unsettled me. There should be ghosts. There should be screaming specters racing through the hallways, considering how bloodthirsty we were and how many we had killed. But nothing. Just a deep emptiness that echoed through the Barrow.

"Why does this feel so alien? I lived here, it was my home, and yet it has no life of its own. Maybe that's it. This feels like an empty house that was abandoned but that never took on a personality."

Lannan surprised me by speaking up. "Barrows, from what I understand, are almost as much of a living organism as the Fae who inhabit them. But this place can never quite be the same. Myst is an unnatural creature bent on achieving something for which she was never destined. I think she may have created it in almost a mockery of the Barrows she coveted but wasn't allowed to rule."

That made sense. She could never create a true Fae Barrow because she was hybrid. The Vampiric Fae were neither vampire nor Fae, but a demonic blend of both, and so anything coming out of the Indigo Court would be as alien as the Shadow Hunters were. And this Barrow? As devoid of charm and any sense of welcoming as Myst.

I crossed to the opposite wall and searched. The stone was cold and unyielding to the touch but then, after a few moments, I felt the shallow depression and pressed it. A secret door slid open, and I glanced at the others.

"We found it. I guess . . . it's time to go?" It took me a moment to figure out they were waiting for my orders. I swallowed my fear and motioned for Check to take the lead again. This was as far as I remembered, and I'd never been down this secret passage. We'd all be flying blind from here on out, and I recognized my duty to my Court. I couldn't go in the forefront now that we had found the passage.

As Check stepped past me to enter the passage, he stopped then turned to say, "We won't need illumination here. It still glows. Her heartstone must still be at its core or the light would die out." With that he moved forward, followed by Fearless. I was third, then after me, Grieve, Hunter, Lannan, and the rest of the guards. Now that Kaylin was gone, we were thirteen, not counting Ulean.

Once again, for the third time in the past two months, I was following the path in search of a heartstone. One of those times, it had been to retrieve Lainule's gem in order that she wouldn't die. The other had been to hide my own. This time, I was in search of one to use as a weapon—to destroy Myst.

Third time's the charm.

The corridor in Myst's unnatural Barrow was dark, but an icy-neon-blue light broke through the darkness. Considering she drove the snows, I had expected to find this place set in a world of ice and snow, like my own, but instead, it was deep rock and shadow. Myst might fancy herself the Queen of Winter, but she had stolen the title and was co-opting the storms. A thought crossed my mind as we hurried along the corridor.

Ulean, when Myst is defeated, will I gain her power over the winter? I am the Queen of Snow and Ice, yet I'm a wind witch.

You already have power over the winter; you just haven't had the time to learn how to use it.

Her answer startled me and set me to thinking. If I had been given the power over snow and ice when I'd taken the throne, why hadn't I known about it—or at least been told about it? And how long would it take me to learn how to use it? Could I possibly use it as a weapon against Myst now?

Ulean—can I—

No. I know what you're going to ask, Cicely, and the answer is no. You don't have the power to use it against Myst. She's too well versed in the energy, and you would be like a child trying to code a complex program. You're new to the realm you now rule, even though you were destined for the throne. Just because you wear the title doesn't mean you can claim the power yet. Once this is over, Strict and the shamans will help you learn to control the winter storms. You will be more powerful than most other Fae Queens, save for those in the Great Courts.

How so?

Because you already can summon the winds and you are half magic-born, which increases your ability to use those powers.

I'm a hybrid, like Myst, then.

A hybrid, yes—in a way. But like Myst? No, never. Not even though you were her daughter. You may find yourself to be more stoic than others because of that lifetime, and because of that life, you will wear the power of the throne well once you discover your confidence, but Cicely, trust that you'll never become Myst. You have heart, and you have love and compassion. And those three things cancel out whatever heritage she may have left your soul.

Somewhat comforted, I studied the walls as we passed through the tunnel. "What is this rock?"

Hunter gave me an odd look. "Rock is rock."

I grinned at him. "No, I mean is it granite or basalt or . . ."

"Ah, yummanii terms. I don't know the definitions, but this rock is lava rock and came from deep in the world, uplifted by a great force and pressure as the mountains folded under the earth's plates. The rock tempered over time. And here it exists both in the world and yet outside of it, as do all lands within the scope of the Barrows, and Barrow places. But yes, it is a hard, unyielding stone."

"But how did Myst create this? She was one of the Unseelie—the Dark Fae. But she wasn't a queen, and she wasn't, I gather, particularly powerful compared to the shamans. Even though she was turned by Geoffrey, how did she end up as . . . well . . . as the great and powerful Myst?" I grimaced at my own pun, even as I said it. The wizard of Oz had been a charlatan, illusion and parlor tricks. Myst was far more than that.

From directly behind me, Hunter laughed. "I can tell you a little about that. Live as long as I do, hide in the forests and shadows long enough, and you learn things. When my son, Wrath, took the throne of Summer, he kept in touch with me, and I was privy to many secrets that would have otherwise gone untold."

A shiver raced up my spine, but it was a good one. My grandfather had stories to tell me. The thought that I might spend years to come curled up by a fire with him, learning about our people while the winter raged outside our Barrow, sounded positively delightful.

"You know the story of how Myst and Geoffrey plotted to seize control of the Unseelie Fae and the vampires by working together?"

I nodded. "When she found out she was more powerful than he, she double-crossed him and killed most of his men. That's what started the war between the true vampires and the Vampiric Fae, right Lannan?"

Lannan grunted but pushed a few steps closer. "Yes, that's right. Both of the fools were mad, if you ask me. But then, it takes a madman to think he can be so wanton and fly in the face of established order. The Crimson Court only kept Geoffrey around after that incident because he was more dangerous to let go. Keep your friends close and your enemies closer, and all of that folderol. I think, too, there may have been some sort of misguided loyalty in letting him remain alive, but it was not our place to speak up. Even my sister doesn't understand the reasoning of our Queen at times. It's not up to us to question her motives, however. We are to simply obey."

Check pointed out a root in the floor, and I skirted it, in turn pointing it out to Hunter and Lannan.

Hunter lithely hopped over it. "Well, after communications broke down and Myst and Geoffrey had established their feud, Myst went into hiding. She knew she wasn't powerful enough yet to take on more than the handful of vampires she already had. So she and her fellow companions, all of whom she had turned, first returned to the Fae Barrows, but nobody knew what to do with them there. They retreated into the wilds. I believe it was about that time that the Shadow Hunter nature began to exert itself, and they were exiled from the Fae communities for good."

"So it was sink or swim for her." I tried to imagine what she might have felt—alone with just her few companions, disowned by her people and knowing the vampires were out to get her. No wonder she'd gone a little nuts.

"Don't feel too sorry for her. Myst was power hungry before she was turned, and the transformation only left her more so. She went into hiding and began ordering her people to kidnap whatever Fae they happened across. They started turning them to increase their forces, but it didn't always work right."

"So they started abducting Fae . . . but what about children? I know they can breed." What I wanted to ask, but wasn't quite ready to, was *When was I born?*

"Around that time, one of the women found out she was pregnant and the baby was born vicious, changed—more powerful than the parents themselves. That was when they realized they could still reproduce, and so began to build their community through forced breeding. Because of the cerulean cast to the children's skin, Myst named her realm the Indigo Court, and firmly punished anybody who tried to go up against her. I gather she was gifted with a knack for torture, and her people began to fear her."

Enforced breeding, kidnapping, anything for survival. "Did Myst anticipate being where she's at now? Did she always look to ruling the world?"

Hunter gave me a sad smile. "Don't dictators always anticipate wielding great power? I don't think she thought it would be in this manner, but yes, I think she always wanted to rule the world. She had kidnapped a couple shamans first thing, from her people. While I'm not sure how, she forced them to develop rituals to transfer more power to her. Somewhere along the line, she ended up with power over the winter weather, and over spiders, and she became Queen Myst, of the Indigo Court."

I wondered if she'd killed them, to absorb their power. Or maybe, turned and obeying her, they'd been willing to help her grow and evolve.

"In some ways, I have to admit I admire Myst." I didn't want to say the words aloud, but it felt like they should be said, as an acknowledgment to my enemy's strength. Never underestimate your opponent, and always remember how strong they are.

"Why? Because she was your mother?" Hunter wasn't being a smart ass. He was asking a real question.

"No. I mean, yes, she was my mother . . . but no, that's not why I admire her. She took a situation that had gone terribly wrong and turned it to her advantage. She didn't give in; she stood up and took charge. She's a survivor, and she does whatever she needs to in order to see her people thrive. It may be some real freaky-assed crap she pulls, but she has goals, and she's following her dream."

Lannan snorted. "Just because you *can* do something doesn't mean you should."

I glanced over my shoulder at him. He grinned. "True enough. But what can I say? The woman is ambitious. Just because I admit that, doesn't mean I won't do my best to destroy her."

"Good to know." He started to say more but then stopped, pointing ahead.

I turned. There, in front of us, stood a door. Most likely it would lead us to the first guardian. Meaning the first adversary. And all guardians of all heartstones were set to fight to the death.

Taking a deep breath, I turned and motioned to Check. "Everybody at the ready. Weapons at hand, please. Expect trouble on the other side, if this follows the usual pattern of things. Check, once we're ready, open the door, and let's see what we're facing."

As Check reached for the handle, I clutched my dagger, the hilt solidly implanted in the palm of my hand. We might find a monster on the other side, or a ghost, or a riddle or . . . who knew what?

Check opened the door, quickly to take whatever might be on the other side by surprise. And there, in the middle of the archway, blocking our path, was the first guardian at the gate. We were facing a gigantic snow weaver, and the eight-legged freak looked overly delighted to see us.

Chapter 16

The snow weaver made no move to attack, but waited, blocking the entry. We were facing Myst's first guardian, which meant we were on the right track to finding her heartstone. But considering it was a guardian, the snow weaver was bound to be more powerful and magical than its kin.

Check jumped back out of reach as the rest of us took a step back.

"Lovely. Just lovely." I tapped my dagger against my hand, trying to figure out our best approach. "Watch your ears, guys. And eyes. The snow weavers are deadly, and they can charm the hell out of you. There won't be any reasoning with it. It's either *My way or the highway.*"

As we shifted into a semicircle around the door, the spider's crafty gaze followed us, taking in every movement. Most guardians seemed to be able to talk, so I thought about engaging it, but the fact that snow weavers were versed in luring in their victims meant a conversation wasn't all that appetizing of a thought. At least not from my side of the fence.

Ulean, what do you suggest?

This one is cunning and wily. I sense a great hunger, and

she cannot let you pass; therefore, you must fight her. Be watchful for her magic. The siren song is deep within her, and I think you may have a difficult battle on your hands if you let her speak.

Great. A female? They tend to be more deadly than the males.

Always the way, Cicely. Always the way.

I turned to Check. "We fight, but if she begins to speak, we have to silence her." Before we could move, however, a faint whisper of song sprang up, and the first few bars instantly plunged me into a deep sadness, filling me with regret. The music shifted then, ever slightly, and promised hope if only I'd reach out and embrace the singer. I struggled against the desire to move forward, all too aware that this was the snow weaver's trap. She really was a siren.

Cicely—don't listen and tell your men to fight her song!

I shook my head, trying to clear my thoughts. *I know, I'm trying to shake out of it enough to—Fuck!*

One of the guards—one of our men—had lurched forward and was nearly within reach of her long, jointed legs. Check leaped forward, grabbing the man by the arm and slamming him back, throwing him to the ground. The guard groaned, but his eyes cleared, and he struggled to his feet and scrambled back.

The snow weaver let out a noise that sounded like a heavy sigh, and the song intensified, but Ulean swept through with a huge gust of wind to divert the music into the slipstream, away from us. The resulting static disrupted the spell and the spider fell silent, but the feeling of malevolence grew stronger, and I had the feeling she was pissed out of her mind that we'd put a stop to her magical song.

"We have to go in. She's probably not going to try to lure us again, and if she does, Ulean seems to be able to disrupt her. But she's deadly, so one bite can kill." I glanced back at the guards. "I hate to say this, but Lannan, one of your men might be the best bet. You guys are already dead."

He gave me one of *those* looks and shook his head. "No, we are not dead. Well, yes we are, but there's a lack of respect in your words, dear Cicely. However, that aside, I concur. Her poison cannot harm us." Motioning to his burliest guard, he said, "Mort, get your ass in there and do your best to skewer her. She needs to die."

Mort—I supposed it was short for Mortimer—stepped forward. He was tall and stocky, a barrel-chested man who fit the uniform he was wearing, which happened to be a pair of dark jeans, a Metallica T-shirt, and a black leather jacket. He wore a motorcycle cap that was studded with little spikes. As he moved toward the spider, he pulled out a wicked-looking knife with a long serrated blade.

The snow weaver shifted as he moved toward her, and the glint in her eyes told me that she recognized he was ready to rumble. She scuttled into a better position so she could use her web for balance and yet rear up, ready to strike.

Mort gauged the distance between them and eyed her soft underbelly. That's where the majority of spiders were most vulnerable. As he jockeyed for position, so did she, and it was like some macabre dance—the vampire and the spider, trying to find their perfect balance.

And then, because somebody had to make the first move, and she was obviously waiting for him to, Mort leaped forward, sweeping his blade through the air to land in the belly of the snow weaver.

The spider reared up again, then fell on him, plunging her fangs deep into his shoulder. He let out a string of curses, but pulled out the knife and struck her again. She scuttled back, tearing herself off the blade with a sucking sound.

I thought I detected a hint of confusion in her look. Mort wasn't dead; he wasn't on the ground. Which meant chances were good that she didn't know he was a vampire and immune to her poisons.

Mort followed her, but she stopped at the edge of the door. She wouldn't run away. She was a guardian, bound to stay and fight, and she was doing her damnedest. She leaped forward, oozing blood and fluid from her abdomen, and landed on Mort again, once more sinking her fangs into him. She missed his heart—a good thing—and one last time, he brought his blade up, directly beneath her as she straddled him. The snow weaver shuddered, and the lights in her multifaceted eyes went out. The vampire shoved her off him, and then stabbed her again to make certain she was dead.

"Good work." Lannan helped Mort up and examined his wounds. Though the gaping holes in his clothes were still there, his wounds were already healing over. He'd be fine. His heart was intact, and therefore his body would heal.

"Thank you." I didn't know what else to say, but acknowledging that he'd saved us a good deal of trouble and lives lost seemed important. "Are you all right? Did she harm you?"

Mort gave me a long look. It was impossible to read what was behind those dark eyes. "Thank you, Your Majesty. I'm fine."

Well, he was certainly more polite than his boss. There was no sarcasm in his words, and for once, I wasn't left with a sour taste in my mouth. I motioned for Check to take a gander through the door. He quietly sidled up to it and peered around the corner. After a moment, he leaned back.

"A wide cavern, Your Majesty. Like a field of boulders across a plain of ice. Dark, but illuminated lightly from a glow within the frozen wastes. I could detect no movement, but that doesn't guarantee there isn't something in there waiting for us."

"Oh, you can bet there's something there. We'll just have to figure it out when we get there. From what I can tell, there are usually three to five guardians set by the Queens. They get progressively harder to pass the farther you go along. I'm not looking forward to running this gauntlet, but now that we're over the first hurdle, we'd better get a move on, because the others might figure out we're here."

I wanted to add that I knew for sure they would. That, when I'd set up my own guardians, they'd formed a network. If one went down, the others would be alerted. But that would be giving away my own secrets, and I wasn't comfortable doing so. I was also aware that, by protecting myself, I was putting my friends in jeopardy by not telling them what I knew. Either way, it was a losing situation. But self-preservation won out. I kept my mouth shut.

Finally, I accepted the wisdom of what Lainule had tried to teach me—the Queen must protect her heartstone above all else. The Queen *was* the heart of the Barrow. It felt both a selfish and conceited thought, but it was true. And sometimes the truth wasn't politically correct.

"Are we ready, then?" Check gave me an odd look, but when I met his gaze, he simply smiled softly and turned to lead us through the door. Sometimes I had the feeling he could look through my skin and see everything going on beneath the surface.

We entered the cavern and found ourselves on a sheer sheet of ice. Boulders—large blocks of granite that had cleaved off the mountain—littered the enormous chamber. The other side was difficult to make out. In fact, I wasn't even sure if we could really see it from here. I thought I might be able to make out a distant wall, but the light was too dim, and the chamber too large to know for certain.

The ice had a peculiar sheen to it. Unlike the ice in the realm of Winter, it bore only streaks of blue through it, no pinks or purples. Faint slate streaks that raced along the glassy surface. Pinpricks of light, sparkling like silver stars, shone from within the ice through the pale, hazy film of frost. Was this a giant ocean frozen over? Or simply ice on the ground? Or was it something else entirely, something Myst had managed to conjure from whatever magic her shamans had been able to manifest?

I leaned down and trailed my fingers across the surface. A faint pulse echoed from deep within the frozen waste, sending a tingle through my skin. For a moment it startled me, and I just about pulled away, expecting it to hurt, before realizing it actually was making me smile. There was something familiar about the sensation. And then I understood—it was the ice itself that tickled me.

Perhaps it was different than the ice back in my realm, but the feeling of the frozen water was comforting, and all ice came from the same underlying source. Myst might be an upstart, but she *had* managed to tap into Winter's energy, and she *did* understand its nature.

Which makes her even more dangerous. Ulean, how much do you think she knows about me? I mean, she knows I was her daughter, but how well do you think Myst understands who I am . . . and what I am becoming?

Ulean gently gusted past. I could feel her swirling amid the frosty air. She liked the winter. Even though summer winds might be fun to work with, I knew that Ulean preferred the cold, blustery gales of the dark months.

I think that she knows you better than you might wish for. Myst may be lost in her desire for control, but she does not underestimate her enemies, and like it or not, the two of you have commonalities. Cicely, you may have to try to understand her better, in order to defeat her. Find your similarities and you will find her weakness.

But finding her heartstone and destroying it seems easier.

Never count your storms before they brew. While you may find her heartstone, I have the feeling you will have to face the Queen herself.

And with that to chew on, I stood, surveying the vast chamber. I closed my eyes, searching my intuition. *Ulean, can you tell me which way to go?*

I will scout around, but I think . . . I think you can figure out which way without me. I'll return in a moment.

As she swept off, I inhaled, then let out my breath slowly, searching the slipstream, trying to feel my way around. To the right the wasteland of ice continued, and I could sense nothing stirring. To the center? Again, a long uninterrupted stretch. But to the left—to the left, I caught the faintest hint of motion, and then, a hush as whatever it was felt me probing the slipstream.

Did you sense it? Ulean returned.

Yes, to the left. What is it?

I honestly don't know, but whatever it is, it's big and lumbering. I can't give you an estimate, though, because it feels like it phases in and out of this plane. However, I can tell you that it isn't really an Elemental. Truly? It's like no creature I've ever before seen.

That was so not reassuring. A large, lumbering behemoth

that wasn't an Elemental. Not much to go on with regard to
what it was, or how dangerous it might be.

Did you sense any malevolence?

*Like the snow weaver? No. I'm sorry I'm so vague, but
I'm perplexed. I've never encountered this creature before,
or anything like it. There is sentience, yes, and intelligence,
but it feels distanced.*

Maybe it was an animal of some sort. Which would make
it harder to kill, at least for me. An animal wouldn't have any
personal motivation against us—it would just be doing what
it was summoned to do: protect.

I told the others what we were facing.

"How big is it?"

"Good question. Ulean says large, but she doesn't seem to
be able to pinpoint what it is, or how large it is. Apparently it
phases in and out, so it has to be magical to some degree. But
there's no deliberate ill will there. The thing was probably
summoned rather than being one of Myst's creatures."

Hunter frowned. "That doesn't give us much to go on, and
it doesn't make for confidence. Let me go up front with the
men. I've seen many things through my life; perhaps I'll be
able to recognize whatever this is."

As he moved to the forefront and we continued on, Hunter
suddenly turned. "The temperature of the air has just plummeted at least a good twenty to thirty degrees, all within one
step. Magical cold coming up. A few more feet and you'll
enter it. This is no natural cooling. No, it's caused by something, and I have a feeling we're going to meet up with whatever it is all too soon."

I steeled myself, and sure enough, another couple of yards
and the temperature of the air plunged. If we'd been yummanii or strict magic-born, the sudden drop would have
been dangerous, but without Kaylin here, we were all either
immune or conditioned to the cold.

My breath appeared in tiny white puffs as I pulled my
cloak tighter around my shoulders. The landscape hadn't
changed much, save that we were behind a tall group of
boulders. Clusters of them dotted the entire cavern, and this

collection happened to stand a good ten to twelve feet high, and higher still the farther we went. It was like a forest of stone.

"Where is this creature?" Hunter had no sooner than asked the question when we broke out of the stone forest and into a clearing. There, ahead, was a wall of snow and ice and an opening leading into yet another cavern. But between us and the dark maw stood a creature that seemed to be wavering in and out of existence—plane-shifting as we watched.

I smiled. How could I help it? The creature reminded me of a cross between an elephant and a mastodon, but it was a vibrant blue, with eyes as silver as the moon. It had a trunk, and a tail, and four great legs on which it stood, and yet the fur on its back was long and wispy, looking so silky I wanted to bury my head in it.

"It's beautiful," I whispered.

"Yes, and deadly," my grandfather answered.

"You've seen this before?"

"A few times. The creature is definitely a plane-shifter, and you're right—it's not evil, but it is a summoned guardian and is bound to obey to the death. It's a paralaxium, and it's from the plane of Ice, so in a sense it is somewhat like an Elemental, but not at all like Ulean or the Ice Elementals. It's simply a creature that happens to live there."

"How is it dangerous?"

"Unfortunately, it can kill you with a touch if you are of living flesh and blood." He glanced over his shoulder. "They are rare and beautiful beasts."

As I studied the creature, it studied me back but made no move against us. Most guardians were set to a specific area—cross the boundary line and they would react. There was no telling how close we'd have to get before the paralaxium would charge, and I wasn't quite sure I wanted to find out.

"How do they kill?" Grieve turned to Hunter.

Hunter shrugged. "A touch will drain the warmth of the body, plunging you into instant hypothermia. And I do mean absolute hypothermia. You'll go from your normal temperature to zero in ten seconds flat. The body goes into arrest.

Even those of us from the realm of Snow and Ice—even you, Cicely, the Queen of Snow and Ice, would die."

"So, we don't want to pet the pretty pony." I let out a long sigh. "How do we kill it? We don't dare touch it. So, is there a way to banish it back to the plane of Ice? Can we do something to make it disappear?" Even as I suggested it, I knew that was a long shot. None of us had that kind of power. As far as how Myst had managed to get the creature here, I had no clue. If she could reach into the plane of Ice, we had bigger worries on our hands than we knew.

When I looked over at the creature, it met my gaze again. The giant silver eyes were incredibly soft, almost gentle, and I wanted to talk to it—to get to know what it was like. Ulean was right, there was no malevolence here, no hatred. The creature would guard this gate because it had been bound to do so, but not because of any anger toward us or loyalty to Myst. And that knowledge left me furious. I didn't *want* to destroy the paralaxium. It was, as Hunter had said, a rare and beautiful giant, deadly but without guile.

"What do we do? I don't . . ." I paused, turning to my grandfather. "I don't want to destroy it—I don't want that on my conscience." Collateral damage was unavoidable, I knew that. But Myst had put me in a place I hated right now, and I wished she were here so I could unleash all my frustration and anger on her.

"The only way would be to break the binding, or to banish it back to its own plane." He cocked his head. "I somehow doubt any of the guards have the knowledge of how to do this. And neither does Grieve nor I. Nor, I doubt, the vampire— Lannan."

"That would leave me. And I . . ." I studied the paralaxium, skirting around the creature, trying to assess how close I could get before setting off its alarms.

Ulean, how do you banish a creature back to its Elemental plane? Do you know? Can you find out?

Cicely, there are ways, but you do not have the knowledge. I might be able to find someone to help you, but who knows what kind of cascade such an action might bring?

Then tell me, is it possible to distract it so we can slip by? Can we outrun it, do you think? I was searching for anything that might allow us to let this creature live. The more I examined it, the less inclined I was to attempt an attack. Not just because our chances of fighting it were pretty much nil, but because it was trapped here, like Myst had trapped the Snow Hag.

Wait . . . the Snow Hag! She was bound to the snow, and maybe she would be able to help. I made a split-second decision. *Ulean, I need you to go find the Snow Hag and bring her here. She should be able to travel swiftly through this storm—it will be like old home week to her. If anybody can help us, I imagine she might. But you must hurry. I'm afraid if we try to attack the paralaxium it will destroy at least some of my men, and in the end, be destroyed. And it's a death that might not need to happen.*

I understand, Cicely. I will return as soon as I can. And with that she swept away.

I turned to the others and told them what I'd done. "It's the only way I can see to get through this gate without a loss of life. And truth is"—I glanced back at the paralaxium—"I don't want to kill it. I don't know what it is I'm feeling, but I think we need to free it. We need to get through this guardian without shedding blood."

"You make me proud to be your grandfather," Hunter said.

Check and Fearless flashed me smiles, and I realized they, too, had been taken in by the creature. Grieve said nothing, but rubbed my back as I stood there. Finally, we stepped farther away from the creature and settled down on one of the boulders to wait for Ulean's return.

As we huddled in the dim light flickering up from the ice, I contemplated the future without Myst. I had to keep some hope. Kaylin was gone, that much we knew. But he wasn't dead, so at least we had some comfort there. Grieve and I would live in the unending winter, while Rhiannon and Chatter would live in a world of summer and sun. The prospect of days stretching into decades into centuries and millennia suddenly felt daunting—more than I could take in, and once again, I felt overwhelmed by the changes through which I'd gone.

But I'll get there, I thought. *Every day my life will become a little bit more my new normal. Every day my new life will become a little more engrained.*

"Penny for your thoughts?" Grieve bumped against me, his voice soft and soothing. "You seem a million miles away."

"Perhaps I am." I cocked my head to smile at him, then took his hand. "I think it's just . . . shock. The shock of this war, the culture shock I'm going through, the physical shock of the transformation. It's enough to send me spinning, and sometimes, when we pause long enough for me to listen to my thoughts, I feel like I'm sliding into a deep hole, unable to sort out all that's happened. If we defeat Myst, I'll have the time to puzzle out who I am and what I'm doing. Until then, I feel like I'm making things up on the go."

"Flying by the seat of your pants, so to speak?" His eyes twinkled then, the stars shimmering softly within the luminous black void. "And yes, when—not if, but when—we defeat Myst, then you will take time to rest, to learn more about the life you've entered."

"Lainule tried to warn me. Several times she warned me that if I was successful, things would never be the same. I didn't understand what she was talking about, and of course, she couldn't tell me." I worried my lip, wishing once again that the former Summer Queen was still with us. She'd been a fountain of strength, and even though I thought, at times, that she was hard and cruel, now I understood why she had been the way she was.

"What would you have done if she had been able to tell you? Do you know? Would you have let her die? Or . . . would you have gone through with it?"

The question had run through my mind a thousand times in the past month. By finding Lainule's heartstone and returning it to her, I'd not only saved her life, but I'd set into motion the events leading to Rhiannon and me being crowned the new Fae Queens. When I thought over the alternative—Lainule dying, with no one to take her place—the answer was obvious. Though a little part of me still rebelled, still wished I'd never returned to New Forest.

"That's not a fair question, and you know it. I may have had the illusion of choice, but there could be only one outcome when you think about it."

Grieve laughed. "You always had a choice. You could have said no and walked away."

"But what kind of person would I be if I'd have done that?" I glared at him. My love was boundless for the man, but sometimes I wanted to clobber him.

"You would have been the kind of person who could never have successfully taken the crown. You'd have been more like Myst than like yourself. You think Myst would sacrifice her own future for anybody else?"

He wrapped his arm around my shoulder then, and pulled me close. "I love you, Cicely, because of all your flaws and all your wonderful attributes. I love you because there would never have been a question in your mind as to what you should do. You had a choice, yes—you did, regardless of what you think. But you chose this path. You chose the harder road."

"And am I now all the better for it?" I thought of all the permutations of what might have been, but they were so much fodder for fantasy now.

With a deep sigh, I swept the whole conversation away. "It's too late in the day for philosophical musings. We're in the midnight of this battle, and we just have to hold on till morning. Best to leave the musings for after—for when we look back and say, *'Do you remember when we were sitting in the cave, waiting for Ulean to help us with the paralaxium?'* Then we can decipher the web that brought us here."

"No ghosts of the past, then, while we wait?" Grieve brushed my lips with his but stopped as Lannan sauntered up. "What do you want, Altos?"

"I wonder, the guards are keeping watch, but the question remains, does Myst know we're here? Why aren't we dismantling that beast? My men will not be harmed by the kiss of cold." The look on his face told us he thought we were making a mistake.

"That beast is a creature from an outer plane, and I don't really think it's wise to go killing it off if we can help it." I let out an exasperated sigh. "Lannan, you are not so far up on the food chain that you have no enemies. If the paralaxium's people—or whatever you call them—find out we killed an enslaved member of their tribe, we're all on the shit list. And while you vampires won't be destroyed by the cold, even I am not immune to that bone-chilling touch. What if they came to New Forest and rampaged through the town?"

Lannan let out a harsh, short laugh. "Cicely, by the time we're done, New Forest will be empty. Myst and her freak-show parade drain the life from the city even while we're sitting here twiddling our thumbs. By the time this war is over, the town's going to be dead. Do you understand? People are dying right and left."

Grieve broke in. "I thought that shouldn't bother you, considering how little regard you seem to have for anyone not part of the Vampire Nation."

"Wolf-boy, watch your manners. You may be a king, but I'm Regent and blood brother to the Emissary. We are both nobility." Lannan crossed his arms, staring with open hostility.

"Enough!" I was tired of the testosterone games. "The both of you stop this. It's time to have this out, and you're both going to listen to me and then shut the fuck up. Yes, I fucked Lannan, and I liked it, and he saved my life. But I'm married to Grieve, whom I love with all my heart and with whom I've thrown my lot. Lannan, show some respect to my husband—he is the King of Snow and Ice. And Grieve, Lannan saved my life. Don't forget it."

They stared at me, both openmouthed. After a moment, Lannan shrugged, nodded, and returned to his guards. Grieve stared at him with a shadowed look, but my wolf was silent. I'd had some impact on the pair of them.

I was about to say something when there was a noise from the direction in which we'd already come. Turning around, I saw a swirl of snow come whirling in—a tiny vortex about four feet high, but fierce and thick. And then the snow twister stopped, and there, in the middle of the cavern, stood the Snow Hag.

Ulean swept past me. *I found her and asked if she would come to us. She agreed. I think she may be able to help, though I don't know how.*

Thank you—we need all the help we can get.

Turning to the Snow Hag, I chose my words cautiously. "One might welcome one of the Wilding Fae, though caution her to proceed carefully, for there are many dangers in this place."

The Snow Hag grinned, her snaggletooth glistening in the dim light. "And one of the Wilding Fae might question a queen as to what the Winter would have her do."

"A bargain might be struck, if one of the Wilding Fae would agree and could help. But the danger is real and the task, great."

"The Winter Queen might realize that even the Wilding Fae know that there are times for bargains, and there are times for great deeds. And this would be the latter. What would Winter's service be?" With a touch of her nose, she as good as offered me her help for free.

"A few yards farther along, one will find a paralaxium from the plane of Ice. A dangerous beast, and yet, a Winter Queen would choose not to destroy it, but to send it home if possible, unscathed and freed from the snare by which Myst bound it. One might wonder if the Wilding Fae know of a method of doing so?"

Trying to explain what I wanted in the strange cadence of bargaining speak wasn't quite so easy, but I had the feeling I had gotten my point across by the look of delight that spread across the Snow Hag's face.

With a quicksilver laugh, she whirled, sending a shower of snow to cloak me in white. "Oh, the Queen of Winter might just prove why she is worthy of the crown she wears. Yes, some of the Wilding Fae have the knowledge of how to do this—present company included. So, a queen might wish that the paralaxium return home, safe and free?"

"If one such as the Snow Hag could manage the deed, then yes, the Winter would bid her to act, but to also keep herself safe."

And then, without further word, the Snow Hag set foot ahead. We followed, at a safe distance, and when she came to the paralaxium, the Snow Hag began a singsong chant, in a language that was so old it made me want to weep.

The paralaxium trumpeted, its trunk rearing into the sky, but it tossed its silky blue mane from side to side in time to the cadence of the Snow Hag's song. A moment later, it began to fade, growing translucent, and then—with one last, long look at me with those glowing silver eyes—it vanished, and the path was clear.

"Such an act is done." The Snow Hag turned to me. "And the paralaxium knows who ordered its freedom. If I were a Queen of Winter, I would expect one day to receive a call from the plane of Ice, a caravan of visitors, to perhaps thank a queen for such a deed as this one."

I nodded, feeling both sad to see the creature go—I'd felt incredibly linked to it—and yet, relieved. We didn't have to fight it, didn't have to kill it.

"And now, the Queen of Winter travels forth to the last gate?"

"Only one gate left, then?" That was news to me, but welcome news.

"One gate left. And then the hardest journey to come." And with that the Snow Hag moved to the back of the line. "Perhaps the Wilding Fae will stay for a while, to observe. To lend an ear."

Grateful she had decided to stay with us, I motioned for Check to resume his place. "Let's get on with this. One gate left. And then . . . if we are lucky, we destroy Myst's heart-stone and with it, bring the Long Winter's end."

Chapter 17

One gate to go, one last leg of the journey and perhaps, the nightmare would be over. The chamber beyond where we'd found the paralaxium sloped up, quickly becoming a narrow tube. Reminiscent of a lava tube, it was ragged and rough on all sides and circular in shape. We could only go one abreast here. Check took the lead, then Hunter and Grieve after him. I came next, then after me: the Snow Hag, Lannan, Fearless, and the other guards.

The going was harder than crossing the frozen surface in the large cavern. Going uphill was always more of a chore, and the rocks in the tunnel were jagged, thrusting up from the floor as well as from the sides and ceiling. While we weren't dealing with stalagmites or stalactites, we were facing rubble large as our fists and boulders that had tumbled down the passage from whatever ledge or chamber to which we were heading.

I glanced back at the Snow Hag, wondering if—with her short stature—she was having a rough go at it, but she appeared to be moving along smoothly. She caught my eye and winked at me, then touched her nose with a crafty grin. I was beginning to like her more and more, and it occurred to me that, once this was over and if we prevailed, she would make a fine ambassador between the Wilding Fae and my Court.

After another ten minutes of increasingly steep climbing, I asked, "Can you see anything ahead?"

A moment later, Grieve called over his shoulder, "We are nearing an opening. I expect it's the last gate, so we'd best be prepared for whatever barrier Myst has erected. Unfortunately, it's hard to wield a weapon and manage this climb at the same time."

He was right. We were no longer even hiking, the grade had grown so steep. In fact, we were nearly at a fifty-degree incline and were forced to use our hands to help us scramble up. The rocks cut into my palms, but gloves would have made the surface too slick. As I pushed yet further, my left foot caught hold of some loose rock and slid out from under me. While I wasn't in danger of falling, I pressed myself against the path until my heart stopped racing, and then moved on, hoping the pebbles hadn't rained down on the others.

"It is a bit of a climb, one would think, but nothing a queen and her company cannot scale." The Snow Hag's words echoed from behind me, making me smile.

"Encouragement is always welcome, from friends and allies alike." I glanced over my shoulder, grinning.

"Almost up top!" Check called back. "I don't see anything at this point, nothing barring the way. I'm going to stick my sword through the opening first, however. Stop climbing for now."

We pressed against the side of the tube, and I welcomed the chance to rest. Who knew what we'd be facing once we were through that opening, and after a tough climb, I didn't want to be thoroughly winded. While we'd managed to pass through the barrier with the paralaxium, thanks to the Snow Hag, I had my doubts we'd come through the final gate without a fight. Or at least, damage. It might not be a sentient guardian, knowing Myst. It might be a trap.

I waited, but there was no word or sound that Check was engaged in a fight. Whatever was up there apparently was either biding its time, or had somehow managed to miss all our commotion. Again, guardians tended to activate only within a certain radius, so we might have still been outside its range, but that didn't mean that it didn't know we were here.

"Nothing. I'm going up. Be prepared." Check's voice echoed down, and then, at the sound of him scrambling through, I held my breath.

Please be okay. Please don't get ambushed. The guard had wormed his way into my heart, and over the years, I had the feeling our friendship would grow. I wanted him there to protect me as time went on. I'd come to trust him, and that was more than I could say of most people I knew.

A moment later, we heard the welcome sound of his voice. "Come on up."

Again, we began to move, and in another moment, Grieve disappeared through the opening, then turned to lend me a hand. I took it, and he pulled me through the mouth of the tunnel, then returned to help the Snow Hag.

I rolled away from the hole, scrambling to my feet as I pulled out my dagger and looked around. We were on a ledge, all right, next to the entry into the passage out of which we'd just come. Behind me, past the tunnel's mouth, was the opening into a cavern. Another few feet in the other direction led to the ledge's end. I cautiously sidled over to the edge to find myself staring down into a dizzying drop into the blackness below.

Caves within caves within caverns.

The ledge on which we stood was a good ten feet wide, as rock strewn and harsh as the climb had been. It was solid though—cut into the side of whatever mountain it was the Barrow was buttressed against. Here, in this realm, we were far away from the Golden Wood within this Barrow. I had no idea what realm or plane we'd entered, but then again, within the Barrows time and space were all mutable. At times, with all the realms jostling for position, the whole thing reminded me of a giant game of Tetris.

Wandering over to Check's side, I gazed into the mouth of the cave and gasped. "It's beautiful in there."

"Yes, Your Majesty, it is at that."

Within the cavern were thousands of tiny lights—blue and pink, purple and luminescent white. The lights twinkled, like

Christmas lights, flashing in an array of patterns too hard to
follow, but that registered as having some symmetry. The
cavern was abuzz, but from where the sound emanated, I
didn't know.

"Incredible. What are they?"

The Snow Hag joined me. "One might think one was in the
realm of the night sky rather than the heart of the unholy terror. But beauty can be deadly and is often an illusion."

I nodded, captivated by the brilliant lights. About to ask
what we should do next, once again the reality that everything was up to me hit home. I was in charge. I was the
Queen, and it would forever be this way. I might ask advice,
I might seek counsel, but from now on, people turned to me
instead of me turning to others. A knot formed in my stomach and, overwhelmed, I could only gaze at the lights.

Then, fingers entwined with mine, and I looked down to
see that the Snow Hag had taken my hand in hers. The feel of
her skin—so alien and yet so solid—against mine, gave me
comfort in a way I had never before felt. She was solid as the
ice, solid as the rocks beneath our feet, and yet there was an
ethereal cloud around her that reached out to cushion me.

She squeezed, just lightly, but the energy that raced from
her fingers through mine was immense, and it recharged me,
strengthening me as I dropped my head back, letting it flow
through my body.

"One might think a queen needs no counsel, but truth is,
a queen often needs the most support even as she supports
the world that rests upon her shoulders. One might find a
friend in the most unlikely of people."

Tears sprang to my eyes, and, impulsively, I crouched
beside her, resting on my heels. "One might value friendship
more than gold. One might say a thank-you, as long as that
thank-you is not taken as a bargain nor a debt."

"Neither bargain nor debt." And then the Snow Hag
reached out with her long, jointed fingers, and stroked my
hair. "Neither bargain, nor debt seals a queen to one of the
Wilding Fae. No, simply friendship. And understanding."

"Your Highness—look!" Check's shout startled me out of

my thoughts, and I smiled at the Snow Hag before standing again. She squeezed my hand once more, then let go, and I ran over to Check's side.

"What is it?"

"We are all topside now, but look—in the tunnel."

I glanced down into the passage through which we'd come. Below, I caught sight of a glistening shimmer, and I could hear the rush of water. The passage was filling up, and it seemed to be . . . could it be?

"Is the water freezing as it rises? Turning to ice?"

"I think so. There's no way back. We have to go forward now. What are your commands, Your Majesty?" He waited, sword point down on the stone floor.

I considered our options. We had to move on, but the fact that there were no obvious obstacles to entering the cavern with the lights made me nervous. It felt like a trap, and it probably was.

"Search the outside of the entrance to the cavern, please. Look for anything that might indicate a trap or a snare."

Check called over his men and they scoured the edges of the cavern's entrance. A few minutes later, he shook his head. "We can't find anything, Your Majesty."

That pretty much took care of that. There was nothing to keep us from going through. One last look at the tunnel through which we'd come showed that it was packed full of ice, no longer usable. But at least no one would be coming through after us.

"Check, you and Mort take the front. Hunter and Grieve next. I will come after, between Lannan and Fearless, then the Snow Hag and the other guards in back of us."

And so we formed our marching order and, without further wait, Check and Mort crossed through into the cavern of lights.

⚓

Sparkling lights, twinkling lights, lights everywhere, like the most decorated garden during Christmas. Like the brilliance of a faerie-tale scene. The cavern was not large, but it was mesmerizing. For a moment I stood, gazing up at the illuminated ceiling. Just what the lights were, I didn't know, but they were everywhere, like a thousand gleaming sparks in the black of night, and they made me want to just stand there, watching in wonder.

As we moved toward the center of the cavern, I could see an opening on the other side. But I had to wonder: Was Myst's heartstone hidden in here, beneath the shower of light? Or was it beyond, through the opposite door?

Ulean, do you sense the—

Cicely, run—run! Now!

I froze at her cry, but then stumbled forward as the lights suddenly surged off the walls and ceiling and began swooping down on us. What the hell?

"Your Majesty—run!" Fearless grabbed for me, but the lights swept down on him, and he was on the ground, rolling and screaming. I turned, meaning to go to him, but then someone grabbed my arm and dragged me forward. It was Lannan, and we were heading for the opposite exit.

The men were shouting now, but I could barely see anything in the swirl of lights that dipped and swarmed. I struggled against Lannan, desperate to find Grieve, but he was too strong.

"Grieve! Grieve! Where are you?"

A scream startled me, and I jerked my head to the side. One of the guards was being stung to death, swelling up like a balloon everywhere the lights stabbed into him.

"Grieve!" Frantically, I screamed for my love, but he was nowhere in sight.

Lannan let out a shout. "I have Cicely! Save yourselves!"

He pulled me through the door, with the lights still swarming after us. One managed to land on my shoulder before I could make it through and sent a shockwave of pain through my body, like the worst sting in the world. I spasmed, screaming in shock, and Lannan scooped me up and swung me over his shoulder, leaping through the door. The second we were out of the cave, the lights stopped trying to follow us.

Lannan set me down, and I slid to the floor, moaning. Just

that one sting had nearly incapacitated me. I thought of the men still in there and let out another moan.

"Grieve—Hunter? Are they . . ."

"I will try to find them." Lannan knelt beside me, tipping my face up. "Will you be all right for a moment?"

"Yes, I'm all right. Just a little system shock. Please, see if they made it through?" I didn't care if I had to get down on my knees and beg. If he could find my men, I'd kiss his feet.

He patted my shoulder, and then was off again. As he plunged back into the cavern, now a vortex of swirling lights, I gingerly pushed myself to my feet, leaning against the wall for support.

Cicely? Are you all right?

Ulean, yes. . . . I will be. Grieve—Hunter? Do you know where they are?

No, but I cannot leave you unguarded. Lannan is looking, is he not?

Yes. What are those things?

I don't know—it seems they might be some sort of stinging insect. They are deadly, I'm afraid. I know at least two of your guards fell. They don't seem to be able to harm the vampires though, so maybe there's hope that Lannan's men are able to guard some of your men.

I pray so.

As I began to look around, trying to see through the shadows cast by the lights from the other chamber, I realized I was in another corridor. I searched my pockets and found a tiny flashlight. Bringing it out, I flicked it on and turned back to the cavern where the insects still swarmed. I couldn't make out what was going on, other than the hypnotic swirl of the lights. I placed my hand over my stomach and summoned my wolf.

Grieve, if you can hear me, if you can feel me, let me know. Let me know if you live. Where are you, my love? Are you alive?

But there was no answer, only the continuous swirl of motion. As I watched, waiting and praying for Lannan to return with good news, a sound caught my attention. It was from the corridor beyond. A gust of cold wind blew past, but it wasn't stirred by Ulean. I heard a faint laughter.

No. . . . I know that laugh. Please, not now. Not here like this. Ulean, can you find out if it's who I think it is?

A beat. Then another. And then . . .

Myst is here. She's waiting for you. Do you want me to go up ahead?

My blood froze. Myst was waiting for me. If I sent Ulean, she might be able to disrupt her or banish her.

No. You must stay behind me. I have to go. If I don't take the offense, she will. Better I make the first move than struggle for defense. I have to go. I have to face her.

Surely, not alone! What about your men? What about backup?

There may not be any backup! For all we know, they might all be dead. If I wait here, she might release the light creatures from being trapped in the cavern. Then it would be over before it began. I have to go, Ulean.

Then I will be by your side, Cicely.

And with that I began to creep through the corridor, Ulean behind me. I was sweating cold bullets. This was about the worst scenario I could imagine—facing Myst, not having her heartstone as collateral, not having my men beside me. She had all the toys, and I was going in unarmed.

I thought about pulling out my dagger, but then decided the fuck with it. A blade against her? Might as well tickle her fancy. No, I had two things to my advantage. One: I could turn into an owl and fly away if need be. And two: I could control the winds.

Sucking in a deep breath, I began to run. No need giving her any more time to prepare, and she knew I was coming. Otherwise, she wouldn't be here. Something must have warned her. The guardian we killed, perhaps, or the disruption when we banished the paralaxium to its home realm. Or maybe this had been her plan all along.

The passage abruptly ended, opening out into yet another chamber. But this chamber had a large opening to the outside world. From where I stood, I could see what looked like an incredibly steep drop-off into the forest below.

And to one side, on a throne of bone and crystal, sat Myst.

Myst, queen of the Indigo Court. *Myst*, the mother of the Vampiric Fae. *Myst*, the woman who had long ago been my mother. She was tall and thin and mesmerizing with her terrible beauty. Spindly, and yet stronger than the reeds that will not break in the wind, she stood. Her hair cascaded over her shoulders in jet locks, with crystals of silver running through them. Her dress was gossamer silk, deep indigo embroidered with sparkling silver threads, and her skin—a pale alabaster with a cerulean tint. Her eyes were, like all of the Shadow Hunters, pools of ink scattered with stars. And sitting beside her, glittering on a pedestal that was no doubt rigged to high heaven, was a shimmering stone. Her heartstone. I could feel the pulse of its heartbeat from here.

She simply waited, watching as I skidded to a halt near her. I braced myself, but she did nothing. Said nothing. Just smiled a cunning smile.

After a moment, I steeled myself and stepped forward.

"And so we meet again. This time it is not Lainule's heartstone up for grabs." The last time I'd faced Myst was in a desperate race to recover Lainule's heartstone before Myst could destroy it. I had won, but not by much, and though I had driven Myst away, it had only been temporary.

"Welcome to my lair, Cherish. Of course you remember the Barrow. And of course, you figured out that my heartstone would be here. When my first guardian fell, I knew that you were here. So I came, quickly, to wait for you. You did not disappoint me, daughter of mine." Her voice was throaty and rich, with a hint of madness behind the laugh.

"I'm not Cherish. Not anymore. That was long ago, far away—in a different time. I'm no longer your daughter, but Queen of the Court of Snow and Ice. And you are an upstart who has disrupted the balance."

I thought about making a dodge for the heartstone, but that would be suicide. It didn't take a degree in rocket science to know that she'd snatch me up if I got within arm's reach. But we couldn't stand here talking. One of us had to make the first move.

"Cicely!"

Gasping, I whirled to see Grieve stumbling into the cavern. He looked dazed, but he was on his feet. Behind him, Lannan was helping Check, and behind him, the Snow Hag. Whether anybody else had escaped, I couldn't tell.

"My disloyal lover—how good to see you again. Perhaps you'd like a taste of my gratitude?" And with that Myst was on her feet and she held up her hand. A pale beam shot forth, hitting Grieve in the chest, and he went down, screaming as convulsions racked his body.

"No!" I threw myself at the Queen, body-slamming against her. Startled, she broke off her attack and turned on me. She let out a low hiss as she laid her hands on me. I screamed as her nails dug deep, burning where they penetrated my flesh. Leaning down, I bit her, deep, sinking my teeth into her hand.

"Bitch!" She let go and slammed me back. I went flying against the wall, landing to slide to the ground. Grieve was on his feet, and he lunged at her as I scrambled up again. She managed to grab hold of him and wrapped her jointed fingers around his throat. He gasped, struggling as she tightened her grasp.

"Leave him alone!" I frantically looked for something to attack her with—I knew my dagger wouldn't make much of a dent, and then I saw it. On the ground beside her. She'd dropped an obsidian blade when she stood. I darted forward and grabbed it up.

The obsidian blades were like crystal meth to the Shadow Hunters, fueling their destructive urges, and that tendency was still there, buried within my soul. As my fingers closed around the hilt, a shiver of arousal ran through me, and I came up, laughing. Here was power—the power of the stone to bite and claw and suck the life out of my opponents. The power of the blade to sever through muscle and bone. The power to destroy, to rend and tear and maim.

"Taste this, you cunt." I lunged toward her and sank the blade into her arm, twisting it as hard as I could. The joy as her blood began to pour escalated, and all I could think about was making her hurt, making her scream, feeling her bones break under my pressure.

Myst spun around, but she held on to Grieve. I let out a

growl—he was turning blue, an unnatural blue, and I knew she was killing him. My only thought was to take her down, to save the man who was mine.

"You're playing the wrong hand, Myst." I jumped back, letting go of the blade. There was only one weapon I had strong enough to destroy her. As the fury took over, I closed my eyes, lowered my head, and then, I began to raise the winds.

Come to me, my winds; come to me, heart of the storm. Be part of me, sweep through me, take me in and devour me. Embrace me with your power. I give myself to you. Lift me up and carry me forth.

And then, two words: *Gale Force.*

With a howl, the winds stirred. And then they swept in, down on me. The noise was deafening as they caught me up, sweeping me aloft on a crest of air.

I rode the storm that swirled below me as it formed into a vortex. *Hurricane. Tornado. Cyclone.* Whatever the name, it swirled into the chamber, and anything not nailed down began to blow over the side. The mad joy of the winds began to overtake me. This power was stronger than any blade, any desire, any hope or fear or dream. I wanted to ride the storm into the open, to mow through the forests, to uproot trees, and to blow the roofs off the houses.

But first, there was Myst. And she met me play for play. She towered into the chamber, icicles shooting out like lightning bolts to crash against the ground. Grieve was still in her grasp, though she was holding him like a ragdoll now, but whether she was aware she still held him, I couldn't tell.

"You are done. Your time is done. Your reign is done. It's my time now, and I reclaim the long winter from you." I threw a gust of wind barreling at her, and it struck her in the chest, knocking her back.

She shook it off, but it had hit, and hit hard. "Contrary. Oh daughter, you should never have returned." And with her free hand, she shot what looked like a bolt of lightning at me, only it was forked ice, and it raced toward my heart.

I swept to the side and watched as it impacted against the wall, shattering as it did so, rocking the cavern.

"I will destroy you for good, and then I will take your land, and despoil everything you hold most precious, like I did your aunt Heather."

That was all I needed to spur me on.

Caught in the pure joy of the storm, the power of the winds surged through my veins as I raged toward her, streaking like a twister, spinning madly as I fell on her. She was in my grasp as my winds shook her ice.

And then I had her throat between my hands. I called the storm to strengthen me, and began to spin, holding her by her neck. Her body stretched out as we whirled, our speed so dizzying that everything around us became a blur of motion. She let go of Grieve in order to claw at my hands, but I held fast, and my hatred and anger fueled my storm.

And then I let go, sending her flying, and she crashed into the wall. As she fell limply to the floor, I struggled to rein in the storm, but it had me in its grasp and wouldn't let go. Caught by the heart of the wind, I fought for control, but my mind was slipping, and I phased in and out, unable to focus.

Then, below, I caught a glimpse of Myst crawling across the floor. Grieve was lying near the edge of the drop-off, and as she approached him, I suddenly realized she meant to push him over the edge.

"No! Grieve!" I fought with the storm, bucking the winds.

At that moment, a streak raced across the cavern floor. It was Lannan. He glanced up at me, then—with his golden hair glistening in the dim light—he pushed Grieve out of the way to safety. Myst managed to snare Lannan's ankle, and, slowly, like a tree toppling, she yanked on his leg and he fell, landing half over the edge. He slowly slid forward, the only hold keeping him in the cavern that of Myst's grasp.

"Lannan—no. Myst, stop this!" With one last push, I shrugged off the madness and dove, landing hard on the floor. I scrambled forward, ignoring the pain in my side, toward Myst. She was holding Lannan by one ankle as he dangled over the deep ravine.

"You *love* him, don't you? You love this vampire as much

as you love your Wounded King." The words cackled out of her throat.

Then, before I could say or do anything, Lannan shifted, dragging Myst forward with him. Startled, she turned to see what he was doing, and before she could let go, he jerked again and they both plunged over the side, into the darkness below.

"Lannan . . . no, Lannan!" I crept forward, peering over the edge, but in the darkness I could see nothing. They were gone. As I turned, Check was staring at me, wounded but alive. He met my gaze and gave me a soft, sad smile.

❦

I dragged myself over to the pedestal by the throne. Myst's heartstone still glowed, though its light was fainter, and the beat, a pale sound. I pulled out my dagger and touched the edge of the stone plinth in which Myst's heartstone was embedded.

Nothing happened so I took the chance. It was now or never, while she was weak. I began to pry the stone out of its bed, and after a moment, with a sucking sound, it popped free.

I wrapped my hand in my cloak, to cover my skin, and cautiously picked up the glowing stone. Here it was. Myst's essence, trapped so long ago and so carefully hidden. I was holding the heart of terror, the heart of the unnatural winter. Ragnarök come to rule, in the form of a beautiful woman with cravings for power not destined to belong to her.

By destroying this stone, I would be destroying the woman who had once been my mother. I had loved her, and then I met Grieve, and that love turned to hatred. I had loved her, and she had turned on me. We had betrayed each other throughout time, until now. And it was time to end it. Time to break the cycle. Time to put to right all the damage that Geoffrey and Myst had engendered.

I looked up to find Grieve standing there, holding himself upright by the throne. Check struggled to his feet, and then, the others straggled in. The Snow Hag. Hunter. Fearless. Mort had survived. Lannan's other vampires.

But the rest of our men were gone. Kaylin was gone, back to the Court of Dreams. And when this was done, Luna would be offered up on the plate of her own sacrifice. Lainule and Wrath had been forced to leave. We had lost Heather, Anadey, Rex, Leo. So many of the townspeople. All sacrificed to Myst's thirst.

It felt like I should say something. This was a pivotal moment in our history. An enemy thousands of years old . . . And we had come to her end. But there were no words.

In silence, I placed the heartstone on the ground and raised my dagger.

Ulean, will this kill her? Will my dagger do the trick?

Oh, my dear Cicely, how can you still ask me questions? You are the Queen of Snow and Ice. Trust in your power. Trust in your intuition. Trust in yourself.

Thank you. Thank you for being with me. For staying till the end. You mean more to me than anyone.

I have your back. Till the day that you die, I will stay with you.

Lannan . . . is he dead? Do you know?

I can't give you an answer. I don't know. Maybe . . . maybe he lives. Vampires are resilient.

I suppose . . . it's time. I watched Krystal kill herself. I lost one mother already. I helped kill Heather after Myst turned her. I saved Lainule's life but lost her in the process. And now . . . now I'm killing the only other mother I've ever known.

Sometimes, life sucks.

Yeah, sometimes, it does.

I raised my dagger high above the heartstone and plunged it down. As the blade met the stone, it fractured slowly, a web of cracks spreading across the stone, and then—with one last shove, I let out a shout, and the stone shattered into pieces, the shards flying. And Myst's light went out. Forever.

Chapter 18

And so there will always be an ending. All stories come to an end, even if it's only to open out into yet another tale. The hero begins his journey, unsure where the path will take him, and then, after the darkest hour, he emerges victorious. But there's always an after. *Happily ever after* may play true in some faerie stories, but it doesn't hold true in the world.

After Myst's heartstone shattered, her light went out, and we knew she was dead. As I knelt by the remnants of what had been her essence, we heard a terrible shriek from outside and turned to see a silver streak rise into the air, soaring upward, to vanish in a shower of sparks.

Myst was gone. Truly dead and forever out of our reach.

I forced myself to my feet, then struggled over to Grieve. "Are you all right, love?"

He wiped his hands across his face. "I think so. I am hurt, but I'll survive."

Check managed to drag himself forward. Mort helped him. "Your Majesty . . . there are no words. You have saved us all."

"We will have to hunt down all her minions. We must

eradicate all of the Shadow Hunters." But in my heart, I knew there would always be two still living. For my own soul bore the blood of the Indigo Court, and Grieve was still part of that hybrid race. We would never be free of the taint, but then again, was anything ever 100 percent clear and good and pure? Black and white were mere concepts, with a thousand shades existing between the two extremes.

Weary beyond counting, I stumbled to peer over the drop-off and stared into the blackness. Lannan was down there. Lannan had sacrificed himself to take Myst with him. He'd given me the chance to destroy her heartstone.

"Please, be alive. Please, be down there . . . still alive." Vampires weren't easily destroyed. But if he *was* down there, and sunrise hit, it would kill him. I whirled around. "We have to find Lannan—we have to rescue him if he's still alive, before sunrise."

Grieve shook his head. "Do you know how far of a drop that is? No one could survive it."

"Myst did, because her heartstone was still beating when I destroyed it. Lannan is a vampire. We can't just assume he's dead." I gazed at my beloved, pleading. He stared at me, and I knew that he could see into my heart. I loved Grieve more than life, but I also loved Lannan, and I knew that now. I'd hated him, I'd despised him, and part of me always would, but I needed him.

"I'll go looking for him. I'm still in good shape." Mort strode up beside me. He gazed over the edge. "I can make it down there."

"One of the Wilding Fae might be willing to navigate the drop with a bloodsucker, without a bargain struck." The Snow Hag gazed at me. "But only if a queen returns to her home to rest and heal."

"How do we get down? There is no path from here. I can fly, and so can Hunter, but Grieve, Check, and Fearless . . ." I looked around. There was no path from here, and we couldn't go back the way we came.

"Worry not, my granddaughter. I have called for help on the slipstream. Even now, our people are winging their way to us, and they will be able to safely transport the King and your guards." Hunter wrapped his arm around me and gave me a long hug.

Sure enough, within a few minutes, several owls flew into the cavern. The storm had died down and the clouds were breaking. For the first time in a long while, the stars shimmered into view. The Uwilahsidhe brought ropes and harnesses and all things needed to get Grieve, Fearless, and Check out of the cavern. Hunter and I shifted into our owl forms and flew out into the night, on calm winds, heading toward the forest below.

✦

Except for Mortimer and the Snow Hag, we all met back at the Veil House. By now, the temperature had risen a few degrees and the blizzard was gone. The snow would take weeks to melt, but the long winter was ready to give way, and as I flew over the yard, circling before I landed in the branches of the great oak, I thought about my life and the strange sequence of events that had brought me to this point.

I shimmied down the tree, leaping to land in the soft snow below, and stared at the glimmer of lights in the house, suddenly missing Heather again. She had given this house its heart, but now she was gone, with all the rest, and our lives had taken twists that we never could have expected.

As I headed toward the house, Hunter followed behind me. Grateful he had survived, grateful that we had come through with as few losses as we had, I turned to him and held out my hand. He took it, and we silently crossed the top of the snow banks, dancing along the crust, under the watchful eyes of the moon.

✦

Ysandra welcomed us in with hot mugs of coffee and chocolate. A chicken was roasting in the oven, along with biscuits. As I looked around at the signs of normalcy, it was hard to take in. We'd done it. We'd destroyed Myst. Peyton approached me, a question in her eye. I knew that they wanted to know where everyone was. Who had come through safely, and who remained behind, but I wasn't ready to speak. I needed to breathe. To walk through the house and know that we were safe.

After a few minutes, I peeled off my clothes, right there in the living room, and Luna hurried to bring me a robe. I slid into it, and then sank into the rocking chair, still mute. Hunter shook his head as Ysandra started to approach me, warning her off.

Another breath, and another. And then, as I accepted a hot cup of coffee spiked with chocolate and the fragrant steam rose to fill my lungs, I finally let out a long sigh and nodded for them to sit.

"Myst is dead. We destroyed her heartstone." How could I describe the battle? How could I explain the storms we had raised? There were some things too powerful for words. "I . . . We fought. Lannan helped kill her."

"Lannan . . . He is . . ." Luna's question hung heavy in the air.

"We don't know. Mortimer and the Snow Hag are searching for him now." I swallowed a catch in my throat. "Kaylin saved our lives, but he gave in to his demon to do so, and he's gone back to the Court of Dreams. His demon had to take over to keep him from dying."

Luna let out a cry and pressed her hand to her mouth. She hung her head and Peyton reached out to stroke her back.

"Grieve and Check and Fearless survived. The Uwilah-sidhe are helping to bring them home. They were wounded."

"And the rest of the men? The rest of Lannan's men?" Ysandra reached out but stopped short of taking my hand. Something had changed. There was a gulf between us, and I could feel it, even though I hadn't been the one to create it.

"Our men are dead. So many have died. The town will never be the same."

"Maybe not, but we'll revive it. We'll make it stronger." Peyton bit her lip and looked at Luna. "Strict, your advisor, showed up while you were gone. They found Zoey. She killed

herself before they could catch her. She must have felt Myst
fall."

Luna let out another choked sob. I caught her gaze. There
was something in her eyes—a fatal vision that stared back at
me. We'd won. She would have to make good on her promise. I
wanted to ask her what would happen now, but too much
had passed this night. Too much water under the bridge. We'd
lost too many people. I didn't want to know when we would
lose her, too.

"I suppose I should call Regina." But I made no move for
the phone. There were so many things that we needed to do.
Aftermath was almost worse than the actual battle.

"And so . . . what next, my friends?" I looked up. "What
the fuck do we do now? All our focus has been on destroying
Myst. And that's done."

"Clear out the Shadow Hunters. Heal the wounded. Bury
our dead. Count our blessings that the world won't fall to Myst's
rule. And plan for what happens next time someone gets it in
their head to create an empire. Because you know that there
will always be another time, another enemy, another power-
crazed fool ready to destroy the world in their attempt to hold it
in their grasp." Ysandra laughed, but her voice cracked, and she
began to cry. Luna followed suit, and Peyton. And I sat there,
devoid of tears, because I felt so numb that I didn't know if I'd
ever be able to feel much of anything again.

⁂

Even with my apathy, I forced myself to place a call to Regina.
She dispatched a host of men to go in search of Lannan. By
morning, we hadn't heard word one from her, and I could only
pray they'd found him before the sun drove them back to their
lair for the day.

Grieve was hurt, but he would heal. The same with Fearless and Check. The Snow Hag had vanished, but I expected
to see her again. Kaylin—I had no clue what happened to
Kaylin, and once more, I could only pray he'd found his way
to the Court of Dreams safely.

Rhiannon and Chatter returned from the town, where they'd been leading their men in routing the Shadow Hunters from New Forest. They were covered in blood, but unhurt.

And now my cousin and I stood on the back porch of the Veil House, staring as dawn broke in the east. The rosy streaks shimmered across the sky, and though it was still icy cold, the edge in the air had worn off, and here and there we could see icicles melting as the sun rose. It would be weeks before the snow was gone, but the worst of the winter was over, and we were on our way to spring.

"When I came back, I had no clue . . ." I stopped. There was no use in chewing over the past. What was, was gone. What was to come, would be here in good time.

"Was it hard to kill Myst? Were you sorry at all? She was your mother. Once, long ago in a dark faerie tale." Rhia gave me a smile, and the warmth of her eyes filled me with hope. She was the summer, bright as the sun, and I realized that any time I ever needed to bask in the light, I just had to meet her for lunch.

"You know, there was one point where it all felt so pointless. Where I felt like we were all pawns—including her—in one big joke the universe decided to play." I paused, then let out a long breath. "But . . . Lannan . . ."

"You mourn him. With all he did to you. . . ."

"With all he did, I miss him. I hope to hell he survived. Tonight, I'll contact Regina and find out what happened. If they even know. But he saved me. Rhia, Lannan gave me the time I needed to finish Myst for good. He sacrificed himself for us."

"Maybe he escaped. Maybe he managed to survive." She put her hand on mine. "Cicely, let your heart be happy. We've lost a lot of people, but now, New Forest can recover and be safe. And you and I can go about putting the pieces back together. Summer and Winter."

"Fire and ice." I turned to her, taking her hands in mine.

"Amber and jet."

"We'll never let them separate us, even though we are worlds apart. The balance must be maintained. Even though we are at odds, we'll always work together. Promise me that no matter what, we're still twin cousins."

Rhia leaned down and placed a kiss on my cheek. "Always, Cicely. Twin cousins. Never to part."

*

The town was digging out. As we made our way through the streets, Regina had told Dakota—Lannan's main day-runner—to spread the word that Myst was dead. And our men, the warriors of Summer and Winter, were out chasing down the last of the Shadow Hunters, destroying them on sight.

As soon as we managed to reestablish communication with Seattle and the Consortium, we'd enlist their help, and soon, if we were lucky, we'd manage to destroy every remnant of the Indigo Court. Without Myst, the Shadow Hunters would be plunged into chaos, so now was the time to finish them off. And this date would always be a holiday—the day we vanquished a monster.

As we passed what had been Anadey's diner, Peyton stopped, staring at the building. I slid my arm through hers.

"Are you all right?" I asked as she stared up at the silent neon sign. A FOR SALE sign was posted on the building, and I knew that Peyton would never again darken the doors of the restaurant.

"I don't even know what to say. I lost my mother when she tried to kill you—and then again when Geoffrey killed her. I lost my father too soon after I found him again. Just so much destruction." She shook her head. "I'm going to call my father's Pride in a few weeks and make arrangements to go stay with them for a while. When I come back, I'll open up my business."

"What do you think will happen to Luna? Do you think . . ." I didn't want to ask, but Peyton was the one Luna was talking to most.

"I think that her ancestors and Dorthea will come for her when they're good and ready. Maybe today. Maybe in ten years. Or twenty. Who knows? None of us ever really know when our time is up, not until we face it head-on."

"That's true enough."

"So Luna's life is forfeit. She bound herself to a pact, and they fulfilled their promise. She can't back out of this. But it was something she wanted to do, and our paths are our own to walk. When will they come for her? I have no idea, and I don't think she does either. But she made the choice willingly. Don't take away her sacrifice to help us. Don't make her feel guilty over it."

"That's what someone told me about Kaylin, you know."

"They were right." Peyton looked like she wanted to say something else, but was holding back.

"Out with it—what is it?"

"Only that . . . Luna was marked the first time we saw her. You saw it in your cards, and so did I. Maybe she was destined to die young. Maybe we saved her for a time, but we can't stop the Fates. We can't preordain who lives or dies. You might have the power to kill—to order someone's death. But ultimately, if that person is meant to live, fate will find a way."

I let out a soft sigh. "You're basically saying that if Luna's meant to go, then nothing we do will stop it."

"Yeah, I am."

"I know. I know. I'm tired of losing people."

"Cicely, accidents happen. War will come as it will. People die. A bullet, a vampire's fangs, falling on the ice and breaking your neck . . . There's nothing you can do. No matter how much you want to stop it, nothing you can do will prevent what's meant to happen. You may be a queen, but you aren't a goddess." And then she wrapped her arm around my shoulder. "No matter how much you wish you could control everything, it's not going to happen."

"Well, fuck. You just ruined my day with that." But I was laughing with her, even though I didn't want to hear what she had to say.

*

Ysandra sat in the rocking chair while I perched on the ottoman, watching the flames crackle in the fireplace. She was studying me, and finally, I turned to her. "What are you thinking about?"

"You cannot lead the Moon Spinners now that you are Queen. I'm sorry, but it's just not possible. I thought I was done with the Consortium, but I've decided to remain in my power there, and to change the institution for the better from the inside. But the town needs a witch, and with Magical Charms being Luna's shop . . ."

"Give her the power of the coven. Let her take over. I don't know how long she has, but maybe by doing so, you can help her with this damned pact she made with her ancestors. Luna's a strong bard, and her powers are growing. I don't know where they're taking her—I doubt even she does—but I know she could use some guidance." I reached out, warming my hands on the flames, but they were too hot, and I pulled back. Even though I loved the cozy glow, there was something off-putting about the heat now.

"I was thinking the same thing. I'm glad you concur. When will you return to your Barrow? As much as we love your company, you need to be there. You and Rhiannon need to leave the reorganization of the town to those of us who . . ." She trailed off, then her voice hardened. "To those of us who make our home here. Your Majesty"—she held up her hand when I started to protest—"No. You must wear that crown like you mean it. Your Majesty, forgive me for being blunt, but you don't belong here anymore. Your people are waiting. They need you."

I felt like a fledgling being pushed out of the nest. But she was right. The Veil House was no longer my home. New Forest wasn't my city. This was all a different nation, and I needed to go home.

"We'll leave tonight, after I find out about Lannan."

"Go before then. We'll get word to you. Go home, Your Majesty. Go home."

※

Grieve and I stood on a snow bank, under the moon, staring at the sky. Rhiannon and Chatter had branched off, with their guards, at the fork leading to the Twin Oaks. And now, here we were, standing above the Twin Hollies, staring at the portal that would lead us back to our home.

"Did you ever think we'd end up here?" I turned to my beloved. My heart was still aching, but now it skipped in anticipation. It was time to move ahead, time to step into our future.

"Honestly? No. But long ago I told you that we'd end up together, in the future, and now the future is here, and we are free from the shackles binding us to the past. We're free to be together, to rule a nation, to create a future."

And there, in front of our guards, he pulled me to him, and his lips met mine. As he kissed me, my heart swelled, and my wolf growled deeply, but it was a happy growl, a satisfied growl. I sank into the kiss, feeling his love surround me as he embraced me with all of my faults.

"I don't believe in happy ever after, you know," I whispered as we pulled apart. "I don't believe there's ever an ending. Life just keeps going, and when you finish one adventure, another begins."

"There's no such thing as perfection. I don't expect life to be perfect. I just never want us to get bored with each other." He stood back, holding me by the shoulders. "We'll find out about Lannan. I promise you—we'll find out one way or another."

"And if he lives . . ." I couldn't finish the sentence. Grieve had heard me in the cave; he'd heard Myst and he knew.

"If he lives . . . well . . . we'll have to figure arrangements if and when the time comes. Meanwhile, our kingdom awaits." And he took my hand as we passed through the portal, into a world where winter never ended, where the snow and ice forever covered the landscape. Where I was Queen of a frozen realm, and Grieve was my King.

❧

I soared high over my icy realm, reveling in the freedom flight gave me. Hunter swooped past me nearby, and then another owl—and another. My grandfather had brought a host of our people into the realm of Snow and Ice, to live under my rule, and now we took to the skies every moon. It was our tradition, flying high on the wing, hunting in the forest, rejoicing in the feel of the wind on our feathers.

Ulean swept past, laughing as she disrupted our flight. I steadied myself, and then, joy filling my heart, I pushed forward, leapfrogging with her under the light of the moon.

I never thought it could be like this.

Cicely, life is never what we think it will be. If you stop expecting it to look a certain way, to flow in a certain direction, then life has the freedom to become what it needs to be. You just have to remember that your life is not what Rhiannon's life is, is not what Luna's life is . . . or Peyton or anyone else you know. Destiny wears a different face for every person.

And then, she was off again, and I swooped, gliding after her. My people turned, following me, as we flew through the chill. The snow would soon be falling again, but here it was natural that it should. As I caught sight of the Barrow, glistening in white, my heart swelled, and I let out a long shriek of joy. I was finally home.

Epilogue

TWENTY-FIVE YEARS LATER

"Cicely! It's so good to see you again." Peyton ran up. She stopped to curtsey when she realized people were watching, but I laughed and grabbed her hand, pulling her to me.

"Fuck that. Hug me, woman." I held on to her, breathing deeply as the warmth of her body filled me with a heat that I seldom felt anymore.

She smiled, shaking her head. "So . . . another cycle, another solstice." And then we stood in silence. As the years went by, it was harder to find things to talk about. Oh, we discussed her business—which was thriving—and my kingdom, which was also thriving. But sometimes the past was still so raw, so over-whelming, that it intruded on the present. We reminded each other of darker times, of people loved and lost.

Twice a year, New Forest held citywide festivals for the summer and the winter solstices. Rhiannon and I attended both—one of us ruling the celebration with the other an hon-ored guest. Now, it was summer solstice—our birthdays. I was here to enjoy myself, while Rhia presided.

New Forest had grown into a real city, and though it had never been the same, it had turned into a thriving metropolis for magic-born, vampire, and Fae alike. We were cutting-edge in terms of interracial cooperation, and were considered a role model for the nation. But beneath the veneer, everybody who had lived here twenty-five years ago remembered the days when Myst had tried to destroy us. There was no getting away from history.

"How goes the business?"

Peyton laughed. "Lots of cases coming my way. The Veil House has never hosted so many people. I'm working on a big corporate case for the Consortium right now, though I can't talk about it. But it's going to boost me into high demand when I'm done." She paused then, the smile in her eyes fading. "But you know, it's never been the same here, not since . . ."

"Since Luna died." I finished it for her.

Three years ago, the ancestors had finally come for our beautiful bard. She'd been in an accident. But she'd left Wind Charms to her daughter, who had also taken over the Moon Spinners, as well.

Kayla was an extremely potent witch, with a personality to match, proving adept at vision magic, water magic . . . and dreamwalking. As to Kayla's father, Luna had never told us who he was, though we had our suspicions. We also suspected that Kayla herself knew. Five years after we defeated Myst, Luna had disappeared for a week, and when she showed up again, she was pregnant. Thrilled, she'd never once talked about where she'd been. But we knew—we all knew.

"Kayla's doing well with the business. Ysandra is mentoring her, and it's working out well. But . . . she's not Luna. You know how that goes."

"Yeah, I know." With a smile, I hugged Peyton again. "I need to check on the kids, but I'll be back." As I turned to go, I glanced over my shoulder. "Still no boyfriend?"

Peyton shrugged. "Casually dating, but no one special. Don't fuss over me, Cicely. I'm good on my own. If there ever is anybody, he'll have to complement me, not complete me. I'm content. Now go tell the kids to come give their Aunt Peyton a hug."

"Will do." I wandered through the backyard of the Veil House, and waved to Rhiannon. We would carve out our time to talk later on.

As I wandered through the expanse of yard behind the Veil House, I saw our children gathered over by the border to the Golden Wood.

First, there was Andy—the boy we'd rescued from the house. Rhiannon and Chatter had adopted him, and he had grown up a strong, trustworthy boy. He was skilled with herbs and had become a healer. Andy was also in love with my youngest daughter, Krystal, who was a telepath and a wolf-shifter, like her father. Krystal and Andy wanted to live in New Forest, so they would be marrying soon and taking over the Veil House for their own when Peyton moved into her own home across town.

For two years, she'd carried on at the Veil House after Luna died, but I couldn't help but wonder if Peyton hadn't been a little bit in love with our bard. I'd never ask her, and she'd probably never volunteer the information if she was, but part of me whispered that Peyton had fallen for Luna long ago.

To my left, at a picnic table, sat Rhiannon and Chatter's son, Talker. He was eating alongside my second daughter, Amber. They were also headed for the altar. Or at least, Rhiannon and I suspected they might be.

The pair spent every moment they could together, and since neither was heir to the throne, we saw no need to force them to stay home all the time. They had to deal with the brunt of security guards and all that being the children of royalty entailed, but Rhiannon and I were determined that they grow up to lead their own lives. We were changing the rules of our realms, as much as we could, and integrating the Fae into the mainstream of life.

Lastly, our oldest daughters walked hand in hand. Rhia's daughter—Hawthorn—had hair as red as the morning sky. My daughter, Yew, mirrored my own coloring. Once again, amber and jet would rule. Fire and ice. We had given birth to them on the winter solstice. Yew was born just before the stroke of midnight, when the night was at its darkest. Hawthorn was born twelve hours later, just after midday, when the Wheel had started to turn toward the light. Grieve and Chatter had been proud papas, that much was for sure.

With Hawthorn and Yew, tradition would rule out. We were grooming our daughters to one day take our places. They would remain with us, in the realms of Summer and Winter, until the day we were ready to return to the Golden Isle. They had accepted their fate and were content. Destiny would have its say, even when the future intruded.

Grieve slipped up beside me, wrapping an arm around my waist. "Enjoying the festival, my love?"

I nodded. "Yes, though each season, I feel a bit more alien-ated from the town. I suppose it's what this life does. This is the price we pay. I spoke to Peyton. She's doing well, but she misses Luna."

"We all miss Luna. And Kaylin." He pulled me close. "Tonight, you will stay with Lannan?" The old jealousy was long gone, buried under the strength of our love and of our children who cemented us together like glue.

With a shy laugh, I nodded. Two nights out of each year I spent with the vampire. We had come to an understanding over the years. Lannan would never mellow, but he respected me now, and he and Grieve even had found interests in com-mon, though they would never be close friends.

"You do not mind?" I always asked, even though, after twenty-five years, the routine was down pat.

Lannan, of the golden hair and dark soul, had survived the fall, and for his bravery, he'd been handed the permanent keys to the Regency. Together, he and Regina ruled over New Forest without question.

"I do not mind. He saved your life once, and he saved my life. And then, he sacrificed himself so that you would have the chance to destroy Myst. You can't fault a hero." He grinned at me. "I know your heart belongs to me."

And it did, even though Lannan and I had our fun. The truth was, at times Lannan and I just spent the night talking now. While the passion had settled into a comfortable friend-ship, when I needed him, I had the outlet twice a year to play in the dark, to safely vent out the memories of Cherish and Myst.

Now and then I met with his sister Regina, and we went shopping at night. The stores would open their doors to us. I'd learned more than I ever thought I would want to know about their lives—both before and after being turned—and I had developed a deep respect for them. Our friendship was forging new inroads for the relationship between the Fae and Vampire nations.

"My heart is in your hands, my love." I kissed Grieve on the nose.

"Go. I can feel you're antsy. Go flying for a while. You need it." He slapped me on the butt, and I laughed, once again marveling that I had found my way back to him. The journey that had started forty-six years ago, in this lifetime, had ended up here. In this yard, on this night, under the summer moon.

I headed toward the oak tree. Grieve was right. I needed some time by myself. With every passing year, I enjoyed my time in owl form more and more. My grandfather and I had spent a lot of time together, and I was beginning to understand the true nature of the Uwilahsidhe, though—as he put it—it would be a lifelong journey. One day, I would meet my father again, and I hoped he and Lainule would be proud of how far I had come.

As I climbed the boughs, I remembered my first time. Pressured by an unknown force, I had climbed the tree, removed my clothes, and then plummeted headlong toward the earth. And for the first time, I had spread my wings and found true freedom, and had begun my journey toward finding out about my lineage.

Now, as I stared up at the glowing moon, I could hear the sounds of the festivities from below. Our people were content. We had relative peace. We had rebuilt New Forest after vanquishing Myst.

And the future? Only the Fates knew where it would lead.

Ulean, are you ready?

I'm here, Cicely. Where do you want to go?

Let's head out over the forest. I want to fly hard and long. I'm ready when you are.

You've got my back, Ulean? I always asked—it was our tradition.

And as she always did, Ulean laughed. *Of course I do. I will always have your back. Forever. Call up the wind, Cicely, and let's stretch those wings of yours.*

And so I called to the wind, and a stiff breeze sprang up as I plunged forward off the tree, arms shifting into wings, body transforming, tail feathers growing. I spread my wings and turned on the wind, and with Ulean dancing and leap-frogging by my side, I flew into the night as the moon rose high over the trees, and the Golden Wood glowed with an unearthly, beautiful light.

Character List

CICELY AND THE COURT OF SNOW AND ICE

Check: Cicely's personal guard.
Cicely Waters: A witch who can control the wind. One of the magic-born and half Uwilahsidhe (the Owl people of the Cambyra Fae). Born on the summer solstice at midnight, a daughter of the Moon/Waning Year. The new Queen of Snow and Ice.
Druise: Cicely's lady's maid.
Fearless: Cicely's personal guard.
Grieve: King of the Court of Rivers and Rushes. One of the Cambyra Fae (shapeshifting Fae) now turned Vampiric Fae. Obsessed and in love with Cicely.
Hunter: Cicely's grandfather. Wrath's father.
Silverweb: The treasurer of the Court of Snow and Ice.
Snow Hag: One of the Wilding Fae. A friend of Cicely's.
Strict: Cicely's chief advisor.
Tabera: The late Queen of Snow and Ice.

RHIANNON AND THE COURT OF RIVERS AND RUSHES

Chatter: King of the Summer Court. Grieve's best friend.

Edge: Rhiannon's Court Advisor.

Lainule: The former Fae Queen of Rivers and Rushes. Grieve's aunt and Rhiannon's aunt. The former Queen of Summer. Destined to fade back to the Golden Isle.

Rhiannon Roland: Cicely's cousin, born on the same day as Cicely, only at daybreak, a daughter of the Sun/Waxing Year. Rhiannon is also half Cambyra Fae, and half magic-born, and she controls the power of fire. The new Queen of Rivers and Rushes.

Wrath: Cicely's father—one of the Uwilahsidhe (the Owl people of the Cambyra Fae) and originally a member of the Court of Snow and Ice.

PEYTON AND THE COURT OF THE MAGIC-BORN

Anadey: Traitor; was a friend of Heather's and mentor to Rhiannon. One of the magic-born, Anadey can work with all elements. Peyton's mother. Deceased.

Kaylin Chen: Martial arts sensei, a dreamwalker, has a nightveil demon merged into his soul.

Luna Saunders: Yummanii bard.

Peyton MoonRunner: Half werepuma, half magic-born. Anadey's daughter.

Rex MoonRunner: Werepuma. Peyton's father. Deceased.

Ysandra Petros: Member of the Consortium. Yummanii and powerful witch who can control sound, energy, and force.

THE INDIGO COURT

Myst: Queen of the Indigo Court, mother of the Vampiric Fae, the Mistress of Mayhem. Queen of Winter.

Heather Roland: Rhiannon's mother and Cicely's aunt. One of the magic-born, an herbalist, first turned into a vampire by the Indigo Court, now truly dead.

THE VEIN LORDS/TRUE VAMPIRES

Crawl: The Blood Oracle: One of the oldest Vein Lords, made by the Crimson Queen herself. Sire to Regina and Lannan.

Geoffrey: Former NW Regent of the Vampire Nation and one of the Elder Vein Lords. 2,000 years old, from Xiongnu. Deceased.

Lannan Altos: Professor at the New Forest Conservatory, Elder vampire, brother and lover to Regina Altos, hedonistic golden boy. New NW Regent of the Vampire Nation.

Leo Bryne: Was Rhiannon's fiancé, a healer and one of the magic-born. Leo was a day-runner for Geoffrey, turned to a vampire by Geoffrey. Deceased.

Regina Altos: Emissary for the Crimson Court/Queen. Originally from Sumer with her brother and lover, Lannan. Was a priestess of Inanna. Turned by Crawl.

Playlist for *Night's End*

I write to music a good share of the time and have been sharing my playlists on my website. I finally decided to add them to the backs of the books for my readers who aren't online.
—Yasmine Galenorn

A Pale Horse Named Death:
   "Meet the Wolf"
A.J. Roach:
   "Devil May Dance"
Adam Lambert:
   "Mad World"
Agnes Obel:
   "Close Watch"
Air:
   "Moon Fever"
   "Astronomic Club"
   "Napalm Love"
   "Surfing on a Rocket"
   "Playground Love"

Android Lust:
    "Here and Now"
    "When the Rains Came"
    "Saint Over"
    "Stained"
Antaeus:
    "Palm of the Prophet"
Atlas Sound:
    "Angel Is Broken"
AWOLNATION:
    "Sail"
Black Angels, The:
    "Vikings"
    "Don't Play with Guns"
    "Young Men Dead"
    "Manipulation"
    "You're Mine"
    "You on the Run"
    "Indigo Meadow"
    "Haunting at 1300 McKinley"
Black Mountain:
    "Queens Will Play"
    "Wucan"
Black Rebel Motorcycle Club:
    "Feel It Now"
    "Shuffle Your Feet"
    "Fault Line"
Broken Bells:
    "The Ghost Inside"
    "The High Road"
Buffalo Springfield:
    "For What It's Worth"
Chris Isaac:
    "Wicked Game"
Clannad:
    "Newgrange"
    "Banba Óir"

Cobra Verde:
   "Play With Fire"
Crazy Town:
   "Butterfly"
Cure, The:
   "Charlotte Sometimes"
   "Pornography"
   "Cold"
Dragon Ritual Drummers:
   "The Fall"
   "Black Queen"
Eastern Sun:
   "Beautiful Being"
Eels:
   "Souljacker Part 1"
Faithless:
   "Addictive"
Faun:
   "Lupercalia"
   "Pearl"
   "Zeitgeist"
   "Hymn to Pan"
   "Sieben"
Foster the People:
   "Pumped Up Kicks"
Gabrielle Roth:
   "The Calling"
   "Raven"
   "Rest Your Tears Here"
Garbage:
   "I Think I'm Paranoid"
   "Bleed Like Me"
   "Only Happy When It Rains"
   "Queer"
   "Beloved Freak"
Gary Numan:
   "Melt"

"Dead Heaven"
"Hybrid"
"Dead Son Rising"
"In a Dark Place"
"Walking With Shadows"
"When the Sky Bleeds, He Will Come"
"Pure"; "Dominion Day"
"The Angel Wars"
Gotye:
    "Somebody That I Used To Know"
    "Hearts a Mess"
Hedningarna:
    "Grodan/Widergrenen"
    "Räven"
    "Tuuli"
    "Ukkonen"
In Strict Confidence:
    "Silver Bullets"
    "Snow White"
    "Tiefer"
Julian Cope:
    "Charlotte Anne"
Kyuss:
    "Space Cadet"
Lady Gaga:
    "Paparazzi"
    "I Like It Rough"
    "Teeth"
Ladytron:
    "Black Cat"
    "I'm Not Scared"
    "Ghosts"
Lindstrøm and Christabelle:
    "Lovesick"
Lord of the Lost:
    "Sex on Legs"
Low:
    "Half Light"

Madonna:
    "Beautiful Stranger"
    "4 Minutes"
Marcy Playground:
    "Comin' Up From Behind"
Marilyn Manson:
    "Tainted Love"
Mark Lanegan:
    "Phantasmagoria Blues"
    "The Gravedigger's Song"
    "Methamphetamine Blues"
    "Riot in My House"
    "Bleeding Muddy Water"
Nine Inch Nails:
    "Get Down, Make Love"
    "Sin"
    "Closer"
Nirvana:
    "Heart-Shaped Box"
    "You Know You're Right"
Notwist, The:
    "Hands on Us"
Orgy:
    "Blue Monday"
    "Social Enemies"
People in Planes:
    "Vampire"
Puddle of Mudd:
    "Famous"
    "Psycho"
Rammstein:
    "Ich Will"
    "Stripped"
    "Wollt Ihr das Bett in Flammen Sehen"
Red Hot Chili Peppers:
    "Blood Sugar Sex Magik"
Saliva:
    "Ladies and Gentlemen"

Sarah McLachlan:
   "Possession"
Scorpions:
   "The Zoo"
Screaming Trees:
   "Dime Western"
   "Where the Twain Shall Meet"
Seether:
   "Remedy"
Stone Temple Pilots:
   "Atlanta"
   "Creep"
Susan Enan:
   "Bring on the Wonder"
Syntax:
   "Pride"
Tamaryn:
   "While You're Sleeping, I'm Dreaming"
   "The Waves"
   "Violet's in a Pool"
Toadies:
   "Possum Kingdom"
Tom Petty:
   "Mary Jane's Last Dance"
Verve, The:
   "Bitter Sweet Symphony"

Dear Reader:

I hope you enjoyed the final book in the Indigo Court series, *Night's End*. I have loved writing this world, but as with all faerie tales, it's time now to close the book on Cicely's story. While not everybody found their happy ever after (and like Cicely, I really don't believe in HEA), I am content with how the story wrapped up, and I'm ready to turn the final page on their lives. This has been a journey, this mystical, icy world I've created, but now it's time to move on.

However, even as one door closes, others open. Next, I bring you an e-novella, *Flight From Hell*, in August 2014—the crossover story that links the Otherworld series with my new Fly By Night series. And then—book sixteen in the Otherworld series: *Priestess Dreaming*, coming October 2014. Camille goes in search of the Merlin, and her journey takes her far into new realms and new dangers. After that, I'll have Delilah's next book, *Panther Prowling*. For more information, see my website and follow me on Facebook.

I'm enclosing the first chapter of *Priestess Dreaming* to whet your appetite for the next adventure coming up for Camille and her sisters. For those of you who are new to my books, I hope you've enjoyed your first foray into my worlds. For those of you who have followed me for a while, thank you once again.

Bright Blessings,
The Painted Panther
Yasmine Galenorn

I contemplated going back into the house, purse over my shoulder. Should I, or shouldn't I? Utter mayhem lay within. Absolute chaos in a kitchen, complete with spilled food, a huffy dragon, one very pissed-off house sprite, and my sister, the wide-eyed, *catch-da-giant-bird*, turkey-chaser. Add to that the rest of the milling—and by now, thoroughly confused—throng that was our extended family, and I made my decision. *Not a chance. Nope. Not gonna happen.*

I was perfectly fine out here in the pouring rain, getting soaked. Let Smoky take his lumps from Iris. This was all *his* fault, not mine. The only part they could blame me for was that I had assigned him the chore of bringing home a twenty-five-pound turkey for tomorrow's Thanksgiving dinner. Was it my responsibility to remind him to make certain it was already dead?

Not. My. Fault. And neither was the Three-Stooges aftermath that followed. Now, with Iris and Hanna both on the warpath, I had no desire to go back in there and subject myself to their outrage.

As my gaze wandered over to the turkey pecking around

our backyard, it occurred to me that the bird was eyeing me with an evil glare—like some demented ostrich. The fat old Tom was closer to the woods than our backdoor, and I wondered if he realized just how lucky he was.

I stamped my foot in his direction. "Go on, you dumb bird. Make a break for it while you can, before Smoky comes looking for you." As if he understood me, the turkey turned toward the treeline back of the yard and slowly began to waddle off into the sunset. Or rather, the pitch darkness. It was only around five-thirty, but by this time of year, the Seattle area was swathed in night. Sunset had come and gone about an hour ago.

I snorted. "Have a happy Thanksgiving, bird. You lucked out so give your thanks to the Great Turkey or whoever it is you pray to."

As I watched him vanish into the woods, I wondered where the hell Smoky had found him. No doubt he'd stolen him from some turkey farm or something. Wild turkeys generally didn't go running around the streets of Seattle. But I wasn't going to ask. After this fiasco, I had a feeling that my dragon-shifting husband wouldn't be in any mood to discuss turkey-hunting.

Thanks to sheer dumb luck, the bird had managed to escape from the kitchen. He'd left behind a trail of walking wounded, though—including me. That beak was nasty sharp and I had the scratch to prove it, but at least I didn't have a hole in my hand like Roz did. Yeah, in the great dinner war, the bird deserved his freedom. He'd earned it. As the last of his tail feathers vanished from sight on the path leading to Birchwater Pond, I saluted him.

"You've got what it takes to make it, soldier. Carry on."

With one last look at the house, I straightened my shoulders and headed toward my car. We still needed a turkey. I might as well head out to buy one. On the up side, by the time I got back, things should have smoothed over.

Families. One thing was for certain: Mine was loopy, batty, and all around a freakshow crew. But I wouldn't trade them for all the glitter and glitz in Otherworld *or* Earthside.

I slid into the driver's seat, but as I inserted the key into the ignition, a shiver ran down my back. A shadow passed through me, cold and dark and incredibly ancient.

Quickly, I locked the door, suddenly nervous. Maybe it was the wind that rattled the trees that had spooked me. Or, maybe it was the driving rain. Or perhaps the darkness and perpetual gloom had finally managed to suck the smile off my face. Whatever the case, I glanced back at the house, anxious.

PTSD, maybe? We had recently come through a horrible stretch, what with the war raging in Otherworld and losing our father. We were all still a little shell-shocked. I had been coping with a lot of nightmares and flashbacks the past few weeks, but this didn't feel like it originated from the same place.

Trying to quiet my mind, I listened, breathing slowly.

Inhale. Exhale. Inhale. Exhale. Listen . . .

At first, I could sense only the wind and rain that lashed the yard, but then . . . below that . . . *there it was.* Something was on the move. Something *big.* I searched my feelings, examining the sensation. Was it fear? Yes, but more. Anticipation? Anxiety? A tingling at the base of my neck told me that deep magic was afoot, and would soon be knocking on my door.

Magic rode the currents, on the wings of a flock of birds. They were there, in the astral, black as coal and shrieking warnings of an ancient wood filled with extraordinary beasts. The rolling mists of time poured past as the ravens cried, their song echoing with magic. Dark magic, deep woodland magic. *Death coming in on waves of flame and smoke.*

As if in sync with my thoughts, a shriek cut through the darkness, startling me out of my trance. I recognized the cry. *Raven.* Oh, fuck—raven was calling. And where raven flew, Raven Mother couldn't be far behind.

And behind Raven Mother, chasing her, was a dragon. At first I flashed back to Hyto, but then caught hold of myself. Hyto was dead and gone. I forced myself to focus, to examine the energy that went rushing past. This dragon was ancient— not a dragon from the Dragon Reaches, but from the depths of the earth, come awake after eons of time asleep in its lair.

As he roared to life, chasing the flock of ravens, he vanished from sight.

I found myself sitting in the car, my hand on the keys. Wondering what that had been about, and almost afraid to examine it, I shuddered and started the ignition. As the car warmed up, I stared into the darkness of the night, my thoughts far from Thanksgiving.

Yes, something big was headed my way and there was no use trying to avoid it. I might as well just open my arms and brace for trouble. Trying to hide from potential trouble had ceased to be an effective defense mechanism a few years ago when the demons had first shown up.

With a grimace, I pulled out my phone and texted Menolly that I was heading for the store to replace the turkey. As I eased out of the driveway, I whispered, "Bring it on, Raven Mother. Bring it on. I'm waiting for you."

A faint laughter echoed over the howling of the wind. She'd heard me, all right. And she was waiting.

✤

"Give me that!" Delilah's voice rang out and I turned, scanning the mob for her face. Somebody was bound to get hurt in this mess. People were shoving in every direction, trying to push their way through the mass of churning bodies. To my left, a woman tripped and fell. I tried to maneuver through the crowd to reach her, but a man stopped to help her back to her feet and she dusted herself off, looking no worse for the wear, but then, a glint in her eye, she was gone into the seething throng.

Still not seeing Delilah, I glanced over my shoulder. Smoky and Trillian were standing at attention, waiting for my orders, both looking resigned and rather frightened. Their arms full of bags, they threaded their way through the chaos as they followed me. Delilah was still nowhere to be seen, and I made a unilateral decision. She'd just have to catch up to us later.

"Over to the pet section, pronto!"

Pointing toward the opposite end of the store, I began to traverse the aisles. Wordlessly, they filed along behind me. Gauging the easiest, quickest route, I wound through the rows of merchandise, narrowly skirting a table of precariously stacked crystal dishes. Motioning for the guys to be cautious, I held my breath until I was past the display.

Once we were out of housewares, the crowd began to thin out as we maneuvered our way over to the pet toy aisle. Along the way, I caught sight of an insulated lunch bag in fuchsia, with a cat appliqué splashed across the front. It really was cute. Another woman was eyeing it and I had a split second to make up my mind.

"Nerissa would love that." I snatched it up seconds before my opponent could grab it and, once again, we were on the move, leaving her sputtering in the dust. A few moments later, we reached our destination: The pet care section. We had the department to ourselves. Most of the crowds were over in electronics and toys. Chase and Iris were fending their way through the latter and I silently wished them luck.

"Are we done yet?" Smoky grumbled. "Haven't you found enough loot? It's four-thirty in the morning, woman." He didn't sound that angry, though. In fact, the twinkle in his eye told me he was putting on a show because he thought it was required. Just like a man.

Trillian, also my husband, snorted. "You really think that's going to work? Dude, you should *know* your wife and her sisters by now. We've got at least another hour to go. Remember last year?"

Trillian's obsidian skin glistened under the fluorescent lights. He'd braided his hair to keep it out of the way. The silver strands rested smooth against his back, shimmering with the faintest of cerulean highlights. He had worn a sleek black turtleneck and black jeans, but left his jacket in the car, claiming it made him more aerodynamic in the crowds. A Svartan, one of the dark and charming Fae, he usually managed to get what he wanted by smooth-talking whoever was in his way. But on Black Friday, all bets were off.

Smoky, on the other hand, was attired in his usual getup: white jeans, V-neck pale blue sweater, and long white trench. At six-four, my dragon towered over the crowds. Though I kept him near, even his imposing nature didn't offer us much protection during the early hours of the most terrifying shopping day of the year. He, too, had braided his hair, though it was ankle length instead of mid-shoulder like Trillian's. Luckily, his hair moved all on its lonesome. If it hadn't, his braid would have gotten trampled several times tonight.

"Don't remind me." Smoky rolled his eyes. "Last year was worse than this, I'll give you that."

"The others aren't done yet, so just hold your horses. Remember? Hanna promised leftover turkey soup along with fresh baked homemade bread if you guys play nice." I picked up a catnip mouse and shook it, frowning at the *squeaky-squeaky* sound. Delilah would love it.

Her toys were constantly ragged, she played with them so much. And then, the thought occurred to me that we should get her panther form a toy, too. One that could withstand a good mauling. Also—why not one for Nerissa? Her puma liked to play and, on occasion, Delilah and our sister-in-law went hunting together in the forest behind our house. They never really caught anything, but the big cats liked to prowl through the trees.

"After we're done here, we're heading over to the stuffed toys. So gird your loins, or whatever it is you boys do in order to stay sane."

Oblivious to their groans, I began tossing toy mice in my cart, before we pushed onward.

Delilah had driven her Jeep, Menolly had brought her Mustang, and I had driven my Lexus. Morio had also played chauffer, driving his SUV so that Iris and Chase could come with us. That way, we had enough room for all the packages as well.

Hanna had stayed home to watch Maggie, our baby calico gargoyle. And Bruce, Iris's husband, had begged off because he'd promised to help Vanzir and Rozurial with some secret surprise they had planned. They had shooed us out of the house, instructing us *not* to return till early morning. I wasn't sure what they were up to, but could only pray it wasn't something stupid like turning the house into a giant video game or something.

It was nearing six A.M. as we pulled into the driveway to our lovely old three-story Victorian with basement. Menolly still had some time before she had to be in her lair to sleep. Vampires and sunrise? Not such a good mix, so we always made sure she was home in time to get to bed. But we still had nearly ninety minutes before the sun crawled over the horizon. Or up behind the clouds, as was more often the norm here in Seattle.

As we piled out of our cars, the men gathering all our loot for us, I glanced at Trillian and Smoky and wearily smiled. "You do realize how much I love the pair of you, don't you? And Morio, too." Morio was my third husband. I was one hell of a lucky woman.

His hands full, Smoky winked at me as a strand of his hair unbraided itself, slowly reaching over to caress my cheek. A smile creased his face. Dragon smiles were always a little sly, a little coy.

"You can show us just how much you love us after we haul all this stuff inside." His voice was husky, and I caught my breath as the touch of his hair sparked off an ache that rose between my legs. I wanted him and I wanted him *now*. It had been two days since I'd had sex—we'd all been busy. But that was two days, too long.

Trillian brushed past me, arching an eyebrow. "That's the best idea I've heard all night."

"I wish." Shaking my head, I forced my attention away from my nether regions, which were now up in arms, demanding attention. "Go on, the pair of you. You know what waits for us inside there. An early morning brunch, and then Iris and Hanna are going to put us all to work. Except Menolly, of course. Honestly, how Iris manages to have as much energy as she does after having the twins, I dunno. It's been less than a month and she's raring to go."

As much as the thought of an early morning tryst with my men appealed to me, the morning was given over to homely duties. Today we'd all be decking out the house for Yuletide, from bottom to top. With Iris and Hanna in charge, it meant we'd fill every nook and cranny with some sort of decoration. But I didn't begrudge the time spent, especially this year.

With Father dead and so much upheaval in our lives, it was important to keep our traditions alive. We needed these touchstones to ground us and keep us on track. My premonitions of the other night had faded, and I had put them down to skittishness. So far, nothing had happened, and I hadn't bothered telling anybody about them.

Trillian laughed. "Fine. We'll avoid facing the wrath of the house-maidens. But that means we're on for this evening, though frankly, I'm going to need a nap before then. The few hours we got after Thanksgiving dinner were helpful, but not enough."

But I lost track of what he was saying, because as we approached the porch, the front door burst open and Vanzir came racing out, the look on his face somewhere between guilty and terrified. He scrambled down the stairs, leaping to take the last few.

"Run! Get out of the way!" And the dream-chaser demon pushed past us looking like hell itself was on his heels.

Confused, I glanced back at the door. Holy. Fuck. It couldn't be—no, no . . . I couldn't be seeing what my brain thought it was seeing. Could I?

But there, on the porch, with gleaming yellow eyes, stood a very large, very burly creature with white fur covering its body. It was bipedal . . .

"Fuck! *Yeti!* There's a freaking yeti on our porch!" I dropped my purse and backed away from the steps, never letting my gaze leave the creature. Trillian and Smoky were doing the same.

Yetis were unpredictable. Like their cousins, the Sasquatch, they were large and muscular, but their hair was white, compared to the deep brown of the Sasquatch's fur. Camouflage, no doubt. But what the hell was a yeti from the mountains of Tibet doing here, on our front porch? And more importantly—at least for the moment—what was it going to do?

The creatures were wild, almost alien in nature. In fact,

back in Otherworld, there were rumors that the entire Sasquatch-Yeti family were originally from another planet, though nobody knew if this was true. It could have just been an urban legend. They were considered to be Cryptos, but they weren't found in Otherworld and they sure didn't mingle with the Cryptos over here, Earthside. Or with the Fae. Pretty much everybody but monster-hunters gave the primate-like creatures a wide berth.

I searched my memory, trying to figure out just exactly what our options were. Attempting to communicate wouldn't do any good, not unless the creature was willing to talk. And so far, nobody I knew had gotten close enough to one to invite it to tea without getting mauled. Usually, approaching beyond a certain range would trigger off some sort of defense mechanism and the creatures would attack. And an eight-to-nine-foot-tall agitated primate who was feeling hemmed in, wasn't the safest of critters to be around.

"Anybody have any suggestions about what we do with the big white giant on the porch?" I tried to keep my voice even and neutral. No use setting it off with any loud noises.

"My babies!" Heedless of the danger, Iris broke into a run, heading around the left side of the house. Her home was in back of ours, and her twins were there, waiting for her with their grandma. I pitied any fool who tried to get between her and the babies, that was for sure. The house sprite might be a gorgeous, buxom hottie, milkmaid pretty with golden hair down to her ankles and cornflower blue eyes, but she could turn a grown man inside out if she got mad enough. Literally.

"Astrid!" Chase followed Iris at a dead run. He and his daughter Astrid lived with Iris and Bruce. No doubt, he was just as freaked.

Startled by the sudden movement, the yeti let out a roar and bounded down the steps. My men moved immediately to intercept—Smoky, Trillian, and Morio dropped their parcels and darted to cut off the path so it couldn't follow Iris and Chase.

I backed up, looking at the sky. The clouds were thick. It was almost cold enough to snow, and there should be enough energy around to summon the lightning. I raised my arms and called on the Moon Mother. She was huge tonight—not quite full but nearly there, and I could feel her shining down even though she was obscured by the boiling clouds.

As I drew the energy into me, a crackle of silver racing through my arms, I began to feel giddy. What the hell? Her magic made me drunk at times, but never like this, and never this fast.

I wanted to dance, to spin and cackle and laugh. Trying to focus, I forced my attention back to the tingling moon-fire, but it was no use. The next moment, I heard music, faint at first but quickly sweeping up to surround me. Bouncing with a deep rhythm, the song enticed me to join the dance, the voice deep and guttural.

I began to whirl, laughing as I looked toward the sky. The Moon Mother, she was up there, and I felt her singing along. But whatever the words were, I could not understand. Guttural but delightful, they sang of adventure.

The sky shimmered, a thin veil of sparkling lights flitting around me, and enchanted, I reached out, trying to capture the twinkles in my hands.

A low growl startled me. To my left, Delilah, in her panther form, bounded by, chasing a translucent figure with wings. Tiny, it was barely a foot tall. Oh hell! Some semblance of coherency broke through. I knew what that creature was! A *pixie*. A freaking pixie.

We were friends with a pixie, but the majority of them were annoying pests and worse. They liked to lead people astray, and they had it in for Witches like myself. And this one was darting around, sprinkling dust right and left.

No wonder I wanted to dance. But then, reason escaped me as, once again, the music lured me in. I whirled, holding my arms out, and the energy I had drawn down from the Moon Mother suddenly cut loose in a volley of bolts as I became a spinning wheel of silver fire, sparks flying from my fingers.

Delilah snarled and lumbered out of reach. I heard Nerissa curse as I hit her with one of the mini-bolts. I wanted to stop, but my feet kept moving, I kept twirling, and the sparks kept flying.

"Stop me! Somebody stop me! Pixie dust!" I managed to shout between the violent fits of laughter that were erupting from my core. I had no clue what was so funny, but I couldn't stop that either.

By now, it occurred to me that if I had to be shooting out sparks, why not move to where they'd do some good? I tried to catch sight of the yeti in my dizzying spin and realized that if I moved in a northwestern direction, I'd end up near the creature, who was now fully engaged with Smoky and the boys.

As I danced closer, still spinning like a crazed top, Smoky let out a shout, and then Trillian. The next thing I knew, the smell of burning fur filled my nostrils, and with each spin, I found myself facing one very pissed off and scorched yeti.

One circle around and I caught sight of him gazing at me with those glowing, angry, topaz eyes. A second circle, and a big fuzzy white arm came flying out. The third and I staggered to the ground as his big ole' fist met my crazed body.

I landed on the frozen driveway. Apparently the temperature had dropped enough for frost to form. The fucking dirt was hard and cold. But even getting smacked by Mr. Abominable Snowman couldn't shake the pixie dust off me, because I began to struggle to my feet, still needing to dance. The next moment, Smoky had grabbed me under his arm, dragging me behind him as we raced through the yard toward the studio that had originally been a shed.

The minute we hit the door, he swept me up and barreled into the bathroom where he shoved me—clothes and all—into the shower. One more second and he'd turned it on full blast. The water was cold, and shocked me into silence. As the spray warmed up, it began to wash off the pixie dust and my foggy thoughts began to lift. My body was still jazzed higher than a kite by all the energy I'd drawn in, but at least I didn't feel the need to go gallivanting in a crazed polka around the room. I stood there, mutely under pounding water. *Yeah, this outfit was a goner.*

After a moment, Smoky turned off the spray. "Pixie dust gone?"

I searched for the dazed feelings brought on by the dust,

but the only thing I felt was wired and bedraggled. After a moment, I nodded.

"Yeah, I think so. I'm pissed, but I'm thinking clearly and I don't feel quite so possessed to go frolicking with Mr. Yeti. *The yeti!* Where the hell did it come from, and more importantly, what are we going to do about it?"

"I don't know. When I saw it attack you, all I could think about was to get you out of the way. You were in no shape to protect yourself." He held out a towel. I stripped and, leaving my wet clothes in the shower stall, I stepped out and wrapped the thick terrycloth around me. The soft cloth against my skin felt good, and I suddenly realized that I was rapidly growing tired—another side effect of too much pixie dust.

"I need to find something to wear and then we have to get the hell back to the house. The fact that pixies are having a field day in our yard is bad enough, but a yeti bounding out of our front door? More than a little scary." A sudden thought hit me. "Maggie! We have to make sure Maggie is okay!" Pushing past him, I rushed out of the bathroom.

"You can't go racing out there in a bathrobe." Smoky motioned toward Rozurial's room. "Grab something from the incubus's closet and I'll go check on Maggie." And he was out the door before I could touch the knob.

Wanting to run after him, but realizing that dashing naked through the storm wasn't exactly the brightest idea, I hurried into Roz's room and tossed my way through his dresser. I found a tunic that fit over my Double-D's, and a pair of pajama bottoms. Tying them firmly, I realized I'd have to go barefoot. My shoes were ruined and I couldn't wear any of Roz's boots—they were far too big. Sopping hair and all, I headed out of the studio, back toward the house, my feet freezing. The frozen soil and frosty grass made for a slippery mix, and I struggled to keep my footing as I raced back toward the house.

All hell had broken loose. Trillian and Morio were still fighting the yeti and from what I could see, the damned thing seemed tougher than a dubba-troll. But that was only the half of it. Glimmers flickered from all over the yard—and every glimmer seemed to have some sort of creature attached to it.

The pixie was still flying around like a crazed maniac, and to my dismay, I spotted a couple more nearby. *Hell.* They were bad news, in general. Mistletoe was the exception to the rule and that's only because he was our friend.

Beneath a huckleberry bush near my herb garden, I could see some sort of frosty hedgehog-like creature. Not certain what it was, I decided I had better get dressed before investigating.

Trampled shopping bags were scattered all over the yard, and I scanned the area, trying to locate everyone. I finally spotted Nerissa, in her werepuma form, and Delilah, who was still in panther form. They'd treed something, and both big cats were standing up against the trunk staring at whatever it was they'd managed to trap in the branches.

Menolly was up on top of the roof. She was after—what the hell? It looked like some sort of gremlin. She was climbing along the shingles, but the creature scampered over the tiles as if it were running on flat ground.

Rozurial was nowhere in sight, and Iris and Chase had taken off for Iris's house. Vanzir was struggling with a figure beneath a cedar. They were rolling around on the ground, locked in a wrestling match, and I heard Vanzir utter a string of curses. Shade was chasing another glimmer around toward the backyard.

Motherfucking son of a bitch, what the hell was going on?

Just then, one of the Fae guards who patrolled our land ran over to my side, panting. "Camille—we're overrun. Four of the men are out back fighting a group of barbegazi. And two of the men are chasing a couple of ice wolves."

"*Barbegazi? Ice wolves?* What the hell are they?" I wasn't sure I wanted to know, but then again, there was a lot I'd learned the hard way that I wished I didn't have to know about.

"Barbegazi are creatures from the Northlands—very much like dwarves only smaller and, in a way, hardier. Usually they're kindly natured but this batch appears to be a particularly surly lot. As for the ice wolves—they are also known as amaroks, at least to one Earthside tribal group. They're wolf demons, dangerous and hungry for human flesh." The guard glanced around, shaking his head. "I don't know what hap-pened, or where all of these creatures came from. The wards suddenly went off and we were swarming with them."

"The rogue portal out back? Could they have come through there?" I motioned toward the porch steps, which were surpris-ingly clear. "I need to get dressed and get back out here."

He followed me up the stairs. "No, the portal hasn't been active at all. I—"

As we entered the house, he fell silent. First of all, the foyer was filled with snow. White, cold, sticky, wet snow. And it was snowing up a storm. *Inside the house.* Second, a loud humming emanated from the living room.

"Well . . . this is new." I stared at the snow on the floor, all twelve to fourteen inches of it. My feet were beginning to freeze.

"Wait here, Lady Camille." The guard plowed his way into the living room, then within moments returned. "There's a portal in your living room. The snow's coming through there. Ten to one, that's where all of these creatures came from, too."

A portal? In the living room?

"Okay, then, well. I don't know what to say to that. But, come with me. I need to change and I don't know what else might be rampaging through the house. I'd rather not be surprised while I'm getting dressed." I darted through the snow, wincing as the sting of the frozen water hit my feet. The guard—whose name was Dez—followed me, sword out and ready.

The living room was, indeed, filled with snow, and it was beginning to drift up the walls, and out into the foyer and the parlor. The room was also decked out in the most garish holiday décor I had ever seen. In one corner stood a ten-foot-tall tree, blazing with neon flashing blue and green lights that made my eyes hurt. The lights ran the length of the room, following the ceiling around to form a terrifyingly bright border. Huge acrylic ornaments bedecked the tree, catching and reflecting the lights like crazed prisms.

"What the fuck . . . it looks like Crack Santa and his methed-out elves descended on our living room."

"I don't know, Lady Camille—I thought perhaps you decorated before you left for your shopping trip."

"Oh, hell no. *This mess*? I have better taste than that. And you know Iris . . . yeah . . ."

The thought of Iris allowing such a gaudy show in our living room almost made me laugh. Thoroughly confused, I turned to the portal, which was shimmering in the opposite corner near the window. It was swirling with icy blue sparkles. I had no clue to where it led, and I sure as hell wasn't going to dive through to find out.

"Okay, upstairs, to my rooms."

As we headed up to the second story, the chill followed. It was still snowing when we reached my suite of rooms and by the time we reached my bedroom, I could see my breath and my toes were numb.

Dez made a quick survey around the room and ascertained that nothing was amok—or at least, nothing was running amok.

I stripped down as he kept watch. The Fae—including half-Fae like myself—generally weren't modest or embarrassed by nudity, and he stood by the door, guarding me, without so much as blinking an eye.

Slipping into my ready-to-rumble cat suit that I wore when I knew we had a fight on our hands, I zipped it up and slid on a pair of kitten heel granny boots. Then, slinging a belt around my hips, I fastened on the sheath containing my silver dagger.

After dressing, I made certain my unicorn horn was still safely hidden away in the secret compartment in my closet. For what we seemed to be facing, I didn't think we'd need to use it. I wasn't about to deplete its power this far from the new moon unless it was absolutely necessary.

Once I was finished, I slipped a capelet over my shoulders for extra warmth and quickly mopped the streaked makeup off my face. My eyeliner and mascara had survived—they were waterproof—but everything else was a lost cause. Less than ten minutes after we hit my bedroom, I was finished and ready to rock.

"Okay, back down to the first floor."

But as we reached the landing, I paused. Someone was coming up the steps. I pulled out my dagger as Dez held his sword at the ready.

As the sound of footsteps rounded the turn, I held my breath, but then let it out in one big exhale as I saw it was Smoky, looking grim.

"Maggie's all right," he said before I could ask. "I left her hidden down in Menolly's lair with Hanna to watch her. But that portal in the living room? I know where it goes. I hopped through to find out what the hell was going on."

"Where does it lead? And can you close it?" We followed him as he turned, heading back down the stairs.

Smoky shook his head, glancing over his shoulder. "No, I can't close it. The gate was opened by powerful magic, and I can't do anything about it. But as I said, I crossed over to see where it led. I'm not sure who the hell did this, but the portal? It leads into the Northlands, as far as I can tell."

My heart began to beat faster. The Northlands could be reached via Otherworld, and through perilous routes up in the higher reaches over here, Earthside. I had a lot of bad associations with the lands at the top of the world. And there were a lot of harsh, volatile creatures who made their homes there, including dragons like Smoky's father, who had imprisoned and tortured me.

"So the question is, who opened this portal, and why?"

"Right now, I think the more important question is: just what all has come through so far? And what else can we expect before we manage to close it down?" Smoky's grim smile deepened. "Let's get back outside, woman. We need to do something to stop that yeti from trampling the yard."

I turned to the guard. "Dez, stay here, please, and guard the portal. Don't put your life in danger, but if something else comes through, try to stop it if you can. And if you can't, get the hell outside so we know what we're facing next."

With that, Smoky and I headed back outside, into the fray.

New York Times, *Publishers Weekly*, and *USA Today* best-selling author **Yasmine Galenorn** writes urban fantasy for Berkley: both the Otherworld series and the Indigo Court series, and will soon be writing a spinoff of Otherworld called the Fly By Night series. In the past, she wrote mysteries for Berkley Prime Crime and nonfiction metaphysical books. She is the 2011 Career Achievement Award Winner in Urban Fantasy, given by *RT Magazine*.

Yasmine has been in the Craft for over thirty-three years, is a shamanic witch, and describes her life as a blend of teacups and tattoos. She lives in Kirkland, Washington, with her husband, Samwise, and their cats. Yasmine can be reached via her website at galenorn.com and on Twitter at twitter.com/yasminegalenorn.

A Queen can never let down her guard...

FROM THE *NEW YORK TIMES*
BESTSELLING AUTHOR

"Lyrical, luscious, and irresistible."
—Stella Cameron, *New York Times* bestselling author

Galenorn.com
facebook.com/AuthorYasmineGalenorn
penguin.com

M1442T0214